YEH HELL OW

YEH HELL OW

A novel

by

JUDYTH EMANUEL

*Dear Denise,
are beginnings more
important than endings?
See. The end is open.
Life!*

A
BOOKS

Adelaide Books
New York / Lisbon
2019

*JUDYTH EMANUEL.
2019.*

YEH HELL OW
A novel
By Judyth Emanuel

Copyright © by Judyth Emanuel
Cover design © 2019 Adelaide Books

Published by Adelaide Books, New York / Lisbon
adelaidebooks.org
Editor-in-Chief
Stevan V. Nikolic

For any information, please address Adelaide Books
at info@adelaidebooks.org
or write to:
Adelaide Books
244 Fifth Ave. Suite D27
New York, NY, 10001

ISBN-13: 978-1-949180-66-4
ISBN-10: 1-949180-66-2

Printed in the United States of America

For Ben Sewell, Sasha Burnie and Hannah Burnie

Content

4

5

6

7

The important thing ached to sing.

This then the song it screamed.

My nervous first twenty years.

Whole lotta shakin goin on.

Began with a small gulp...

1

went backwards

HELLO manky me over the moon. Bested approach, deciding maul into growl fragmented fiery flinch fuckit. Grrr the rundown. RANTED. Be prepared for loud off-key what comes. Anyway, gawk. At. Me plunked bitty bits of the sum total. *Looky here.* Helpless wayward way to begin. *There. There.* Ooohed cripes oddwacker times drowning in vodka and rusty-tasting tea. Him crouching down, eyes on cunt, my nightmare, *hold yourself together, quit licking,* the housework mops another nightmare, same again the next spitted and polish fuck me, fucked in the. I was a small girl scarce one point five meters, *what are you going to be when you grow up?* A drunk. The portrait of me child, I rode a merry-go-round at a standstill with the world revolving around me where it stopped nobody knew, got bored and married and buried and every Sunday best in the last pew at the round and round. This carousel sang Pop Goes The Weasel, aha, I was a popular amusement, five hundred, fifty watt light bulbs ON. I rode painted horses frozen galloped a curling mane, huge nostrils, whitest teeth and crazed twinkle in his eye. Just pretend. A puke resemblance. *Explain.*

Well, we were hippies, we were feral, we were strait-laced, we were boring, we were poor, we were average. We grew fangs. We wore angels wings. We were irritated. We cherished our grievances. We obliged. We hesitated. We were suddenly uncertain. We began to hate. We kept our distance. We coddled our distance. We ate our distance splotched with cream and sugar.

Distance changed the love I had for you.

Er, but I felt quite tipsy.

Oh. Look what I done, how dreadful.

(She was so self-effacing!)

I did not find searched moving the wonderland. Honeysuckle, a figment of my dreaming and identical to the dormouse, I murdered the gift of time. Asked riddles, puzzles, questions, verses without answers. Riddles? Double meanings, wits, veiled verbal's, enigmas, misunderstandings oh real funny honeyed, holes in my top and bottom, holes in my middle. What was I? You had a tail and a head, but no body, you were not a snake. What were you? What ran, but never walked, had a mouth but never talked, had a head but never wept, had a bed but never slept. Three eyes in a row, but when the red eye opened, everybody stopped. What got wetter and wetter the more it dried? No sooner spoken than broken. Silence. I was weightless, but you could see me. Put me in a bucket, I made it lighter. What was I? Her bright fragile, when you said her name, you broke her.

We dwelt in Places built of creepers and sharp uneven ground, pitted roads, mostly shacks, single story houses, the flat roofs looked as if the roof blew off. Where I flew the freak flag, southern real cross with piddle stars kicked back the sunburn. Moosh. And Fichus shrubs pruned into impeccable ball shapes. Shaved balls on the brain ha. Everywhere tittle yellow petals of roses proliferated blooming. The pebble paths rough on bare feet, weathered palings years of windblown leant at strange angles. But every surfboard upright beside garish beach umbrellas, paper lanterns, salt bush stayed alive in sand. The rare seahorse letterboxes, pert creatures with musical cleft bodies and cemented fins reaching for the mail, a beautiful quirk in this deserted suburb of Honeysuckle. Where. Kinds of fairytale people here the ex-nun, fleshless friendlies came rattled for dinner, meet Gull and Etcetera and Mr. Winkler wink wink. In the shade of a fig tree planted in a parking lot, parked this smiling Kombi, a copulating couple inside, but for the slight rocking ahhhh. Somewhere over the. And on the counter in the corner store, lolly jars in rows of temptation yes Conversation Lollies with *sweet kiss, dream girl, my hero, good pals, lush lips* printed on them inside a heart shape wow rainbow jellybabies, boiled jawbreakers, all sorts, Jaffas, Colombines stuck to gums, fruit tingles ooh, tootie-frooty, choo choo bars, steam rollers and musk sticks his favorite apart from sex.

Imagined deadly imagine. We lived by the sea you see and we were dead. A miserable goddamn excuse. You misunderstood. For I lost me poor little Everything. That time I needed Something Old. Something Borrowed. Something Blue. Something shabby. When. Ewww. Us became one. And the sameness. I real something rotten worn fucked shitshocker.

Yeah did you find her sapphire crucifix? A locket and her silver chain looped around my neck. The cross fell into cleavage. Snug and deep. The beauty magazines eternal young airbrushed Dolly, Vogue, Teen, Cosmopolitan a twiggy chic on the cover and pages of in-depth articles. *Accentuate cleavage with blusher.* Blush helped. Me. Every *every* night girl of me positioned in front of the gilt mirror, found in an opportunity shop finders-keepers. My spine straight and settled for soap the deepest cleanser, reached for the tissues wiped the Max Factor caked on my wafer face and waterproof midnight shadow and sweet lipstick sulked gloss and smooshed moisturizer over, reflected a brittle monstrosity with black smudged eyes Whatever Happened To Baby. Bleached hair (hers browner, plainer, a natural brunette) and wider eyed, thick lashes flutter girl-next-door, snow white pinched my lips parting, *what have I done now.* Dressed a thinning, most days, sundress the style. A halter neck tied with a sash, cool, in fashion. Loose rayon above my knees. The yellow dress clashed wrong blurt raucous. At ragdoll buttonholes. Tatty pompoms. Wore that frock again and again. I pinned to the yellow, a tin brooch of a dung beetle, bought for a dollar from the pitiful Saturday markets had to scrape a quid. And accessorized velvet headband, all the rage. It fell forwards, covered my eyes, blinding sea of second-hand clothes, threadbare girl, limbs falling over themselves, bucketing clichés. My precious button collection. I told you junk.

I ranted chin bristle, forehead pimples. Rats! Crap! The absence of fun, wild, fierceness, the end of days, the second coming, sniffs, scratches, licks in enemy WILDERNESS.

Stop.

This was my story, this was my song. What. Ohhh, nothing. Much.

B-B-B-Breathe Breathe Breathed

The Past! Died before I got myself b-b-b-born. I launched in birth same as entire everybody them All Creatures (great and small) got birthed. This a blinker previous unremembered. After themselves were. Spat out. Squeezed out headfirst. The difficult part. Why so bloody narrow?

Birth of me me me. I heard the midwife urge, *push. Stop pushing.* Rah rah rah. Said this to the woman soiling fresh laundered bedsheets. The woman bearing me, expelling a squished football from her uterus. Spontaneous expulsion. This sporty fetus hurled into the arena. Tangle of membranes, placenta roped by the umbilical cord according to blood everywhere. This sparkled of sterilized instruments clamped and cutted. Shocked from the starter pistol. My skull, you see, transparented. I blinked at the one splitter second. Startled by blinding yellow of. Brain-searing flaming spotlights. And black baby eyes the size of poisonous berries, opened wide haunted as a storm at sea and.

I choked. Airborne lost. Oh, baby turned a bit blue. Defective heart *breathe, breathe, breathe.* But I would not be told. Kitten baby mewed soft and helpless and angry blue veins. Blood sugar, pressured low sugar, lower tension, high blood up. Respiration depressed and heart rate slowed. Brave heart slithery sticky abrasive hurt heart pulsing a pulsebeat. The beat did not go on. Scrubbed medicos, silicon gloves snapped, emergency masked faces and whisked bundle of flesh to intensive or somewhere oxygen cribbed. Real back of beyond. Of the garden, my planted baby bean in soil mulch. *Why won't she touch me?*

Born traced me right to the twinkle, birthing my phobias. Bright lights, crowds, high heights, moist objects, a body falling and falling, you. *Stop complaining.*

Lying in the began cradle. Utterly Nakedness. Bundle baby weighed as much as three blocks of butter. Parcel of emptiness contained the dignity of quieted sorrow with a solemn expression summoning my doubtful. Of a melancholic stare. Baby mouth pouted. This strawberry pondering a somber future. Should I howl adorable? Or muted grizzle. Discontent followed needling my. Disenchantment snapping at the heels. If I got to Here from There. Always I wanted to go straight back There. But no possibility of joining the dots. What dots? The stepping stoned wow star patterned vertebrae of the Milky Way, stargazed constellation clusters, big dipper, southern cross, globular cluster, omega something and a black hole somewhere sailed a ship at sea, my keepers named me Shipley.

And dotkid Shipley stewed grew, of course, ha, ha, blah the growing process bloody obvious, ripened into a plain, silent, fat apple cheeked. The keepers loved less, allowed sun kicks on a bunny rug. The light dappled blob-baby. And yes, mostly ignored. Stuck in the middle ooh ooh. Not belonging. Left out. Hand-me-down child. A lump, just a lump, interesting, but just a, should had a voice, but never made a sound. Or a croak or a whimper or a yowl or a toot or a boom.

The beginning years chased the unreachable. As if skipping after a hat hurricaned. This lifelong girl couldn't let go of hands held, paper, friends, china swans, religion, letters, vividness, a damp cloth, men, embroidered linen, keys, magic spells, chess pieces, fries, true love, lace. Not bras I outgrew, those I threw. Every goddamn sticks and stanks and skanks and stuckers stuff vanished, got mislaid, fried, bolted whoosh nowhere to be found. Drama done and finished with. Irretrievable Emotions lost. I moved on to find a different. The core of me the lump of me. But in the going, the going changed. Never the same again. A lucid of lumpy molecules. What about the thing? I had no idea. You see. I was only a baby, baby.

At two or three years, dressed in a cotton singlet, sun bonnet, terry toweling nappy. A child played in the sandpit. Messing mud pies. Ate sweet juicy clover. I chewed green. Scrumptious gritty sand chewed yellow in and exhaled the breath in my stunted lungs, blowed dandelions shhh. Those drifting weightless weeds. Of such virtues, honesty, trust, cared careful, not yet discovered, like first memories. Weedy parachutes floated on the summer breezes of.

Was I a sucker, *you can't be not at that age*, sucked my forefinger. Index finger, pointer finger, trigger finger. The finger God waggled *dirty girl* digitus secundus. *Grow up.* The finger God what pointed at Adam frescoed on a chapel ceiling. Finger of Baptist pointing heavenward. *Don't look.* Leopold simpered with his forefinger down his throat. Freud frowned pathological, masturbatory, auto-erotic. Who blew knew. This such bollocks. How could a child know that. But I knew why. I stuck my index finger into my mouth to stop my face falling off!

Chubby counting reached through more twelve months to four five six. Seven witch, the rot set in, stripped a flowering bush of all her buds, oh look the tree! This amazed and wonder sounded of birds came at me mixed heroic mind-screwing brain-cell killer potions. Jam jars filled with muck, flour, grubs, dirt, dead flies, black tea leaves rotting. Cast spell of gave me mega. The delighted shebang gave up counting the hedges caught between road and ditch. Chose a direction what ruined me. Okay flew enchanted carpet, beanstalk, flying saucer to some exotic destination where, *you know*, what I read. The magic faraway dug a garden with a spade. Which for a witch, the only way out and away and up was down.

The beginning of my brilliant ideas. Often. Mostly went nowhere but I did...

FLY! FLY!

Peas rolling off my plate. Crusts cut off white sliced. Stopped eating peas and the crusts on edge any sandwiches. Spat sog on plate bread crusts caught in mouth half way dangled. Dribbled beans peas mushed heaved almost.

And this horror of freckles.

Flight future tasted flight. It tasted free. When this me. Eyes turned skyward. Held the breakaway longing for fly high.

But did what told always did. Even though so bound up could not shit didn't ever knew that word. Then. Spoonful of castor oil. Sat on the toilet. For hours to a child memorizing pink tiles looked like faded lollies.

Got nutty ideas from the backs of cereal boxes. These games sometimes a plastic whistle. Girl snapped crackled popped. Hair orange whiskers frizz. Someone. Not God. Maybe devil planted carrot seeds under cotton-thin skin of this scalp. Banged my head wished for fair hair instead of a mop of carrots. And a silver watch. Eyed same as dainty Timex. On Carol Smart's wrist showed off. This need for jealous but just felt left out.

Mostly I school uniformed walked kept one leg stiff imitating Beverly's unbendable leg wrapped in leather straps buckled to a steel brace. Spastic what kids sneered. The parents whispered, *polio.*

Back in those times of leafy streets. My keeper sank in dishes, suds, laundry *out damn spot*. Busy so busy closed the windows to stop tonsillitis. Worn out mealtimes scolded believing,

"Eat your crusts or your hair won't go curly."

And I said,

"But look. My hair is already curly."

Really tight wild. Oh, she banged wooden spoon on the kitchen table wood on wood. Winked the spoon.

"Hoity-toity. Eat your peas missy. You must eat what you're given. What about those starving children in Africa?"

Puzzled this logic. Sat on my hands shifted bottom waited for punishment. Didn't understand how why I should eat the starving children in Africa.

"But that's cannibalism."

She stared at me.

"Cheeky. Go to your room."

I flew into the bathroom and threw up all the peas.

Not too stupid flashed in my mind memories, think faulty lighthouse. Pretty confused by Christmas cards. Fa la la la la picture of glitter snow cottages laden roofs some thatched. Another land. Far. I never saw snow. Here. This beachy Newcastle. Town clown names. Fort Scratchley. Nobbys Bogey Hole. Red nose glow. Paddle footed striped every mild season milder, blurred into the next on. Weather cool warm hotter. Sky not normal hazed of coal, copper, steel. No snow. Just Iced Vo Vo's. Just sugar flakes sprinkled on pink and white coconut ice. Treats at the yearly fete. I hoped for snow. Real freeze. Not just glittery puff printed on a ripped up card.

School walked all the way. And ran it. Miss Hassel, deputy headmistress God of us. God was dull miserable crabby with no slaphappy in between. Miss Hassel prowled corridors darkened by brick walls hung with framed prints picture dead heart of the desert a few painted bush scenes go creamy ghost of gums bark half stripped off as if shedding a crusty scab. Art. And classroom kind of cheerful. Riot of crayoned stick figures. Violent sunshine pictures fences kept everything us drawn on the page in.

So lunchtime at school. From midday lasted an hour. More kids played. Wintertime no brightness. Sort of mild weather children barelegged. But must wear short tan socks scuffed brown school shoes matching ugly uniform with neat pleats in fabric colour of the dung crapped.

Skin all over me thin as tracing paper. Held bones together. Did not wanting to be nondescript homogenous dung. Not needing to be same scuff as everyone dung children. In own clothes, part of who I really was. The thing just started learning. Among other things. Fuzzy discontentment. Tiny girl seven. No friends. Child born on an island shaped by red dirt. Sand on the edges. Oceans closing in on me. This ache to be somewhere magic. Far away. No clue where any such place might be. Thought thorny stuff, of why was all that? Had to find a witch soon. Get her to cast a big spell.

Oh so what. This what of. Failure. My first spelling test. So what. It was too obvious to spell words correctly. "Spell Wish upon a star," said Miss Hassel. Wish why. Star when. More interesting to misspell every single word. Which I did. Even 'a.' With such lovely handwriting. *whish apon i starre*. Teacher frowned marking large black X. On my careful failed. I stared at large black X looked cranky asked,

"What's that's for?"

Then later when this. My own height got measured and recorded, got that wrong too. Quiet announcing was to, was to, told Miss Hassel,

"I am ten feet tall."

One foot tucked behind the other, sat alone. Hard bench bottom glued to the wooden slats. Playground ignored shy child. Paralyzing tongue-tied shy. Nibbled a spiral of apple peel then boring jam sandwiches. Soggy bread last bite of swallowed. Lump too big for my throat.

A cold day. This might have nearly cried. Felt sting watched nearby, classmates played, swooped here there. Handball, jump rope, elastics. A step forward, hand reached out whacked tennis ball, bouncing thwump. On the concrete. Plump kids chalked hopscotch squares. Just girls hopped. Gayle jumped first wobbling on one leg. Annabel giggling, lost her balance crashed on bum. I sat very still. Very stuck. Cast a wicked abracadabra spell at those girls. Guess what! Half their faces disappeared. Half nose eye cheek left. Top of their heads as well. What no brains. Now noses clamped to chicken necks. Mouthless eyeless speechless stumps ha ha.

So awful mean nasty what I imagined. This invisibility invisible child shivered shivering raw knees attached to thighs dotted with goose bumps. Goose dots when oooh astonishing idea flicked on. Amazement sparkler erupted teensy shooting stars. Spelled starres, tick. Somewhere inside my own brain. I OWNED THESE TWO LEGS. I did! I did!

Logical. But still. Mighty revelation eclipsing carrot hair, bitchy girls, mushy peas, tough crusts. Precise instant. I was child understood being inside myself beyond any doubt. Yes was. I was here. Here in my skinny wrists the tiniest pulse like a button throbbed. *Here.* Hooray inside my own body. Used both little hands, patted my knees, my tummy, my chest. Hugged myself I did happy. No other people lived inside me that was that just me. Beat my heart just me.

Well up until then. Right up too that second, I had no concept idea of existing the separate thinking person. Thought child blended into with keeper often sad, baked bread pudding from bruised bananas. Blended with grand keeper knitting little squares to sew together into blankets. Blended around with grandfather not believing what Charles Darwin wrote.

Now I understood. I was. Real nobody but myself my own being big separate. I being whole stood on own two feet flesh child breathed. Separate in the whole world universe from unfriendly girls. Idiots. Not allowed to say idiots.

And no thunderbolts. Not voices from above no descending doves not miracle. At tiny moment clear. Everything brighter clearer revealed new thinking world. I child got wings. Wondered how could take me further high than I knew where. This go asked what to do. Should do this. Silly was that silly. No I should. Fly! Fly!

Next day of usual ready but different before school. I did. Ready for it packed lavender scent, arrowroot biscuits, a compass, my Pinocchio puppet, a jigsaw puzzle, a set of binoculars. All fitted into brown Globite school case. Cardboard in those days. One clasp broken. Got sneaky knew I snuck everything. And huge black umbrella. Got it all somehow out the front door. Past curlers in her hair keeper, slapping jam onto Tip Top white sliced kept crusts didn't notice. Phew. I thought somehow got on the bus. Myself kept to myself another moment soon.

Miss Hassel rang ding-dong school bell old-fashioned brass with a wooden handle. The bell, not her. Crepey flesh wobbled ding-a-ling very funny at the top underneath her arms.

Children dawdled did. Some skipped. Whooped, others rough boys, measly girls, playtime. Yippee finger buns strawberry milk chocolate wagon wheels. All of them rushed now. Swept by a wintry breeze. A paper bag danced across the asphalt. Miss Hassel frowned. Loud teachers bossed kids. She pointed at a small boy.

"Pick It Up Please Christopher. Put it in the rubbish bin."

"But it's not mine Miss."

It. Her thin lipsticked lips sprayed droplets of spit.

"Do it."

I hated Christopher.

"Hate means kill," said my keeper.

What happened the week before. This. Christopher played in the street outside my house on a quiet block in a cul-de-sac nice way of saying dead-end. Rangers Retreat Road named after that old gentleman bushranger probably didn't get far without a sawn-off shotgun. Christopher snot smelled grubby. Aimed his toy pistol at my red head. Boy shoved me hard. Yelled rude names.

"Gonna shoot snotface carrot top stupidhead poopyhead."

I came a cropper. In fright almost wet my undies. Tears bloodied knees stung. It seemed. I had a giant's voice. Came out of nowhere. Roaring the worst words I knew. Did know worser.

"Dirty horrid rotten rat pig poo."

Neighbors flapped shocked ears. *Children these days.* My almighty god-fearing keeper embarrassed hands on hips anger wiped clammy hands grabbed. She dragged me into the kitchen. Pressed her hand against my flaming forehead. Bent me backwards over the sink. Thought my body limp didn't struggle. Got ready for it. It. Dipped a coarse bristle brush in soapy water. Sunlight soap. My keeper got rude away of me. Scrubbing filthy words right out of my mouth. Might have choked, squirmed. All these desperate things soaped by. Cake of not real sunlight. Bright yellow gentle on the hands. Purity mixed with truth was Free, said advertisements, Of Adulteration. But ferocious scrubbered shut innocent me. Soap, suds, sunlight massacred small bit of self-expression poking through. Little shoots, flower buds throttled.

And for such a long time. Imagined my keeper forced blistering sunshine down my throat. Burned dark sunlight cleaned guts inside me more retching foam. Never said much again. Closed mouth introvert child. Could not get rid of the taste. Ever. Sour. So why not. I thought I might fly away. Soon why not.

I did. This. The day I gathered my things. I walked across the sports oval. Right into the middle very center centered. Stood on the grass. Middle grass bit damp. Good. This was. So much I needed plenty of space. Lots and lots. And very very determined, opened the umbrella. Rather dramatically. The sound of indescribable not a creak, but a whoosh.

Sensed a change in the air I did. Which way the wind blew licked my finger. That way. Snapped my fingers, snap crackle pop. *Please cut the crusts off.* Myself I was. Red-head but not fiery. Everything went faster quick. More than any time it took to think a thought. I thought. This fast.

Keep one arm straightened. I kept one arm straight. Blowy wind almost. Brewed windy. I clutched the handle tiny hand grip cold. A strong gust of wind as if big hands maybe giant turbulent from spelling bee. Rushed under the canopy of the umbrella that became the parachute opening. Brolly another whoosh shot up took me. Into the clouds. *Here we go Pinocchio.* What I did grasped bagful of goodies. Pointed my toes. Light as a cupcake went with it. Dangling blew swayed. Up up up high above upturned faces of those boys' mouths gaping little pinpricks. Stunted girls with half noses chicken necks couldn't yell. Miss Hassel, almost hysterical. Easy to spot in a bright pink cardigan. The other teachers many mostly cupped their hands around mouths. Whistled called,

"Yoo Hoo. Little girl...can't remember her name."

"Coo-ee get down from there."

"Right this minute."

"Or there will be consequences."

Kids small as insects. Hair blown far back amazement. Ran waved shouting,

"Look at whatsit."

"Hey watchamacallit."

"She's insaaane."

Insane the girl could fly. Lived to tell it. Whirlwind of freaky ideas seized. Well. I almost peed my pants. Again. Really truly hook of an umbrella dangled me in blue sky might be blue door opened to the anything of anything. Lucky looked saw everything from up there through the binoculars. God was supposed to be here. But he wasn't. Anyway, I looked forward to sight of reindeer. Soon. And there snowflakes. I gathered melting to my lips. Eat the bikkies I did and finished my puzzle. So organized prepared for this special life. My keeper read about me in the newspaper. Beautiful crumb on a cloud. The shining pearl shone somehow. Rare bean, little pebble, here there everywhere.

Careful I carefully set my compass. What direction. In the direction of what I said. What was ahead. Fly! Fly! And I did! I did!

It Could Hurt Anyone

More now confession of uninteresting, but imperative fizzle of fireworks, rockets, bungers and listening to bible thumpers a nuisance from an early age of Methodist church childhood of Sunday dresses trimmed with ribbons, of my hair in too tight pigtails, of my fringe trimmed straight as a page in a book and somehow American evangelism, fund raisers dry humped praise be the teenage years, alternative Christian groups, cults, fellowship, prayer nights, asked this question, *what does 'conjugal rights' mean?* And a baptism dunked in a motel swimming pool. Baptized wearing a calico dress tied at the waist with a rope, God I thought and believed but felt nothing oh wetted and stank of chlorine my ruby mouth and freckles nodding as the congregation hummed *swing low sweet* or *when the roll is called up yonder* onlookers gawking, the devil in white, the angels hoot and cross their talons *best of luck*. Fuck. Conclusion. Eternal damnation clouded pleasure. And done with the lot, I quietly strayed to better and worse.

Piddley littled. Ignorant girl knew nothing about men. Except for my imaginary friend. Little Chinaman Wang in a green satin suit brocade hat a long black braid. Wang let me play with his red Chinese dragon and fly his paper kite. He poured me a cup of plum blossom tea from a terra cotta teapot.

A miniature elephant glued to the lid. Searching dredges of the cup, he read in the tealeaves. *Wish from your heart.* Tears of the tea did not drain away. *Ahhh, much sadness* sighing.

"You are an old soul."

WOW. I didn't know this old in soul. The young did not know the real of old. Until I got older. Of realized I definite an old soul when I miraculous young. Too late. Just. Be. Yourself.

Hell Bounder fraught the. Damn damn damning. Did not know my alarm of. Unusual suspicions moaning. The time I overheard, could it hurt anyone. Sex. I heard it, puberty woken by unfamiliar groaning and I lay in the bedroom next to. My keepers and their strained noises. Alive at the time. And I heard them. Strangest spanks heavy breathing. My female keeper groaning higher singsong ah ah ah ah ah cries muffled. What sounded. Supernatural. Eeek ran from the house. Down the road. Into the forest of. What I knew nothing about. It never occurred to me to find out, to get out or. Ask. Someone.

And why the burning. Book borrowed from the library. Scorched me, remembered the flush flamed up legs. Chapter Four, I read, a man put his fingers inside a woman's fanny. I thought, how odd. Who would think of doing this?

And why the persistent need to explain to inquisitive children. The biology of sexual reproduction or where babies came from I wasn't curious. I did not ask what origins. Girl the entity. In the forest. I simply knew. And I somehow learning to deal with myself as a being inside the body I owned. A body didn't think of myself as created or born or growing, or changing. But being In The Moment. The past didn't exist. I didn't know I had a future. I thought I had appeared, like instant pudding.

Even as a girl. Hell bound for hell hic hello bragger in the yellow sundress Yeh Hell Ow remembered mystifying. Mother and Daughter Evening. Sex education night instigated by the

Christians. This event for mothers and daughters seated and silent now, in the primary school assembly hall. Some squirming and shuffled, scuffing lace-ups. The authorities concluded we should be aware. No pill in those days.

The evening invincible a thundering of an excitable middle-aged woman leapt onto the stage. Miss Flint, The Mistress in Charge of Girls. Her left hand raised in a frozen salute. Legs planted militant this plump, short such a square. Intensity bugeyes of an owl. And straight jet black hair combed into an unflattering pageboy style. Her turkey wattle neck snorted into the microphone.

"Good evening mothers and daughters, my name is Miss Flint. I am going to show you some slides. I'll begin with two important diagrams."

Mothers and daughters flinched. Where the curiosity disappeared just. Resignation remained. As. Miss Flint took a deep breath turned clenched crimson with a swallow gulper and dived in.

"This image is a medical graph of the male reproductive system."

The projector whirred. Slide number one a picture cartoon, appeared on the screen. This pinkish indeterminate shape. Miss Flint struck the diagram with a long wooden pointer. She said unintelligible.

"Yoo-ree-thru. And see the hep-ih-did-uh-mus. Beside that tes-tih-kulz or tes-teez." She rapped the pointer.

"This tube is called the vas def-uh-runz."

My misunderstanding fogged meaningless through. And through. The mechanics why functioned each organ. I stopped listening. Miss Flint's cane hovered over a violet sausage arrow. She whispered,

"The pee-niss."

Her voiced dropped smack to the floor. Got out a mumbled jumbly. This sperm-a-toza swam in a fluid called see-mun. These fast swimmers speeded to the eggs. Babies grew inside a woman. I felt my tummy for the eggs. Were they raw. Or did the heat of me boiled them. Slides slid past me. Weird drawings. Mustard tubes, lolly holes, wiggly ovals and another lopsided rounded arrow. No mention of the arrow expanding or changing appearance. Then a headless menace appeared with stunted arms raised in a kind of fury. Headless waved deformed cauliflower fists colored orange. Miss Flint's determination, another scarlet breath. Authoritative pointered at the menace.

"This is a diagram of the female reproduction system. This part here is the vuh-jeena-nuh surrounded by a rosy area called the lay-bee-uh. The hi-mun covers this opening here."

Miss Flint rapped the pointer hard against the cauliflowers.

"These tubes are called the fuh-lo-pee-un tubes. They connect the yoo-tuh-rus to the o-vuh-reez. The male see-mun comes from the pee-niss and meets the zi-gotes which are eggs living in the vuh-jeena-nuh."

She and the pointed poker firestick bowed triumphantly. But I wondered. Where were the eggs? How did they meet the arrow? Things usually met at some stage. I knew this detail. But the process. The why. The non-existent eggs. Meant I never discovered. Penetration, orgasm, masturbation. None of that. Pleasure. Nothing but diagrams. An outraged maroon womb, a purple penis.

The last remaining slide. Of a man in a navy suit. A woman wearing a sunny yellow dress with an apron. They stared at each other. We all did. This mediocre astonishment as if they had never met. My burning question. What happened to their clothes while when babies were made? Did the suit, frock, apron remain? Did nobody undress?

Then mystery frightness of Miss Flint launched. Breathless. She concluded the lecture with a warning. A portrayal of man's insatiable appetite for lust. She exhorted stunned mothers and daughters,

"Girls! Girls! Don't you ever let a man drag you into the bushes!"

Even in the long shy ago went whoop. I forgot. The girl fourteen, ingrained with very yellows. Scout android spy bluffer darkside of a seventies moon turned. Lurking counter-culture hippy. Painted my bedroom walls yellow. Then black blackened surround prison cell. Theory of lone goth before goths existed but fragments of yellow peeped. Hidden in my bedroom girl of dwindling luck, in the introvert wilderness shot bow and arrow code name cool alien read The Whole Earth Catalogue. Fled the earth flatted my frame against the moon path of destruction. This wished for blonde waves of Cinnamon Carter in Mission Impossible. But settled for long mousey Age of Aquarius. Watched PYE TV teak box a window to the world. It beamed black and white unwinnable Vietnam war. The lest we forget brewing anti-war movement. Wondrous Woodstock. That Girl of diamonds, chestnuts, sable and gingham. And an evil queen of a prowl knucklehead. God death reaper sneaky. Begat not, my did not. This image a girl must be.

The ballerina picture once treasured, as in pressed to my boobless. Ballerina music box tinkled teensy ballet tutu, golden hair, painted lips, twirled to nutcracker, gathered dust under the bed. Girdles, pantyhose tossed in the trash. Girl teen posed in fox blue flared jeans, a shiny yellow polyester shirt, buttoned collar and cuffs, sometimes maroon crepe pantsuit. A jarring match of sunflowers, denim and port wine, drenched in Plath angsty Ariel. The wanderer gathering facts of trees communicated with other trees. Listened to Cat Stevens followed by a moon shadow. Ploughed through The Fear of Flying confused about the zippers. Puzzling over Kerouac hopping on and off freight trains. Ideal man yuppie George Jetson. Meh George sparkling in triangles and spirals, so slim on those moving footways flying cars off to the office. George George! Then home, plummeting through glass test tubes. The Jetson's house. My dream home. The float of lived. Push button refrigerator popping out hamburgers. The hoover with a mind of its own. Dreamed this life. With Rosie the robot maid. But I worried. Rosie without the convenience of feet.

A teenrobot fifteen age, dressed in a yellow uniform, entered the workforce. Sunny of me worked in a nursing home kitchen. Saturdays and Sundays. Seven hours, a dollar an hour. For drenched in sweat. Gargantuan dishwasher sputtered steam. Sapped weary remains. Set hundreds of breakfast lunch dinner trays, slotting them into towering trolleys. This relentless rotation. Unstacked, scraped sticky plates. Cold corn flakes. Congealed gravy. Half eaten scraps of roast lamb. Dessert bowls, peaches, ice cream licked clean by toothless sweet toothed oldies.

Those wages bought me a Mini Minor. Four hundred dollars. Yippee. Taught myself. Bounced from one side of the road to the other. Rounded a corner. Mounted the curb. Front wheel rolled off. I booked a couple of professional lessons. I practiced for three years.

Driving test provisional driver's license. An examiner wrote four pages of driving errors. Top gear. Forgot to change gears, lanes, give way, stop at stop sign. Turned right into three lanes of oncoming traffic. Handbrake start, rolling backwards down the hill. Drove through a crowded pedestrian crossing.

Reverse parking dented a fender. Jumped out of the car. Left the engine running. Ran from the perspiring examiner. Four attempts but no? No improvement. But the fed-up examiners gave me a license. So I would never return.

For gorging the specter of self-loathing, trash talked and howling this bitter fragrance of living on the edge of bohemia and not knowing you were a little bent, perhaps the opposite of fancy, the lack of dramatic extremes growing up, some fleeting encounters with being not quite filled with The Holy Spirit. Lightly stroked, but not penetrated by the pedophile piano teacher. Stricken with a choking illness, half drowning, but not. And a number of minor awards, not tsunamis, but concentric circles of ripples, a pebble tossed into the pond, ignored by bottom feeders below. And not grateful dead. The scrawny girl ignorant of steep mountains, true love, gin, a broken body, high heels, anarchy, food processors. But wanted to join the party, dance in a ring around the sun, take off my shoes, walk barefoot along the golden road, try on my wings and find where *it's at*. A girl plucked from a withered bunch and. Loser girl at least bright meant weaker, and by set alight flowers. Virgin sixteen weeny ween.

My Precious Star

Groan. The Future! You were plumper and young and intense, *bear with me.* An internal monologue of a rabbit here. Morbid, more trash talking, *so deal with it,* I couldn't wriggle, but kept harping the harpy and wet my pants. You mowed the lawn, you dug around, gouged a find in me. Beauty? Some. None. A lump? A portion of pie? A grain of glass? Beauty truth, truth beauty, that shitsimper Keats, jogged me in the ribs, his smug advice, *all you know on earth and all you need to know.* But I didn't. Did this compare to the end of the road? *Rubbish.* The girrrl unmasked by Aristotle the tire kicker, quick tire changer. His clay feet grounded to the graveyard. Of plots feigning impertinence. I grew into piss Plato with my sights fixed on the heavens. And my authenticity pulverized into mincemeat, glinting excess jewelry, chalky and rouged shuffling, dumb-founded, rabbiting, quavering, lyrical, waxing my armpits. Without claws, I lost ambitions, deficient in cut-throatness and no candle to illuminate my incandescent lives. What? *Are you joking?* The Reality was. The sun went down. I lost blood. I collapsed on the bed. *You will suffocate. I am already.* Hey a kiss made an indescribable sound get me. A tin of sardines to restore my sensitivity, alone in the desolate landscape, I gazed mute clawless at a speck of light twinkling high in the precious. My very own star. Flickered fuck. Just went out. *Shit.*

Never. Ever. Dreamt

Nowhere. To live. Parallel life. Trapped in the effort to re-member and the squirm to disremember. This random. How the fuck did I get so unlucky. Thin girl of mind-numbing hand to mouth existence. Hung on by my. Teeth. Ribs in disbelief.

Footsore blistering hours and hours delivering pamphlets, brochures, newspapers. Of garish hundreds. Spotlight, Specials, Free-Giveaways, Agency Queries sealed with a kiss, dear sir/madam, we have buyers looking for a mansion similar to this, *I swear,* here, the lush houses money moneyed, *I wish* stone walls, elaborate doorbells sang you ding-a-ling nobody home. I shoved myself into gaping slits, trekking vast distances between the manors' mailboxes out of reach blimey. Uppity the steep hills of Beauty Point, a sight bleeding picturesque. Ginger tabby Russian cats on the roam, ignored sweating girl buckling under a back-pack. I delivered my deliverance, chased by gnashing Alsatians, Dobermans, guard dogs hungry for fear. A vicious terrier, its sharp fang needles, bit me on the ankle. Droplets blooded dan-gerous. Risked my life. For thirty dollars. I dashed the littering, flung the offers, dear homeowner, looky what we have for you a bargain, stuffed into shiny Receptacles. And eavesdropping pass-ersby, so overheard snippy. *You can thank your lucky stars he wasn't armed. I am on my way. I bought coffee and bubblegum. Little bugger. Can't keep his hands to himself.* And yippety yip, Christ almighty, my salvation around the corner, a high rise tower of three hundred apartments welcome concrete ambush. I filled the boxes, ticked the boxes, paper trail rid of the gross lot and lived. The sun in my eyes. At least. The sun shone. And I was alive.

This much dreaming. of. Bah. A shimmering gate shoved holy people through to the mighty mouse paradise. An angel brandished its notebook. With a fountain pen, the angel ticked off the names on her list. The ticked ones and there weren't many, were allowed in. Nobody knew particular content of par-adise, but it must be fabulous. The angel sent the wickedest lot to a shocking hot place on fire with a blazing moon and no fresh breezes. The angel said, wicked. The angel cried, I told you so.

Never mind. Keep quiet. Honey. Did not expect me to pull a claw hammer from my tartan pocket and tap the nearest skull as if an egg shell gave me.

A headache, I whined. Nothing emerged, except gentle quiet hiss ssshh steam, dream on baby. Whoop-de-do-dah brain throbber. My threat dreamtime of. Batshit. Bullshit cartwheels. I dreamt of an animal, half panther, half panda popped over my shoulder-pads. Unsure this happened. Even the wolf in sheep's clothing walked by my side, prepared to rip the abominable guts *what.*

Almost myself of stumble, no buckled monsters in my closet, checked under the bed. Needed a roof over my head.

I hoarded. Clothes stuffed in bin bags. I folded my clothes, clutched at shrapnel money. Empty wallet persuaded me to hock a linen blouse. Pure 1940's. A woman in love with vin-tage clothes, well she gave me ten dollars. The arduous nothing of what to wear rummaged me in charity stores. Vinnie's, the Salvation Army, thrift stores, dressed me fancy anyway. Fully

clothed in clothes outfits matter. Bullish dreamgirl in front of
the looking glass. I swanked old leather jeans, double-breasted
tartan blazer shoulder-padded with sharp lapels and a sailor cap.
Sometimes I dressed in a man's jacket. Tweed and silk lining. The
brand of coat men died in. I sported a soccer sweat shirt and a
red net hoop skirt with a green sock and a red sock and Chinese black press-stud shoes. Sometimes wore a yellow wee willy
winkie nightshirt with a wide indigo belt like a strip of ocean
in a sea of sand. Or 1950s grey faded jeans nipped at the waist
with a striped bijou vest exposing my midriff and a saucy beret.
Hey swaggered a light green bowtie with a long white petticoat
swirled me swing circle skirt trimmed with broderie anglais. Fine
white cotton and floral embroidery made me think of aristocratic
garden parties, cucumber sandwiches, delicate throats, pinkies
aloft, a sip of Earl Grey. I dyed a chef's jacket and karate pants
a matching grey. The dye streaked across the fabric in a motley
pattern before acid wash became fashionable. Went walkabout, a
rambled shod in marching girl boots with a rose satin bed jacket,
a Balinese sarong, no baton and no knickers.

Car boiled over, the engine broke for a while. I sometimes
hitchhiked. In four-inch platform soled shoes, oh for a soul and a
side splitted maxi skirt, *laugh till your sides split*. Pointed my forefinger at the bitumen road, or thumbed in the air a ride. On an
isolated stretch running through dense bushland, not a house in
sight. A semi-trailer screeched to a stop. I hoisted myself up the
enormous step. Sat in the cabin of the prime mover. Wondered
with horror what if. Had I left an egg boiling on the stove? So, I
hitchhiked straight home to check. Impractical Danger every day
or so. What Miss Flint warned. What if dragged into the bushes
by a hairy truck driver. What if it violated my body, not found
for days. But nothing happened to me. I decided puny plainness
acted as a deterrent. That and the toy gun.

Burning Down The House

Needed a roof over my head shelter from the storm, *may I stay here a little longer until the rain stops*, so share houses. Doors slammed in my. *Show me the money.* Vagrant roaming, a knapsack on my. But I believed there must be. Some house, some for me, somewhere. With minimal funds, obliged to renting low rent rooms. Ship-wrecked mariner scanning the accommodation classifieds. A month in advance. Moneyless caused the necessity to move me *we shall not be moved* a thousand times. The nomadic existence. From house to house filled with hollow sounds, bunk beds, dope fiends, a varied sense of doom, smelly from cigarettes, stale fish and overripe fruit. Still the attempt to be courteous and discreet to create a favorable impression. I smiled and spoke clearly at various derangements. I found comfy houses, but bleh contained dubious one-eyed people loading a joint. Or the dingy room, crowded of seedy tenants suffering from foot fungus, and playing head-twisting hip hop songs. Hungry child lookin' wild childish in the city. Hey one *abode* had a motor cycle parked in the living room and incinerators jammed with pizza boxes and a headless rocking horse and doors without locks. Pig pens crowed of critters sitting on milk crates. In their white gleaming kitchens, the hellish chilled of an operating theatre, I met sets of porcelain professionals, mostly couples afflicted with oxygenated blood. They blended dry martinis. The males full of enthusiasm,

"When can you move in?"

But the girlfriends refused to share a house with the sixteen year old girl wearing medals and dressed in peculiar outfits. I was not anyone's cup of tea.

Situated in a north shore suburb, I rented an enormous bedroom with a little sunroom in an art deco house owned by a distant Asian investor. These housemates, bad-tempered hippies from Nimbin, Marnie and Hep slept on a loft bed in a windowless room next to the kitchen. And they were always naked. I asked,

"Aren't you cold?"

A blonde Swedish couple rented the room next to mine. And downstairs jerks Derek and cousin Alistair, spent three months of the year in Bali, dope dealing Scots built of red faces and ginger curls. Included Beth, the scrawned mean girlfriend. Derek responsible for the lease on the house. Every time Beth showered, I pressed the door buzzer and turned on the hot tap and witchy cackled a simmer at the sound of her yelp. Beth, the buzzard, owned an MG, the interior knee deep in candy wrappers. Late on a Sunday night. Derek got escorted from the premises by a policeman. We all whispered,

"Drugs."

Good riddance the lease-holder arrested, yay the house was mine. I searched for coins under cushions and carpets. Of course, only dust, dried orange rind, plastic pegs, a used a band-aid spotted with blood, baits, a dead bumblebee laid on its back. I got busy rearranging the pictures and furniture. I threw away the rotting bathmats, the fishless aquarium, the logic, the certainty, my identity, the flair for interior decorating. Beth hatred eyes yelled at me.

"Who do you think you are?"

"Superwoman."

"Bitch."

Learned from a spaghetti western.

"Life's a bitch motherfucker."

The Swedes counted a thousand crumbs I left on the breadboard and they whining a furious disgusted. But I saved the life of the Swedish girl. She looked the wrong way and stepped into three lanes of oncoming traffic. I grabbed her arm and pulled her onto the median strip. This simple act of bravery ha broke the ice. The Swedes forgave the crumbs. I gave them a packet of peppermint lifesavers.

In the city, I shared a semi-detached, smelled of cabbages and disinfectant did the flatmate, an unemployed actor. Electric emerald eyes, a Commie, consumed a capacity of frugal packets of two minute fifty cent noodles. The actor spent time, many farts, his hunger head in the refrigerator staring at food he had not bought. The other tenant, a pasty-faced receptionist. She looked like a chimp, that looked like a potato, that looked like a lump of clay. I wanted to ask her, what have you done to yourself, have you ever seen the light, are you lacking in Vitamin D or red blood cells, have you seen a doctor, have you swallowed to much cum, too much gum, too much smog for sure. Pasty girl sexed a married man on Wednesdays at six thirty pm raced up the stairs, licked his chops, humpa humpa storm rode him, spluttered a yahoo, heard the whip crack, caught sight of a dog collar and a leather pouch. At seven o'clock, the man thumpa thumpa thumped down the stairs and pulling on his coat and tie and zipping his fly flew out the front door, pretty fly for a mite guy, guessed late for his din din. I never saw his face.

Then Wheat Street overrun with brambles, beside the highway, a house without curtains, an empty swimming pool full of mud, eerie hush lurking in the bottom of a shot glass, a lizard on the rocks. This house owned by Phil Jürgen pet philosopher, a supercilious grin, dour self-contained, walked with a limp from a broken pelvis, sucked air through his arse, the image of an Indian feathered headdress tattooed across his chest, well-read man in a constant state of unlearning Nietzsche, did he shit straight. I thought. Bloked smoked some. Cigarette after cigarette. Cell mate drummed nicotine stained fingers. I ignored easy. He told me,

"I am a bastard. I am color blind. I have no personal history. The individual exists. Only The Self Matters."

I said, "Great."

Left me to burning incense, my nerdy inhibitions exploring the process of myself, in other words, was not how you died that mattered, was how you lived. Was it okay to store a bomb and a baseball bat under my bed. Beginnings ended at the beginning, endings began at the end, loved the mind-bending complication of this idea, but I kept this to myself huh ruts we fall into. Dicing tomatoes and onions wept for congealed stir-fries and no washing machine. Television Thursday nights, Dallas soap opera sorts. And the hair-do's blow dried sprayed into frozen upturned flips. The plastic eyes cheeks attacked of buffing and blusher. J.R. shot. And bang on ten o'clock, every Sunday morning, Phil played the song, Cheeseburger in Paradise. Chunk warm bun, hunk of meat, medium rare, ketchup, kosher pickled volume on high. Hamburgers. Phil, the veggo. Over and over again. And he never sang. The Words.

I rescued a bedraggled terrier from the middle of the road. Swerved off the fast lane, hit a pothole. Last minute thunderstorm and I dashed, skipping puddles, slick the wet, picked it up, cuddle drenched smelly dog. Hello Samson. What heartless person done this deed of deserting a. Joyful little spark.

Filthy starlight in the night. Hotchpotch eager wagging its tail loved at first sight hello. I spoke to the dog. The authority voice.

"Entrust yourself to me and I will bathe and feed you treats and kibble and brush your matted matchstick body."

"Courage my canine friend. Do not overreact."

"You promised not to overreact."

Its broken promises. Samson, the dog, overreacted and crapped all over the house. Piles of diarrhea in the middle of Phil's bed. Phil wanted to kill the dog. Phil screaming a lovely brand new philosophy,

"Shit shit shit shit shit shit."

"Yes it is," I said.

I tossed him a roll of toilet paper. Samson chucked a seizure. We discovered in the coming days daze, Samson doggy was a horrible savage, incontinent, raging, dog hating, child hating, epileptic terrier. Samson bit cars and people and babies. Sometimes they bled. So I gave him to a dreary couple.

"Samson is a doll. He's a toy."

"What brand."

"Um. A Shitsu."

"Is he housetrained?"

"Of course."

I stared into Samson's eyes. Evil black dots.

"He loves everybody."

The house became infested with fleas. Before going to bed, I sprinkled the sofa cushions with a tin of flea powder. The lid fell off fuck. Slacker. Left the pile of flea powder there. Phil rushed in and without looking, sat down fast on the sofa and froze as an enormous white cloud of powder arose around surrounded him like a flour bomb. The coughed puzzling and clouded of Phil's wrath. And the wasted space of me lay on the kitchen floor and laughed myself. Sick.

One cold evening my brrr lit a fire in the fireplace. The rug caught fire. Phil's eyes blazing the walking dead wearing Bludstone boots, stamped the smoldering. He went outside. He blinked at the stars. He pointed his chilling logic. At the roof.

"Shipley. We have no chimney."

"Does that matter?"

"Are you trying to burn down the house?"

Yeah, I ought to stop pfaffing, get organized being individual unbelievable incredible at housework. I emptied the contents of the vacuum cleaner. In the garden. Somewhere in the hoover-fluff lay dormant marijuana seeds. Weeks later, a crop of healthy marijuana plants sprang. Accidental cultivation. Phil spluttered with pleasure,

"You're a clever girl Shipley."

And frugal. For three dollars, I bought eighteen kilos of carrots. I cooked masses of revolting carrot dishes. Carrot casserole, ten carrots vertical in a circle crown stuck in brown glug. A carrot cake caved in the center. Underdone half-baked carrots in cream and wine and peaches.

"It's a tart."

Phil wretched. And carrot slices boiled in oil.

"Chips," I announced carrying them dripping oil through a colander. The carrot pudding stank of cider vinegar and crunched of orange zest and peanuts. Carrot juice every morning bullied. *You loves carrots don't you diddums.* Phil's skin turned orange, his eyeballs bulged shrieking,

"No More Fucking Carrots!"

"But the roughage," I cried.

2

Monk

Footstep barefooted along the golden road. A twenty-minute walk to the bus stop. I whistled and sang, and carried on. I waited hours for the bus with its green stripe down the side. Did not fly far. A shy two nights a week. No diamond lighted. No living on the street. I wasn't looking for religion. I needed to be part of a group, dodge loneliness, pretending I had friends. And joined a youth outreach coffee shop called The House On Fire. Two narrow semi-detached houses. I wore a black duffle coat, discount jeans and navy sneakers to Wednesday night prayer meetings and frayed jeans with a batik caftan to Saturday night beat generation counterculture coffee house on fire. Laughter in my eyes. Danced in my feet. I was a neon-light diamond. And. I could live on the street. I picked a peculiar party. No dancing in a ring around the sun. Just the walls of The House On Fire painted high gloss going-to-hell red. The floor scattered with grubby cushions and old mattresses. The hum of beatnik meets rock n' roll. Lost souls ambled through the door. Drank innocent free coffee listened to live music. Everyone unaware. Redemption was closing in.

My crush seepage on the dusky tough-talking streetwise Italian boys. Vince, Dominique, Antonio. In a clump. Jostled snickering each other. Their parents owned the fruit shop around the corner. Should I convert their lost souls. But I giggled flirting, no holier than thou. And lapped up their smooth olive skin, velvet eyes mocking my merciless virginity. While those Christians group of solemn shaggy seventies hair, pimples and beards *we shall not be moved*. They plotted, prayed, boiled water, washed cups.

I the youngest. Fresh from high school. Introvert, red-faced, stuttering, pigeon-toed. Who else was a virgin? Everyone, sex before marriage was wrong. And Monk there. With my one eye open while praying, I spied on him.

And I discovered the name Monk, meant 'in the valley of oaks.'

By the by, monks had deep desires to inspire people in a higher cause. Monks shared strong ideas on spiritual matters. Monks tended to be humanitarian, broadminded, generous, loving, kindhearted, sensitive, romantic, with magnetic personalities. They followed professions serving humanity. But were often easily hurt and quick-tempered.

Monk, the image of Neil Young, clean-cut hippy harbored a god-complex. Holier than thou funeral director innocent air and a religious nose. Hooky. Trickled of virtuous pleasant. His hazel eyes misting a mystical air enchanted by my nervous tic. A boy oh boy, destined for the vicarage. He lived with the doting mother in a high-rise council flat. Where milksop mommy beated her dear me's. Mrs. Quill always said, Dear me dear me dear me, same as him. Ferretface woman this Mrs. Quill. Little fairy queen lady inside the wizened of a coat-hanger body. Hung with girly frocks and pastel cardigans. Tripped about in low-heeled Mary Janes lithe as a reptile. And

Monk not adventurous Mummy's boy. As a child, he played hopscotch the girly way. Got picked on by the bullies. Cried a lot. Had no cheek, no grit. Valued nothing. Grew disinterested in life. His addictions, roast chicken and tinned sardines and a ploughman's loaf for dinner. Nothing but blandness in his bearing and a reddish concentration of capillaries under his skin. Made for sensual lips.

"Kiss me," begged his mother. Her own lips like crushed carnations.

"Kiss me," I begged.

"Kiss me," cried desperate women.

"Kiss me," demanded the frogprince.

Monk spent most of his time yelling,

"Get away from me."

He didn't care how cranky he sounded.

And the dear quaint madam language Monk and his mother spoke. Dearies, whoopsadaisy, lovie, heavens to betsy communicated fractions of his feelings. Blurt called later alligator. But I refused to reply. Whatever crocodile. He named me cutie-patootie doodle-bug flitter-mouse angel-puss chick-abiddy. Double barreled to him. I managed bang a rump-diddle asking him,

"Hey do crickets fart?"

Well, Monk did this his wait and that wait. Was I in love. No. How long before him hazed and haloed learned I was not his. Monk. It began with a wink at my poker face. What a catch. Nicked his face shaving. When would the weather clear up. Six months our Courtship, put the car seats flat down. On the sexless night. Sometimes. Under a concrete stairwell. Him scrunching tissue balls. We of fumble intimate rare times. Private parts never kissed a foreign land. Too twisty to touch. Still waters of the deep ran. Snaky girl snaked his snake. We did cautious pash, no tongue, kept duffle coat on. Was it swivel hook, this iniquitous unseen pressed against my slit, protected by thrilled cottontails.

And there was no affectionate way to say Monk.

At midnight Monk turned off the lights and locked the front door of The House On Fire. Beside myself. Beside his rusted Renault. He leant on the bonnet of his car, a mustard color. The engine was cold. And dawn fell upon him that he would marry me and I would be his wife. I twiddled my hair behind my ears as jazzed. Yep. His hand jingled not much money in his pocket. He stared directly at me. Was. There. A. Pause. Were my bags straight was my hair in place no artificial flowers. It came upon him that he would marry me. The gist then. The snapshot then. The upshot.

"Shipley," he said. "Would you."

He asked me to marry him. He did not say please. And no diamond ring. No bended knee, he should kiss my toes, but for socks. Oh and no gondolier. No terrace facing the sea. Not for me. Stood shyly beside him and yawned at the asphalt surface of the road. Did I cry a silent wolfhowl. For a cold motor. For romanticism skimmed past my bewilderment. I would be - I would be - I would! Mebbe. Of course. And I hellbent the married. Be his wife sorted of. Hyper meta uproar wife. Bubble and strife, hen pecker, bum and tongue, shrew, rib, lawful blanket. The Sunday Roast.

I waited. Of course, I replied,

"Yes. Alright."

His exquisite lips parted.

"Alrighty."

Gosh, you thought. Big blunder. It was colder. The darkness folded. We never even flirted. Now a rush, this dashed into MARRIAGE. Blimey half-hearted once the question done dusted.

I snuck him into my bedroom not in love. Him a virgin too there there loved. Pashed desperado higgledy-piggledy not in love. A limp trout, not in love, I lay on the bed, its broken springs just old, not from any bounce. Whoa skewered. Thought we had done IT. Before the vows. Doomed us evil wizard, clobbered the purity vapor. Lovedovey. I unglued my cowbelly, pushed his bone off, worried about sinful plunge us down hellfire. Came close. *Please do not touch.* Said stern admonishment.

"We're not allowed."

I took a bath, locked the door, soaped the sins, my belly, my breasts called,

"I won't be long".

I could imagine a murder here or a coughing fit. Didn't wash off the soap, another layer of protection dried on my skin toweled and dressed. Pulled the plug and somewhere pipes gurgled. Colder the weather, nothing cleared in my room. Monk sulked not to worry and gave me a hug. Of knotty not *not* genuine. *There there.* Sensible Monk pulled in his penis deflate until after the wedding.

Beachy

Woo whoopee. My mind hurtled to friends. Monk's friend
sure Fergal, a well-made solid man, buzz cut hair, tight jaw
resembled a male model on a billboard advertising cigars and
cognac. Not my friend after he pounced. And his wife, my
older sister Alison, her son Jason. Their mansion at the top
of Mad Mountain. I remembered touch of the beach, Sunday
afternoons. Of course, the sea below gnashed teeth. Crushing
choppers to came futuristic. Hungry waves chased the rocks,
right I remembered the. Bright hard skyful sun. And those
seagulls squicking *look at the seaview what a view.*

   Alison and me kinda virgin cake. We laid our lazy. Side
by side on aqua canvas patio chairs. Her slim and my skinny
sat in bloom fullness. Tinny bodies of starved sullied. But cute!
And we body slick slippery. Pinkies linked best friends, blood
sisters, sistersky. Lemony fresh, we rejected yellow wine for red
red wine, burping fake of girl sophistication, spice summered of
gossiping. Hotties. Jason only four. Naked toddler still feeding
at her breast flop from skimp bikini, not stopping her from
drinking. Gossip wine loosed our tongues, skinned better times
of driftwood, sand spinning lovesick. Chin chin cheers. Ice
cubes melting on our belly buttons. Huh. What. Mad girls escaped of the attic. Little housekeeping persons. Bitchin twitchin.
Ignorant of what we girly crazy nothingness canker. Million

dollar midriffs bare legs tanned. Two sets of fine eyes serious blue/grey and oval heads, contour of a jewel balanced on gabble chins, chicken necks swallowing. How much alike we were. But Alison quiet of ordinary, a soft inscrutable face and her behavior at times secretive and insecure. She parted her long brown hair in the middle. Hair that framed a high forehead, watchful eyes.

We Cared. About Everything.

At the beach, we faced the ocean, ignored soar Mad Mountain glaring behind us, cragged rocks roaring, *I am bigger than you.* Mad Mountain wanted to kill us.

Two sunbathers, beach umbrella in a flap. And Alison always wrapped a lemon sarong around her waist and straw hat and her long slender legs and my nobbly pale legs, a wrist tattooed symbol of eternity looper. Kicked off our rubber flip flops. Sand between our toes. Sunblock smelled of jasmine rubbed it in stung my eyes. I was not crying. The time we had the whole afternoon scampered to the waves, to the fierce and salty and beachy and she dived under. Her an excellent swimmer. I flailed about. I told her,

"I can't put my head underwater. Water gets into every hole. I will drown."

Alison floated in a calmer sea. We talked pretty lips. Alison of absorbed air, flushed the tremulous avoiding stormy weather.

"I need peace," she said.

We complained. A lot. Our lot. My lot ratty swimsuit worn elastic stretched to the limit, bargain basement.

Sometimes she snuck up behind me, put her arms around my neck, pressed her cheek to mine, said,

"I'm sorry sorry sorry."

Her voice fading, her body shuddering into my weak, my worry, my incredulous. What for?

She bought two pairs of angel's wings from TEKS. Real white feathers and the conundrum what to wear with wings, I said,

"Black silk."

"Pajamas," she said.

She owned black silk pajamas and I teamed cut-offs, flip flops and a grey K-Mart shirt nearest to black why we slipped the winged ties over our shoulders. Wings on our backs surely protected that day I followed her walking in the rain.

"Feathers are dead." she claimed, "And they are waterproof."

I pitied the poor bird, its feathers ripped from follicles. Those feathers got soaked, so not even water resistant. Dragged, these wet and muddy angels without umbrellas.

"Our bright plumage," Alison said, "Light burdens."

Your thoughts of a downpour, goldfish and the shedding of. This, I thought, was what not making sense was about.

"Remember." I said later. "The wings. You wasted twenty-four dollars."

"But we were angels."

"Not for long."

Sometimes at the beach, we sang medleys, soft tones *wouldn't it be nice if we were older, let's go surfin' now, chug-a-lug chug-a-lug.* I sang the theme songs to Yogi Bear, Star Wars, hummed Jaws. Unstoppable, we dropped our prude jaws at nude sun bathing, how could they. Disgusting.

The old closeness.

"You know that song 'I touch myself'?"

"Yeah."

"I have a confession."

"What."

"I never touch myself. What other women do. That."

"Ohhh. Well. Not a problem sweet. I'll demonstrate on myself."

"Alison!"

"How else are you gonna solve the mystery."

Her the teacher and me the grasshopper. The shy of me gasped, "Oh God okay."

But month of crimson tide. Period. The mess of it. Red-sticky pad stuck to my lace underpants.

"Don't worry," she said. "I'll teach you the skill to get yourself off."

We snuck into the enormous white. Spotless bedroom rejected a g-spot. She careful laid a towel to protect. And plopped on the bed. She arched her back, bared herself from the waist.

"Watch closely."

Dread thought, what if Fergal interrupted cripes. Her hand moved between. And the longest finger, the third finger. Alison shining fingers cleaves herself a fraction. These two baby quenelles of pink mousse, made the spoon sure sultry and wet. Revealed precious nugget. And she showed me. The method.

"Use the tips of your fingers. Start gentle circular vary the pressure until the buzzing."

My fingers covered my eyes peeked through.

"Ewww."

"Some women prefer carrots or a cucumber or sex toys, vibrators, lubricants to polish the pearl under the hood"

We roared. At the idea of endless touch teasers, sensual bliss, extreme thrill. She giggled at my hesitancy of w-w-what. What if my eyes fell off my face and I knelt and the light streamed from skylightheaven. She pressed harder.

"I can't." I said. "I can't ever do that."

The harder they came, the harder they.

Fell.

Alison thought too hard, too deeply. Delicate mind-body her and me. Our matching ovarian cycles. Pituitary gland located right at the base of the brain. Where the hormones marched to battle. A recognition of these facts. The riot mind sent endocrine glands into such a frenzy, a woman appeared screaming. But her of talking whacky hormonal forebodings. This made us moody gloom. And guilt thoughts, be better as superwomen. Yet the world. Humanity surrounded by.

Irritabilities itching itching scratched itch, sewed it a stitch irrational outburst. Unreasonable impulses such a temper tan-trummed.

And uncontrollable infatuations. She acted much older. I admired her excessive knowledge. Her hair in a French knot and sometimes high heels covered with glitter and diamantes tottered through the house just because Fergal went apeshit over small dents in the polished wood floors. She enjoyed his hyperactive spasm after the barbeque exploded and singed off his eyebrows. She told me,

"He covers each foot with a shower cap and stands on the dining table to de-cobweb the skylight. He expects me to be a hellcat in bed. I can't have anymore. Children."

She opened the refrigerator and grabbed an iceberg lettuce. A firm head, until she tore it apart. Each leaf the layers of transparent green tissue.

"I keep busy or I'll."

"Don't even think about it."

Alison read Madame Bovary, Classical Mythology and first-aid books on proper bandaging and artificial respiration. She sewed animal shapes onto a patchwork quilt for Jason. How she constantly indulged Jason.

"You're spoiling Jason." I warned watching Alison cook burgers slathered in sauce and scoop ice-cream sundaes.

She stuck pins into a silk rainbow pincushion. She collected smooth pebbles and made pot pourri scattered in little wicker baskets. Alison. Her tiny tasks, the pincushion, dried petals, weeding around the daisies and poured wine into petite crystal glasses. Alison stuck with a rotter.

"He never speaks to me. He is always on the golf course or in the garage."

Men, we sipped. I remained tightlipped about. The worst. Dizzy fucker wet with serpent sneezed on me. Hey ho what if I grew a dick ha ha blather pretended reinvent sad and sorry, his hefty cock revealed to me, it filled of honey treacle. I Laughed and Laughed.

"I am a plane. I am the walrus. I need to pee."

I asked her, "What's your favorite color?"

"Blue naturally," staring at the sea, wiser at twenty-five.

Alison always cried bluer and. Yes Lord, I meant from out of the blue. She gave me a hug. The last scrutiny, different and the same. Alison went into her blue. I should hate blue. That would be logical.

And a vulture memory plucked me with its hooks. Did Alison ever think. Wherever she slips evaporated to come. Did she ever *visualize* us. Of me. In the fog search, pissing myself, ghosted bad and weeping. Surrounded by a thousand trick mirrors smashed glass flew at me. In my mind, you know, this flying. But not yet.

You understood. And gawped at what controversy. Seaspray, spittle vanished quite the rapid. Blue disappeared. Puffed the vague magic. Dragonbreath. WARNING! Missile the whoosh. Never the same again. What followed to be wrenching ow. The shock. Ha mountains much blood. Might be mine. A nicer way of saying, what really happened. My turn skirmished in the wilderness. *She'll be coming round the mountain.* In about fifty years. Blue and bright above. Bared feet, hands and elbows crawled like a blubber wombat. My sugar tummy contracted. I persevered. Blubber earthworm wormed forward. Faced on the ground chewing deathdirt. Through poisonous plants, dead leaves, sharp sticks, Coca Cola cans, discarded tissues, campfires. The fallen crackling. *Oh we'll all go out to meet her.* She tried to save me. Jesus saves. Money? I always wondered. Of a wonder, I slouched There from Here. Metal teeth savored this. I was human. And humans yes forgot ninety-two percent of. After a year, the dreams. Marry me made me marooned. It was about Me Me Me. Not unbearable to be self-obsessed. A martyr, the muttered at sixteen going on seventeen, dear me, thin waist the waste. Did I get too? In the proximity of. Ahead lifer. What a marvelous way to die.

3

yeah well. Burnt. In. Hell.

I kept secret. How Monk screwed up his nose when he proposed. He asked the screwy girl. Just six months ago. Both of us hotted and hellish under the collar. Did I detect hints of sarcasm or mercy or lust must be. Under sin threat lovie. It came upon him. Monk Quill tip of his tongue licked my ear, proposed his mustard. A drop of spittle flew, landed on my blouse. See-through. Unromantics on the street. Next to his car. His proposal casual as if asking me to pass the salt. And pepper girl only only only a girl. Her chug-a-lug inhaled. At the time. Leant against, beside myself, whatever crocodile. Put my hands on the cold bonnet of his car, cried the alright. Yes. Ready set went the yes! A voice splitted marriage. Voiced in my heart, in my brain cracked my low lying heartvoice. Alright, I cooed. Yes. Ahem. From a bellyvoice lower the nethervoice. The brainvoice of lightheaded. Of registering a judicious life in my head. I decided dip my toes to test the temperature of marital waters. The sand between my toes, the sea thumbed its nose. *I told you so.* Caught a cold that night. The car hood of extreme coldness. Got the engine started. My vroom purred. Shame of branded sexual awakening. That Girl. Vulgar buzzing between my legs, stumble, goaded me in directionless, a cowgirl of the shoddy shot. If only I were a knockout, requesting a birdcage made of exotic wire crammed with canaries. Or experimented with drugs and not believe Mrs. Quill's mental admonishments. What God commands, what the blinkin bible states. Marriage or burn. Those Gospels of the New Testament did not split hairs. Bibble bible recommended waterproofing, darn the holes, airtight. *You ain't allowed to be fucked girlie.* Dimwit wanting to incinerate thoughts. What god joined. Let no man. And the Bible, probably every religious books maintained the shout, sex before marriage Was Immoral. A raging, snapping SIN.

Without mentioning the word. SEX. Mrs. Quill, incapable of letting that particular word stain her skin thin lips. Keen eyed her sharp at the Friday night dinners. She served chicken, not fish, even though the Lord suffered and died on a Friday. Her justification.

"Abstinence means not eating from the meat of four-footed cloven animals. Chickens have two legs and fish have none. White meat is acceptable. It stops us from being greedy and selfish."

She would not let me near Monk. He flinched when I squeezed his thigh under her teak table in her dull dining room of laminates below popcorn ceilings resembled cottage cheese spreading asbestos, ideal for lung cancer. And the lively spot of patchwork cushions errr. He scuttled to the bathroom, tiled in mawkish mauve fluffed with nylon mats. I wondered at Monk, in there an hour. I heard a flush.

Mrs. Quill threatened brimstoned fire. *Go to hell. Oh darling where do you think I came from.* I told her rhinoceroses stamp out fires. I told her, the devil on my shoulder said, hells bells what are you doing. I told her, Satan barbeques sinners over blistering coals and eats the blackened flesh. I asked her,

"What in the name of God is brimstone."

"An expression, my dear, of God's wrath."

I raised my pencil brows.

"We haven't done anything."

"I saw that look in Monk's eye."

"He was hungry."

"You can't, you know, have relations."

"I don't have any anyway."

Her firmed over and over judge mental judgement day.

"Sexual purity must be retained. You will burn in hell."

"Yeah well."

In the hellish pit of the earth chockers with fire and sulfur. Pinking her cheeks, she flustered.

"Think of yourselves as cars. If you drive only one car, you'll be content and you won't want to know what the other cars are like to drive."

A small bird, a sparrow flew at the window, slammed into the glass and fell. HELLO. Mrs. Quill waved the purity flag. She lowered her head as if a Roman general about to charge.

"The following happens if a couple has 'intimacy' before the wedding night. They both become unconquerable."

Were they an army, a country, a herd of feral pigs? This battle to keep arousal doorways shut and barred and dead-locked ruined the fun. Her sniffer determined to keep us apart and this distraction burned the dinner.

Before I stutter married him nothing else to do except collected bride dolls, baby dolls, empty photo albums of tissue pages. I packed these godsends into a hope chest. My glory box. Hoping for glorious. This hoarding of absurd ideas, birth death certificates, pressed flowers, china figurines, Noddy books, pennies, potions, pimple cream, erasers, spades.

He dug me. Thought I believed in love. With him. Life together unending I promised anyway the idea of it. Could not *not* admit. For I believed. In a magic carpet, wished from my heart. Tears drained me tethers. Ahhh sadness, claimed my wrinkled soul.

Ready set went the bride dream. Armed with gloves, roses, a surrey with a fringe on top, lingering glances, clambakes. Preconceptions here. Marriage a rollicking duding roadkill. A courting, blessed were the meek, turned the other cheek of larking sparking fussing cussing. Holy shit. Seven brides coddled clobbering him around girlish smiles, woman wiles for seven brothers, fired a gun, caught a rabbit on the run.

Took a run at the contraceptive jungle. The unfit girl fitted for a diaphragm. Family Planning Clinic bit sordid for free. Clinic such a brutish word. Bleak ante-chambers. Pile of filthy toys tossed in the corner. Framed prints of pregnant bellies. A daisy somewhere made it wonderful when the weight disappeared. And on a high bench, I noticed the gruesome anatomical model of a full term fetus. Clean and plastic and cartooned.

I was ushered in by a masculine middle-aged nurse wearing white leather shoes. The kind of shoes that skulked without a sound. Maybe a squeak. I baulked at the sight of the surgery. Stainless steel, antiseptic forceps. Gynecologists probed their greasy. Skulker shoes pointed at a narrow examining table.

"Please stretch into the dorsal lithotomy position."

"The what?"

"Lie flat. Bend your knees. Focus on the picture of a sunset on the ceiling."

Ok the picture on the ceiling unavoidable. A setting sun fell into oranges and yellow surround gangly palm tree *now let me see.*

Nursey snapped on latex gloves and eagerly inserted her index and middle finger into my vagina. She said,

"I am aiming for your posterior fornix."

Really. Right then. Hallelujah. Where was. Err, she took her time. Her wiggler fingers up me. Did she believe thingix far-flung to the furthest haunts. Poking my pixie cervix. Licked her lippy. Donkey teeth spiked spittle. Her repeated boa constrictor snaked into my innocence. This maggot writhing inside a fig. She lubricated, folded in half and inserted numerous different sized dome-shaped caps. Silicon shallowed. Upside down bowl smacked of the beautiful pea-green boat. My lovely pussy! Oh pussy my pretty. A popper pussy. You were. You were!

Her hard monkey eyes darted guiltily, avoiding my eyes. She muttered,

"Deficient muscle tone."

Bollocks always difficult in the pipeline. Christ in heaven, mandatory fitted for vaginal invasion. Pickling me over and over were her probing my private parts intended a type of molestation?

And after the marriage, the use of contraception began. Botched wrestling the rubber cap. *Most effective if used correctly.* Slap forgot to put it in. Bugger lost the spermicide. Help slow maneuvered the diaphragm into me. And often the die diaphragm was pushed aside by heavy thrusting. And if rubber left in for too long. Shit I forgot rubber still in. Buggered difficult to extricate rubber. My fingers aye blast too short.

I disregarded the rules allowing silicon longevity to lasted two years. Slap. Dear me inept at the cossetting of my little diaphragm. This taking care of protection. Washed with mildness soaped rinsing warm water. Ah no forgot. Allowed to air dry where I no. What this practice of air dried anyway. Powders caused infections wronged for the diaphragm. Oil-based lubricants, Vaseline, cold cream damaged the silicone. Examine the diaphragm by held up to the light. This anyway showed weaker spots. Diaphragm filled with water revealed leaks blah somehow. Old lady silicone yellowing with cracks, wrinkles, pinpricks.

The pill. My swallowed attempts of arbitrary. I neglected to take the pill following menstruation. Each month became a bullet spun in the cylinder of the birth control gun. Held the contraceptive muzzle against my head and pulled the trigger. Odd months of this gunning. Twenty-one gun saluted stupidity.

Twenty-one gun saluted stupidity. And hey, I pulled the trigger. Pistol lip shooting bullet kisses killed us.

Any the way, at heartless, every girl the same. In 1978, besotted with the idea of married state. In love with David Frost, Cat Stevens, my high school math's teacher, The Monkees, Mr. Rochester, Ringo Star from a far every star. I busting at the holies to married anyone. But I engaged me away to Monk. *You do not have to do this alone. Let's ask for plastic knives and forks. Have you heard of the word feminist. Have you ever tried acid. Is it truly spicy. Can I sample your honey pork. Do you hate it.* Brilliant unspeakable truth. Love came and went came, went uppers downers, in out damn spot, inner sea of rush. The guilt gilt tawdry gold, red tassels *am I too spicy. Why do we fall.* Were you serious. *What's in the glory box.* My hope chest. However, the but but *but choose life or death. What in hell is brimstone.* Did I feel lucky. The questions. Could it well be okay? Right then. If you made a bad marriage, become a philosopher. But why did? This claustrophobia. This sunken Shipley. Burning boats, burnt her bridges, ignited the forward. Why this time? When. Life seemed so mixed up.

Question Could It Well Be Okay
Wrong Then

A chop chop Chinese restaurant chooed every town. This small lurid tucked in between shops on the main street. Merry woks tipped, chop sticks clatter, sizzle of peanut oil at Yooks Yu, Dragon Palace, Chang Kong, Hang Sing Inn, Wan Win. Wha wha flaunted tawdry gold décor. Rooster waddle red of fire crackers, of the riotous brassy, of Oriental lanterns with skimpy tassels and paper shades filled with dead flies hung from ceilings. Of claustrophobic velvet wallpaper scattered with pictures of junks sinking in Hong Kong harbor. Sunk. Sticky tables, red napkins crown-folded into indecent peaks. Red what a color deserved to be!

Saturday night attempted the treat takeaway from Fook Yuan. Picky Monk his priss tasty buds, after a lifetime of his mother's baked potatoes, boiled peas, plain roast chicken. An entire life deprived of Chinese food. I talked him into it. *Try.*

"Monk. You do not have to do this alone."

Questions empty pockets, breathing bless in my King Gee overalls and I tied around my head a 'Come On Eileen' bandana. My fumbling for greed and fried and,

"Shall we ask for plastic knives and forks."

Got to know each other over takeout Chinese and I compiled questions. Monk scooped chili spiced soy noodles from greasy Cardboard containers. Deep fried pepper prawns heaped on a mound of oily fried rice. Deep dark deeper darker spicy but.

"Can I taste your honey pork?"

Sure, pushed his pork with the fork, rolling in lemon sauce and honey. Sweet and sour witnessed the saucy droplet messed his shirty and sweetly I asked,

"Have you ever heard of the word 'masculine?'"

Monk fussed. Pulled in his turtle head. Gutted, churning echo chamber, hollow bounce of chow mein, this crispy bunched into balls, let loose in his stomach acid another question.

"Have you ever tried acid?"

I gnawed on a battered chicken wing. Bitesize same size blitz cute.

"Do you hate it? Is it too spicy?"

He grimaced and chest retched. He drank a glass of beer. Forehead beads of. Inside his oral cavity the warring sour salty bitter heat, his tongue hanging, gasped for water, drenched his rioting nerve endings. Behind his kissable pucker. The pallid. Plain eater. Spoiled by his mother. Starched the boy, ironed the man, not lifting a finger except to turn pages. Of his newspaper. I wondered. We didn't get to choose life or death. Just sauces and spices and cuts of meat. How would Monk cope in life with such delicate taste buds.

I told Alison about the face he pulled. Alison and I escaped random fuss. Under matching straw hats shaded fair skin. I tugged at my dress. Yellowy rag Me broke to broke. Her rich, the unhappy. Presented me with hand-me-downs, silk slips, a pleated skirt, Levis, espadrilles, beaded cardigans.

Beautiful. She gave me. Those limited hours each week. Sometimes we talked mostly. She smiled

"Run mad, but do not faint. Ah ha."

The modes of fainting should vary, be as different as possible to appear diverting. For a man needed diversion.

"At least Fergal has the cat."

At least, we breathed same as ghosts. Our breathing in unison peace and quiet. Calmed. By the view from our decked chairs on the deck breezy. Always counted on the waves crashing. Jason a year older, scooted about. Other times, we picked clover dreamy. The dream of. Our wafting. Weighted last memories arcing that way, this way. Over tipsy on chilled glasses of pinot. We sang *rama-lama-lama-key-ding-a-de-ding-a-dong*. I played air guitar, Yeah Yeah Yeah. I threw my hair full forward and back imitated heavy metal rock'n roller. Frightened the flies. We sang *the harder they come* and Rocky *trying hard now it's so hard now.* She laughed and laughed. I asked her why, what was. Funny. Which made her titter radical.

"Don't you understand?"

Choices, the future, proved hardest. But our glitzy grease disco fever. Alison hummed *you gotta friend in me* and I schmaltzy believed her.

I created a childish story. Special for her, the telling.

"This is a good girl tale. Everyone loves this unnamed girl. She becomes ultra -lovable, the world at her umm, she reverses in time, gets younger and fabulous beyond belief and gooder, a real goody goody, she says goody goody gumdrops, everyone loves a goody two shoes, she appreciated the brightness of a morning, what is average morning, but a waking up to her fantastic shine magic, she cast her wand, waved her spell, everyone groveled, but not the someone who shoved her down a well.

Alison said,

"Really. Purity and goodness are not very interesting Shipley."

I turnabout dying got on with it.

"Okay evil then. Nasty woman everyone hated, unbelievably unloved, humans shunned her, she put herself, dug herself into the well."

"What well? The same well?"

"Just a minute, there has to be a well."

Panted a bit, made it nauseating foul, but fragrant.

"This wicked girl dug deep, you know."

"No."

"From exact spot the water diviner pointed."

"Where?"

"I dunno some field. Dug in many locations. What was she thinking? She returned to the original hole and kept digging. The new Well downer hundreds of feet deeper. She played, she festered in the Wishing Well of endless springing bloodmuddle. Which in reality, is the unknown depths of what she couldn't recognize. Get it?"

"Nope."

"Me neither. Anyway, she built a top bit, a chocolate stone covered with sprinkles. A bonbon Well."

"Right. Are you serious? What in hell."

"I just thought of it. A tiled sugar roof. Raspberry tiles. Cute. And steep steps descending into. Da Dah. Liquorice Allsorts leading to an unpleasant pit made of toffee rock, yum, delicious, surrounded by a butterscotch wall drizzled with fudge, dented from ropes used for lowering marzipan buckets brimming with miraculous perfumed bloodmuddle. Ingredients combined to ease the hurting. Got that?"

"Errr. No."

"She closes the Well and…."

My voice went its husky,

"Traps her dismal spirits. Hooley dooly. But the Well comes alive! I don't know how it happens. Sugar, the hunger, a game and the Well starts eating itself ugh horrible. It eats deluge of junk and explodes missiles of lollies shot into the clouds or whereever, any reason to get the furthest extremes from her, the unloved until nothing but her bawling and boiling and swimming alone in bloodmuddle, an uncomfortable revolting goop. And she blames humankind for hating her. And the world over-the-top hates her, it's obvious she has nobody to blame but herself. The End. So there."

I remembered her joy. Alison laughing staccato yelps,

"Shit that's not scary. It's a fucking fairy story. What in hell is bloodmuddle? And why did she stay down the dumb Well?"

"I got stuck." This shivering.

"You're nuts Shipley."

Alison deeped understood a lifetime more than I ever could. She reached the top of the Well. She slid the stone lid across and disappeared. I waded below in the bloodmuddle. My quieter daredevil talked shit bounced against the.

"Jeezus Gawd almighty. I am fucked."

"We both are," said Alison.

"I know."

"Fergal fucks the shit out of me. Don't tell Monk."

"I promise."

"Thanks. I discovered life somersaults this backflip. Life slaps you in the face, it tramples you. I read that somewhere and I thought it *does,* it absolutely does."

Without an answer. A questioning.

"We are not very normal, are we?"

"God forbid."

"What are you gonna do?"

"No idea. I should make a run for it. But he put bars on the windows. I lie down and rest for hours and hours. Sometimes I don't sleep. I hear him creeping about. I get afraid. The house smells of bleach. Sometimes I shake the bars. I rattled them because they rattle. That is all."

Peppered summer when. Hot hot hot. Girl married blue deary. Dimwitted lost me, lovely blah deary. People said girl terribly blue dearie. But her blah blah seized by sea.

"We are screwed." I said.

Okay Could It Be.

I watched this funeral procession. A polished puppet drove the hearse of bright chrome. Passerby ogled the tiny white coffin and it whispered, a child dead. The mother of nowhere and everywhere, this fascination with grief, a foraged for bleak and 'at peace' was such a beastly phrase.

Right Then.

Alison suggested a run. Somewhere.

"You mean jogging?"

"Yep. Get in shape for the big day."

"What big day."

She frowned her should-I-tell-her frown. The marriage circumstance gradual crawl of Never. Be. Free.

"You really don't realize do you."

What I was getting myself into.

he did it this way

The Week before The Wedding. Late she was.

"She's gone to the shops," said Fergal, lone fisheyes careering over me.

I recoiled as if he were. Radioactive. He began fondling his fatcat, a whopping puss, a fur bauble the color of a carbuncle. It purred, gracious me satisfaction. What type of man loved *felines* brandishing the meow. Fergal and cattysphinx rubbing noses. He beckoned,

"You can wait for her in the sitting room."

Fergal dropped the cat, let out a yowl. He advanced two fingers pointing closer and closer his fingertips closed my doll eyelids. Gentle in the beginning, weirdo prickled the back of my neck hair rearing. He grinned,

"I shall return."

He slithered, but not far enough.

The facts of that sitting room. Scared of cat hair filth taboo. Cold mountain white galaxy of hard glare and shag pile rugged. I removed my shoes and soon living wool between my toes and ears and stood in. A common lounge room where nobody ever lounged. Where. The murderous phantom did not actually kill, but kept her dead. How could she bear to live inside the unbearable. HERE. Alison, the lady of the house, seen according to the temperament of the lord of the room. The body of her hidden from everyone, but herself. Whiteout woman, without shadows. Everywhere the gleam of it. Turned awful.

Click of he entered tip-toeing this sneaked of him. Savage skuzzbucket skeezy locked the door. The fellow a creeping across plush. Snailed he of long-tongue. Crept over *hello gorgeous*. His face a horrific faceted crystal. Insolent pigeyes insinuation expression said,

"You know. The strongest muscle in the human body is the tongue. Wow. Eat, swallow, talk. The tongue gets quite a workout."

Fergal had knocked Alison up. She forced to put up shut up. And now his arms outstretched, was he herding chickens? He of the piggy shifty said to me,

"Come to daddyo."

"'ARE YOU OUT OF YOUR FUCKING MIND?"

Songed in my mind Bad To The Bone. But Determination clean shaven. Nicked the cheekbone. Shifted sneaky. Loosed at large *oh baby*. My glow worm gleamed, not in a good way, attracted snakes.

How should we begin. His second coming. No his thirst. For the juicy bits. It returned to that that sick sick the retch the wretch. He knelt nose level with my. Cunt.

"We'll do it this way," he whispered.

"Keep you virgin."

The sixteen of me reeled, but the granite bar, the black stone bench blocked escape and his lewd wrestled at me. Hands grabbed my thighs full circle the muscle. Wet his Slobber toe-tip tongue twelve feet long. Up my legs gentle pulled off my undies. Beastie ate succulent morsels of cunt fluff.

He cried, "Get me off."

And hung on, he upsomed gripped. Scratch of his fingernails nailed to the cunt crucifix, not a joke, the shame, the chaffing. Immoveable girl of quicked horror froze terrified.

"What are you doing? Monk is your best friend!"

Tremor in my voice, gave him buzz pulse of pleasure. Caught cunt in his flytrap. He flipped on his back.

He persisted wrapping arms around my tight. Gorilla arms longer than. "Let me go. You arsehole."

Face up my. Cunt sucked and slurped licky lickies. Gymnast tongued tip urgent rutting his nitpick in. Just a cunt. Did not reach the cherub chamber, the kiddie sack, the baby bog.

Where was that piano man to free me. Quiet lashed. Hungered for ugly food. Strawberries smooshed. Thought oyster slimy. Thick pea soup, raw chicken skin, chicken necks how they felt to touch. I thought of raging bulls, minute coffins brimming with blood, a uterus lining sliding away, no he pulled it out with pincer fingers and shouted, "URK YUCK." This man with a mule brain, a horse dick. Heehaw burrowed and burrowed. Fergal the biologist nosed. Got his fingers in. His fist in. My barefoot stuck in the stocks. Neck wrists pillory humiliated restricted by his. Wooden yoked.

"Stop it."

Those inhuman. Spat at him. Had to run. And stamped on my mind the image of his neatly ironed. Chinos, yellow chestybond cotton holeproof, flat packed attacker, flat on his, straining the veins, even tan, golden hairs, white socks, loafers pointing to hell. Go to hell. Why this punishment what had I ever. Woman the whipping post. The victim stood. Body collared quiet could not escape from his grasp. Got his tongue lashing. Pulled me plummet onto him, rolled dolly over, pressed my forehead to rug glug, the shut my eyes as he. Slapped and tickle his lizard between excessive urgent. Trapped my head rug muffled BASTARD. Rubbed tickled zealous and strong. Careful not to ruptured my maidenhead. Kept me intact. For the wedding. Could not explain finger pilloried carpet burns. Paddled winker under yellow sundress. Dogpaddler bugger groaned and groaned, sure he popped once his skyrocket. Did it fizz fizzerman. Another wet patch. Of dreaded dirty dirty boy. Pants on fire, stone by stone, limb by limb, ceaseless shrieked shit head and I let him get away with it. Balled where *she* went. Barnacle Fergal the fiend who scrammed. This offender against public morality. Locked the bathroom door. *Lock up your wives.* That gonner. And while he was gone.

4

HURRY

Mrs. Quill her eyes irk shining. Showed me the sepia. Her wedding picture. The happiest day of her life. Slender twig woman. Petiteness neatest wore a silk wedding dress. The palest cream, the kind congealing on the top of milk clung to peeled back tinfoil lid of the milk bottle. The satin covered buttons fastened with hand-sewn silken loops ran in a line down her spine. Mrs. Quill visioned of a white satin me. Enveloped layers of creamy magical lace. The tulle and a string of plastic pearls. But. Non-existent funds to buy fantastical farces on a budget of nothing.

The forced to conform by a virginal white wedding dressed. I wasn't sure if I remained virgined. Monk done unspeakable rubbed against. But I shut my eyes and kept my underwear on.

The Dress. I tried on dresses fifty percent off. Half-price sale for half a bride. The White Gown too haughty. Glamor Closet target for a joke. A Special Occasion. Doubting it really supposed. Eternal Bridal got closer. Off the rack vintage secondhand nothing under a hundred bucks. Thought of sheep at the sight of. Curtain style dresses with tits everywhere queuing.

Sheepline. A flock of sheep formed a line mirroring the profile of the land. A few lambs random. A grassy field. Sheep followed blind over the edge, fell into a sweet water well, bride mined it.

The sales assistant at A Bride's Blessing clicked her long shoes, clicked her high red fingernails this blessed of claws, clicked her heels. Such presence, she resembled a conquistador. Her eyes sparkled with admiration.

"You have the most beautiful breasts."

I flattened my self-conscious titties and the nipple murmured.

"Thanks. Er."

Her name tag of Marilyn.

"Thanks Marilyn." This untapped asset pair kept hidden inside nylon skin tone nanny bra. He slipped a hand in once and prig slapped it. But what the fuck did that matter. Feral heatheart boiling in oil, fuck the dress, wasted of money. Plague the Saturday, whatever a lamb. Just show up at the church, lamb, in a comely billowing sheepish egg white dress of every fantasy, gashed the stuffing out of me, would take care of. Itself.

Mrs. Quill sighed in defeat at sighting the new dressy. Wrinkles deepened charting her surface with double misery. Her hang dog eyes, watering at the frock I purchased. Seventy-five dollars at the Indian import store crammed with punjabs, hippy skirts, batik caftans, bandanas, patchwork ponchos. A modest cheesecloth of yellowing dress, whimpered anti-weddingness, touched of lace and minimal frill, minus netting. The dressriver long enough to trip me over, flowed past my ankles. Sparks. Had to be careful On The Day. Her discomfit despaired at my bare hair.

"You are not a bride if you have no veil."

Unbride me, the failure veil, festering and shrimped my short in height. Shrimp, the kids called me. Mrs. Quill frowned deepest lines at the uncovered top of my head in the sight of God. Demanded cover my naked tsk-tsk. God gave me hairs, no disrespect for traditions, once pagan. Brideless girl skulked a sheath of silk tulle from the depths of her wardrobe. Bought it from a craft shop sometime without knowledge. The use what to do with. Sin synthetic. Last minute shroud. Remembered dead keepers of old this drowning, simple nun folds. Bride of none.

On the biggle day. White knuckled Mrs. Quill did a twee skip grand entrance of a little curtsy. She wore green crimpalene matching jacket, three quarter sleeves, pencil skirt hem, a fraction below her knees, petite heels, sheer stockings showed missed hairs on her stick legs. Sticks and stones, my immediate thought, break my bones, but birds, was it time, was it words? Yes words, nervous words never hurt me.

"You look nice."

And the words almost broke her bones.

For on the nobiggie afternoon. There. Was. No. Plan. All thumbs. Jingo confusion. Doolally of dreamy hairdresser, church, reception of sandwiches and cake in the Sunday School hall. Fergal devilman wheedle offered,

"Come back to our house for champagne."

"Yes," said Monk. "Alright. After the tea party."

Disaster needed an outfit for the afters. Be changed after what into what. Charged into the bedroom. Oooh cripes shit snatched a fitting anything damn would do. Selected a 'going away' blouse. Haircloth burlap whipped me, the old yellow nylon hitched and knotted at the waist *cover your navel* hells bells, stayed in the theme, bordered with fumble crochet unlined exposing bra and navel. And a red miniskirt skirt mismatching. Torn mini slit on the side. Sexy. Alison would hate it. Monk might think slutty, but I under pressured to start the motor. Last minute, I sewed repaired the tear it fitted unholes unholy.

What I heard then. The agonized screech. Mrs. Quill horrored herself. Flung up her hands screamed and steamed in circles as if a toy train run of its tracks.

"Shipley! What have you done."

The screen door banged, its fly wire let in the flies and flowers arrived. Florist plunked a bucket or two of yellow roses, wilted baby's breath, bunches of daisies. On the kitchen floor. Last week, I ordered random flowers. Mrs Quill sterned and hoarse,

"Why why why in God's name, didn't you request bouquets?"

Swore sugar shit and her hasty flurry. Puffing billy to right this disastrous. Ribbon snatched from wedding gifts. Flowers ribboned into tight bouquets slight of bashed with thorns intact pricking. I ouch muttered,

"We should remove the thorns."

"Shipley! No time for fiddly stuff," roared birdy Mrs. Quill puce-red in the face. Her frustration same red as my chicken miniskirt, hung on a hanger, hangman for after the ceremony. I sniffed onions on her breath as she wheedled,

"Hurry. Get dressed for the love of God. Do your hair."

I hurried. Pulled the cheesecloth over my head and smeared the neckline with. Cheap foundation. Mrs. Quill rushed at me with a soapy chux. She sponged off the marks. On my mark, got ready go. Ten bobby pins fastened the veil to paper flowers either side of my Farrah Fawcett flip. The shock of veiled netting sprang from my scratchy scalp. Clouded my garish bleachers hair and makeup caked dolly. Novice bride in hippyclothe, ivory bracelets, lace gloves soaked in Lipton's tea the night before. Handmade bruised bouquet. A bunch of hurry. Late for a very important. But where. Alison wasn't here. I rang. No answer. She must be already. Zero time to wait.

Mrs. Quill whirled around. Panic-stricken chook biddy. Another highest-decibel shriek.

"Shipley! How are we getting to the church?"

Fergal drove Monk earlier, *we can't be late.* No limousine waiting. No chauffeur in shiny black boots. And I never ever rode anywhere in a taxi. The bus or? I indicated the Mini Minor.

I crashed the gears, floored the accelerator lurched poor Mini. Mrs. Quill and me, just us bonded. Bonnie, Clyde, Thelma, Louise, Ned Kelly on the lam. Sang a nonsensical song, *make it to the church on time,* we charged straight through every red light. A stop sign. Switched lanes, screech wheels, like a demon race derby hotrod car. Slammed the accelerator harder, determination extra splendid. The celestial speeding. Skidding into a parking lot and parked in the disabled space. Engine boiling. We were. Forty-five minutes late. Organist played *morning has broken* sixteen times over. My aged sweet sixteen going on. Blackbird had spoken, morning had broken. Rain sweet well, new fell, great day for a wet wedding.

Leaving the keys in the ignition, the car doors wide open, I lashed the dress, the limpet, the disappointments. Mrs. Quill clutched my arm. And we sprinted.

"Go through the side door," I yelled and she bolted for it. The Mary Janes nimble splashed in the rain. Without her trusty raingear.

How she carried on about that for the rest of her life.

Deep breath. Alone in the dark vestibule. The dim chill. The wars. The barren beasts asked yourself this. *What if I am a body of air. What if if I fall on a knife. What if if if I earthed under my afraid. Why didn't I find someone to give me away. Gone Away fade fading get away. Leave me alone.*

Alison supposed to be acting the role of the maid of honor. Made of where suppose already in attendance suppose should. Flibberdegeegibbetty host by my side. And rows of church pamphlets tucked into a display box. The headings (ooh ooh) What To Do To Go To Hell, Atomic Bomb and The End Of The World, Judgement Day Cometh, A Miracle In The Desert, Trust In God, Jesus The Way, They fashioned Jesus as white and blonde and blue-eyed angelic. Are You Ready indicated a big fat zero, what emancipated me. This absence. The organ played Here Comes The. I straightened the cheese cloth, rustled my tulle. Lips glossy for a dollar. Sweetness of the wet garden. Mine the sunlight. Mine the morning. Born of the lighted this. Life of endless fucking bloodmuddle. The shimmering gateway Jeezus the way. Angel ticked off my named doodle-cutie angel uproar. Smell of roasting chicks. Whoopsadaisy heart beater. In utter naked brainless.

Could not wait for her. Alison. Must be late, but she was Never Ever. Late. Had hatchet henchman dragged her into the bushes. With this thought. Gave myself away.

Da Da De Dah

Wedding. Not my kind of day. I didn't care for the day. Had to get it over with. Not as if I was about to jump off a cliff.

Could a girl marry for throwed herself into. Sex without guilt? But science witchcraft New Testament villain roared willynilly, Abstain! Abstain. Until yoked. Could she dabble. Not. At almost seventeen. Dreamed within a dream. I wanted to growl. *Grrrrr* grunt. Were brides permitted a growl? A grunting? Now and Then.

Cringe viewed wild west yellow of sunlight wanged da da through the church windows. Sharp angles caught cobwebs. Triangled. Steamy and streamed. Lightness of a wincing. Unable to protect myself. Hurt my eyes, forced me cross-eyed. Feverish, as if light could kill. But shade the veiled my tears blamed the brighter too. Bright. Jeezus. Was the light, the way and the approximate drummed into me. Were brides allowed to squint? Let the bride me distorted eyes must get them opened see.

My *grrrrr* growled stood at the beginning began forward on. A narrow strip of red nylon carpet ran like a stream of blood down the center aisle. But why why walk down the aisle? Of prized idiot pet on show. Hated center of attention. Preferred the backdoor ha da. Aisle of questioned, future regrets went de da on wobbled heels. Faltering once, cowered.

But I kept going. God hand diddle her pushed to the wind-up where. Pastor priest solemning. Pudgy man bulked religion. I remembered, stuck in my craw. Pastor priest with gold-flecked eyes. Hazeled. And drooping cheeks serious tucked of those partial. Vows waiting behind fatted calf pursing. He held his palms facing the rafters *bless this couple oh ye lord*. I lordy curtsied. My coy careered callow judgment, heard me uttered those vowings. Oblivious to gravitas gravity and significance. Gathered together. Everyone forgot dreams. Join this man, this woman, in what, holy matrimony. Sacred consecrated sanctified hallowed divine blessed union oh. Convenient excuse. HOLIEST of bonds. Not to be entered unadvisedly lightly. But. Reverently, discreetly, advisedly, solemnly da da. Excuse me the justification of desire whirled inside my mind. I did not want to live alone. I wanted my curious, what this experience was. Nudged my tootsie into. Marital swamped get me Sexed, not a fuck fully unfucked. No, me the fucked, not fucking. And if we changed. My noncommittal would skitter. Find another woman. To love, comfort, honor keep for better worse, richer poorer, in sickness in health and I could leave. Forsaking all others. Faithful as long as we both shall live. I could leave again.

Years meant zilch. Da Da De Dah. Nothing completely happened except whatever whatnot happening. A shimmering glimmer gate shoved holy girl into the sweetie well. Ooohed soap drama, bleated, rain on the roof. A thunderclouding. Ex-aggerated dramatic lots of memory.

And this Baptist church built from blonde bricks. What price per brick. Must be bargain bricked. Dollar a brick. Cut-rate. Soulless bricks. Senseless thought bricks did not possess a soul. Same as blonde brick pastor priest. Him stolid edifice man behind the pulpit. And lace sun clotting in a sour wasteland.

Of wooden pews dotted with stunned relatives. Strait-laced Christian crowd. The rattled skeletons. And housemates the Swedes, Phil, Marnie, Hep, electric eyes starving. They little belittled stunned of tittered,

"What does she think."

"She is doing."

"Too young."

"An orphan."

"And not wearing white."

"There is mud on the hem of her dress."

"Her veil is crooked."

"The marriage seems, ummm, rushed."

"Is she?"

"Possibly."

"I bet you ten bucks she is."

Nobody said, Up The Duff.

And you dearest spite concerned. I shocker thought I was. Up. The. Freaking. Duff. The bloat of when late. Absented of bleeding for weeks and weeks. Endangered spell of the monthly, every woman girl got herself a wonder, oops, I didn't think of purchased a test, those exclusive for the rich and practical. The readied money ones. The delighted women wanted a bub bought cradle, a navy blue perambulator with suspension. Wheels. And the others, same as me, of pregnant possibility, staggered disbelief. At a pip in the pit of a womb. But I knew this mmm improbable, even though said my yes to his wetted. Foamy at the mouth, the blatant hide of me. My hoped, but please god not that yet. Girl designed to be pristine virgin Mary, every pure ever unsullied.

Unrealistic the bee, the buzz, the bloat, float my boat, this phantom fetus, size of a peanut dissolved. In my head, not my wicked womb of churn eggs scrambled (ha) for whatonearth to love eventual this. When a baby bit-nipped a girl in her craving cave ache.

The future closer than I anticipated, junk of middling craziness created from yikes. The fermenting material girl? Kept my zipper zipped. Honest, I did. Throbbed at the memory, unruly imagination worse. But it was, what it was. Me explaining pain, changed plain me, young bite my tongue, here home of my, yeh wed rhymes with dead. The.

Rough roses sighed heaving in. Christ. Bitter rose in my thorny. Throat. Watching the pastor priest and my blushed virginity through concession layers of creamy silk tulle. Thicked my lull.

Dear God if priestman serious read my mind! And terrible what if. God her-his-self snooped in my foolish? My lash brain smacking of guilt-free fucks and lots. Head throbbed hazy netting. And trill in the front row I shiver sensed damp shrivel, mother Quill threatening her brimstoning banter. Of a shocking hot place.

"Let it rain," glib said.

And the blank beside me. Fussy too bound in spectacle follied. But this. Reckless. I guilty of awareness the missing. Girl of disappeared. Alison promised to be a bridesmaid honored. Alison intended to be. Here. Here. She did not appear. Plum frosted fled the scene. Told me Fergal wetted his willy. Soon her, soon of so soon she got to twist. The sickening where. The where, we found out too late. Rattled her cage. And I disgruntling over and over my selfish.

She promised. She promised. She promised.

Not to her went. On at my side. But she. Wasn't. Left me stranded in my hello dear, doing the wrong fad. Alison the dreamer probable mislaid today of all days. Did she lost and dreaming and sat swellsky too near edged of the cliff. How high was. Favorite fervent summered. Waves clashed on the shore and welcomed. Alison confirmed.

"Don't worry, I'll be there."

At my elbow bested beside me supposed to be. Where. Could. She. Maid of honor, a breath of fail to showed. Promises promises deliberated removal thorny thought from. But thorns halted the dreaming. Of bunch yellow chosen. What I had. Pistol posy of quick tie quickdraw. The hasty neglected cut off sharps. Bunched my hunch tried to hide the glance around. Pricks stuck into the palms of my hands. Should made me choose primroses prim particularly suitable or daisies sweeter of innocent. I hand-picked the weed, roses. This of a stigmatizing the approximated sort of stigmata. Crown of thorns Christ who pressed it into his skin.

Christ, I thought. Good afternoon, was it a good afternoon? What was I doing. What was I thinking. I was thinking what was I doing. Entering a mousetrap, the inescapable. But I would leave. What was I thinking, a tumultuous sea, silhouette of a boat? Her face the bloom of a rose. What held by hands itchy from lace gloves. Pricks stained lace these of blood dread.

Go into the world and create a man to love. I went into shed preconceptions. The past not much of it. The ideas, particular tastes, this entered unknown geography here. Of complete surprised, Monk materialized. Till until death deader did us part, hair parted, splitter to have in-depth fuck and to hold. Each other. Prisoner. For ever and ever. Whew sounded so nice.

Monk exultant at the conclusion. His beige shirt, unbuttoned at the top, a leather string with a wooden cross hanging from his neck. Our long seventies hair bohemian chic straight, mine disco sexbomb curled like lilting wood shavings from my scalp. Equal lengths stacked layers of a rock and roll halo. And Monk beside himself myself us. Shrank on the verge of broken.

Expectant wrong the word anticipating holy life of us. I crazy bones desperate for him to be the One. But near seventeen age of knew zilch. What else, but I amplified his mother, the persona of flabbergasted her. Not much except condemnation at this stage, learned in the future, harmless and talk doted her dote on him. Draped myself in the adoration beloved of him. I turnaround complete gasper, what his mother always gasped,

"Why. Hello. Dear."

But mine a whisper veiled. As Mrs. Quill, within earshot in the front row. Monk almost heard mouthy Fergal, his low softest, penetrating my plundered.

"Hi gorgeous."

My skin crawled shivery sicker. Monk's friend, not mine. I barely tolerated. The best man not the best. Niftyswifty stood next to gloomgroom. Fergal thin as a broom. Hair brushed gelled strawbroom stiffed the stiff. His uptight trousers. Tight arse panty waisted. An inoffensive mauve of the purple arrow from primary school. Sheen of pointy shoes polished to perfection pointed at me. Last week he peeled off my skin. Church bells pealing wedding day.

My eyes wide questioned. Fergal. Where was she? My sister. Why wasn't she with him. Monk whispered.

"She felt ill."

This apparent. And Jason near, shiny kid in his snazzy suit and bowtie. But her absent. Vacant spaced. I thought she promised. She bought the dress flowed hippy flowered peace and love. Of a disappearing. Fergal attempted the hunt for her. He dodged my anxious eyes and shrugged a quiet migraine excuse,

"She had to rest. Twenty minutes she said."

And it began. She was just seventeen. Almost. Not quite. *Know what I mean.* His heart went boom. Crossed the room. Held my hand in his. So loved me, sweet, with all thou art. Loved me in the lightest part. Loved me in full being. For me. For the girl in-curable, illogical, impractical. Careless. Budding dazzled. The vile, yellow-bellied. Certain my dream of wedded bliss would somehow become as real as a bewitching television show. As real as a peach-fuzz life residing in the dead-end of Morning Glory Circle. The husband arrived home at five. He flapped his over-sized ears. I twitched my nose and rattled ice-cubes in a tall glass jug.

"Can I mix you a martini?"

What was I thinking? Flap twitch rattle.

I do I do I do.

Did I crackled, wriggled and snapped to it. Fifty years in a jingly suburb. The poppet picket fence family living in a cute cottage decorated with brocade curtains. Ugh. Brocade every-where. Homemade shepherds' pie in the oven. *Mmmm.* Moon in June hung motionless in the sky. Silence was that new silence. Cloud clambered a climb towards the sun. Snarl of weeds grew large. Roses ceased to murmur. Hubby on the brink of impo-tency. His velvet hands never had a callous. Held his nose when taking out the trash. Owned a sledgehammer, a mallet, plenty of chisels, a socket set, zillions of spanners and never sang roller old folk song, *Daniel Boone was a man. Yes, a big man.*

Yes. My Dumb. Misunderstood every important words. *Do you take.* Hellfire licked at the harebrained crime of will you take this man. Enough. I saw. Slanting light. *This man.* I thought dumpermoon misshapen other awkward yellow. Thorns. Them lined on his cheek. My crap longing for shitty love. The sheep-outline of landscape. Scape goated. *Be grateful goddamnit*

Crazes flashed *by this ring.* Monk's stubble chin. *I thee.* The glare of a gold. Monk neat pressed taupe shirt receding a feeble. Cardboard cutout. Musky man brimming with love caught me. Ring a dopey. Ring a ding. Ring around the rosy. Ring to large slipped on my finger. *Wed.* My cloak-and-dagger shrieked, fuck me dead. Pearly gates definite for sure opened and transported me to high kingdom come heavenly. Both of us said,

"I do."

I did I did I did. You may kiss the. Not longed lingering but a brush of lips. Managed the difficult parts. Heaven realer truth. Together. *I do I do I do.* Later Monk joked. My shining expression made him think of how brightly lit bathrooms attracted blowflies.

Derrr duh. *Did you.* Da da de dah. Ha-har-de-ha. *This woman.* Chug-a-lug-chug. Da roo ron ron. Chugda dah do do. Lug lugger bugger. Har har shrug mug. Da de hoo hoo poo poo. Cheaper de da. Chirpy chirpy cheep cheep

Frankenstein bride *you may kiss the bride.* Bride wore boots. Bride sixteen shook her bootie.

Threshold possible Inside The Room on the flipside. These contrasted, hostile or the concept of joy. Behind the laminated alter. We signed the marriage certificate. I bit my top lip. A row of black and white photographs of dead Baptist ministers watched from the wall downcast met their devils. Devil-may-care expressionless devoided.

The organist squirmed on her hardy ha ha wooden stool, pressed her plain brown shoes onto the foot pedals and pumped the wedding march. The bittersweet together marching along the aisle. Monk of handsome and sheepish, smiling, slim, clear skinned, angelic. Proud did it smile on those lovely. He held both his hands together in front of his genitals to hide his hard on. The bride, shy as a gunfighter assessing who would shoot first. Eyes rounded the innocence. I held his arm. Bruise yellowed roses. Gold ring on my finger, wrong finger fatter finger, but still it slipped. His mother cringing in the church pew. A fixed pasty smile. Pigeons fluttered in the courtyard. Handfuls of rice were thrown. Hit me, hit the pavers with tiny thuds thudded. Where. Thud. Was. Thud. She. Thud.

Owls Cried excuses excuses.

After the day, after daisy day of COMMITMENT, after chicken, apple-pie, the floppy blouse did not match ill-fitting miniskirt, this ensemble clashed with scrawny. Monk dragged me up Mad Mountain.

"We have to go. Why do you hate him so much?"

I smacked at the salt air. Stars crazy winked the missing, the clouded faces, the stifled me and I tore off my mouth.

Fergal's cube. The shag pile weighted me down, tied my toes in knots, tickled my curious spots, my funny bones, my hot to trot. Monk and Fergal floating on air, a few feet above. I demanded to know. I blurted rushed, a nuisance sobber.

"Talk to me. For pity sake, tell me what happened. Send for a search party, why don't you. Do something to find her."

Did she want to be found. Let it slide, sleep it off, she was a ghost the whole time. A figment. You invented her. These thoughts made me queasy, a putrid tang. She did this on purpose.

"MY GOD GIVE IT A REST."

Fergal made excuses. Said Alison wanted a break. Fergal assured us, she had not gone. Anywhere. But home the whole time, didn't we remember, she was there. Fergal made light of it, oh sister where art thou, jealous, a joke. Blew me impulsive kisses meant, blow me. The arsehole. I sharpened my teeth. Alison would return sure.

"I am not concerned," Fergal said. "She does this a lot."

I yelled, "No she doesn't."

But. What if he told her. His assault. To get a reaction. Alison such a high-strung jittery creature. A flight risk woman. And the many kinds of vanishing. The multiple steps. A master plan. Destroyed photos of herself. She did that anyway. Cut ties that bind. Her slow and slow of isolation, rationed hours with me. Avoiding, excusing, deflection, chronic misleading, many white lies got her vanished, bit by bit. The prisoner's dilemma. Variations of uncooperativeness. Her gradual decline. The degradation effect preached lies of a new reality. Blend in with the crowd. Maybe she dyed her hair and bought bargain clothes from Best and Less. Did she drain her bank account, hide cash under the floor in a cave, a crawlspace, a hole in the garden. And went somewhere nobody suspected. How would she survive. In a jungle city or an isolated town. And the sense, she left on purpose. Or had he forced her to leave. Did she copy the name of a dead baby. Falsify her identity, fake her own death. A newborn died on her birthday. A baby named Lucy.

Alison always said,

"I need to make a stranger of myself."

And I always said.

"What for."

And the missing farewell note? *Explain that.*

Made me turn to lies, what lies beneath. She invisible and in her disappearance rendered her visible. And her vanishing caused curious changes in what remained of me.

Monk complained,

"You're being a nuisance."

"In pain," I said.

No place to live after the wedding. And what to do a heartache happened after the. A blur. Of the blinding, pulled the shades married. Insensible thought who would, the woman, the man wash dirty dishes piled on the kitchen sink. Who would the woman, the man take out the garbage. Who should wipe his arse. Who loaded the wringer. Who heaved the beef stew. Fed me. Clothed me. Hunted me. Prayed for my sugar soul. Who a million more the chores. Whoo whoo! Owls cried the shrewd fierce merciless.

And the ring adrift on the beach somehow. My cavorting blistered got burned, the wedding ring fell off. In the sand. Many many billions of grains swallowed it quicksand. I told him *I told him* loud to infinity and back ring the incorrect size. But a wedding band. The circle of love without end. The lost. Somehow the end.

Brided stop me wishing for a passionfruit moon. Stood fright at his grey rock. How could I be so careless. Roses harrumphed leant in. Phew almost jumping off the cliff into what the sea. I walked on water. To the brink. Could not fathom the why. I thought I did see moon river yellow. But indifferent to the yellow thorns. And Monk the outline of his landscape. Hung him motionless below the sky. Dreary yellow. Yellow desert rosed. And me sighing number of weeds. Silence imitated an old silence. Was it okay then. The mislaid ring. And heaven tons livid. Flooded the ocean, the sea, the tormented rivers foamed. Water-lilies shrieked in their beds. I made my bed, cried my river of. Gave up the pursuit. I settled for waiting.

"We have to go, I paid a deposit." Monk spent weeks saving for the holiday.

And we went on our honeymoon anyway.

5

A Cabin In The Woods

Began Shipley extreme virginal spread moonhoney my puzzled of incalculable dumb ignorant about the attachments, those protrusions, that meaty of him. And Monk average in height. But the bounty, a whopper thangy jabber ready and waiting and wanting. At the sight of his erect smolder missile, I screamed,

"It's gone the wrong way up."

And honey shut the front door, fear shaked my brick body, hairline fractured the foundations. Monk the Man persevered with his spectacular failure to coax my, to prize apart virginity…
Hear hear!

Here here, Monk rented a cabin in the woods, a relaxing honeymoon, a quiet ten kilometers from town. Total nineteen human beings, spook humans and lone pub, no post office, no newsagent, butcherless none of that, but beer and spirits and cask wine. Monk chose this remote rustic loneliness.

"Where we can get to know each other Properly."

"Okay."

Wooden ramshackle humbled in an overgrown uncleared clearing. This house fitted with inadequate drainage systems, pipes erupting dribbles and windowpanes rattling in the wind. Light at least. A single forty-watt bulb, without a lamp shade, switched on heaving from flash to extinction. The interior of ripped rattan blinds and pallets for shelves, three bricks between each piece of timber. Single-bar heater and the water cold. No no no. I said.

"I have an idea. Heat the water in the kettle."

"Say please."

"Please."

His command planted double bitterness. I went murder quiet and behind his back, I punched the air, *please,* like a boxer attacking holy joe the punching bag. Forced into 'say please" got blood from a stone, go on, give the devil his due, this plotting began from grain of hatred, niggling haunted grew, yes the beanstalk in fop fairytale. Hate hurted me as dead woman told no tales.

Outside the outhouse loo, in them olden days called a dunny, of a forlorn corrugated fifty meters from the cabin. I dashed through lantana and overreaching blackberry, bushed of spikes, caught me sharp, tore my yellow halter neck a million threads pulled. Bracken and branches tackled my ankles. I stumbled forest wounds and a leaf in my hair shouting,

"I'm busting for a pee."

Dark finger marks tiptoed on the bowl. And a cake of cracked Palmolive soap sat proud on blocks of wood beside a garden tap. That level of quality civilized. For miles and miles, humming miles and miles, nobody to peek at me so I left the demure door open and gazed across these fields of waving wheat or dense dead or growth of disappear and yes fiery sun setting flashed between gum trees. Their edges could be a spirit stealthed. In the corners of the outhouse, nervous noticed cobwebs thick as mesh. Those spiders absent, a fly caught. The spider dinner. *Just you wait for the fall.* Spiders loved the heat.

I rested my head against ruin hewn timber and peed in peace. A magpie crowed, no toilet paper.

What ho, I blah done packed necessities. The basic what to last us two weeks, scrap of meat pies, picnic basket, chutney and sauce, tea bags, salt and pepper, roll of clingwrap, the bandit crusty loaf of bread, pat of butter, potato chips and a frozen chicken for his lordship's Sunday luncheon.

This at last, this peace, this escape and genuine nature surroundings, learning by heart the leafy scents, wet and heavy hovered over pine needles, brackenish, eucalyptus trees ah spice. The flannel flowers feathered my cheeks soft as velvet. Could I run wild, rustled the wilderness, enough. Miniscule mounds of kangaroo poo. Along goat tracks sticks and stones underfoot. Gallop the vines, the branched of a choking jungle, beat the bark. Half alive, I lay in tall grass. I sat in trenches washed of rain and breathed, *ouch* bitten on the bum by a bull ant made me dance. Imagined the moors, the heather, the valleys hazed from mists, the bugless landscape of a wuthering pictured the heights, different from this country here the mozzies, the flies, the snakes slither venom. Found a creek rippling over pebbles of forgotten slights, pounded them behind me. This time enjoyed. For Once. My callousness scrambled eggs over the hill. And somehow faraway, a widespread army of hairy flowering Paspalum weed disturbing pastures, woodlands and footpaths begun my. Life as blackberry crumble.

And dreaming vows faded and vanished the yellow pining for shocked expanse of a desert. This holiday same as zebra stripes blending from afar to match the arid ground, when seen by moonlight. Monk whistling,

"Where are you?"

Slept in late morning. Sleeping untouchable under knitted squares, the blanketty blank blanket of mixed wool, nylon blend. Colorful woken. I woke and remembered I was dead. Not dead as in death, but dead as in the slow killing of every emotion a type of death. I woke and confused myself for Monk, beside me, right snoozing deathly lay on his stomach. How the poor guileless bloke, pajama shirt buttoned to his Adam's Apple, emptied his innocent eyes behind closed eyelids. My turn time to rolled my eyes and tumble from that bump double bed near the cozy hearth. Joyously hallelujah chorus of toasty toes on scatter rugs, fur skins lifted from the backs of cows and now flatted one dimensional on scratchy floorboards.

Brand new newlyweds. The two of us without speaking, rocked on identical rocking chairs. Rockers slight squeaked on the porch, thought of a hick granny with her pitchfork and redneck Pa aiming a weapon loaded with buckshot. Swung my feet, one two, one two, one two, sang *stayin alive pick up the pieces I will survive.* And fuck bravado, this was pleasant. Forgot the owned binding Us Me Him each crammed into a single body. Well we. Air considered in the fresh, an axe and logs arranged for the chop. Monk lighting the wood stove, fired smoky reeking warmth. Baked beans on toast and boiling the billy, tin mugs, we wished. I ached for certainty. Even if staying meant meagre supplies, stale loaves, butterless hours. If we could live here, logged for the ever. And ceased this rotting strict, the thought rotted. The early bid birdsong, sounding bells, clear as a, let me. Stay here, faraway from a future of scrubber shit piss, rashed hands, endless shifts, footsore mouse on a wheel.

But fraidy, the minute worry, the sabotage myself and him any minute. A billion bushes rustled rabbits, wombats, or some worse monstrosity yikes cripes shit bigfoot. Vowed I heard a crocodile, a camel gnashing its choppers, a fox quick as silver. Or trots of wild boar scuffling its snorted. Creatures beyond the trees, behind the trunks scuttled branches.

"Monk Monk! That scary thing. Go see."

"Please," he said.

"Please."

As if I met him yesterday. *Must I beg*. And this demanding 'please' reared image of ugly church scrubbed sandy bricks, passing time. Brought me here. Final. Thoughts hooked the edgy in my guiltbrain. Girl at the mercy of religious imperatives rigorous chastity no. Self-denial. Self-latching. Self-locked criminal. I committed the crime of marriage for the sake of safe married. Here the connubial state, naïve knave and cheeky bride. To howdy experienced as dragoon married. Etc etc etc yes folks, scrubber sand vowed, giddyup girl and dour. I got here from. Scared of a hellish fate in the pit of eternal fires. Wrong! This wicked wrong-headed theory. Failed to do the trick. Ahhh. *Promises promises* scolded my stun opposite of special. And too young. Purity nature's abhorrence. And tender. Ripe mouthwatering yellow as a restless fruity. Creamy as a pear. I got ravenous bloaty. A silk stocking thrown into the sewer. Of wondering about the biggest miscalculation in a lifetime. Honey.

Monk explored the woods, this quest for mushrooms and koalas and gum nuts and interesting stones. I banged two saucepan lids together the old cymbal call, dinnertime. Somber slop of red tonight.

I called to him,

"I cooked spaghetti bolognaise."

His face appeared ruddy with terror.

"I found a freshly dug grave."

"But I thought it was a disused graveyard."

"You thought wrong."

Wrong! Jutted my jaw. Monk's mouth unmoving ate sloppy choking,

"What in the name of god did you put in this."

"Blood," I replied.

An abrupt pain in his bladder and in the darkness, he sprinted across the field into the outhouse of outer. And he too Left The Door Open. Stood his whimper at relieving himself. Nicely dimmed. The distant picture of the back of his shirt, khakis around his ankles and bare buttocks framed in the doorway, obscured the arc of piss. I knew what he held, light as a stone. Cupid zipped it. He turned and signaled, resting his cheek on praying hands, came towards me. He walked through the waving wheat sure smelled sweet. He got closer and closer.

"Time for bed."

Right skimmer thought ached for a donut. I grabbed a box of tissues. Half a packet of sweeties. An ice-pack, a glass of water, pen and paper. Hundreds of cotton buds without a clue. The correct procedure. Silly regretted not bothering to read Our Bodies Ourselves, hating gawk detailed illustrations of female genitals same as onions sliced through the center. Hundreds of layers.

Dear dud me. Monk blessed by a tether of wife. The canoodled backrub pucker up. Time For Love lusted, self-love, garden of earthly sexy delights appetited. Anyone else might done the deed already. Sure, pure pigmaid should have sucked his topper. But always available a began for. Sexy not once grasped until the present. His initial tackled on a brightless night, mournful as loose ends, the awful dank and evil clowns ooh spooky right. Conjugal juggle commenced seductions in complete blackness, was I the bride of grave ugly, should I turn on the light sweetheart. Monk groped the room, *come out come out wherever you are.* The syrup voice pouring into my ear. I swallowed my chewing gum without meaning to. Bed of rickety reached for me. Him without clothes. But he kept his socks on. I covered my eyes to the touch of his and hair of him smooth as a Siamese cat yowling a wide-ranging. I tensing grand. Had a go, had a stab, had a crack AT remembered the diagrams, the pointer stick, Miss Flint, the purple sausage, raw eggs, did I have bad breath. B-b-b. But here a Victorian maiden grinned and bore it and laid like movie stars in love scenes on television faked moans as if ravaged by a minotaur and thought of. Another biosphere. What if God saw. My vuh-jeena-nuh. Ugh. Refused to examine. Prostrated, legs apart, knees bent to my chest. Honeymoon of this honey not over the moon. Temptress offered girly me of shy ignorant quite. Prudish repressed, for my pussy bubble boiling the billyboy. He struggled to pluck off the blushing petals. Kissed my fallen leaves, the tickle, the itch. And ferreted for the secret of the rose. La la la. Shoved a pillow under my pelvis.

"Are you comfortable?"

"No."

Monk pitiful bloke prepared for a vixen, but given a straight the corset lace whaleboned woman who. Hoo Hoo. Boo Hoo. Hazarded some whispered dirty talk where the smut, the nonsense, what to be said,

"You're a naughty naughty girl."

"What???"

"A cheeky minx."

But I mistook *what.*

"Uh?"

What had I gone and done. Killed his shredding confidence for.

"I'm too scared to go on top."

Monk and me. The We of Us. Could not seem to fuck properly. He tried again and again. He struggled to enter my oh my. Oh my. Prude pleats tensed predicament with misery and shame. Sex the snagged, it fucking failure and shallow girl sighing, crying and worried more mostly breathily.

"Monk. Are you sure you're putting it in the correct hole?"

"Yes."

"Take off your boxers."

"It's no use."

He said, "You're so small."

Faulty piece of the puzzle cried,

"It's my fault."

I cried

"I am somehow flawed."

I cried real tears.

"Some men and women don't fit together."

I softer of insisted.

"Push harder."

I waited for him to say, say 'please.'

I shouted, "Please." Right in his earhole, *do you hear me. Push as hard as you can.* When that midwife commanded my keeper. Pushed me into the yellow. Hell. Ow. I turned a bit blue. At the beginning, I returned Azure ha by fluke and tinny Shipley folded her flesh fabric. And Monk gentled his afraid of hurting. Banging a lamentable struggle to enter the pearly gates. He moaned,

"I really truly can't get it in."

You are not alone. Does it happen with everyone. Try a new hobby. You don't blow it, you suck it. Vilification. Punishment botching the penetrate. Not a joking, ha not a laughing, ha. Matter. What could the matter be. Honey.

"Do you think this is funny?"

"Kind of."

Giggled ineptness from the perpetual virginity of the soul. Yes, mattered the growth. Our frustrated sodden. The boggling importance of penetration. The girl an impenetrable fortress. Banged my pipes tough this steel. I suppressed a suction, shut me pipe. The nether regions knotted princess. Wet creases, my knotted shut for months. Why would I be. Clenched. Should be swoons. And the problem went deeper. The penalty for my flouting sexuality, moral frailty constricted me in watery. Those microscopic caverns, how could they be sopping slammed shut.

Nights square hole for the round peg. Emotional disconnection the unsexing frightful. Collapsed pent-up impulses. And sperm did not pass go. Monk and me suspended like a rooster and the egg. The mysterious egg inside my womb. The puckered egg uninvaded. Unfucked pretty fucked. And the rooster wasn't sporting a satisfied smile. And us of nonetheless, no idea what in hell. *Don't be afraid of sex therapy.* Huh. Nights we pushed and plugged the screwing moonhoney jab jab jab. But lost the sizzle. Until finally. Monk got frantic, shouted,

"Shipley! We need help."

S.D.S.

Monk an absolute picky stickler for details and me, the drain-pipe. The narrow tube, no light shone at the border of desperation, my feckin unfuckable tunnel. The necessity to hasten solve this fuck problem, the man determined, To Make It Better.

"We need to find an expert."

"On what."

A fortifying. This bracing against. "Right. My problem eh."

A Mr. Fix-it, a how-to fella, a blokey lackadaisy enthusiast to unblock the biddy old blockage. Eh devo, Monk leafing through the yellow pages, index listing problematic intercourse under horses for courses and was she a little lady. He rang doctors and explained, cupping his hand over the mouthpiece. His worry of the world listening, wiz bang found a Sexual Dysfunction Specialist. An S.D.S and the S.S and the S.A.S. and S.V.U anyone to crack the case. A sadist careered licking its chops at embarrassment relayed Our Problem. Who cared. Monk booked an appointment, a week to look forward to a stranger's beady eyeful of my twat.

Anyway. A summer day wouldn't it be luverly. We left the logged cabin, the bigfooted peril, the sun looting sorrow and drove the hours, my braindead chomped treacherous road to the city of the innocent to consult this Sexual Dysfunction Specialist.

Suppressed my amazed gawking gasps at the butch of looker Sexual Dysfunction Specialist, her grotesque oatmeal skin and hair cropped freshly mown lawn, dull but not green and stick-out ears. *Grow your hair.*

No delay, Monk demonstrated the dilemma of our private nethers. While my deep blushed, couldn't get a word in, just sat watching stilted Monk. His forefinger jabbing at a closed fist. While. The three of us grim, heard in his invisible grunts and mealy croaks. Cripes, I cackled like a cuckoo and the S.D.S and Mr. Pokefinger stared at me in horror, but I was now used to intensed scrutinizing, bleep bubby.

Began second my wonder mystery of what verdict would the S.D.S. pronounce. She of salivating authority kept an absent mirthed, straight laced, no expression. For it was deemed unprofessional to crack up at ridiculous couple, thank God or make any hopeless hopping bounce of the ignorant.

The S.D.S. identified the problem and the hideous fluff above her lip released a droplet of drool.

"Young women experience Vaginismus."

I thought. I begged. I prayed. Jeezus. God goddy Goddess Lordy Lord. Help me. Don't let terrible killer vagi-whatever disease strike me down.

Monk frowned of wondering what vagi, what nis, what mus. And the pocked and furried made no exertion to sooth monstrous rattled of me. Us. Rational to avoided messy hysteria. The S.D.S. talk talked talking voice monotone explained,

"Vaginismus is an underlying muscle constriction. The contraction of muscles surrounding the muscles at the entrance to the vagina."

Crick crikey relief. The unseriousness. My entranced sign, No Admittances. The triviality. My access entry front door muscles, twisted of involuntary spasmings and surprise shocker rejected cock, every tampon, toy dildo and complete misunderstood biological goings on.

I huffed the sigh, glad not carrier of rampant infection, thank you dear lord, demon, universal gods, unknown entities and random supernatural powers faffing about the cosmos.

The Sexual Dysfunction Specialist continued.

"This symptom of vaginal shrinking causes the vagina to become unusually tense and the muscles tighten."

The thought. The picture made my entire muscles, sinew body, stomach, lungs twitchy and tightened. At the idea of my blatant clueless. A bossy sign down in the nethering, *Go Back You Are Going The Wrong Way.* Had he ragged me with red hot poking.

Monk glistened sweating dripper brow. His ropey neck veins of strung out, gulped his hoarse,

"Dear me. That sounds serious."

Pious held my hand. His blanding a poker face. Did it comprehend. My shranken tubes. My creases toughed not soft, unamenable, unwelcoming. A fortifying. This bracing against. Wasn't there a drug. Medicinal relief to numb the dumbed.

The S.D.S. elaborated.

"To solve the problem, Shipley needs to relax."

I shaked my very quaked vulnerable soulsoil. Old soulless muttered,

"Well that's not going to happen."

She heard. He heard. Himself his selfishness earnest exhortation.

"Shipley, you must try."

The S.D.S. cast a glazed eye in my direction.

"But in this case, I do recommend surgery."

She listed the rules of what to be done before an operation. Battery-operated game. She dealt the cards among the players.

Exclusive the doctor card or the specialist card, manipulated a pair of bolt cutters, removed the ailments, wrenched ankle, broken heart, water on the knee, butterflies in the stomach, wish boner, leg cramps, brain freeze, blunt cunt until a buzzer sounded and the red nose lit up further instructions. No food or fluids for twenty-four hours before. The Operation.

Shit a yellow brick road. Brutal easier to wield the sledge hammer. To hack the hacked. A prognosis, the diagnosis, my dilemma, my sexual dysfunction. He called it, Your Problem. And little lamb obedient complied and waited baa.

My painted faces made me up and I sexed to young dearest. I lost me poor little sexed dearest. People said I terribly sexed dearest. But. I poor shopped. Thrifty cooked chicken, cheapest mince and chops and no change.

His gristle of shrunk bent out of shape. My waxed apple, my yeasty, we bumped into each other. If husbandman rose, cautious handled his thingy unhandled hoe. Sometimes the hungry masta masta baited. His secret roundabout for masta-batoom. Him of a tugged it, rubbed it, face down on the sofa, bum in the air. Donkey man. *I saw you do it.*

Vinegar girl shoulda offered him relief. But fruitless igno-ramus me didn't know The Manuel Method required. Scien-tific lubrication applied slippery non-stinging fragrance free gel. Woman must jumped right into clutching the shaft, both hand languid stroked got him going. *You'll be surprised how tight you can squeeze!*

I missed every chancing cuddlies. Missed a nibble at his feast. His long lute of longing married a dry dud. Monk forced now to wait for his merry seeds to get a swimswamswum.

Nice & Sliced

The night before my gamer operation, the two of us unspoken, was it the uneasiness for a while. The thirsty victim protested.

"I'm so scared."

Monk hiding his tortured,

"Shipley. You're being a tad dramatic."

I thought how sharp his blade of unsympathetic. Botched the gotten his mind around Reality. But if Monk knew, if he visualized the process. His brain would detonate. His skull erupting and splattering its contents across the cosmic whatever. The idea. Me human sacrifice on stone slab of lambchop imagination. I should not have read The Bible.

What if a supercilious anesthetist thought himself whale of a know-it-all. What if dangerous anesthetic if a mistaken overdose jobbered and fully stopped my heart. Would thump-blood restart its pumping.

"Monk! They might make a mistake. What if the knife slips?"

Monk's face turned ashen. His struggle of perpetual pretentious.

"Shipley try and stay calm. I'm sure it is a routine procedure."

Fluent through my taper windpipe.

"I have a narrow throat. Would you make me get it scalped wider?"

"Shipley!"

We went to bed. I slept like a nervous corpse. Anguished further the night, we both dreamt of scalpels jiggered sideways and rivers of blood. Got him massive constipated.

Monk steered the car slowly to the hospital. He cried,

"Thank you very much Shipley. I had nightmares of the knife slipping sideways and rivers of blood. All night."

His concertina foot on the accelerator jerked my stomach full of butterflies the suffocating breed flew me carrying my toiletries and spare underpants in a shopping bag. The martyr arrived at The Martyr Hospital.

A nurse instant writ my name manifesto on the plastic band and latched my identity around my wrist purposed to identify me. Nursey commanded,

"Wear this young lady."

She rustled a drafty paper gown. I shivered goosebumpy blind and murmurs and hands reaching for me, a little push into razor bed, tinker tinker winded it higher *here we go wooze*. Another louder sterilized gassy voice of an important man held the hypodermic low and spurted enthusiasm.

"This should do it Miss."

Gleeful, it glanced at my glee chart. Was my cunt marked with an X? It rubbing his antiseptic soap and breathing excitement, surgical masks ballooned neat. The daft sidestepped the air bubble injected earlier. Into arm or buttock the jab of calm float. Sight of fluffy meringue everywhere. The air fluff fluff whip it whip it good went into. I began gaggin fishy.

"Monk don't let them."

Those cannibalistic medical maniacs.

"Monk save me."

My fucking jerk anesthetized. OW. Needled fine fine lance, spear, ultra-thin slipped into my vein. The heart stopper.

Under hazy mindcloud. Hammered me a bitter, got me a pint. Sized loll, but sulked unconscious conscious supernatural me, hi hello, a sarcastic way to begin.

"What's wrong with you?"

Monk's every hair on his scalp stood up to his petrified. And disingenuous encouragement trickled into inaction. He patted my hand.

"Let's try to relax."

I groggy drifting off horrible fluorescent above then clear and soft.

"I wouldn't be here in the first place if I did that."

Quiet my cinder call.

"Monk…"

My hand raised, imitating a condemned woman sent to the death row guillotine. And they wheeled me into surgery. To the sudsy ocean. Rushed in and out waves did she. Where doctor taking me. I begged,

"Don't let them garrote me yellow."

A nurse leaned over me.

"It's perfectly normal to be slightly incoherent at this stage."

I thought, err fine and started moaning.

"Don't let them put a pie in my oven pit. What if they murder my baby tunnel. Pitch dark at the end of. Don't let them stick a lizard up me. Don't let them ram a broomstick up my witch witchettygrub."

Dim sensed the heat of Monk about to explode. I waved again. A weak wave at him. He walked backwards, incapable of daring to turn his back on me. He watched me go. My hand fell, lights out. *What if the knife.* Trapped price conked out.

I at no time, figured the before. To inquire particulars of the procedure. I just accepted without question, letting the delighted cutter hack his way. Into me.

And while the sleeping heart, my out of body girl levitating above, I watched. Man of mine sat on a seat. Alone on a synthetic chair for hours in the windy waiting room. May as well be comfortable in the empty. A biscuit on his knee and cuppa tea balanced on the armrest. Lukewarm the grey swill. Crunched him crumbs bit his moochy bitten sipped Lipton's and sobbed.

His maggoty sex loved botched Shipley livid in the misty. The bloody mist of his unused cock. His terror terror terror terrorized chewed his sugar-free bubblegum, lip smacked the smack smack smackeroo. I knew in my deep. Monk refused to picture my cherry made to measure. I remembered him baulking, found it unspeakable to chortle the word, cunt.

"It's demeaning," he said.

"Too right."

Bile rose from his agony meat. Churning his butter stomach, he searched for the mens, the mens *over there little man.* Bathroom scrubbed shiny, the tiles whiter than pearls, suds germless forevermore. Monk sicked up the biscuit in the urinal. Wept his donkey rush peed yellow dying for a whisky to bitchslap his worry. He vomited fear foam, this spleen without substance. Such a bad aftertaste. His furry tongue. His scurried. His flurried. The agony jig, dump truck, earthmover clenched his balls. His thigh muscles tightened and he squeezed his knees together unable to tear them apart. And torment never let go.

Sir, were those white coated doctors masked robbers? The reparation questioning? Did doctor giggled bind my shins to my knees? Stretched it did they did they did they? Applaud, sweat, dicks bulged in surgical pants as they wielded steel instruments of tongs, tweezers, clickers clackers into my clack eh. Click unlocking locked door created accessibility yay. Penetrating my jesustheway. I betted. They allowed a trainee tweak my pinkish, my teensy buttony. Maybe those doctors laughed, woop woop she's a tender little. Executioners pinching my clit for the hell of it. Ha just for jollies. Fixed of admiring,

"She's a perfect peach."

Peachy keened. Before the nick in time. Surgeon sliced. The tiddley winks. A millionth of a millimeter. Ah this should open her candy pockets a notch. And Sister sutured the score.

"Sweet," said witchdoctor.

Nurse stapled the vagina. V vied for victorious. The blokey always won. And hellish God watched the severing, scarring and embroider of my pure moistened lump.

The Patient comatose, snored deep, instincted of how to get back from out of body to into body. I visualized a universe of crucified visions. Priest waved a scalpel. Surgeon carried a yellow cross on his shoulder. Cross to bear heavy. Yellow light scorched my haystack brain stacked with yellow bricks, straw bricks, cheap bricks swimming in a lake of hellfire. Mucked the muck. Tripping on a stream of blood. A million fetus peanuts sewn into the maiden veil. Bright lit bathroom flies caught in a spider's web. Eyes whites behind turned yellowy spindly veins frighting, electronic guts. Eyelids weighed as much as the boulder thundering toward my heard. Abba singing, *I do I do I do.* My mouth crammed with lace, this tickle choker itched hair ball down my. Threads protruded through ooze the crochet. Laced with thorns. Mad woman in the attic. Alison where? Somewhere. She yes action stations! Her supposed to remove the thorns.

She must be here some awaywhere. Flowerwhite body, white sliced, she rolled with the clouds. And nightmare infiltrated a Fergal of smolten shlong enjoyed rolling her twinky. Fergal thought me the ninny. The last words Alison spoke to me. *Wait for me.* I tremored the visual of her under. Water. Beautiful. Her zippered into. The yellow cloth. Similar to those times children built sand castles for the smashing. My ring of gold lost in the sand. Sorry I said to him. Sorry. The fiendish omen. And in my mind expired. *Breath your last.* Because *I saw her.* Magic godforsaken figure. Apparition woman with long brown hair. Lashed to the mast. Pirate ship Shipley. This vision hovering at the finish of me. The me crawled under a rock. Rocked the boat. Raced the reefs of her crush smoke and mirrors. *I saw her.* Alison dressed somehow in aqua as a lagoon, Hawaiian shirt. Sapphire cross spooled easy around her neck. Legs sheer barelegged under a white chiffon skirt. Reached the floor, the smelly floored. I pointed to a shaggy rug on gleaming surfaces. Clean as clean, disappeared every speck, fleck, turd and puddle from the floor reeked the floor, shagged the floor. Wet the wool, pulled the other one. Alison asked,

"How did that stain get here?"

She wrung her *wait wait for me* muffled,

"What have you done?"

Hardly conscious I lay. Anesthetic fading me and paper wall melting. Eyes shrank to slits. Eyes half-opened crook. Eyes woozied. C-C- Coming around the mulberry bushed, I hailed brain flubber. Half-drugged, but coming round. On the gurney. Up to my neck in a white sheet. Sanded sheeted wrapped like a gift. Girl the spud. My gut quizzed what, why would I think baddest snorting mucous waked.

Semi-Conscious trance seesaw a stranger, seeming young man standing at the foot of the bed. Might be a surfer. Might be a lemon meringue pie, yellow sty in my eye. Might be a courier delivering flowers. Or an angel. But he wasn't. This innocuous sort minus the surfboard or a bunch of flowers or angelic stuff. Had he wandered in from the street to chat with his friends in the operating theatre. What if holy fuck those intentions of skewer sinister. A voyeur creep, tempted to stroke my unconscious body.

Fully Conscious wiped me stale breath lambikins wetter. Ouched my scabby privates stiff stitched. Pussy fully plundered a little. Bleaked beaky a little. Severed a little. Oozy a little. Crowed a little. Gnarly a little. Surfer courier angel damn fairy gone. And I fully opened my eyes blinked haze stinking of Dettol, eucalyptus, linoleum along the corridor ahead, hallucinating nurses. Starched flags flying along the slippery lino. Pelicans loose. Paper planes. Was it The Flying Nun? Hallo Mother Placido and Sister Bertrille. *Hang on.* Now then, before then, after then. The operation remembered. Fucking fabulous. My fucked fabulousness. But behave and. Be happier pussy. Catwoman pulled the caper in what the cape. Be panther pussed to his woody. More space for his dipstick. Broad sparse arse girl, arse grinner. Git thee git thee licked to the wonder thong. Yum rum of willingdone. Wider. Open wider. Mmmm. That much better girl. Sex gage caliber bursted the mercury in the thermometer. Monk blasted to kingdom of come. This performance I acted goody goody clapped hands. Handed scalding cheek. Openings to pest pleasure. Cool sensational. More freedom gained. Wider. I wided gapper open to the magnificent entire. AND. I would come hundred and two hundred times. SHHHHHH. I would march ten thousand times. Sex the war plugged my pores. Got me nice and sliced. And what? Jellied brain stammering song. When it came, when it came, when it came. *When IT COMES to being loved, the first cut is the de-ee-ep-est.* Jelly shit hadn't thought of unreality magnitude. How un-the-real was here along the yeh-hell-ow. And the first cut. Cutting the deepest.

Make-Believe

The second coming of. Jeezus what a mess. Sought somewhere. To lay our heads, lay each other, lay the missus. A home to dump of homey, with shelves for trash crap. For a shelf to store his bottle collection, stamp collection, coin collection, rock collection. Christ. Mean my snide, what day was the rubbish collection. My scorn candid at him.

"Where did you get. This. Shit."

Shedding the remnants. Trapped our traps. And my pile of inconsequential. My detritus. Which sounded Greek god-ish, jetsam owned flotsams, satin petticoats, a set of watercolors for doodles, unreadable books and mirror mirror on the wall fairest of everyone. A small number of wedding presents scraps of useful. Many doo doo dishes, kitsch salad bowl, a toaster, mugs, antique teaspoons of silver shell shape scooped a spoonful of. Sugar. Shitcrikey stacks of flowery porcelain plates and chipped and cracked. Ugh. Evidence, madness and fleas lived in cracks.

Home. We/he leased a crappy shed-type *abode*. Twenty-five bucks per week. Long lease. Security of utmost in an old pickle shed, sweet exactitude tit sized, zero square meter length of a shoe size eleven, boring white shack, doll house, once a garage converted into a barely livable dwelling. Owned by an evangelist couple, Ollie and Molly, grainy humans crunched of *healthy*, but I noticed fungus on furious feet encased in chunky leather sandals. And the two of identical flesh, this swapping of skin. Both rubbery faces earnesting The Word Of The Lord. A month's rent, plus security bond. Supplication held out their hands for. The Money. On the plus side, a convenient location, Monk the man double triple closer to his mother and Fergal. Small town Eden, beachside town of closed doors and shuttered windows. And our hovel on Honeysuckle Avenue, named after dense honeysuckle bushed, grew at the edges from nowhere, along this road fastened to the bottom of Fergal's crag, too high for humidity sank consuming the avenue lined with holiday houses mostly uninhabited, reason for closed and shuttered shatter, each careful lawn, shady porches, humble brown went dead privet, spontaneous weeds ra ra ra greened mossy pavers.

A giant's peak blocked the views. Finale and the began. The cliff the edged of reason. Scarce tall as Everest and lonesome dangerous. This ominous. This presence. What would Jack and his beanstalk say. Woofed the size of! Heartened elevation high as herohigh. A thousand meters above sea level. Right rough choppy. Cliff frown top peaked spectacular as rock ragged drop the other side. Our viewed the other side of steep. Almost vertical trod the stony path up and up and up twists curves same as my heart. The path like a broken spine. The path of a dinosaur backbone. Infinity of it, this abrupt bended, yow of synch and forced to keep going. To a wire fence ridging the summit, part of lookout. Beware our explored, how hard the gusts propelled hair, clothes into vertical whipped. Woowoo wild. Missed and seaspray hissed.

Once, I winced halfway to Hopeless wooping Nothing was. Impossible

And always in plain view. From our every window. Gnarled pine trees in full chase up up up to Fergal's temple materialized. The king's featureless treat house. Architectural marvel as if spaceship sprawled its outlines. Enormous white cubist on top of the headland. The angles, the slanted irritated my eyes. Clapped on shouting impertinence, scotched efforts tried to murder the spectator. With its looming. And the cube mansion blazing. Bulbous eyes replaced portholes. Frogged eyes. This windswept citadel owned by turnpike piker, below the garden of eerie delights and Fergal the conk.

Fergal. Spruce washed the Volvo every Saturday afternoon at precise the time two o'clock. He pressure hosed the house. He polished rag howling the windows. He swept the bird droppings, the fibfib fabrications. Of a tidy savage. His touchy nature of perilous. I told Monk this and this fraction of underhand awfulness. The rest of it.

"Alison reckoned if Fergal found the tiniest speck of dirt in that house, he would scream and scream. He's worse than your mother."

Snort.

And Alison. Not the textbook woman, never met his high expectations. Made her break out in boils. Made her jaw tremble. She glided around the outside. Stayed near the edge. Disliked the indoors. Fergal sinister spied through keyholes. His kingable listening from behind doors. That creaked. In private. Volatile fist smashing her nerves, like a pile of twigs. And away she flew. No sign. Except this interminable grilling of blood seeping steaks by shitface Fergal donned his 'licensed to grill' apron. Fustian ironsides strode his jackboots. The man couldn't keep his fingers out of dainty maidservants, cute little girls, other men's wives.

The black cat next door gliding for a visit. Tail vertical and airy sailing meow meow. Helloed first year of heaven the air, the smells, the fresh we breathed, tree sap, seasalt, saltbush, sea-food sauce, fish and chips squeezed of lemon lovely distances.

But Life. Inside cheapest cocked quarters.

"Monk it's so tiny, so noisy, its claustrophobic. I. Can't. Breathe. You have to help me. I CAN'T STAND THIS FUCKING Shithole."

His roasted chicken coop. We sank. Boxed us in. Two prisoners inside a cubicle. His forehead bumped the door-frame, architraves, even the ceiling sometimes OUCH. Plaster fell, left the warped outline of a pear. Pared back, I swept the fragments. For. Truth chopped into rationality. Did it. A cower, the plugged ears as corrugated iron roof louded from heavy raindrops, purple rain, bang bang, banged my whines.

The kitchenette equipped with a bench-top stove, two burners tot tot, low heat, very very small. Saucepans fell off. And the day after the rain, I dried my wet shoes in the oven. Which refused to work now.

"No heat," I said contrite. "I insulted the stove."

I gently shut the oven door to avoid additional aggravation. Excellent housewife solved the problem by cooking dinner in an old Sunbeam electric frying pan.

"It's non-stick," said Monk trying. To. Be. Helpful. Urgh, his stomach heaved, watching me hurl curry powder and honey into concoctions of rice, raisins, spinach, chuck steak, mashed zucchinis, orange segments, turmeric, garlic. Mush stirred glutinous lumpy spicy fired yellow. Shocking chef, bopper handy ooh, I announced,

"It's vindaloo."

Hoping a label gave the meal authenticity, made the food taste better, created a genuine gourmet treat reality.

Thwarted wart Missus in crumple. Prickle wife in a pickled. *Find a project to do, make it fancy for the hubby.* The compulsion to improve and convinced Monk, to paint boring white hardiplank with Dulux gum-leaf low sheen, his shocked.

"Are we allowed?"

"Just do it. PLEASE."

Monk painting planks greener than green, the doubt, his furtive, a watchdog for them landlords. A man walked past and stopped. The man stared incredulously. The man yelled,

"Hey mate! I gotta tell ya. That's a god-awful color!"

My wife forced me.

A previous tenant or possible Ollie and Molly left a bedroom dresser, stank of shoe polish and soiled nappies. Maybe they kept a baby in the bottom drawer. I found eighty dollars tucked under the drawer lining, a sly hoard of the evangelist's wife. Why hide money. Saving her for a surreptitious sins of Violet Crumble Bars, red rouge for her sallow face, a bottle of cheap perfume. I had noticed the whiff of musk about her. Should I, as a brand-new wife, accumulate a pile of hush hush money. Hided coins in a sock snug under the scented lining of a drawer. Discovery species Molly typed wives, snuck the dollar stashes.

I fancied Mollie's staghorn. Whoop-de-do, she owned a gigantic. This spectacular specimen grew on the trunk of a eucalypt. I crept into her garden and stole fronds. Yanked from the barking. Plants belonged to nobody but themselves.

A week later this determined knock at the front door. The evangelist's wife in a shitty mood.

"Shipley. Do you happen to know where my staghorn is?"

"No." I lied.

But behind our shed-lean to. A tall gum tree rose resolute amongst the dust. In full view, attached to it tree trunk, the lonely staghorn. Clung *help me* to the bark of. The stolen staghorn lived for eternity, but I ignored it's stalwart and isolation invisible to me, where did you come from.

Interior Decorating some. Fuckoff wife chose blazing orange for the sitting room walls and ceiling. Summery pumpkin coach cinderella off to the ball smoldering color warmed to the atmosphere.

"It's cozy," I explained to aghast.

And then beetroot crimsoned the entire bedroom walls, ceiling, chipboard floors. Monk's head spun, *can you see your brains sweetheart*, at brightness of this midget vegetable house.

"Can't you smell it?"

Sickening Sulphur tint closed us in. Four-walls moved closer every day. I held back the walls. I armed myself with a meat mallet prepared to attack an innocent wall. And this shed of sorts infested with flying cockroaches batted at, scuttled into cracks in the floorboards and holes drilled into skirting boards for no reason.

From the kitchen, a low door led to ramshackle bathroom. Rabbitty size of a rabbit cage. Pfft, luxury decided to create a rainforest effect. I painted the woodwork mellow yellow. The walls pine-o-clean green. I miscalculated enamel surfaces and painted the whole bathtub inside and out. Ochre. The color of diarrhea. And each tiddly night, Monk soaked in a warm bath. His soak of relaxed to disappear cares of the day. My ear to the door. Heard his prayers.

"Dear God dear God dear God save me from."

Exhortation to rescue him from me who muddied the waters. Where he developed his irritated of, *what Shipley git girl gone and done now.* By hook or by crook. For the major complaint in the water. In the black sea unparted. And in the mud puddle bath floated. A million bits of paint peel. Same color as poo invading his water-puckered skin. His bathing roundabout little little night of every night. Shit in the water.

And wifey unable to bear. Bare surfaces that stunk of airlessness. I covered the walls with postcards, rusty horseshoes, maps, a broken violin, whatever stuck. And time for that poster. Peasant Wedding Feast, hundred and fifty by a hundred and twenty centimeters. Famine drunken hungry painting. Taped, fit the whole wall. Pleased with the effect.

"The colors are lovely."

And Monk stepped back. Critical angled his expert head. His arms wide the width of the. This emphasis sang my dead cold and he *observed,*

"Yes. They. Are. But the poster is a bit on the large side. It completely dominates the room."

I bristled, easy the rile pile of infuriated. The man constructed of a cardboard character. Miser elected to live in a box. I huffed.

"And *please,* what room are you referring to? We have No Room. It's a cupboard. This slum the size of a cubbyhole."

Monk glummed.

"At least it's clean."

"And colorful," I retorted.

Furniture. I nicked milk crates from outside the grocery store and balanced scrap wood scavenged from the tip.

"Voila. Bookshelves! What do you think?"

I bought a bed from The Salvation Army charity shop. Ghost mattress lumps, squeaked hard life, the ding, the dong many slept in and a timber bedhead with faintest pattern of roses. A softball bat and my hope chest under. Gathered dust and lint.

And for the sofa. I wrestled a fully sprung baby mattress from the curb.

"Here give it to me," Monk slung the mattress over his shoulder, omen what baby slept here, how many this history of cries in the night and we went, the three of us, home, no thought for any future. Legless baby mattress, length of a toddler, on the floor against the sitting room wall. I covered the stains with a knitted rug from a church bazar. Masqueraded as a lounge suite, meant for stunted halves. Persons. Ha the other half sat on the periphery sacrificed *I am the skinny one*, allowing plenty of room for Monk.

Husband. I looked and looked and looked into his satin eyes. Scoured my deep into those abyss eyes. Fell into hazel holes. The ceaseless wondering.

Did. I. Love. Him.

Well, trust existed. He admired his own pious humdrum, wised and firm. The feather pattern of his chest hairs. Displayed his hair shirt starched. For a laundered life. To some extent. The tactics of a much loved booby trap. His excellency. His Christlikeness. Cuts my bruised self. My puny of ineffectual fed cowardice stayed with him. His lovely bone structure. Keep shutted my maw. I lacked sense. But developed a sense of Humor, burping yawn coooed coughed, ahem. Along the way. He lost his. Funny about that. Ho Ha real everyday of every every. Reality.

I often caught him in front of the gilt mirror. He turned his head right and left and right again, experimenting with his profile as powerful or stern or humbly keen for the events of the day. Mirror swallowed the jokes on the brink of telling.

Yesterday. Heard him start the car and the sound of screeching brakes on a bend in the road. I held motionless as a lighthouse at the kitchen window. Watched and waited. Breathless, anticipating a crash, hoping for a tragedy. Monotony wished him dead. Wish widowed me. This played at the tragic wife of not wanting to play anymore.

And Monk wanted to fly the helpful flag. Racing over the dependable of. His supportive punchable. Praised sod be the sober caring.

"I want to be helpful," him-as-him said, with a little sob tangled into helpful.

He said,

"What about Tiddles? Mr. Winkler's cat. Tiddles is adorable."

Helpful hogglebully wept for my help me.

"And Mr. Winkler is friendly."

Our yard shared with next door Mr. Winkler. Oversized beans stalking in his vegetable patch. Old Mr. Winkler, bore a resemblance to Mister Magoo in safari shorts exposing nubby knees, long white socks, checked shirt, a tie tied tight, the man pruned his geraniums on Thursdays. Without fail. Grown him upped in Depression. Years. Hungry years. Humpies, dole, stew, barefoot children lived on bread and gravy and families made do with a single bar of Sunlight laundry soap.

With a crooked finger, Mr. Winkler beckoned Monk.

"Sonny! I got something to show yous."

Steered Monk into his pantry. Monk must have felt uncomfortable, Mr. Winkler and sardinish breath. Mr. Winkler hoarded tinned food in preparation for the coming famine. The shelves loaded with cans, Edgell's peas, asparagus, sweet corn, Golden Circle pineapple, Heinz baked beans, John West tuna, tins of tongue, stacked in towers. Mr. Winkler grinned gold tooth glinted goldmine this.

"Young man, when I depart this life, you can have the tinned food."

His promise thrilled Monk.

Couple dumbfounded the newlyweds supposed came this jolly. But perished from. The cured wife, brined wife, too salty and sliced. His tremendous relief, those private parts fixed for good. Oy goody. Yet Monk scarcely identified the me, he admitted,

"I don't understand you."

What he really meant, *I made an error,* what he really meant *I will steal your power,* what he could not say, *I am starting to hate you.* Might knew enough certain of I started to dislike him. This hunting for dollars. The scrambling for a livelihood. Set aside days. Sure, he misunderstood. Bitterness. I pondered. Sang my song, did I blooper? I intended to go on and on. About IT. Well I kicked the legs from under. The table set with knives and forks for cereal and bowls his wheeties against my cornflakes. A flake and corny crunched the chill what The Abyss of Meaningless. He sneered,

"Typical of you, to tackle a heavy subject early in the morning."

Well the alternative then. Meaningful shut the fuck up. We talked about nothing much. And breakfast hid behind the newspaper, dipped a spoon into a bowl of Weetabix, sipped a cup of milky tea. One. Two. Three. I danced a kick and a shuffle and talking heads trilled,

"How do I work this?"

Him muttered in italics. *"This is not my beautiful wife."*

A song began. Lyrics stabbed at my troll-heart.

"And I may ask herself, my god, *my god*…what have I done?"

What the fuck had I done? Snapped my frickin' finger lickin' fingers, did this to myself, *stop complaining* but I. Bored need brazen times at seventeen. A scream oodles oddity. Unbelievable the tired. Nails bitten until they bled. Chewed. Fingerless. *Stumps.* Raked through the hair of a girl. I inspected my raw hands. Half expecting the skin to and a a a disgusting liver bog to spill out. This happened, told if you suck thumbs, chew knuckles gush of stigmata laid on thick. And Monk soothed sticky *nonsense,* calling me *oh my honey.*

"*Hunnee.* Don't worry. Girls always bite their fingernails."

Real men never bited. With that fuck off fact, he spread his hands in front of me. And showed me the delicate half-moons emerged from his cuticles.

"These white half-circles indicate excellent vitamin B levels."

Kicked in the.

"Who the hell cares?"

As customary. This Monk Quill assumed defeat. The smarmy chained to a barking mad girl. Pled bled ignorance,

"I try to be nice."

I cried,

"I know. I know you do. But it isn't enough. I'm at the end of my Wits."

This blurt of ending wit. Shit I thought. Our knees touched. Eyed seen through him, you were clear plastic and water. He turned on the tap, tapped my foot. I blamed myself. Not a real gadget. Ummamumama. Dreamplans uncontained lacking weight. Shock of the reality truth of myself. The year before coy glances and affection generated love brimming behind his dour faces. I dissolved into a useless beast of confusion. His sour breath. And donkey's years of damp twisted underpants. Gazing at me playing wifedom. The unskilled buttering his toasting. The man's patience tested daily. I forgot to unplug the iron. Left it burning fused to the flowery fabric covering the ironing board sizzle. Horror accused,

"Hon. Hon. You'll burn the house to the ground."

Hon left the water running. Hugger buggered. Lost his respect. Lost her minded. Lost the house keys, car keys, hub caps, license to kill. Climbed in the window. Let the bath overflow. Left the hand brake off. Always left an egg boiling on the stove.

"Look," I yelled. "A rainbow."

Sometimes he stood stiff-legged, sugary wheedling.

"Honey bunny booboo. Wassamatta?"

I held up both hands as if measuring the length of a fat alien. This wanting to get him in a stranglehold for. Endearments weakened a despairing soul cosseted in a kinky manner. Which a marvelous. Or not. A certain amount of protection in some instances signified caged. And sometimes people disappeared. Sometimes the wife jumped. Sometimes the wife put her fingers in ears, peg on her nose groaned. Was a wife allowed to groan? Monk wished for my happiness. He absolutely did. Because there was torrid in the oven. His lured.

"Sweetie, let me hold you."

Stunning sucked at my. Clasped me the wind. At least the opening wider. Drafty. His opened microscopic pores, to that unspecified whatever. I got close.

"Kiss me! Not like you kiss your mother."

He pressed his lips himself against mine. Should I swoon? Should I bash the moon? Eyedots dilated as. The artillery shell explosion in the whites boomed. And I rancid inside the warm of him. I thought sausage and mash and trash. Tripe, I thought, his surface rippled with tripe. His fingers, sticky loops of gristle, circled my body. This pressure of octopus tentacles round and round got tighter and tighter. I could only think of tripe, a pile of heaving tripe. A cunt replicated tripe, the part that got constricted. I touched it once and it touchy touchy tripe. Tripe with onions and goosebumps. He married tripe and it raw and cold with soft welts on my body. He got it into my tripe, his gristle into my cunt. My peachskin buzzy, *shall we dance.* His lovestalk boomed messy. Monk said.

"This is love."

Cagey and blank and loved and blind and wiping myself. After his banana. Kaputted my stopper seal. In the climb-over-the-bed beet beet root bedroom. What if someone peepertom?

I hung tie-dyed sarongs on the windows. Tied and dyed, sheer our authentic shedded of shedding our shade existence, here streets away from the beach. The dead sea. The raging ocean. The waves. Arggh. Wonderful.

The man persisted. The pestering for a baby.

"Let's have a."

"A what?"

"Give me a baby. My own Flesh and Blood. A child completes a woman. Proof of genetic data. We'll live on freedom, on air, on benefits."

But I swore, I belched, I maximum objected.

"It's too soon. I'm too young. We have no money. I won't survive. I refuse to touch a baby except with a pair of tongs."

And how could trippy life wonderful come from tripe? Okay buy him a baby doll motor inside its chest wha wha instead said,

"Here. Have this. It won't cry. It won't shit. It won't eat."

"You keep it," he said. "It'll be an inspiration."

Goodness. Bawly groaned. Glugger dazed his fiddlee dee. "Fiddlesticks."

He blushed. Soul of a corn cob needed a drink, poured himself a frustrated vodka with a twist of lemon. Just the way he liked it. His yellow. Wife yellow. A corned cannon ball, it's chain failed to clank or roll. At the end of my wits, of all places. Imagining these particular witless wits were a long piece of string, with a firm knot hanging from the end. Ugly thumbed its nose at the yellow cord. Or preferred the thicker witty? A rope for tethering some forlorn mortal or circling the neck. A rope the same as a not-so-nice noose from which to hang Gulping. Pinned and needled. Triggering fragmented memories of tinned food, a pregnant ? And dreams of a murky gone wondering what judgement means. Murky gone. Foggy forever. Madly un-mad. Extreme, damned the extremes, went on. With the day. I made the bed, did the washing, washed the dishes, chipped the cups, a dish. My favorite. Hand painted petunias for the dishy miss of purpled. I dropped the dish eventually. And Monk tut tutted,

"Your Aunt Florence gave us that."

Aunty Flo and George her whistling budgerigar cheered the yellow laminate kitchen. Aunt Flo wore flesh-colored nylon stockings. Her hair teased into an up-do hairdo sprayed with Hidden Magic kept it high. And radiant complexion dabbed of face powder changed wrinkles into the loveliness of film-star glamour. Her cul-de-sac cottage beside bushland. The bush, I told her. Where flat rocks. Carved by the Birrabirrigal clan since the last Ice Age. Aunt Flo's eyes darted like the budgie.

"Hells bells anything is possible."

She selected bruised apples and pears, she called stairs, to mashed into cake batter. And hells bells, Aunty Florence educated me. The importance of womanhooded *you identify, you twig yes?* About infinite disguised. Midnight bride. Frankenstein bride. Zippety bride. Marriage required a Hills Hoist. The divinest present a stay-at-home bride could ask for. These smarted homemakers loved *loved* Formica. And a Sunbeam Mixmaster made life *so* much easier. I didn't know that.

Of course, Aunt Flo thumbed those pages of the Women's Weekly and read Surprise peas chose a single pea in three. Which was what good enough for Surprise. She laid on thick Coppertone, a faked browned. She went and bought vanilla self-saucing pudding in a hurry. She learned. A good thing that Mortein. Bugkiller. Spray, she thought, smelled unpleasant, but just stick to it.

For Sunday best, *I don't go in for shoulder pads,* Aunty Flo dressed in a tangerine chiffon frock and pinned a little metal brooch onto the pussy bow at her neck. The brooch of ribbons tied in a cute knot glinting, but not real gold. her favorite word, Fabulous! She poured herself another cup of tea, milk in last and sighed,

"It's gold plating over brass. But it's fabulous."

And George whistled a happy tune.

Did Aunty realize reality mauled us. Bet she somehow. The grind life trueness of real. Realness insinuated every damn thang thung it meaned. She-woman-to divulged me. How the self-sauced grownups lay bloated from a billion surprised peas. Dead from inhaling Hidden Magic. Those crazy paving stones rioted and danced along a path over ragged ranges. Aunt Flo enlightened around me. The scorch gold hush shriveled at noon on the boiling. How the Coppertone skin of a sunburnt country peeled and peeled. The truth Aunty? Yes. Verily verily merrily merrily. Fact faceted her me sincerely. Yours.

"I am sorry I broke the dish."

Broken platters. I painted and glued the pieces. Together left faint brown lines. The color of apple bruises. I didn't remember. The contraption of it not practicality, but actuality.

I stood on the welcome mat doorstep, key mid-air facing the keyhole and my body hair rose. Something landed. Tickled. Shit. Creature light pattered on my head. Something skipped over my ear. Fast. Down my arm. These teeny fingertips playing a piano scale along the hairs. And a gargantuan hairy spider leapt from my fear to floor and its eight legs. Daddy-long-Legs. Huntsman on the run disappeared into a shrub. Leaves everywhere. My mouth opened screaming a soundless suburban scream. Aaaaaaaaaaarrrrrrrrrrrrgh. Of stagnant nowheresville. Diluted girl on the outer spidery, trapped. Paling fenced desert of grinning garden gnomes, seahorse letterboxes, off-white fibro, compressed Bessa blocks. Voided days of familiar began.

Beginnings moved on to new endings burning for something. Special. I was I was I was bragged of my heart, savored slow leaking tire, hissing of tedium. Nothing probably happened. Four walls lived the life, living a life, its own damp sweetness of. Bewilderment, put on second hand clothes, three-dollar Indian sandals with holy socks in the rain, hand to mouth, cold cups of milky tea and me. Floating immature mellowed merciless raw incompetent kook. In reality. Here. Elbows leant on tiddly stove, me watching the clock numbers ticked little clicks from 9:00 to 9:01 lasted a lifetime. The time it took for a nightmare to turn into a television game show of life gone on forever, but it wouldn't and had nothing to confirm my extinction, which clicked over and on and into this infinity of ending up where I ended. *What did I think. What should I do. Where could I go.* Grocery shopping, St Vinnies, bake bread, a cake, cookies, another pot of tea. Paint the front door evangelist fury red. It not much of a rush in fantasyland. And never went to a pub nightclub, never shopped for new clothes, new furniture, never a proper job. *Sob poor you.*

Work. Penniless applied for a job. Night shift in a private psychiatric hospital. Of bleak lights, long hallways, locked doors, sleeplessness, exorcisms. The suicidal, obesity, housewives, drug addicts, souls riddled with demons. Prowled the hall. I fell asleep at the front desk my nightmare of the queerer gods surrounded me crowd of dancing, howling, torch-bearing patients dressed in animal skins. Worshippers flew their flung frenzy, shout Boo, pajama party stoned me. A nurse woke me and said,

"Wayne is threatening to kill himself. Can you go sit in his room?"

I went and sat in his room. This young man pock-marked skin, a glint in his eye. Begged,

"Why don't you give me a little rub down here? I won't kill myself if you touch me with kindness."

Uncertain kept her sat on a chair. Boy pleading, could I. Meat his leap secret suckage untold. Sweet persistent please, him miracle cured, if I stroked his penis. But naive confusion. Misunderstanding why in hell he wanted me to do this. Never heard of such a rubbing incident. I stayed sitting rigid in the chair. In the darkest corner of the room.

Night of the obese. Sedated naked woman slumped in wheel chair. Eyes rolled back into her head, bulk of flesh dumpling woman persisted in falling sideways. The other nurse helped me lift the lolling immensity into bed. We could not find her clothes. A thread of cotton hung out of her vagina. We left that tampon in. Her. Covered her with a blanket. Treatment sleep therapy. The drugging. What they recommended. Women slept off the fat. Fed on their misplaced fat. Yearned for lasting love. Lucky if they woke. Many died. Before the invention of lipo-in-a-box, extra wide heavy duty toilet seats with warm water rear washing, total body lift, lap band surgery gastric by-passes.

Midnight Woman possessed by evil spirits sealed in Room Nine. Her head did not spin. She did not wee uncontrollably in the hallway. But lay quiet behind beige curtains and mumbled to her personal poltergeists. Her complexion of abnormal shine. My nervous carried skinny-fright her supper tray. I maintained a cheery tone.

"Guess what we have for dinner tonight?"

Put bland soup, salad, lamb chops before her mutter gruntens.

"Soupsaladbloodysoupbitchsaladwolfwoofwoofsoupshit-pisssalad"

Another inmate, a dusked of aging gay man, golden tan lined face, bleached blonde locks, stray hair on black velvet jacket, stayed in bed, curtains drawn. Subdued dimness dramatic. A vase of red roses scented the air, heavy with nervous breakdowns. Confined the pain and rejection.

The night shift of suicidal housewife dowdy shapeless floral dressed her. Wifeworld frockful of fickles. Pale potato face. Depression wrought. Escorted by well-meaning husband through the front doors of the hospital. Got voltage shot through. This the ECT. Random blows to the head numbed the troubled mind contorted crackling lightning electric shock. Mania danced to a cerulean brain light. Broken souls ebbed slowed of body arched and quivered.

I glimpsed same fed these fades. Red flashing strobe, but the future ignored warnings, I resolute as for example staghorn plastered to a gumtree, pushed the tea trolley through the hospital of unmaddness.

Yellow Not A Thing!

Sometimes. Monk crooned sweet nothings. These rare romantic flourishes.

"Darling. *Oh me darlin...*my sweet canary."

My ears wicked up, it struck thought yellow belittled me.

"Don't call me that."

"It suits you."

"Does not."

Canary such an insult. What was a canary supposed to be? Book skimmed me. And I discovered. Canary birds fell silent as winter approached. Their brain cells died. A single cell at a time. But the chill. Got bonus cells born. Ready. Birdsong in the spring. And canaries were color blind. Lucky bird did not recognize atrocious yellow. Monk said,

"Try on your wings tweety bird."

This proved it. Serious ideas always confirmed a stupid mistake. For yellow got me by its jaws, lockjaw, jackdaw shrilled a sound. Of a. Voice to be suppressed slapped into my wild blue yonder.

"Guess what I hate?"

Eyes his rolled way way back, this a snotty little boy boasting, *I can roll my eyeballs around and see my brain.* Abnormal how the whites showed. What with that going on ball whites hairy red veins. Monk feigned his nip impatient. His expression pained, what in hell was her problem now.

"Ok Shipley. Spit it out."

Hey, I spitted. Shipley romantic rabbit knew my senseless stampede.

"I hate the color *yellow.* Yeh Hell Ow. Say it. Go on. Hello. Even the meaning of yellow. And I bet it means something disgusting."

"Are you serious? Tootie-papooti! Dude! Lamb chop. Yellow isn't a Thing."

Lamb chop?

"Of course, it's a Thing. *Dude.* It's a cross I have to bear. I could slaughter that color itself. I despise those vile undertones."

I picked at despicable. Yellow of rancid piss, the underside of poisonous mushrooms, or furry coatings on the human tongue of an ill person. This hatred of yellow dictated my actions, my decisions. I stopped eating bananas, butter, margarine, egg yolks, mustard. No gulping Vitamin C to prevent ghastliness. Vitamins changed the color of my urine into a greasy yellow. Daffodils, wattle, frangipani and sunflowers were banned from the house. The shriller yellow must be my very exaggerated.

"Yellow is yellow is yellow is...you must *understand.*"

He didn't. Wait. Monk heard blub blub blub.

"Calm down...Don't go getting hysterical. You always do."

I shrieked my bat shriek.

"I bloody do not."

Stampeding got my hysteria.

"Monk. Listen. It's important. I decided not to buy lemons or buttery food ever again. Yellow is poison. Don't you accuse me of being a coward. Ever."

"Forget about yellow."

"What about Edgar Degas? The artist. He declared the color yellow to be a horrible thing."

"Huh," said Monk "Artists always complain about something."

Like he would know.

Did I know nup the incentive to run da dah. Der no. I stuck out my tongue. Which was pink.

Unstuck

Futuristic. Tick. Un-fun I gaped gaper life. The hum drummed of me peering through a gap in makeshift curtain sarongs. Mountain obstructed of. Alison entire ghosted. Must go to the steeped, the boulders waving from an unspoiled sea. This me brideth girling hotfretted called to her.

"I didn't tell you what he did. I had my reasons."

Believe me. She Believed Me

I gained grub my sicker complaints. And the disturbed mind of Girlfriday, proper fried the determination to be honeybee, the finest wifles. Monk dictated the rules. Monk the ruler. My ruler! I loved my twelve-inch wooden ruler measured geometry, drew straight lines, triangles, oblongs, learned in primary school. My ruler, a foot long with a beveled edge and delicate inches centimeters carved. On both sides. Hid the ruler from the ruler. Among mysteried treasures, biro's, notepads, diaries *today we et marmalade on toast for brekkie,* doodles, pressed daisies, notes, *I have two brains, one in the world, the other inside the cosmos in my head. If the worldbrain gets whacked, I crank the sounds of cosmosheadbrain itching to sin. I mean sing. This is not the time or the place.*

Rule of the weakweek toppled FRIDAY. A pissy perpendicular evening of routined. Rolled around the alarm rang, woke sleepy. I grumbled. Friday friggin origin this. Myth of Friday past. The Old Norse woman. Goddess of gold and death. Rode a chariot pulled by cats. Testing much mythical. And every Friday. Wifegirl accompanied Monk on a visit to Mrs. Quill. What? It ain't that dramatic tick tock fossil mother. Uh-oh you wait. Ruled. We must arrive at seven o'clock, even o'clock evening. No later grimmed this. Timed with the going down of the sun. No sevenish. Not five past. Not ten to. Seven on the dimdot. Monk emphasized the dot a lot. Did it make any difference no. But. Late a second, if late a minute, an inch take a mile, That Was War. Imagined him slapping the backs of my knees with a ruler. Giddyup. Hurry shouted,

"Shipley. Get a mooove on. We can't be late."

Deep yeller grew AND tossed his red at Shipley in bed. I slept the day. After I sweated long night shift. Trembled my bloodshots, the ever of exhausted. But abysmal Fridays. Hurried my naked rush hopped about the bedroom. One shoe off, one shoe on. Tore at loose elastic bra straps. Ancient brassiere. Breast flesh spilling from shapeless cups, plain cotton. Hook and eyed stuffed them in. Squirmed into tight Levi's, 'wedgie' design cropped raw cut hem. The coat, an old army jacket from St Vinnies and underneath a black sweater printed yellow commandment on the front 'Dip Me In Honey.' The sight of me in my finery, Monk's scalp stood up. In Frustration. Him bussybozz the boss, shockshouting.

"Shipley! Not that stupid shirt. Wear your silk blouse with the lace collar."

She gave me.

"Hurry. Please. WE CAN'T BE LATE."

Louder. Oooh butted. Beware neat collar strangling me. Broke stringy crying pearl teardrops. Tripped me, repeat lace again and the lies.

"I lost it."

Kept my shirt on. Lied barefaced yellow dripping stained. Ripper blouse, ripped in the last gale. Bent over tied my white laces, sneakers, cost ten smackers and yelling,

"Shall we bring her something? A gift?"

I straightened. Head clunked two brains and the room wobbled.

"I'm so tired."

He pushed me out the door ow shouting,

"I bought OMO. You know how much she loves it. Hurry hurry hurry."

Ten kilo box of OMO $5.99. Boil clothes, linen, birds, anybody with OMO wow added brightness whiteness. Sounded racist. And stony broke too expensive. I suggested pie, crackers, Polly Waffles, carnations, popcorn, choc tops, reminded how a teen missed going to the movies. I grieved this being of. A tawdry cinema date. Teenagers sat in the back row. Thriller hands tickled up thighs. A teenager busked on the beach. The young discoed dancer shimmy a pole. And stoner rocked and rolling. But instead, starved of melancholia romance. I held a box of freaking OMO on my lap, shut my trap, driving to dine with the prune, would it attack me. What gruntled my disgruntled, where were the blasts of funnish? Instead, the consistent bollocks Friday Olympics jumped into the Mini. What if it malfunctioned, omg the what if unforeseen delay and smashed, OMO gush of washing powder. I covered my ears hummed mmmmmm to his constant panting,

"We can't be late. Shipley do you hear me?"

Broken recording started his chant. The whole trip there. Did it his way. Continual the overwrought force of. Prompt. Punched the punctual. We aw shucks, obliged reach the destination by magnificent seven. The luckiest odd digit. Favorite number of most people. Magic numeral. A human slept seven hours. Seven colors somewhere over the rainbow. Monk compulsioned get there by. The sevenday week. God rested on the seventh. I gone carried the seven deadly sins and him the seven virtues *we can't be late*. A mother ladybird with seven spots. Seven times seven, his seven-year itch, mother aged forty-seven. God help the planet if she reached seventy-seven. And burden, Monk of his monotone, Over and Over.

"We can't be late. We have to get there by seven."

And my ick of this wanted to strangle him. But stayed steady proclamation to the seven heavens of the universe.

"We are on time."

"We can't be late. We can't be late. We can't be late. We can't be late. We can't be late. Wecan'tbelatewecan'tbelatewecan'tbelatewecan'tbelate. WE CAN'T BE LATE."

Red in the face, fierce eyes bulging, his hands gripped the steering sped. Got me this him wild animal behind the wheel. The sun going down, put his foot down, accelerated not worth the die for dinner. My cried an unusual practical,

"Monk. Too fast. Stop it. Go slower. The engine might overheat."

And,

"Why why why Monk. Can't we be late?"

"She panics. She worries. My mother gets really *really* worried."

"What in the name of God does she worry about?"

He braked at a red light. I jolted forward, bit my tongue, jeezus hyperventilated. Monk roaring,

"My father got run over and killed by a drunk driver when I was six months old."

"But what has that got to do with."

"You Know Why! Of course I don't remember and I tell her, Do Not Worry. But she worries. I love my mother. We can't be late."

"I'm sorry."

In my overheated unsympathetic uncomprehending, too young, too selfish, gremlin thick two brained head. For Chrissake *Get Past It Already*.

He told me each Friday night. The *exact* the identical speech and I said,

"Okay."

To self-flagellation, whip it whipped it good. Fifty-two inexcusable times that year, I said, Okay. I fretted about this. Regularity saying okay. The sameness. The repetitiveness. Okayokayokayokay. Yoyo ogre of Lochness muchness madness. A maddest un-wonderland. Unendurable, we couldn't be late. Beyond unpardonable for. We rushed to hers. On egg timer. Or the intolerable, the unforgivable, even a few seconds. We did the tedious each and every moldy hour. Drab bleak routine. Of deplorable Fridays. And under my dippy bloused. My cotton singlet said, Dip Me In Shit. And if I reversed it read Shit In Me Dip. I often made dips, sour cream mixed with mustard pickle, an easy jar of cream cheese mashed with sweet chili sauce and a splosh of malt vinegar for sourness split the dip with its curdle. Even so. I researched top-secrets guaranteeing success and planned to make considerable successful dips. Well *life was a rocky road,* I experimented with rocky road dip, challenge the catalyst for success, *believe to be who you are, tackle the dip head on, master your hamster? Hup hup attitude, FOCUS FOR GOD'S SAKE* on the dip, be committed think of a pig and its bacon mmm bacon dip this overwhelming desire, *you can get it if you really want, just try try try.*

Monk yelled,

"Here we are."

Ahhhh, was it dreary, was it late, was it an allusion. No, we made it on the dot of pressure cooker steam driven. *Here we are* Here We Were. The council flats. The Dots arrived, parked the car in the visitors' spot. The word 'visitors' most letters deleted by sniggering louts, read as 'v spot'. We hurried up six flights of stairs. Dippy Dot rapped the brass knocker. Monk stood on the straw mat, a welcome dotty, with his doughface stretched expression of a cheerless gargoyle grin.

Mrs. Quill opened the door. Such gusto as if ripping wrapping paper off a large gift.

"Ooooh."

She coyed and cooed at the sight of her son. She grimaced at me. Alert to my blinks, my shallow attempt to appear enthusiastic about her unblinking avoidance. Thought of my navel. Some people's navels either popped out or recessed. Monk's protruded. I sometimes twiddled it this tiniest punching bag backwards forwards. Again, blackhole screaming inside my gizzard double brain. And Monk heady shuddered.

I kicked at the welcome mat. Mother Quill fluttered her hands, herding us like a couple of headless Jehovah kiddies. She go sugared simpering,

"Come in. Come *in*."

Then. Her miniature protest of barred us. Set in.

"Wait *wait*. Remove your shoes dears. We can't wear shoes inside. Shoes carry sixty million germs."

Shoo she bubble of trivia gained from her precious twelve volume set of encyclopedias. How much did a germ weigh? I untied my shoelaces, pulled off the sixty million germs, revealed holier than thou holes in my socks, curled my toes, curled my regret scowl as. I watched. Ladybug Quill stretched her skinny arms around Monk's neck. This limpid hug. Yet another noose. Smackaroos his stubbled. Her troubles. We heard them little mice of What She Needed. For Example. A dose of paracetamol. Chicken soup. A preacher for a son. New jiffies. Lemon crisps. A lock on her bedroom door. Undying love. A fresh coat of paint. None of which were ever available except the crisps. And soup.

She released her grip.

"Monk my pudden baby boy."

He handed her the OMO. Other weeks he gave her Palmolive eucalyptus scented, Drano she loved, a tin of Vim, a bottle of Mr. Clean on the label a hunk with his arms folded and if money was tight, a Brillo soap pad.

"I make it last," she wiggled her hips and shook the box of OMO, as if shaking a pair of maracas. The granular shakes music to her ears.

"Awww, here we are again."

Mrs. Quill touched her lips, gusted a frown apologizing,

"Shipley dear, I don't ever kiss anyone. Because of the bacteria."

She dragged her mouth down and pressed zipping it. Reminding me of a tight anus.

Her taps dripped. The dryer whirred in the background. Cold tiles under my shoeless. I knew inside her hall closet sat a supreme majesty. Her white leather handbag. Old bag carried to the shops, to the C of A cathedral, to Doctor Peel's. Her three outings on weekdays. Mrs. Quill and her white handbag imitating the queen of England. And constant her uptight. Moaned about frayed nerves, choked chest. Vicks, she needed night and day. One shriveled kidney did not function, too much salty seeped through shrivel. And also the tinkle of raindrops made her ill. Jaundiced gills etched with deep lines revealing years of misery, possible overdosing on lime cordial. Dankness invaded her bones. Her drawers stocked with antibacterial soap. Disinfectant leaked from her dainty body. I didn't understand my mother-in-law's fear.

"Monk! Shut the windows. It's humid. It's clammy."

Rave fiddled of trying avoid stop her ranting.

"I smell damp! Don't get wet in this thunderstorm."

What storm? There was no storm except the one raging in her head.

"You're soaked."

How could we not.

"Stay dry."

How could we.

"Wash your hands *this minute*. The world is a filthy filthy place. Bacteria our biggest threat. Scrub under your nails and behind your ears dearie. That's where they hide."

"Who?"

"Germs. Millions of microbes. Here's a towel. Dry your hands thoroughly."

A guest towel edged with hand crocheted lace. Lumpy and thicklish. Monk's mother, with unlimited time to sew decorative borders onto dishcloths. The insipid bladdered days of dried scrub hunting for grubs slithered across the carpet. Germs hiddenincracks creviced dirty gruesome. Mucky grimed. And I listened, I yawned, I cringed. Strike me dead on the spot my stood. Killed the ever after. Minutes ticked. To priggish blab her blabber. Again and again wetness the killer.

"Make sure you dry yourself thoroughly."

And without fail, same as it ever was, every time of anytime. Exact replica meal cooked every week. Mrs. Quill donned apron frills serving. Monk's favorite. Lackluster vegetable consommé carrot bits floating. Roast chicken slathered of butter. Peas boiled to a sog but bright greened by baking soda and a pinch of sugar. Honest baked potatoes fluffed and salted and peppered. No other flavors, every possible nutrient murdered. Every week. This loved food seemed to regenerate hocus pocus inside her oven.

She confided,

"Monk loves the parson's nose."

The idea livened my questioning glance at Monk picking at the meat.

"Ugh," I said. "The chicken's bottom."

Got me desperate to change subject, enliven the conversation and I blurted,

"Did you know the ancient Romans brushed their teeth with their own urine?"

Mrs. Quill bird throaty choked on a mouthful of peas. Monk spat out the parson's nose. Later sharped me.

"Shipley! Don't you ever…"

Restrained for evermore. Imperfection prospect blanded every Friday. Monk wearied of the perpetual *we can't be late*. To activate change, he interrupted, a casual unfussy. He invited his mother.

"Why don't you come over for lunch on Sunday after church?"

Thrilled she spilled her tea.

"Goodness gracious me."

Her mopped it blathering,

"What time? Can you pick me up? No. No. No. I don't want to be a bother. Don't worry I'll catch the bus. I feel safer on the bus. I'll wear gloves and spread a flannel on the seat. You never know who's been sitting on a bus seat."

"People." I said, trying to be helpful.

Sunday of a borderline scrub sing song. Memories of a beach towel, island on the sand, she lay on her side, the chat chat faded. Gone a while.

Fadie fade sadie sadist the cleaning lady put scented lavender bags tied with mauve ribbons under the pillows. Of worried suspecting Mrs. Quill intended nose her nosy. Me aflapping tea towel rid the dust. The lurking filth leprechaun wormy germy. I straightened the raspberry ripple patchwork on the baby sofa. Vase for roses I stole from the war memorial garden. My erasure forced the bedsitter floor to ceiling germless and warmed and parched.

And a thunderbluster rain and lightning cracked a tin of tuna. Monk appalled.

"You can't serve her canned TUNA!"

Skies cleared. The woman always in a flurry the woman desiccated. Mrs. Quill arrived wearing disturbing layers of galoshes, raincoats, a tower of plastic rain hats, two umbrellas. Jabbing at imaginary devils. I grinned my evil,

"You're three minutes late."

"Mmm, yes the bus…" She sidestepped.

"Why the rain gear?"

"I always bring two as a precaution. Just in case."

"In case of what?" I asked on tippy toes.

Astonished at such ignorance. She regarded me as a pig-ignorant tart. But hell, my innocent faulted of poverty. Mrs. Quill's skin wrinkling dispirit dropped shockopen. Vinegary again.

"Rain my dear. In case of a heavy downpour."

Monk did nothing. Nada nada nada frozed his frosty feeling fluey. Monk, a deadpan block of wood, chewed his cough lollie and stood. Mother Superior Quill hugged the woody woodpecker.

"My handsome boy."

Tweaked his cheeked a wet smooch. Planted hard left a lippy smudge matte sin a lasting finish. Monk wiped his cheek with his sleeve. This transference came somehow to me. Who washed his clothes. She faced me then. She groped the air. Her body twitched set to endure pain. A cockroach waving its jointed legs. False teeth clicked releasing tiniest dribble.

"And what have you got to say for yourself Shipley."

"Um. Welcome to our humble home."

His laconic lordship interrupted. Dear wooden. Put on a tremble pouting.

"I've got a sore throat Mummy."

Her stringent lips sucked in a concerned and firm.

"A cup of hot lemon will soon fix that."

Her eyes flicked over to the fruit bowl. No lemons. No yellow. No kettle. No hot. Water tank too small. The water ran out after one bath. Earlier Monk bathed in his speckled bath. The paint peel floated. Ho hum, steamed his bathing. Played with himself.

I found his queasy. Hard to stomach. Hissed,

"What's the matter with you."

"I don't feel well."

He left me to entertain his goosey goosey gander. And slipped outside. On the footpath stood man and his Sunday paper, under the archway, leaning on the lattice. Sun dappled to somewhere else.

He knew. The drill. Stuck me in the kitchen to prove the good wife. But I was an abysmal cook, the bad baker, melting the candlestick maker. A heathen slut who seduced her beloved son. Let law abiding mother-in-law in. My hominess of small, too chummy, her nostrils quivered. Mrs. Quill fixed nervous eyes on me.

"What are we having for dinner dear?"

Dear me lifted the lid. Da dah!

"A fried pizza."

Sunbeam old faithful fry pan released garlic gusts from glob heap. This pizza fixation piled high with tomatoes, chunks of ham, ginger, frankfurters, pineapple, melted Kraft cheese, ketchup, prunes and dollops of mayonnaise garnished with walnuts that looked like puppies' brains.

"It's gourmet," I said and sunbeamed spiritual satisfaction.

She suppressed a yelp turning a bilious grey of gone rancid.
"Goodness!"

I said,

"Goodness has nothing to do with it."

Did squeamish laugh? For a second. I liked her. The sad
life. I bellowed,

"MONK"

And turned sedately.

"Dinner is served. We have to sit on the floor. Sorry."

I pointed at the baby mattress.

"It's more comfortable than it looks."

Mrs. Quill spread a handkerchief on the undersized sofa.
She squatted keeping her knees together. I asked the convenient deaf and dumb. Husband materializing, I pictured this
body bobbed up in a lake.

"Monk? Can you carve please."

Brave son carved the pizza peaks.

"Oh God, Shipley," he whispered, about to vomit.

I plated the heat of it, mush fell apart, resembling musical
puke imitating pizza. This kaleidoscope in pain. Braver mother
and son, both bit tentative mouthfuls of the fried pizza monster in bits. One bite, innards lurched this happened slowly.
Her on the sofa and me sat on a folding chair and eating what
I could stomach. Monk haunted by the ham, he disappeared
unable to bear. He got busy in the kitchen scraping his plate
as quietly as possible into the trash.

When.

The Peasant Wedding Feast poster gradually came unstuck
from the wall. A creeping subtle. I failed to notice. The uncurling, almost sinister, as if unseen fingers gentle wresting the
sticking plaster off. And the poster began bending like a wave
in slow motion. Came down unhurried sounding a crackling

and again, blackhole screaming inside my gizzard double brain. And Monk heady shuddered.

The poster completely covering Mrs. Quill. Elfin her pathetic gurgle. A helpless shrieked,

"Help."

Her clawing thrashing, she transformed into an electrocuted cat. Paper tearing claws emerged fought her way out from under The Peasant Wedding Feast. Dinner plate up ended. The disaster pizza ruined. Lapful of pizza. A mess on the floor. Mrs. Quill backed in a corner, her sauce handprints splayed on the wall and Monk in a rush bumped his head on the architraves.

"What have you done to my mother?"

A week later, the chance meeting her. At the sighting of me, my mother-in-law windmilling her arms in the street. The bird mannerisms, the noticeable frenetic gestures. She hopped off the curb and waggled her sparrow tail. She pretended not to notice dusty scuffed sandals and the frayed hem of my caftan. Deft fastened the clasp of her queenie purse with a defensive click. Was she expecting me to reach in and rifle through it? Her voice of never recovering from that night quavered,

"Shipley dear, such a surprise. How *lovely* to see you. I am popping to the shops. I need Gumption. I love Gumption. It gets everything off."

I smiled weakly.

"What? What does it get off?"

Mrs. Quill leant close to my ear and I caught the whiff of onion breath.

"The microbes. They are everywhere. They carry viruses. Nasty. Exceptionally nasty. Remember don't ever touch anything dear. Not while you're in public. Bannisters, walls, lavatory seats, steering wheels. Think of the germs. The universe is contaminated. I always wear gloves."

Then she paused and gazed at the sky.

"Gracious. Dear me. Dark clouds. Disastrous. Always a sign of a storm coming. Must dash. I haven't got my brolly. Don't want to get wet."

Babble babble babble. I discreetly made way. But I wanted to run her over.

"I thought you carried two of everything...

Abyss my minded, whistling, too much water under the... rain rain go ...went...it's raining pizza...you'll feel right as rain...come rain or shine...it never rains but it pours...then? Right. Garble garble garble.

I drove home. Newspaper rustled Monk turning sour faced. Pedigree pig paddled my gamy. Snob of the dunny with feet stuck up his lazy said,

"The poster is ruined. Throw it in the bin."

But such a pity. Too painful to discard a wedding. Outrage my squeaked,

"Never."

The hysteria blitzed rising. I swallowed, choking a scream, a song in my crotchety crotch.

Here comes the bride fulled fat and wide. Here comes the bride marching to thee true love united for all eternity.

With a roll of industrial strength tape, I repaired The Peasant Wedding Feast. I repaired thee, the torn thee, the rips thee, the buckled thee. And as a precaution, nailed the poster to the tomb wall. Secure this hammered. Earthy. The doors removed from hinges. The ouch yellowness. It's raw umbered. Bullygrit sundowners. Springtime barny peasants feasted on porridge, bread, milk. The barrel groom upturned. Frothy his tankard. The daffy frivolous wife. In a starvation drunkenness glut painting.

Sure, nothing on earth would cause this picture to fall. Off the wall. I remembered. She laughed that night. Mrs. Quill. I liked her again. The wretched life. Just before I lost my mind.

6

Bonelandia

Twelve months in. Day Mayday. Two anniversaries. For her disappeared day. I sang this song to myself, four words. You're Wonderful, You're Marvelous. Over and over. Monk glowed. Thought I meant him.

What are we becoming my dreamland of the bonies, these failure skeletons. My trance into bonelandia daydreaming. I imagined. Wild wishwashed. Yellow bones. What if. The clavicles came here. At once. In my recurring mare-night this. Tuttle tuttle tittle tat creak crack hinged at the joints. Deboning the safe, unpretentious. Skeleton Friends. With eyeballs. She never a skeleton. She killed them. She killed me.

So the sign of early blossoms on the plum tree, indicated time for bare bones of a shindig time for a dinner party, who the invited. What to cook threatened me the unskilled burner of food. Skeletons ate meat, didn't they? Lost in rambling menus. I kept it simple. Burnt roast lamb. Burnt baked potatoes. Burnt peas. Burnt pears in burnt red wine and cream. Or concocted should a super sophisticated dish. Baked ham and applesauce Boeuf A La somethingy. No, no, complicated matters, stayed with the burned.

I consulted a book, Etiquette The Rules of Good Society. Essential homework for a hostess, guests and guidelines for gits. The bonies. Instructions for special occasions. Garden parties, courtship, engagement, weddings, a death in the family, how to address royalty. The advice translated as priggy proper. Made me act refined in my mind, this genteel girl. Decorous respectable appropriate suitable dream. Maybe not that proper. Shopping to be done limited budget, flowers arranged stole again in dead of night, no broad daylight, split second timing less noticeable, I armed myself with secateurs, snipped white roses, dreamed sophistication, chilled the wine. Send hand written invitations three weeks before the event. Compiled a list of guests easier phoned. These skeletals.

Guest 1, Guest 2, Guest 3, Guest 4, Monk and me. Decided where, at our doll's house. When Wednesday 16th May. And the hour. 7.23 pm. R.S.V.P. Soon. Dress: NICE. Send a reply within 24 hours. Or else! Sort of. Right.

Glitch. We didn't own a dining table. Mr. Winkler lent us two card tables from. Mr. Winkler, amazed on the night, but said nothing about the four skeletons on our door step. On time. Received guests, shook carpels metacarpals, wriggled tarsals and kissed both non-cheeks, for the missing cheeks, barbaric act. Bones clanked. A number of bones mismatched, as if they fell off and reconnected in the wrong location. A mandible dropped to the sternum. Metacarpal fused to its pubis. The patella patting a tarsal. An ischium headbanding the cranium as. Guest skeletons crammed inside the pickle shed of chat. Rattled those bones, alcohol huddled around old silverware, shining glass and patched damask charming. Music, a recording of Asian monks, the high notes made us drink faster and longer, swallowed to choral sounds of shattered howling. My Monk surreptitiously changing the tape to The Smiths.

The Hostess (me) ensured neglect of nobody. Cocktails handed around. Guested drank apple martinis. Followed with whiskey firewater skulled. Women sipped. As many as possible, poured into empty sacks swung from ribcages fueled hilarity. A half hour passed. Surrounded by busy scattering of discreet bowls filled with marinated olives, salted almonds, lumpky pumpkin pies bought from No Frills.

Table. Monk unfolded the two card tables. Arranged guest seating, with particular care in mastering the priority in which guests flesh-less ranked. *Who?* The married ladybones before the unmarried. Husband and wives sat separately. Single guests paired. *I don't know what that means.* Everyone seated to mutual satisfaction. Humerus ulna radius elbows touched honed polished fleshless and cleaned the spinal taps. Of what this must be. And conversation, sometimes I imagined, hurtled about with witted perseverance.

At the head of the table sat a suspicious Monk. His blinded tasteless tactless. *His booming why can't you ever compliment me. Why the mossy cream swirl in sissy boy bowl.*

"What's in the soup?"

"Cream of artichoke. Eat it. You'll enjoy it."

"Will I?"

Monk hesitated before a gloomy mouthful of green slime. G1 glanced sideways. Her eyeballs revolved in bone sockets at G2.

G1 faked her blonde. Matchstick pelvis swivel, toothpick sternum held together by crimson spandex tube dress. Her wrist circled a charm bracelet present from G2. She met him at art school. G1 carved sculptures of gargoyles sometimes goyled in tutus. Named them Fluff and Monster. G2 once managed an interior design business. His sensitive shunned the Client's hysterical abuse of why in hell red satin wallpaper, zebra fur rugs, yellow velvet trailing curtains. The crucifix hung over the marble bedhead caused Client to slap him in the zygo-matic face. G2 packed his bruised ego. Became a shop window dresser, dressing dummies in a city department store.

G1 squeezed his femur under the table. G2 completed a smirk his concha. Difficult without lips to appear serious and supportive. He pointed phalanges at G3. Who wasn't female.

"The girl's writing a dreadful essay."

Wasn't every boned body in the universe? G3 creaked a protest shouted,

"Shut up. What would you know fiddling about with shop dummies for eighteen hours a day. Writing is *cathartic*...I am filled with twisted angst and I need to release it. As much of it as I can."

Once it's out there it is hard to get it back in. This rattled the skeletal eggbeater. And sham merry, I served second helpings of soup. Monk the fleshed fatty man, the outsider, covered his bowl,

"No more soup for me thanks."

G3 pretty boy in a creaturely way. Spent his time reading classical mythology and feminist authors to spout about. And G4 listened in silence. Fascinating faced with narcissism. Opin-ions and achievements added a slight normalcy to the journey of a mud-spattered weary soul as it meandered through the mire of life. The long soup. Mud-spattered? The realization the reality. Nobody liked my soup. They gorged on Turkish bread. The Hostess (me) waved a menacing carving knife.

"Who wants to carve the lamb?"

Sacrificial. G2 farced on his.

"Make G3 do it. He's a vegetarian. Crusty old vegans are the skillful carvers."

Joke! Kosher meat bled, like me.

Monk squeezed me. But I kipped with the bonies.

"Shipley wake up."

Sheesh his excitement stabbed snickle Saturday, time for the barby! Ugh Fergal's bleh barbeque, my why did we have to go. Had me this night skeleton partee. With the minxies, the jinxies, the boozies, the bawdie bones. They fetched me gifts. Old dahlias nodding on crinkled stems. A bottle of honey mead. Date chutney. Cookbook by Chef Reilly and Mr. Tipple thumbed through milksop recipes for devilmen, milk puddings bursting with butter, for cheeky stockpot, onion gravy, rare steak, loin of veal, hag bacon, buggered cabbage. I begged him,

"Just another hour in bed." And fell into dozed peace of Bonelandia.

The G4 spectacles bonestubble bubbleman stared at swill gravy and mound of scorched beef and peasy pees therapeutic dinner, greased lightning, scoffers and creakies. He said,

"It's the absolute effortlessness of the majority to guzzle mediocrity. The great unwashed will tolerate anything except genius."

Hey you mean unfleshed snick snick. Snobber marrow. G1 affectionate thumped G2 on the humerus sternum. Jeepers creepers.

"Speaking of the great unwashed. Come outside for a cigarette you old wildebeest. Keep me warm."

Cockadoodle bonegirl bundled bonehead clink outside. While I the sharp knife, thin slices pleased. Tickled me funnybone. I ladled. Mustard, mint rosemary gravy covered the burnt. G1 and G2 came in from the cold. Reeked of cigarettes. Smoke and mirrors easier to live through someone else. G1 blue eyes misted. Her wet blotted indigo tears. Dreamer longed.

"I long for solitude. I am prolific in stillness."

Her last exhibition a concept of hushed seclusion. G3 pretended misguided hairless,

"You mean them gargoyles?"

"Yes, the gargoyles. Lone rangers of our gruesomeness. Many famous monsters spent time alone, contemplating unhappy childhoods."

G3 persisted.

"Okay so explain the reason for the tutus."

G1 brows-frowned. Tulle tutus represented favorable unions. Like-minded relationships.

"Count your blessings, laugh and the world laughs with you."

Duh everyone such a critic. Fartyartists provoked by a strident chorus. Those uncreative snap expert on the value of creative. Useless work, easy to comprehend. I sighed too much.

"We have so few mysteries left."

G3 remembered The Blind Date Gala. He met a fleshed woman. She managed a hostel for delinquents. Religious, divorced and wow she hated men. G3 turned to sigh.

"Even me and I know more about feminism than Gloria Steinem."

The shuddered bonemoans of rattlers and numbskulls.

"Religious women want God for a husband."

A past beyond criticism. Just perfection. Conversation talked a bubble useless. And without flesh to muffle the sounds of. Paunch sacks rumbled like the ocean. Bowels filled. Plumbing, I thought, the similarity of drains and gurgles and running faucets. G2 asked,

"How about those pears?"

The result a vivacity of miscalculation. The dreariness of old comrades. Desert the bees knees, a black mass floating in glue red wine. Blackened pears garnished with wilting mint leaves, gawked at the horrified Skeletons.

"Eat!" I cried, "The pears are supposed to be charred."

Aftermath, aftermunch hurrah the aftermen segregated bone idle into a masculine knot mute muttered *who won the football, women, have you seen the new BMW, who won the golf, who won the tennis, who won the soccer.*

And the women boning fixated on the topic of an ideal husband. With the silent and absent men qualified. Thanked God in their huddle. G2 reappeared on his way to the. G1 lowered her voice,

"God. He's pissed. Hope he don't pee all over the toilet seat or worse the floor. Yeah, he always remains calm. He never gets irritated. He doesn't even perspire. It makes me crazy. Something quite odd about a man who keeps his temper. I won't stand for it. I mean. Put your ideal man into the universe, the cosmos...He should be level headed. It's hard work keeping men on a leash."

Boneheaded. Men. Drank the entire contents of the bottle. Guest 4, two pot screamer. G3 tripped over the door mat. Hearted walloped scapula. Cartilage flapped. G2 said,

"Got to get up early for cycling."

This hardcore cycling enthusiast, in a frenzy of black spandex, he rode hundreds of kilometers. G1 whispered in my ear.

"Tedious,"

They jumbled together and fell into each other bone by bone, mixed their fibulars tibulars, a gangly tangle,

"Help us," they cried. "We're so confused." And I thought of the game pickup sticks, if a single stick was removed, the others collapsed into a worse mishmash. I didn't need this drudgery. I moaned,

"Why not keep to yourselves? Why this peculiar amalgamation? How will you know which is what. What bone belongs to who. No taxi will drive you home in this state!"

"It is the way, it's what happens you must accept things fall and some of us become muddled."

'But I do," I said. "I don't know why you have to do it here and I am obligated to sort this chaos."

Mass teetered crablike joints crunching the moon full and bright bye bye. And there I was forever picking up bones, emptying ash trays, folding the card tables, salting a wine stain, fuckaduck, there I was washing dishes again.

Did I Mention Demented

Woke. Dredge the slow memory. It not funny girl. Not seeing you after so long, sistergirl. The real of you spilling drowning blow'in in the wind. Let the killer whaleworld swallowed you. Husband slapped your fingers, fingering the wedding cake shaped of dick. Caked got right up your clacker. And the deep-deep band played on. Took all he could take of the take of the took. Stopped her talking. Extinguished the big light. Agony to picture her that way, probable pushy gave her made her. Madder and madder as in explosive. Oh, it not funny girl. I heard. In the distanced, the moan of a person letting another person go. I must. I tried. Honed the clumsy telepathy reached her. Knew she listened somewhere in her hideaway. The song. Always sang meaner. This then was the song. I was singing. Non-stopped anything Elvis both. Different spelled her name Allison. Suspicious my minded. Not burning with love now or never. Or ever the wonder of me happened. The heartbreak steak, no stake. Burnt at the. Toughed the bore singing…She. Louder loudest. And pumped it up the other side of summer. Of I dreamed into idiot universe. And blanket pulled my comfort zone to my ear lobes. Pleaded to Monk *don't make me go to Fergal's barbeque.*

Got myself far below suckle honey, but fever pointed at uppity Fergal's heartbreak hotel. Two story it hurted. Of me loathing maniac Fergal little manic figure, trimmed, hacked, repainted and windexing splatter bucket of soapy. Unaware of my bitter lowdown tried to forget. The underneath.

"Monk! There he goes again. Fucking neat freak. You should introduce him to your mother."

"Shipley! Your job today is to chat and be natural."

"But it's such a struggle to be normal."

"Try."

Helpless as a clam, beautiful clear May day possible for clouds, I checked the sky for treachery. How. By looking skyward, no, by the hallucinatory effects of Dexedrine ha joking, clouds none today, leftover ghosts and the cumulated possibility of postulation, danger, absurdity, the grenade of unseen and cut-price sausages. That Saturday. Monk firmed,

"We have to go. And we need to contribute a dish. Choose an easy recipe. What about French onion dip? Dried soup and cream cheese. No person can screw that up, not even you."

Ummm, unlike Fergal to think of a pot-luck barbequed idea. Lack of control drove him nuts. I laughed at his invitation. Fergal boss, dictated a plan, diagrammed the event, date, time and the designated dishes. Canapes, pasta, salads, sweets. He supplied. The meat. I ignored his command for a salad and made pineapple jelly. Wished for vodka, but only afforded boiling water to dissolve the crystals. My jello the color of piss, poured it into an aluminum pineapple mold. Before its setting, I inserted tiny plastic toy soldiers. Fought the fright fight comrades, these delicate maneuvers. After the jelly half-setted, I topped with Smarties and multi-colored lolly snakes evenly spaced in the shivering fluctuations. Hello fond of the shivers. And the drowned soldiers an optimistic signal. What bested, what better way to go, but in yellowjello. Demon me hoped a guest swallowed the army and choke to perk brighten the afternoon.

Shivered. That day. Meddleday pot-lucked. Somebody better put out the did. Neurotic sex-starved slipped into my party dress. That wedding cheesecloth, its hem shortened high above my knees. Dress dyed the black of unrecognizable. White cottontails tempted pariahs. Push-up bra, stale perfume, dollied girl heavy silver eye shadowed and diamante hoop earrings. My party shoes not even leather, but fabric with a press stud, costed six bucks for barefoot. Was vulnerability predetermined and if so by who? Wished I wasn't Bronte pastel poison turned milk and men sour.

The set of us began the ascent to his house. That rocky path too high, unlucky astronomical peaked. Ghosts lingered. I carried the jelly on a porcelain plate wrapped tight in cling wrap. But it wobbled unsteady, what with the steep. The whipped cream lurked fluff inside an aerosol cannister I failed to get the lid off. Instructions said, if sprayed directly overhead the sweet, well that was committing a serious crime against desserts. Just desserts. Anyway, the cream turning sour in my basket. But I would squirt without wasting gas, a sixty-degree angle worked best. I knew that directioning created lightest creamiest clouds. Daydreamed squirt inadequate at that blue. Today. And Monk ahead yelling,

"Shipley. Come on."

The flustered late again. Why always the irreversible stuck record jammed. Sound of jammy smashed on toast, toasty loads, managed the steps somehow and stopped to itch my skin against a paperbark. Monk barking. Late lated for a very important whatever. Twisting my clavicle, itched me, itch me here I come. Chest constricted the steeped, that solid, the gape of it, limitless. Brought to mind a molestation *we see what we want to see and what we see is not really what's there.* Fergal's house highest, like a falsetto voice, impossible to touch him.

"Too early," I winded and ruby flushed. "We'll be the first to arrive, too eager. Everyone will think we are idiots."

"Whaaat! I don't believe you are worrying about what people think after you act like a deranged diva for a year. In public. I might add."

Young man continuous droned his constant adding. Nothing special. Girl too critical. Wired to the stars. Twelve months in. I might add.

Fergal's stainless-steel front door of heavy hard to get open gawd. The doorbell! Result of everyone bored of the ding dong, so Fergal installed chipmunk voices shouting *someone's at the door* to background noise of barn animals in a panic. And my single pleasant remark uttered to Fergal,

"I adore the doorbell ring."

On the doorstep. And chunka chunka chunk notched my chipmunk impression baring teeth, drew up top lip exposing stippled gums, a scalloped line waving the edges of my teeth and my pawing admiration in the vortex. Monk shoving me, put his hand over my mouth as if I'd contracted rabies.

"Right that's enough of that. Are you going to behave?"

That day. Mayday. Once inside show house. Fergal bogan began showmanning.

"We aimed for minimal. *Unadorned* interiors. Less work."

I thought what we? There was no we. Just him and Jason.

"Minimalism *is* rather effective," said Monk polite-ing about the emptiness.

I shook my empty head.

"You wouldn't know minimalism if it ate your you know."

"No I DON'T."

Monk stroppy crotchety these days. Always full erected drumdrum bore-prickling the worsted. I allowed him to treat me like shit. Took it on the chin, turned the other cheeky chit chittlings.

"Sorry," emptyheaded said. "Let's go outside. Let's leap off the edge. Let's be chipmunks and burrow."

"Not funny," he said.

I followed him, follow follow, into a crackle of vegetation, bright sunlight outback barby. A small crowd formed a jungle casual on the deck. On deck. On board. For a good timed charley. Guested I guess, Jesus flipping Christ! Whelp I *encountered* the Stegosaurus Society of rectum. Dry winks faking small chat chat talkie. The guys wankered in straw boaters. Panamas, loosed rayon shirts, waxed chests, tanned legs, cooked skin the color of barbeque pork. Esky coolers filled with ice slabbed grog bitter and long necks. Barley pop hop juice inky-minky whip belly turps. Men in a clusterfuck sucking at beer bottles. Elbows lifted in a rhythmic motion bottles to lips. I pictured teats on stubbies suck suck you suckers do you miss your mommy's boobies. This mass of male twattering of snorlers.

"Gimme a cold stubby."

"Here wet your whistle."

But those blokes were at an age of chances slipped. Golf, they talked about nothing, but sticks and balls and putts and swings and bogies. The bogie men. The Raptors oozed through palm trees, grassroots and bamboo engulfed. And God in the shade, I saw the slim wives, pressed elegant and dull into linen skirts. The breeze yes, it lilted their careful bleached blondie blowdries. One woman's hair foamed white ching ching from her head, this cash register spitting paper dockets. And breezy lifted the pantsuits, shirties, short skirts a little, revealing hairless. Skin the aging crepe paper from years without bloc in the sun. The bobs nibbling nibbled crackers of dainty. And they small snapping, of vultures let loose truth tittle. Chatty chatted crop gossip gooses beaked snapping,

"Tracy's 'do' what a complete disaster. Remember that dismal town, no liquor shop. Hey to hell with these apricot Mimosas, would kill for a Gimlet with lime. Wonder where Alison went. Yes, read the newspaper article. Somewhat the exposé probably fabrication could he have. No. Here's to her."

Wine glasses questioned that a clink. And the dizzy hush of absent children. The choice of babysitters or child grown too chubby. Jason alone on the trampoline. Baggy cargo pants showed the elastic of his underpants had he adjusted. His shallow leap of forgotten. Already. Jumped. Not high. He bounced listless. His shoulders drooping, cheerless in the center of the crowd. His khaki battleworthy. Tender damp around the hairline in the heat. His back to the cliff. Against the horrific. And panting beside him, Spiffy the Spaniel scattered fur molting. I could observe him clearly. In. The. Heat. Of. Glorious. To God be the glory, ocean views a testament of high above the jagged forcing jagged God rocks, bashed by the waves of an often, every day and on that day by the unpretty brute sea rocked the dead.

"An unsurpassed view," Fergal boasted his expansive.

I thought. Whatever. And leapt out of my. The fossil popped a Champagne cork. Gunshot to my ears. Rat-a-tat-tat filled my glass. Possible slaughtered and be musty hammered merry. That day. Playday. And Monk schmoozed as he circulated a smooth lap of the garden. Danced my uttermost to get embarrassed him. He edged towards me. My roots showing and grinned lipstick-stained teeth bad luck. A pimple. Garbed in black, what appropriate clothes to wear, black tights too constricted. For a funeral. Monk appeared, his whispery close freezed close to my ear.

"Shipley how can you be so crass?"

I turned to him. Turned to stone, eighteen turning to rowdy rocks off my rocker. A slowed turn. The turn of a revolution.

"It's simple. When you don't bleeding care."

Here I went to where. She should be. Visions backboned along my tongue. Dusk clouds, pinker trees, dark orange orangutan of bendy branches. Her beacon glowed brilliance of energy. Fergal built nailed the two planks of wood. I wanted to wrestle that yellow. And she thought, disguised as a rock tied to the end of a string. A yoyo bouncing slamming into the sides of a. This brash roared the earsplitting of me. Blaze in my eyed. My fanatical hearty. SONG.

"The hills are alive with fucking boredom. And you may ask yourself. Where does that highway go? And forsaking all others, be faithful as long as we both shall live. And you may ask yourself. A man will love you forever. Your table will be ready in a minute. God created women as inferior beings destined to serve their husbands. Am I right? Am I wrong? O virgins…o martyrs…oh oh oh greater grating souls contemptuous of reality… full of tears. Your dreams will come true. This will hurt you more than it will hurt me. Slow and steady wins the race. I'm allergic to rubber."

My booming thunderous vulgar.

"This could be the last time. Maybe the last time. I don't know. Have faith…Follow your dreams, destroy your life. Entreat me leave or return from following. This could be the last time. Mayday mayday. For whither thou goest, I will go and whither thou stays, I will stay and whither thou dies, I will die and there I will be buried. Maybe the last time. I don't know. Oh no. Oh no. This could be the last time. And that's it. Mayday mayday. Finito. Finito. Finito. No. Not me. No."

Heads turning. To stone of stoned. Heads of stone. Girl of stony, blinded unfittable position in that crowd on. On the margin day. Mayday mayday mayday.

Fergal appeared. His moonshiner bully expression a question mark.

"What's going on people?"

Carrying a tray of barbeque sauce, hamburger patties, lamb chops, sausages-ages sauce-ages, sliced bread.

I got closer and closer to the marvel meat. I scowled soft murmured vampire into his red neck.

"Bastard. Shall I tell your friends?"

A poke in the grinned ribs.

'Shipley…" His warning line an expression of quiet thunder.

I lunged at him.

"I'm a feral looney tunes you cretin."

My fist belted the meat platter sky high and raining meat, the stunned rushing to catch raw protein. Fergal in a tizz. Merry-go-round Spiffy hoovering hamburger.

I smugged, "Yer chasin yer tail."

Fergal murder hissed at hapless Monk.

"Get her out of here."

Waved my arm sideways, fly-swat gesture. Whopper meatball man this swell, this lingering, this prolonged. Grief. Grew and grew multiplied the missing her. Imitating her. This the day. Feet of clay. Glass chucked sideways. Sloshed wine on the grass. Headfirst or feetfirst. Wet grass spread did the slip. Cotton shoes scuffed the grass, chaffed the blades, stomped the mud, venting hate on that precarious. Sang my secret song of,

"Holy Matrimony! Batwoman. It is the HOLIEST of bonds. Entreat me to leave thee. Theee thou thou ow ow ouch. Swallow it gulp it. Just a spoonful of sweet sperm makes the medicine go down. Let's go. Ah somewhere nice and sliced. Bye bye. Ha ha."

On the ledge, of his continuous, cringed Monk inside his scared. I might blab about operation invasion. The past, a vague smear aimed at me in the salted air. Sea, the enemy let her sink. The water in my lunged, barefoot skimmed the sand. I looked back. Once. At what, at what, him following me. Began again that dreadful singing. Songed of. Grief.

"Where oh where is that doggy in the window. Where oh where did that little girl go?"

I watched his groin stiffen as I. Swayed me dangerously close to the cliff edge. Kicking an empty bottled over. Roll it tumbling for the smashed. On the rocks. Quiet in earshot, popping corks, but fell flat when. Conversation ceased. Guests focusing on mortified feet.

"Terrible. They were extremely devoted to each other. Suppose she misses her. Anyway. No need to carry on. Like a lunatic. Like a prima donna. Like a nutcase. Like a drunk."

A startled woman dropped her sausage. In the dirt awfulness. Seagulls squawked, *shut the fuck up*. Monk reached me. Grasped my arm calm avoided exacerbating. The Situation. No for party already such aggravate anxious, he said,

"Shhh Shipley *Shipley*. Everyone is staring at you."

"Yeah don't care haven't those morons ever seen misery?"

I sensed subtle changes in his expression suggesting ownership of a quirky wife suggested a gentle. Subterfuge.

"Come inside dear and play with Jason. He's on his own."

My removal from the hideous limelight. Of a soldiering on, in spite of. The restless night. His lips widened as if two fingers inserted into each corner stretching expectation to appear compassionate caring. *Don't touch me.* And in between apologetic smiles, a blast of bewilderment popped into his eyes. A terse hand on my shoulder. Force guided firm steering me and his nodding, *nothing to worry about* and winking *she's such a card,* past the looking the other way, the smoothing of dresses, the appalled pull of cigarettes, the huffing *drama queen hysteric,* into the house of mirthless. Left me there, be there. Beware.

"Behave," he said.

"I'll be super sunny."

I promised hell on earth and headed for the bar. The bar where he. Evil constructed of polished granite. Cockup, Alison told me, and tacky, hard the hardest. Found Jason. Palest. Graceful reserved surrounded his honey-colored curls much divine earnestness. Wide eyes awkward boned joints, narrow hands. An elbow leaning on the armrest of a chair. Fell beside him, hello child, shut my eyes. I lived young longtime ago long long once. This storytime for calmed.

"Uh." Jason said, like he'd heard it before.

"Listen. I was. Your age truly the same age as you. I borrowed. A single book from the library at lunchtime and started reading it as soon as I got home and finished it late that night before falling asleep and the next day returned the book to the library and selected another book and each day spent the school lunch hour in the library because of the horrible day ate a Sargent meat pie slathered in tomato sauce almost cold bought from the school canteen and mouthfuls of pastry, chunks of meat, gravy, red tomato sauce spilled down the sides of my mouth, onto hands, meat gravy sauce dribbled through my fingers, cascaded onto my lap, rivered onto my knees, trickled down my bare legs, just before the school bell rang, clang me, rushed myself covered in offensive gunk pie, the sauce, managed to wash off in long stainless steel troughs outside the toilets because meat fright pie too dangerous at lunchtime so borrowed every book in the library, hundreds of books for wormbookish scare of meat and yuk that warm gravy and reading infiltrated myself as otherworldliness the famous five boarding schools, midnight feasts, thousands of cousins, a little brother named Peregrine, the craving for red ballet shoes unleashing me pirouetting onto the stage everything what I didn't have, new clothes, ringlets, a silver cross, a golden sponge pudding with tiny currents sprinkled on top and for reading more books than anyone in the world, the librarian awarded a brown silky satin Reading Ribbon exact color of fright meat pie frightful darling told nobody about the meat ribbon only you know."

Jason laughed. Fright meat ha ha.

Needed a drink, what about you Shirley Temple? Mixing the facts, did I stupor, mixed an absinthe cocktail in front of a goggle-eyed Jason. The boy entranced. Just a spoonful of. A teaspoon of the liqueur dripped onto a sugar cube ice cube. How could someone live in a cube. Why did she. I said,

"This is fun, isn't it? You can light it."

Gave him a lighted match.

"You are the future…"

The flame yes burning fast.

"Quick, I said, "Before it goes…"

Jason lit the substance. Flamed almost his thumb, careful and I instructed,

"Hold the cube over the glass and let the caramelized sugar drip into the absinthe. I think that's how it's done."

Positive drank a mouthful of the cocktail. Gagged, room spinning wooze, but enough.

"Wow. That's strong. No. Jason. No. You can't have any."

And the lord showed no mercy and Fergal entered the room and caught Jason grabbing the glass and the child drank half the absinthe and Fergal's clean-shaven burned crimson with rage and he wrestled the drink from Jason's grip and shouted to Monk standing shocked in the doorway.

"What the fuck does Shipley think she's doing?"

Monk put his head, his sorrowful forehead, his skull filled with infected regret weighed nugget in his hands.

"I am so *so* sorry. She's much younger than us. I thought... oh never mind. For some unknown reason, after we married, she went a bit doolally."

"I'm here in the room," I cried. "You are talking about me as if I am not in the room."

Monk whirled around.

"Your abysmal behavior upsets everyone, including our friends and even complete strangers. Honest to God at times I wish we had not..."

Fergal in his apron, Licensed To Grill. He snarled,

"Keep her away from my son."

He did that. Got her the right furniture. The shined. The shimmered. The scary infinitesimal of nothing existed. Barely a scratch. Damp thighs stuck to the leatherette. Girls just wanted to have fun. And me hopeless with children. I heard her song in the windsong trees. *I'll come for you soon.*

For the rest of the afternoon, Jason lay on a pile of dead leaves. His probably hallucinating, but slept deep for a change, in a long time. And Spiffy sniffed at a pool of greenish vomit staining the wooden decking.

Monk scolded me,

"You are incredibly irresponsible. Apologize to Fergal."

Flamed red. Reeled red. Red sauce, red wine, enraged maggots, goons, maple leaf gonads. Red fizzed a firething. Superior to pus yellow. Red slammed me as abrupt unstable fickle fucked. Red of blood. Fruit of my loins angered. Redstrong slapped my fury face. Red crawled under my skin. Delirious distorted off my rocker red retorting,

"I am seeing red."

"Go home," said Monk.

I spewed red, a red revolution the red army, my stand for myself, express my *feelings* ha.

"You uptight self-satisfied little fascists."

Monk's eyes filled with tears.

Had I won? Beggar fight to the finish, strode down the mountain. Walked the long way home along the beach road. I surveyed the beach deserted that the afternoon. The sunless sea at high tide sending breakers and elongated waves. Steady rhythms struck the shore lazy. Sandland stirred. The seaweed a twisted lot. Starfish in rockpools under the pea sky. A sea cyclical in roar quiet. The unshrinkable expanse. Hemmed by a sober horizon. And I sat on the large sandbank. Thought blah observing every sea sand encountered of solitary habits. The lonely infinity.

Ah, sigh desolated, an unsociable person. But kind of blurried and much distinctive. At the same time. As substantial as her. Jealousy the alien and the traced of sadness. Easy dismissed the girl with a laugh. The forbidden blah blah blah.

The many times, we walked the seawall. Precarious today. Her song in the sea. *I'll take him with me.* Whoosh wish. Bottle of absinthe tucked in my carry bag. Snug swung to the sound humming, *just a spoonful of...*followed by a frightful *dah de dah da da.* Nonchalance gave a damn. But then. The dismayed. What I recalled. A rule that applied to children. Children were not allowed to play with matches.

I remembered. Alison the night warning her trembled before.

"Don't marry him."

Heavyweight scrapped hoarse at the center of me.

"I don't want."

"What? What?"

"To live alone."

My thick as a brick did not expect to be whole of unique or myself. I expected to be a swamp and gravel and thin air. She grab-glared me, *don't don't don't* her desperation.

"You fool. What is wrong with you?"

"Everything."

"Marriage is not a cure."

I resented. The chilling medicinal effect of her words.

"Why are you saying this? Stop bossing me. Get fucked. He loves me."

And parts of Alison not really, toes fading first and her hair, her fingertips. This slow erasure. I reached for her.

"Say something."

But her voice vanishing,

"Don't do this."

My wild and depths heart sank at her misunderstanding my predicament

"I must. You don't understand. You have everything."

Her erasure handless to her lipless, *we die alone*, she threw into her eyes bolts of shadow and sorrow and anger and yanked out dream-hope-possibilities. I went the married and her vanishing by milliseconds. Those angered words branded me guilt horrible. Her vague said,

"Sshhh."

I cried an avalanche.

"I have nothing else."

various ravings and shit coming
that they didn't tell me so, fuck them,
oh you wouldn't understand
I did it for her.

My particular scrutinizing of what came. Walking home under water.

You see, a tortoise passed me on the beach road. True! The tortoise dragged a king-size Turkish Delight. His shell shone frosted chocolate. His little legs shuffled At Great Speed. The tortoise said,

"I can run faster than you."

And I said,

"What of it."

I said,

"You're gonna get fat eating that."

He won the race

Indeed. Because. Right. Bleh, nothing this lot nothing. Might as well be on. A country lane. By a shrub. At twilight. And I sat on a rock and struggled with my stockings. I cried,

"In the name of God. I refuse to wear pantyhose. Ever again."

Exhausting in the tangle tights, gave me up, rested for a few minutes.

Tried again.

"I am pathetic. I can't do this anything."

Shit She-Devil said,

"Nonsense. That's a flaming vapid excuse."

What the? I refused the belief of devilish. Or grasped the idea of vapidity. At a guess, it implied emptyheaded ordinary potato couched chipper blip. Why didn't the devil protect me from panty hose? I waged war against pantyhose. Stuck in my crotch. Twisted in my crack. Stretchy letchie easy laddered made me look slutty yes. Bunched around my ankles of hatred. I brooded the bunch. I mused on such topics as physical exertion like swimming. Swimming unwound for a swam tide in.

After the barbeque, (the color of hotdogs were a terracotta cheerful shade of poo.) I remembered Alison gave me a shirt with scarlet poodles printed on the fabric love chuffed. The shirt enraged Fergal. After the barbeque, I stank of charred meaty smoke, green spirit breath. I cast off the wedding cheese dyed black dress and changed into one-piece bathers, straw hat, tattered beach towel covered my faults. Broken sandals slapped shoe soles swifting to the beach. Where the comfort of seaweed lay in twisted mighty clumps. This dark seagrean, was alive, could be it moved? The sea lapped ever faithful. And I saw a single surfer slick rubber suited eel slither on his board. And I watched his jig jagging, zig zagging waves not that high. He flipped the surfboard knifepoint and the muscles of his arms glistened god of the sea as he stroked wave after wave against the tide to retrieve his board.

The sand trod me to. A shady spot under ah ha the cliff that rose. To her. Behind beached me. And goer scatter of diet coke cans, chip packets, chocolate wrappers, cigarette packets, the hoi poloi. I frowned, lazy swine litterbugs. The Bic lighter worked, if I smoked, but the smoking and breathing failed long ago. I spread my towel near a blackened driftwood fire extinguishing its own past. The sun lowering, I bloc Coppertoned and went in. Held my nose! Seashore beside the seaside, let spent waves wetting my flesh. The absolute necessity soaked by godwetter TO BE cleansed of despair by the rush of yes foam, yes salt, yes coolness water day. And endless waves charged at my ankles wading further into life. Water scurried hard bashed at knees. Water to my waisted real progress. Saltwater dashed me saltspirit and lifted me a float of weightless faraway. On sweet salt. The next wave and the next and the next and the distillation of forgotten. I went the seagreen and swam. My body a ribbon. Forgot ancient history. Needed air and sun, a plus, a boon, blessed yellow today before low disappearing. The holes of me. I dived under, eyes shut tight, pinched my nostrils, surfed the swirl. Forgot the failed. Him, her, the badness, the sadness, the meanness, water extracted those nobs, sinners, assholes, tongue lashers, back biting. Hey knock-down-drown-out damn blast. My stick-on eyelashes fell off. As I bumble swimswam surfaced for pure sky, where it met the sea, the lost me, in lovely invigorated, a body plowed in the choppy, sea scooped me, sea tipped sideways, tasted salty in my seathroat slapdashed at swam and swam, breaststroke and dogpaddle and surf wrestled me downhill to the shore. To the rough of wet sand. My soaked of little lappings. The endless gushed foamy and I lay on my stomach let the salt. Let it. Let it. Please let them. Sting.

That married a year and six months in. Well, it was the Lord's day. Something his Ma would say. On the Lord's day, I ate cheeseballs. I threw them high in the air, opened my mouth, mostly missed. This pointless vigil. In front of the mirror practicing. A treacherous smile with my pink gummy. And an eyebrow arched a quizzical frown. *Wow. Really! How fascinating.* Life built on face foundation. Natural Ivory hinted of peach on my cheeks for him. Because many signs of a dysfunctional relationship. Incapable of fucking like a windblown Argonaut. Where was the roar of stuck in the missionary reclusive. And I trembled this gelatinous substance. Bleeh fungus girl. Moldy yeasty multicellular. Lofty spaces waited inside my sea skull anyway blah.

Anyway.

With the lashing stormy water leaked through listened love. I heard winter pelting our tin roof leaked through the rafters crikey. Yellow patch big expanding heart shaped, the plaster almost caved. In. What if Godforbid the ceiling collapsed? And shit sky sagged onto puddled me.

Anyway.

The sloppy wigged my doldrums ha confession. I experienced overwhelming frights of humans. Those Who Thought They Knew Everything. The disciplined, prepossessing, practical, ruthless know-it-alls them shredded my vulnerable. They flickered click tongues. *For fucks sake.* They dug. What the brazen and discovered a deep-seated terror of denigration. They administered Stern Advice. *Watch where you are going.* I was going nowhere. And thought-provoking suggestions at my earthquaked physique. *Do not judge a body by its quakes.* Constructive guidance. *Moisten postage stamps and adhere onto the right-hand corner of the envelope.* Idiot forgot to remember. Events for fragile leached gloom at terror of dentists, doctors, hairdressers, therapists. The black day I. Said to a hairdresser. Cut it a bit shorter. The bitch hacked off my hair. The time a Dentist stuck a spike straight into my cavity. The whole room spun and turned yellow. I wept and leant over that pristine white dentist chair and vomited my pathetic lunch of chicken soup cubed carrot and slimed yellowing hurl into the Dentist's lap. The day a Doctor what fingered his poke wriggle to my cervix. His finger squirmed and prodded. What was he looking for? A smear, a baby, baby, maybe. And after I sat up and pulled on my undies and put on my rayon circle skirt printed with rosebuds, that prick Doctor would not look me in the and there were much more, but that was enough. *You see.*

The present happened. Cars rear-ended on the Harbor Bridge. A taxi sideswiped a bus. An ancient fossil of a wolf-sized otter discovered in China. A seaplane dived into the Swan River. And should the identification stickers be ditched from fruit and veg? A man found a dead rat in a bottle of beer. Seven escapees from jail spent the night running from dentists, doctors, hairdressers. therapists.

Marriage drifted through work grinding long hours. We were the days. Sundays supposed a day of rested. But I always worked on Lordy day. Better money, vast bucks, double time. I returned the Lord's day to the Lord. *Here you are Lord you can have your day back.*

Ground vague filled the hard to remember hardy ha ha the hard on's, the card games of barnyard snap, old maid, chased the ace, go fish, king queen slap jack, joker in the holed. Board games of snakes and ladders upper downer, prudent deeds upped the virtuous ladder or a mischievous slither downed snake of vice. *Why don't we strip?* T.V tennis, anyone gamey? I didn't want to play games.

Other times, the time of Monk and me spent, did we chat our togetherings. We talked about, we walkabout circles, said same conversation, friends, the weather, his wanted many. He prayed for me. His mother prayed for me to develop normal, feminine, wear sherbet mohair pullovers and strappy stilettos. And always the irritable blowfly of small talk yuss, buzzed and crawled.

"You've lost weight. You seem tired. You looky looky fabulous. I told you so. This looks interesting. Thinking of you. I'm in love with you. I am not in love with you. I hate you. It's nothing special. What's wrong with you. I was going to call. Why haven't you called? Where have you been? I did call. Let's go for coffee. What's for breakfast. What's for lunch. What's for dinner. Drink? I'm free on Thursday. I'm way in over my head. You'll be fine. Try this."

Tried to fit the system. The social-infrastructure hellbent on modifying the behavior of every misfit. I purchased a kiddy archery set. I bought a toy pistol, armed myself with a non-existent intellect. And just fired at any posse of dicks charging at me. I pretended the dolly bomber. Appealing and appalling woman not playing with the full deck. Without a point. Or sane reason.

Inside my head the rant of. Thoughts influenced by trillions of incarnate dreads. This accounted for a delicious portion of countless other mental vagaries. An undisclosed desire to acquire my own personal dick. A disposable dick. A detachable dick. Big enough to surprise Monk. *Look what fell into my lap.*

Yesterday Monk said,

"I'm at my wits end."

Bollocks. I wanted to slap him right there and then. To whack the wits from his end. Walloped thwacking until wallops stung his stinger and he might. Appreciate what Alison already knew. Pain nobody knew. Pain nobody could explain. Real pain explained. This phantom ached heartache. She said something teary, wrong suffering. She suffered here. She blamed heartbreak pain. Pain the god of pricks protective mechanism. Pain yelling rounding wronged with her inner self inside. Pain the sign of the signal slammed emotion. Pain was a good thing. Yeh. Right? Hell. Even though it really fucking hurt. OW.

Monk tickled my armpit. He pinched the skin of my upper arm. Ow. *Ow.*

"Sweetie. Dreamy. Do you hear me? I am at."

"Wits what wits. Shit wits. You have no wits."

"Hush hush we don't want to argue on our day off."

"What day."

Let's not, let's not, let snot go God and the little wife me obedient and act conjugal. But reverent Monk cast his worst at my thirsted. Blustered my biddy. Chief fucker busted my buckshee before. They always did and then the shout at bedevil. Bestill, bequiet, behave, begone. These snuffies did not do the trick for dumbsheila. I guessed it gutted myself in the grind working long shifts and jackhammers pounding next door. Lady bottlebreaker groaned,

"Blessed be broom groom face up my arse."

And upsomdowned my oyster licketty, Monk content in this pickle shed. Kept his dick from yowling. Lusted ham man. That longed peeped his wanting. His battlecock. Hamhock. Rolled onto flatpack me. We knew missionary apparently position under pattern of my body, spread in a star, shaped limp, he scrabbled his ins and outs. His rams and grunts. The rolling yellowish eyes. The tender smooch. The gentle brush of his lashes across my cheek bones. The gratefulness. The blushed of him. At below. Shamed of that viscous goo. The uncomfortable paste semen. Held it in. This deep breath. Disappeared it. Clean me of dribbled gunk meat pie, yellow gravy, tomato sauce and pastry flakes and this was how to bake a baby. When would it dry. What any idea of the removal. And creaky didn't move. And lunacy set fire to the bed sheets, after I fucked him. My marbled eyeballs haunted his wham. I attempted yarn spinner. Humoresque. Should I be stricken, remember the Carmelite caramel? A lying nun with none of. The sanity a nun had. Where to get another set. Of nuns. Of sheets. Of marbles. Of loonies.

Was I okay.

"I am okay."

But no, not really. OK.

He shouted,

"We need milk."

As if a lack of milk would kill him. I walked to the shops. Head down, kept my eyes and steel hoop earrings swung. My denim shorts showing sunburn and rubber flip flops and rumpled. I lacked balls. When events transpired for example. The running into. Someone. I hated fervor, the eyeballing gusto. Infectious zeal this characteristic deluded lost to me. Could not ignite a party or convince the world of the effectiveness of disinfectant and that life-changer the playing of sport. I balled, no bat or ball or guts. And a flummoxed state. Desperate to avoid. A cocksure cocky cock balls of a vague acquaintance baled me against a bare wall. Brick grinned,

"Hi. How *are* you? Remember me?"

I cowered. No. Thief of my personal space, nosing close as possible. *Who ARE you*. A rascal with raucous halitosis. Carrying a bowling ball in a zip up bag. A laser-like bastard bowled. In the glib. It exuded enthusiasm.

"What a beautiful day."

Casual veiled threatenings. This plunder of a crestfallen spirit. Invisibility always lied. I turned from. Bit my sheepish eyes flitted to the left and the right. Of trampled. In quiet despair.

"What are you up to? Shipley, isn't it?"

Red veins spread over its nostrils, blueish veins in odd places. A turnip for a nip nose. A fair-haired werewolf with wiry blonde hairs on the tops of its fingers. He began his savage onslaught. My cold shoulder. Ostrich girl head in the. Huh.

"Yeah."

That enthusiast flaunted confidence.

"We met that time at Fergal's barbeque. You remember? The time he burned the corn fritters."

Did we speak? Could it smell the fuck on me. My confidential. My shams.

"What's new?" Delighted with itself. Hearty obnoxiousness. Spaced out man. I *beheld* splayed feet urg. Did it pee in the shower? I attempted to focus on its earlobe. It thrusted a well-meaning chin sprouting sparse hairs. Devious splendor. A certain type of slacks with a crease matched its wind breaker. Should I fart? I crossed my arms. I crossed the street to rid myself. My assailant following, beamed into my quivering.

"I was just trying to be friendly."

I am not your friend. Dangerous to be bashful and paranoid. Wild in my. Winged the blurred lines. *I don't know who you are. I have nothing to say.* But this.

"It is a lovely day. So nice to chat. I have to go. We are out of milk. Catch you later." *Whoever you are.*

It waved the air, it stepped backwards off the curb, in front of a car. Brakes screeched dented fender on *whoever you are.* Abnormal girl laughed *watch out.*

Truth the doubled lie. Did you realize. Easy I lied. Even tigers lied. But Alison had disagreed. Alison once asked me, how did I see myself. But I wasn't myself at any speed, failed as an adult, into real-self working, so fake considered myself better, an artless lie, I didn't recognize, what I was even thinking, what did you reckon.

I would not be you.

Blurk repelled, when he smelled his fingers after we and. Did you remember my wonder. Were you here. Alison had thumped me not hard but enough,

"Stop raving. You are You."

"I know…"

"Just Be Yourself."

But myself yip yep a super duper proper problem.

Dreamt didn't I. Cross-legged, no underpants on melting iceberg drift, shedding my skin, on the outside of my chest clung my heart piece broken from a puzzle floating on a pond ooh mysterious. Thoughts once dreary, turning iced sliced of optimism. In strode The Cannibal Bladderwort. Wow allowed this contemplating the severing of Fergal! He lived in the pond-life as the Cannibal Bladderwort, a carnivorous plant with teeth true! The Cannibal Bladderwort thrived in quiet shallowest. The shallows inched of watery. A reed, sprouting buttery blossomed. Coiled around our fingers and words spoken in a modulated tone, could be petite dinging bells attached to its throat. Of course, the Bladderwort didn't own a throat. But Fergal the Cannibal managed a quick question,

"And how do you see yourself?"

Bubbles mirrored my face brisk with vengeance floated to the surface pushing aside duckweed. I severed the stalks of this Bladderwort plant. Carried them dripping through the pickle shed. Bunch of bladderwort sweet dunked in a glass vase put it on the dresser beside our bed. Thought hesitated for fresh flowers in a bedroom were for sick people. Phooey went to sleep, but already was asleep in this dreamt the following day stems gone and inside my mouth stung from hostile saliva. I pressed my tongue as if glued with smooth peanut butter, to the back of my teeth. My chattering grinner. Rubbed gums bled gagging. Impossible to rid of this bitterness. Monk always said,

"There is no such word as impossible."

And I cried,

"But that's impossible."

Fergal's wort tendrils circled my larynx and others swam deeper inside sticked to my ribbers. *He's gotcha.* The cannibal bloomed inside me of hauntings. Tiny leaves emerged from under my fingernails like in that movie not sure. On fragile stems radiated from my scalp. Did you investigate? B-grade. Inflated sacs with trapdoors surrounded by trigger hairs secreted a honeyed lure. Thriller if a boy got too close, fiber trapdoors snapped open ate him. Cannibal lie imagined laughable yum. Shadow caught between yellow and red. A lie forever shrunk and forever swelled. My shrunken multiplied lies revealed my linear, my blanked, my various, my sallow shallow identity. Rooted in the shallowing yellow. Roots traveled horizontal surfacing for oxygen. The telling of my lies meant she he were unable to identify the me. As in stinkpot woman tra la lah la lah. Lived unhappy with the grubs, the mice, the flying insects. Provocateur spacegirl bluffed Annie Oakley Joan of Arc Sainted Saint Theresa crouched beside the pond and the reeds reached over. I bound, plaited twisted them tough little buggers, in nobody would ever divulge this shit. Why women disappeared.

I replaced the spaces with loads of lily pads left to grind against green slime, woke me, broke into a cold sweat fear without a resolution. The cannibal was waiting for another go. I swallowed the bladderwort. Sucked it through the pinhole of yellowing lips. Was it poison of me. The beginning of killerings.

But I kept dreaming didn't I? Stupid girl questioned unable to realize myself a woman. Not when I owned such nightmares at night.

Deaf to the practical, drunk drove on the wrong side of the road. Past the stop sign. The red signal *you are going the wrong way.* Reversing the wrong way. In the playground, I hung upside on the monkey bars. The thrill. Clad in black clothes to erase my figure. Left a while in the fantasy freezer. And caves formed ideas. Glaciers butted against the frozen sea stored lamb chops, beans, ice-cream, bait, chicken legs bought with a credit card we never paid off. This empty bank balance held familiar nightmares. Here in the night of the mares. The cougar girl preying on sop soppy gentle love. A mare lonesome housewife sorry her rump withered stood at this crossroad. I slept on two roads forked at a signpost. Each path locked in a V. with signs made of tin. To nowhere no money. Shitforbrains! Everywhere followed to no place.

Another sign, that footpath led to the man and he gave a woman everything she desired. But did such a creature. Exist. And what did women desire? Accomplishments just annoying. Dream me some money to pay the bills.

The other sign it bent wrath and tinned twist, the always of bending in on itself. This work of enraged hands. I stretched our arm and asked where should the second path lead me. Of course, self-destruction an option. Pushed me against a mirror. That mirrored eventual told the truth.

My brutal appearance, misshapen eyes swapped opposite. Full body x-ray revealed meaty selves, segmented of labels. A bloodless carcass hung from its meat hook. Butchered lamb scrag, chuck, loin, breast, flank, shank and chumped. Scragend represented intensity. My rib caged arching like a silver toast rack trapped object of dignity. This made little mouse better right bet it did. Except that vision of those essential two parts chopped. The cheerful shank and the sociable flank. Missing.

Bah yellow deathbed of me. Ate Me Alive. Heck the quietest people grew the loudest minds. Yes, smiling. Woop woop we smiled on the outside. But not the reason anymore. Disillusionment caused of my self-combustion. He hugged me before I killed me. Hell empty every the devils here. But they couldn't stand me so they left. Be livid about this. I loved him, but I hated him. And this fake smiley, inside keened to the screaming. Anger and love hunted me ate me woke me.

Stop complaining and let people think I the fool. Told Monk. There was no angry way to say the word 'bubbles.' And even the nicest people developed limits. Even the sweetest loveliest persons sustained the grins living. And she me of dewy cheek kept my untrustworthy emotions wonderstruck. With angels and wine and warbling's in check.

But Monk barely managed a frown disagreed not acceptable behavior those my antics. Monk downed his worries as a sentry in a box my guard dog watching ready his pounce. Doomster chucked a suggestion chucking his lower lip forward chucks his deadliness. Wised uppity uttered a single word.

"Analysis."

I stamped my foot. My alienation. Fatal rift. Watusied in his face.

"No."

"Yes. We have enough money for two sessions."

I failed the test of a year, two years. I got lost in a forest of confusions. What would loverly Confucius pontificate. Every human object owned beauty, tackled beauty gotcha. The greatest glory in ceased the falling. But. Somehow. Unelaborated of the method. To. Rise every time glory fell. Life of down-to-earth modest earth-to-downer. Urrr not. I insisted on making life complicated. *No.* Yes. I did. And Monk determined to help. Only wanted to be helpful. Monk sneezed the countless.

"I want to be helpful."

"Bullshit."

"Now. Now. My helpless lambkins, you're nothing but embarrassing. And I might add, *dearest,* the drinking is out of control. Get professional help sweetpea. Get it while you are young. You need emotional assistance. Make an appointment with a counselor. Fergal recommends Geraldine Burrows. She meets with her clients in Balmain. Here is her business card. She has letters after her name. MA Psych Clin. She's qualified. More than qualified. Alison had marvelous consultations with Ms. Burrows."

"WHAT."

"Yes, she did."

The man blinked. Manifold combinations. Blinks talked too fast. His blinkingness whipped indulgent flutters charging towards idiot girl. Beated my protests.

"Am I talking to a brick wall?"

Crap bricks again, remembered bricked damnation, dreamed the bricks. Bricked me protested,

"I never mean what I say."

Monk persevered on a mission.

"You don't fool me. I've had two years of this idiocy. Your perversity hurts me. Deeply. You are not right in the head."

"I am too."

My dripping hands stared ahead. At incomprehensibility. Didn't bat an eyelid, batty batgirl gave in panicked. Pardoned. The dangerous rollercoaster. This motion sickness. Inner ear the reason, it moved in opposition to the moving and walking, escalated to running, to fleeing and finished with dizzy sicker. How the inner ear captured unsynchronization, anti-clockwise, the opposite direction to the rest of me. These mixed signals of eyes sent to the brain by the innards ear. Blinded to emotion myself moved such a moving tribute for her without feelings the double brain received jumbled messages. Right so did yours. Well that's fine then.

And I. Discovered the soon enough. A blobbed. The faked. The fiddle-de-dee. Of madder obeyed and applied myself. Obedience tripping what I was told. Monk had spoken. Morning had broken. Forcing me checked a helping person with a helping hand, a missionary. But I already knew that position. The experts, shamans, psychic healers, priests carried little blah black bags, lists of gaggle, benevolent powers, divine intervention found in the yellow pages. They might muck my meandered meanderings and beat me with black magic, dried stingrays, tooth of Dracula, caveman club. But I determined of incapable to let me lose myself in the mire.

And Monk's pitchfork prodding the tiger. She must be cured. The debris. Of rebellious thoughts, real emotions, uncanny intuitions, glum moods, irritabilities, unreasonable impulses, nonsensical outbursts, frenzied dismal infatuations, pisshead vagaries. Cleared. Exorcised, de-demonized, counseled, chanted over, prayed about, persuaded, meditated on, shooed me. I said,

"Okay. Whatever. You want."

And I slept blackout uncomforted by him, a swizzle pizzle. Twisting the night counted the vertebrae of my spine wondering if the. Locked the bones in. Knitted the bones. Knotted the boned. And in many the mornings from long time on, I hugged her shrine intimate with my spinny of doubled upenstance spewing. And struggled to get past. That she walked on air. That she swam. Herself mislaid. This fish tale girl. She should have warned me. In the murk, I thought she cried,

"Wait. I'll come back for you."

The only person. Who got me. Kicked me in the guts. This. Various ravings and shit I didn't see coming they refused to tell me so fuck them and their Analysis crappola, oh you didn't understand.

I would do it for her.

7

Smack Your Inner Sky

Monk ordered my blathering self to book an appointment with a therapist. No delay. No excuses. My throat turning scrappy rawed. How he pulled my string. I sly purred him with devious affection. But Monk got his way. His Way or the highway joked.

"Such a treat," he said. "To dig it all out."

I shuddered spades, kings, joker and said,

"Let's play cards."

A week later pressured minutes ticked. I cycled pressed the pedals, sinew legs, hard little calf muscles and wheels turned. On time. Not a minute. Well trained. Circus trainer cracked his leather. Stopwatched me. Polka dot shorted. Bumpity road of potholes, cracks in the sidewalk. Cars arced around me and the exhaust. A truck swore, "Watch out missy." Missed me by inches. Horned my pedaling and this sudden awareness, the bike lacked trilling. I needed a bicycle bell. A ringer protest at near miss. The sigh,

"That was a close one."

I chained my bike to a post outside an old building, hidden behind a magnolia tree, imagined a sniper, a stalker, snaking along the branches. Snipstalk hurled itself inside an open window and sought treatment for living in a tree, truly I gawped at office block, a pseudo colonial or Georgian or hybrid fussy woodwork curls and trims and brass lamps and dirty windowsills quivered spook, weatherboard exterior extreme weathered, was it bathed in bleach, gave it a licked sloven stare, recognized in the past of probable, the possibility these walls were a deathly shade of red, oooh cried creepy, silently sure before my eyes the boards fading, bored to death, I knew subject red, I knew the fading, I knew bleach, the time I tried to drink it.

I spied black uppercase individual letters on the church noticeboard across the road.

The Most Powerful Position Is On Your Knees.

The letter K at a precarious angle. Oops, those words might be mistaken for porno, rude, crude, bully statement! Here. On Darling Street. Genteel in demand street of the cloistered and moneyed. *Oh, darlin.*

Where to go.

Lost me faulting the distractions, why my joins, body assemblage, copious fabrication, limbs elaborates, a baffled. And I. Forgot directions. Where. Too. Right ripper. Consulting rooms on the fourth floor. Apprehension thudded whump whump whump to the beats of my heart. A constructed creation heart. Lungs lunged wheezing prolific brains unique of.

"You should know the way, what? You don't. Well neither does she."

This was not a movie. I thought it was. A film about a girl grown double brainer and fabricated heart and bloat intelligence. *You overthink. Of course I do, what with the two of them whirring sinning err spinning.*

Should I hurry? Or slowed destined the eventual. I avoided the elevator. Rather the stairs apples and pairs. Pears idiot. I knew that. My new shoes blister sister of sainted soles clunking on the steel steps. Clunketty metal. Concrete wallwell stairwell echoed my clunk, of flameless blameless. I heart beater, better a step to it. Top sweating, I reached Level Four skipped along a long corridor, shuffled to the last door and tentative pushed this point of no return. Of *why why* WHY forced a naked soul to chat with unknown. And troubled lather answered. Easy. I got a screw loosed and shallow. Combined with reckless deterioration. This cocktail that must mustered the reason.

"I am young, I am gorgeous, I am marvelous."

The thrilling wail. Fucking pretty fantastic! Not much else, but to cry.

I didn't tell.

I tapped on a door marked Suite Number Five. Unseen buzzed my shudder into. The inner ear of an industrial interior stripped of character features, therefore a logic defying the outer oldness. And in that reception area, partitions divided mute spaces of unbelievable beige. The color flattened ideas. A color not to incite. Rage.

The receptionist's nametag sported Mrs. Hodge. Written in a friendly typeface. This largest woman florid as a bunch of plastic flowers. A smile annoyed her plump cheeks.

"Yes?"

"I have an appointment with Geraldine Burrow."

Hodge bunches referred to a list. Ticked me off. Tick reminding…*No one knew what was inside paradise, but it must be pretty great. The wickedest lot sent to a shocking hot spot on fire with a crimson moon and no fresh breezes.*

"Is there much of a wait?"

"Thirty minutes."

Walls had mouths and eyes. *And* buzzers. I imagined. Inside these places, doors refused to creak. Ordinary people prisoner of straitjacketed. Women got carted to nowhere inside padded white vans. The barmy trod cautiously, almost a tiptoe on those mahogany floorboards. Safe and sane as can be. Half dead ferns trailed fronds from a brassy pot And more dirty toys heaped of germs special for grubbers. In the corner on a glass side table smudged with fingerprints, piles of tacky magazines splashed with photographs of princesses holding infants dressed in lace christening gowns. Ample lace god help me. Loaded lace. Hankered for grease, why not fries.

And center stage on the wall, a loud picture contrasted the fawniness. A framed print yikes overbrightened the waiting room. I cowered these colors whacked would I get better, would I be faster, god help. Fright Picasso portrait. Smashed at its own features. Caterpillar eyelashes. A squashed hat. And portraited woman shrieking, *Don't stare at maniac me.* Mmmm. I thought, that's bloody insensitive. To hang such a confronting image in a psychiatrist's waiting room. Oh lord. Was the gist, *go to bed, pull yourself together, eat some lunch, worse things happen at sea, your conscience will be fine, get over yourself, get on with it, specks in your head, go right ahead kill yourself.*

Yikes burk nothing wrong with me. Everything wrong with me. Wrong in the bedspread head.

I wanted to be heard. Didn't every human being. Gave myself permission, acted crazy ferocious. Those yellings inside my many selves. These elves imped the mental jig. Odded my put-on. Shameless sham grand slam. My zany show. Blood hamming. Dippy sweet yum yum gawd. Magnificent. And the powdery moth crawling up the window pane. Much hopeless, the moth waved antennas desperately at the sun, *take me.* Outside.

Er. I hung on waiting rooms, swung from the light fitting, waiting waiting waiting. What did anybody wait for unknowable. Anticipation was as good as it got. And the waiting room almost empty. Except for a solitary man. Particles insipid. Oddman unsurprising. His nondescript, fuddle blanding himself, anyone believed he invisible. But his natty glad rags, striped socks and bowtie materialized like fog lifting. Ahh the room then, not that vacant. But a siege. Of nervous sat beside the receptionist's desk. Like a slug suctioned to the veneer. Nervousness apparent from his wild darting eyes. How could wretch keep those fanaticals snug in their sockets. Every ten seconds, gobbit man closed his eyes. Pressed his eyes hard as possible with both fists pushing his eyes back into place to prevent an escape. For under his eyelids, a sack of frenzied ferrets.

"Not long, Mr. Peebles," soothed the receptionist.

Mr. Peebles turned his besotted to her. Mr. Peebles earthquaked with pleasure, rosy for canoodled. Sweatypants geezer. Then. Frowned at himself for feeling happiness. He drummed his thighs with frantic hands proceeded fanning his fettle. Patted himself starting with patting his forehead, cheeks, neck faster faster, bending to his toes. Head between his knees.

Then his poxy trick exploded. Had he scoffed cabbage and beer for lunch? For his otherworld fart silenced the clock. And quite a lot of throat clearing behind the desk. Pathetic Hodge podge woman held a tissue to her nose as. Did she wear a girdle, seemed the compressed type female.

Stink man Peebles muffling,

"Sorry."

I held my nose urk, gassed, pissed. Off. Looney almost a retching. Had to get myself unstenched. Moved away from nervy man, my stupefied collapsing in the furthest chair. More synthetic seat covers. Stickied under my bare legs. Radio softly played country song Stand By Your Man *no* pulled my ape-face, should I gnash?

Limper, Mr. Peebles loosed his chin chin. His nose ran. Got himself somehow calmer picked at a wart on his neck. Inevitable the trickle tried to smile in a friendly way. But he could only manage terror. Did he know. About hellbroth scalding. Baby cauldron bubbled inside this hollow womb. Of mine mined. For babied. Doubled double toil and troubled. Aye enchanting Shakespeare. Torrid hell ha boiled its yellow. Stand by your man. Lullaby girl. Soul choked on a baby poisoned entrails. Stood by my. Stood. Fuming. Black day and white night. Knight in dullish armor, but movie. Baby toe of frog blistering. Baby lizard's leg scorching. Enough. I stood to attention. I said,

"Guess bloody what. Shakespeare never had freaking babies. Too dangerous with yellow hell boiling in those fucking cauldrons." I teased Mr. Peebles. Cheered cheer the stinky a merry chant.

"Laugh. It's straightforward, laugh at LIFE! hah. Life is comical, stand in front of a mirror kak yourself. Have you wiped your bum. Have you washed your hands. Consult your horoscope what are you Taurus unlikely what with the bull, Aries, again doubtful, I notice fireless in your watery. Are you fishy Pisces. Yes? No Libra. I knew it."

He inched. I opened Woman's Day. I read in the princess pages. *Be more authentic be yourself. Coy coiled too cool for her curl. Freak madam lifeliked. Wisherwife full of claptrap. Disgraced honeylamb. Was that ample authenticated. God forbid don't rock the boat ladies, because you can't kill him, are you too needy, ways to be incredibly sexy, give me an excellent reason, hearty dinners, down-do's up-do's you choose sexy hair, newly-wed husbands who kill their wives, blow his mind in bed. Drop three sizes, flatten your abdomen, careers for lonely wives, ladies don't wear hats in bed, twenty-seven and unmarried, natural childbirth can help a coward, be a summer stunner, get an insane body, can husbands be lovers, the secret Cheryl is hiding, my life is a sob story, legs are back and gaining on bosoms, join the foxy boy hunt, the new faces of love, top cleaning tricks, getting to admire yourself, stop being so polite, free yourself from foolish fears, how to overcome dreadful fears of 'unworthiness,' how dropouts and dummies become successful, the 'are you neurotic' quizz, men's deepest fears, how a short girl can rise above it, pamper your party face, nice guys finish last.*

Astounding stupidity. Even better than reality. Opium of idiots.

I flicked pages brisk to the Star signs. Peacemaker enjoys harmonious surroundings. Impulsive Outbursts. Dislikes Unpleasantness. Knows His Limits. I whispered,

"Roar."

Mr. Peebles whimpered. I stamped my foot.

"Your moon is on the cusp of the seventh house. Your moon is descending. Fast. Play catch. Manifest yourself. Spend your savings. Watch the lunar nodes. Smack your inner sky."

I told him,

"For example. Once I draped spaghetti on the blades of a fan. I switched the power on as you would. I pretended the pasta was flying its perilous daring. But it flopped."

As I said the word, flopped, I focused boggle at his unbuttoned revealing tender hairless, *do you wax little man.*

Mr. Peebles staggered his featureless and shifted to a seat nearer the door.

A snap in my thought. She needed peace. I wanted to be free. Let me be. Let me sing song the nutty how now brown cow sang out of my tune, my muddle mind. Noised this bellow.

"And then bananas. And then buttered. And then margarine murder. And then egg yolks gluey. And then mustard snipe. And then urine gripe came upon him that he would marry daffodils, wattle, frangipani, sunflowers and that yellow would be his Wife."

Got Peebles of a quiver again. I kissed the air and flung him a kiss. Made him feeble terrified that I launched a rocket aiming straight for his balls. Little jolly roger dormant in his paunch. Troubled gasbag that bagged baggage. *Fuck forget it chump. We are not real. We are water, under water, under more, guess what? WATER.*

Head tilted caused a slipping agitation in my brain, like a kidney bean shaken in THE QUESTION were there waves. Listen pebble Peebles, I stupor in the gawk. On the white ceiling, an inflamed rash of seeping ugh fungus. Fungal patches puke lesions. Lesions, I said not lessons. A kind of awful. Truth. And true to Monk's mother, I pointed,

"D…D…Dampness."

Another my shout rocketed.

"Don't look at that leprosy sky."

Of course, girdled Hodge woman Mrs. could not resist. Meh sure she was affable, stuck behind the desk, gave the impression of her legless. Without moving her head, her eyes shot high in each socket.

"Well I never."

Mr. Peebles yelped and headed for the exit, for the stairs. I heard steel clunked shuffle. I heard a crash and. Remembered noticing his shoelaces undone. The callous my thought. A head banging might put him right.

Mean madness insisted hunky dory, but misery futiled killing time. And the root of optimism, ha sheer bared dread. That familiar ruffian. Tough the future, wherever near of always. From the future.

From the adjoining office, Geraldine Burrows called,

"NEXT."

Fangs

My paranoid why, but glad I scared him hehehe wicked poor Peebles on the run. The odious smell of his bottom burp. Did he know? A hundred and fifty slang words for expelling air from the anus.

Without looking, little sick entered the type of room always a stifled stale and without looking closed the door, stood without looking in front of the door hands behind my back. Before I moved further into the room. Whiff. Beware this airless space to observe. Where I glowered my, Take This In yep Took It In. Absorbed the sight of wallpaper dancing a pattern of daffodils. Jig petals even nodded fields. Poncey and chaos these busy *busy* floral trumpets of yellows lighted and random.

The deep meaning of multiple daffy dills stumped me. I remembered YES my postcard collection of flowers. Circa 1905. Five and cards browning at the edges. One card of a single daff. Lonely as a cloudme. The Horticultural Society claimed depths of a daffy implied 'esteem.' This languish Language of Flowers on her walls. And I thought should be marigold wallpaper, for marigolds meant 'mental anguish.' I willed the wallpaper to change into a million anguished marigolds. And my dry mouth opened a cracked. Imagine baked earth the pattern inside parching.

My limbs steered further into the consulting room.

The Lady who yelled NEXT. She sat in a comfy armchair in the corner beside her desk, not behind her desk, for to sit behind the desk, might be construed as Far Too Formal. I gasped at the sight of Normal informal Geraldine Burrow. Woman a ball of sunshine. Trim sun-goddess, clothed in lemony pants and bronze leather sling-backs. Her heavy scented tinge of jasmine mixed with gin breath. Her skinnier than me body toe to topped, gobs and gobs of gold jewelry. The Burrow strung with necklaces, bracelets, rings. Every accessory reminiscent of a turvey topsy Christmas tree. Dazzle jingled rose from the chair. Her brilliance moved toward me. Overwhelming amount of alarmed at the situation. I blanched at her bling, Might faint dead at glitter awfulness. Horroring at heaps this yellow. *Relax relax.*

She rattley offered me her hand. *Go on.* Shake-a-handy gold person.

"Good morning Shipley. Please sit anywhere."

I shook the. Headache began fast. Hammerhead. A gong agog. But no escape and I did not drop dead or crackup or foam at the mouth or piss my pants or chuck a fit. I flung up my defensive with stumbling.

"Where shall I?"

She pointed,

"Yes over there."

Past pine bookshelves under a locked window of lightest rattling. Over to a straight-backed chair and a couple of cane chairs plump by wheaty and cushions sewn of daisies galore winking fresh so help me. God. *Choose.* Uncomfortable posture or rickety cane. My hesitation crapped obvious. I should lie down, hand across my brow. With sigh of despair. *Could we lower the blinds.*

I seated myself with the daisies umming,

"Okay fine."

Us cushions pretended a devil-may-care attitude as arm-pits wetted B.O through my T-shirt of limped grey from too many washes. Deodorant too expensive at $3.99. My voice as haphazard as the papered walls.

"Umm, the price of deodorant you know? A bummer, the price of deodorant is a disgrace."

"I agree," said Geraldine Burrow. "You speak your mind."

"Not really."

She began clacking clipboards with cheery determination. "I'll start a little file…"

I grimaced my snore brain of *oh you will, will you?* And wriggled my rebel kickarse.

The Burrow smiled showing enormous teeth. Ear to ear. Ugh. Tusks. Incisors. Deadly fangs. My doubted wondering if natural for a human person to have such massive choppers. I decided her probable sort of woman never content until she devoured the whole damned tussle of inner. But Ok. Made myself pleasant. Some exaggeration here.

The Burrow, attractive showy fine-boned grease skin buttered in spite of. Those black hairs sprouting from a mole in the center of her forehead. Gawd. Circle mark mole. Hole in her head. Geraldine Burrow had triple eyes. Three-eyed person. Cyclops? No, he blinked the one eye. I steeped ideas that a third eye showed the actual manias never wanted revealed. A middle eye pierced the potential. Delving the hidden connections of spiritual development. Argy bargy deep. Anyway, I thought, tread wary if the shine big-brighting. The Burrow shrew this revealed her as exceptionally efficient at her job. That third eye predicting doomsday, of course it did. Its intuition fruited the future. And a third eye came and went without warning.

Every third eye got stronger and stronger, not too obvious, but gradual. Changed the personality and your perspective altered for better and worse. Three eyes lessened selfishness, fed forgiveness, nourished you as the spark of the universe. And third eyes solved problems. What unknown reached for my past. I was. A chubby child island.

"Listen Ms. Burrow, mud pies meat pies haunted me. I ate. Sweet clover. The gritty sand. Who knew juicy grit. I stuck my fingers in my nose to stop my yellow brains from oozing through my nostrils. And oozeyellow followed me. Harmless, I reassured myself. Laughable. How could a girl of this mirth meaningless be pursued by a color? Pursuit happened to people ever. But the yellow followed me, trailed, spreading a distressed residue. Tail of yellow stream, of yellow track, of yellow stripe attempted to catch me. What would yellow do? If it caught my innocent tangle this."

Geraldine Burrow puzzled, I think she was. Well I dug it. Monk had said, beneficial to dig it. He said yellow was not a thing. But to me, it smalled monstrous entity. Vapors yes unusual air. I breathed yellow. Yellow remembered me at age fifteen. Cool girl lighting a cigarette. Sophistication plus. That yellow smoke inhaled and I coughed and coughed my throat firing. Lungs on fire, near death. Lucky this girl incapable of smoking. Left me pithy and cooked meat inside. The earthcore on fire. World peeled the layers and exposed. A body burning the sizzle of useless.

"I remembered, Ms. Burrow, what happened."

But hazy, a maybe it never happened. Fergal stealthboy clean freak cleaned me out. He gambled, rolled the wheel. Merry me the-go-round and him a niggle turd. Hot urgent breath filling my smoke-free lungs. Unable barred him jaws. Unknown. Pretended he, the fun party guy of pathological obsessive mastaburbles. Automatic erotic. Salivation. Pounced me. Fingers and tinny tongues that probed into forbidden. Fingernail scraped my bollocking. Tore tenderized meat from bones. Drunkish tongue pegged me, pushing his mouth, into my. Donkeyhaw pinned me to the fluff flock rug. His rugged dry-as-a-bone. I cried howly rosary. At his his his polished off a girl gibbering, Pig Pig. The man licked his fingers when he was done.

"But did he? Ms. Burrow, did he?"

Doubted that haze-happened unsure fictitious was the attack in my head. Lasted that past recollection. None of the time recalled reflex hindered the beast. Fuck. Two brained drizzle of indefinite. Empty vast in the middle of, I could deceive myself, this wasn't happening why not, because.

"The abuse occurred, Ms. Burrow. While I waited for Alison to come back from the shops."

She never came. Yes she did. If you remembered the attack why didn't I tell you. Did I concoct The Petty Deed and I pictured scuffle flashback. The slurping. I refused consent. A duckling crying for help. Chased after her spark. The cliff, I believed. I told her,

"Be careful."

Everything too late. Wet and bloody and collapsed a fading foretold of the future me. What would happen.

Well it came to this. Smallish suffocated room. Yellowsun psychiatrist. Aromatic candles. Flickered claustrophobic, a girl (me) on the verge of accepting advice from a three-eyed over-accessorized woman. Her sinew almost skinless and fake tanning transforming her skin into the color of wee. Yellow woman of my fated. Could this Burrow undo, unmad, unshatter me?

The woman made me shake. 'Whole lotta shakin.' Why. *Why tell her.* The truth. Should I reveal this load to her opposite. Today fired my thoughts, choking on the memories, a turning Ferris wheel, fortune wheel, wheelie click clicked. Around and around till we all fell down. And I repressed the nastiest stuck his fingers in my privates. He ended pleasure. I cried,

"Pig Pig."

Geraldine Burrow started.

"What's that you said?"

Spectacles slid to the end of her nose. She heard. I know she did. Oink oink. Read my better than dead. Transported me to reality here. Before moonshiny sunburst yellow noodled wigger. Why twitch brat said. Where porker Fergal done put his doodle.

Really and.

Of this beginning session, the Burrow asked predictable questions.

"Shipley. Are you comfortable?"

"Ummm."

She lit five candles. Aroma spiced closeness, sniff.

"Sandalwood clears the air."

She meant evil spirit hooley holy snaddlewood did the trick. Oil of antispasmodic to tackle my irritated. Flashing-backs. Me the inflammation. I inhaled the spice ever hoping. For a calmed self. When honeyed the Burrow self-satisfied, revved her wattage. She sidled into the analyzing and airy. In-toned,

"I do attempt to create tremendous ambience for my clients."

I do I do I do. Her littled flut flutter. The statement veiled as a threat. I had to respond. With. Flame lumps burning through. A flaming throat.

"Okay, right. Thank you. Its lovely."

Here.

Fountain pen, fountainhead, please passed the quizzing. The Burrow wrote a list, a sentence, a scribble on her notepad. *Are you writing about me.*

A girl transformed into a shopping list. Bread eggs butter milked my eyes flitting sideways. I looked around the room. My distraction noticed objects on her desk. A plastic hairless head sliced in half, empty inside. Beside it sat two halves of a model brain. Its hard surface different from squishy sheep's brains blood flecked lying on a meat tray at the butcher. But this anatomical dummy brain was solid, I guessed PVC. Demonstrated to the patient about thoughts. In the mind. And color coded. Red blue purple yellow wormy shapes. Each conveyed various sections. Could be edible candy sour sweet minus sugar coating. Other segments were numbered and tacked together with red cotton twine supposed string section la la la representation of realist arteries. And a flesh colored center. I squinted at a teardrop shape reminded me again of the purple dick from that Mother and Daughter night.

Beside the plastic nobrainer lay a second nasty. Model. The smooth mold of a torso with an open chest, minus arms, nipples and genitals. And the interior without a liver, intestine, lungs. Cavernous contained a beatless heart surrounded by miniature faces expressing many emotions. Sad. Suspicious. Hopeful. Scared. Fury. Happy. Jealous. Love and spared me the gore. Even if synthetic. And this chest full of faces watched.

Another enigmatic object. A mystifying Blobby. Foul. Tied around with a yellow ribbon in the form of a bizarre gift. *Tie a yellow ribbon… Keep still…* It MOVED. This yellow larger than a brain, whizzed faulty synapses and cerebral electrodes. My own PVC brain curdling along my OMG the fated. Yellow. Yeh. Easy okay quite unnecessary to panic yet at. Hell.

Mysterious blobby glowering undefined near a stack of cardboard folders. Bobble appeared organic. Would organism hurt? Should it be contained? In a jar? Should blob be soaking in preservative? *Ask the Burrow for me. No.* She did not notice my darting gobsmacked! Prickly curious cautioned my wonder list. I wondered descending to earth for no-nonsense answers. Was it a lamp? Lunch box? Work of art? Paper weight? Should I *inquire?* What the holy bejeezus is that creature vibrating on your desk? *Do you get off on it?* Ride it like a pony?

I shrugged too difficult. And rude to pry and remembered things revealed themselves eventually.

Her fiddle fixated on the noting mmm. As I settled on the wicker, wind howled somewhere or dogs or crows or banshees. In the land of the Peeble on the run. To kingdom come.

Here many distractions. Sandalwood caused nausea and The Sound of Music sicked in my throat.

"What has brought you here," said Geraldine Burrow yawning with her pages ready.

Time for helloed gripes. For a chanted, more to myself than anyone. Without breath. My voice rising red rose ring a ring a rosy.

"I can't stop myself singing gobbledegook songs."

Was I a Pentecostal possessing the devilspirit? The golden Burrow confused, dropped her fountain. Either impatient or intrigued.

"Err. Can you define gobbledegook."

"Crap. Shit. Idiocy."

Crapshoot nonsensical, my fright watchful gobbled and regret.

"And. Life has not turned out how I thought it would."

"By life, you mean?"

Uncanny anyone explained the meaning of life. A number? Million anythings panged remorse and years the ahead. Fun, I missed. Her. Maybe scared shit. And me mourning, morning had broken. Regrets regurgitated the fear. I thought it was love hark he he joking. Towering fright turned my corner. Afraided myself. Fear claimed, that day fear ceased. Fear ignored end of days, the stopping time to stop. Breathing. Fear devastated. Untypical even if I tried. Fear triggered through my violin vein strings. Type web twine veined wrapping. The time I walked into a spider web it spread over my face I spouted freaking help-bloodyshite scrabbled hands tearing delicate spider crawled up my nose. Small terroring preserved me alive. *Don't tell her every that afraid.* The present was frightening enough.

"Life as a wife. When I look in the mirror, I reflect a girl."

Thin waif girl, funky girl, delicious dowdy scrubber visceral oddest lemon in the bowl. Superheroine caped mermaid Corningware magic whore majestic slut Royal Doulton, raised my pinky in the dungeon. As my chest rose and fell approaching a battalion at war.

"I realized that isn't me."

"What?"

"The genuine wife. It was quite a shock."

"I sympathize."

"Do you? Because marriage is supposed to be blissful. I imagined giving birth. You know. To babies."

PVC puppet babies. Little heads that opened like lids. Heads turning full circle. Pucker pouty made a wha wha sound. Microphoned music box, mechanical limbs with joints and hands that never moved and nylon hair gathered speed. I would treat them to iced cupcakes, fruit punch, picnics in the park, a corgi, ice-creams, sherbet lollies, cough medicine, lacey party dresses. The enchanted kingdom. *King Lace. Whatever it took* for a flawless family with cropped hair and dressed in identical vests. Tartan and tassels. Somewhere. The Sound of. Off.

Geraldine Burrow half listening.

"But you are only eighteen years old."

Only. Really two hundred. I had skeleton friends A dodder dollar bill. Round numbers them. Eighteen. Nah. Hundred in the body better read than red I said,

"I feel a lot older."

"Don't we all."

Oldie moldy misfit. Ms. Burrow listened but failed to perceive. Urk death to perception. Here here. She played the game of gaze. Her enamel disinterested in me the duckling.

"Can I get you a glass of water?"

My duckbrain of. Glass half empty half filled. Juice wine Ribena beer Coke poison. Her deaf steered my blinding. She glanced past. Ah it lasted that pasted me. Narcissist whinger. Of my complained most. I was I was I was bogsider mudsucker shocker. At rest against daisy. I exposed myself as the rattler. The honeyducky. The potty mouth talking sow. Softer softer in a mumble sweet honey cow.

"Monk says I am self-centered. He says I am ridiculous. He says I need help. He says visit a professional helper. He says I need medicating group therapy counseling." Twinged Twiddle the Burrow pondered,

"Do you always do what you are told?"

No but yes but no spat phlegm hand on my heart swore to tell the whole truth nothing but the Signs.

Toil trouble started to come. Slow blushed upping. Worry walloped the fire. Uneasiness grabbed me. Panic left and then and then and then. Returned to itself its retained self in fragments. Cheeks bulged with obscenities. Inside a shout. Not yet, hold horrible in. They gave me an enema, before the cut, held that shit in for ever so long.

"I yelled at Monk. That day."

"Did you?"

"Yes. In front of his mother. I shouted Quill what kind of name is *that*? Quill means you're a dill, you spill, give me a chill. The word is skinny, to flaccid. Quill dick sick prick slick trick lick. Make the gruel thick. Mix it with broken wife angst stank fuck. Monk put his hand over my mouth and whispered *nervous breakdown* at his mother. I screamed, Bitch bitch witch witch, the hedge pig whines, its time its time. His mother told him, attention seeking, ignore her. I wept every Wednesday night at church choir practice. A foolish balancing on the thin wire of then and then and then. The choir sang. *All things bright and beautiful the Lord God made them all.* And desperate, Monk shushed me, For God's sake shhhhhhh hush *hush,* people are staring. I wanted to crack his nuts with a monkey wrench."

Geraldine Burrow frowned the particular frown that frowned at these kinds. Of women. She activated her mmmms. Long longish these mmmmmmmmms.

"Mmmmmmmm. Right. Well. You have a lot of feelings to express."

"Yes I do."

I do I do I do.

Her meaningful vagued and the disappointment kept me talking.

"Monk tries his best. His reasonable. I am no longer his angel. I surpass disappointment. I enrage the man. I buy blunt razors, rippled condoms, a cemetery plot, door hinges, pokers, puns, pills, pork. I let my posture go to the dogs, to waste, the improved sewer self of exceed outshine. Every time a door slams the slamming for a real life. Shut your trap. Shut the fuck. But I can't complain. I should do it. Shut the fuck up I mean."

"I understand."

I wanted to pin her ears to her eyes.

"Do you? Do you really? The compulsion. I feel compelled to sing out of tune. Every song a war. Monk is completely over it. He thought my singing cute and quirky. But he lost patience."

I explained it this way of a fable. The time. Dragon-boots existed. Style of dull.

"In the past. Of dim lighting you know dimmer switches. Think background bark bark bark. I invented a gang of barking dragon-boots. Grew tufts of trollhair. Frenzy bows rested. A pepper of zits. But what. The dragon-boots escaped from the cellar. At dusk sun-sank veil of starry. I the lonesome knightess scorched by love. But that's irrelevant. I swam across the ocean. Dragon-boots rowdy in a mangrove swamp. The swamped reedy. Real swamp. But how a mangrove swamp flourished in the sea. I surprised this scaly band, eating beef stew. Gave me heaped. Plate of. Who knew where they cooked. Knave fool of foolish shouted, Shoo. This frightened the dragon-boots dropped their stew. Dribbled on their claws. They sped in a thunderous. And what the what never to return and I decided. I must. This why. I threw away the stew."

"But," said her the familiar puzzled.

"Hang on let me explain."

This rationalize if magical. I told her dragon-boots the lot. A representation of Ideas. Every Idea apparent ridiculous. Brainstorm stewed pointless. Many schemes wonky daft. Opting for the mangrove swamp, specific for the sinister effected. Drifted gloom vapors. This special effect thriller gamble. Beef stew represented Success. The tossing screamed a cockhead error. You never throw Success into the dunny. This impractical. Blunders gaped a rotted undone. I was downcast miserable starved failure and scared without stew. No longer a swifted expert dragon chaser. And no time left to concoct boiled meat dishes. The stove too conked to cook savory dishes satisfied got no satisfaction. Unsavory. Like stew.

I straightened. Krak quiet volcano rumble below yike spirited. The Burrow gripped her cardboard folders.

"What's wrong?"

Both fists in my mouth.

"Fawful crock ug mug mif god, it's happening. Here it comes. Man oh man."

I slapped myself magic slipper did not fit.

The Burrrow moved quick smart to the seat behind her desk. Barriered, she adjusted her alarmed expression to calm and steady.

My cheeks ballooning, filled with cherries marbles pebbles turds spewed from mouthed grumble bumble. I doubled over as if to birth a monster in the gutter guttural glug.

"Listen."

The growler gibs gabs. My gabbling got beyond excitable. Sang soft roar. Song sounded of music tripping over itself. Happened turvied, tossed its topsy and flattened. A high-pitched, tuneless voice.

"I hosed the flying cheese, the hairy mittens, the copper kittens, the knitted kettles, the creamy drops of rain. Hailstones on hoses and whiskers on mittens, bright copper kittens and warm woolen kettles, wild cheese that flies with the sun on its fins, cream colored raindrops and schnitzel with sashes. These were few of my favorite things."

I wretch bile stopped the singing turned ugly munching sounds schnitz schnitz sorrow. The bang bang you're. Honk-whoop de do I slowed. I slipped into the dead sea. I hushed my tongue sh sh shhhh. *Sorry.*

Geraldine Burrow scribbled on her clippetty clop and said with caution,

"Shipley. You are dreadfully creative."

"Am I?"

"Yes, you are."

"Monk doesn't think so. He says I am just annoying."

I heard faint rumblings. Hunger pangs. Her stomach growling. Lunchtime. I blamed the stew story. I drowned that howled hunger pain louder and louder.

"Every task I overtake."

Freaked my rest of it.

"How do I make the singing stop? I can't help myself. Becomes a piece of snake. A man feathering my nest has no time to rest and then I feel so bad so bad so bad. And Monk keeps asking what nest what feathers. He should *know*. He should be feathering. But he sits and reads the newspaper. I shred the paper. I scream at him. I throw the shreds in the air here make a nest. In this shed. Our lean to. Make space for a nest. I should hose the daisies. Where is she? Where is my pinafore? Where oh where has that little. That shit done. Shit, I can't find the polka dot my pinny. And I ask myself what the hell is a *pinny*?"

A protective smock. A decorative garment. This ridiculous bib. The good ship pinafore. Old-fashioned, frilly, playtime, sheer cotton playing with time. Ridiculous bibs made me half-woman, half-servant, protecting me. A pinafore preserved me dry and revolting.

Alison owned an apron. Her apron said *Luverly wife snappy life, kiss the cook, the kitchen is where I belong, housework can't kill you but why chance it, my wife rules, Fergal's wench, cunt.* Alison of absentee.

The future unfurled, a tight curl uncurling itself. And nothing caused that future. It uncurled by itself. The future gained time unlimited, unself always always the always under my breath.

Lived this grief.

"Life broke her. Life will break us, she said this and I didn't believe her. I should have helped her. Once we were sane. I miss her. Where is she? Yes, I know. I do know. But nobody told me why. At least, she never knew of the molestation. Stunning word. Had she discovered. The arsehole cornered me. He said we'll do it this way and you'll remain a virgin. Virginity intact. Ha. That porker with his piggy cum. He wanted to fuck a mannequin. But he didn't get far."

The ginger Geraldine heard bitty only. The Burrow perking a deduced. Figuring this girl the ingenuous target. Another flame extinguished in the hatefire. Girl madcap as a snake. And Geraldine Burrow was equipped with the tools to change me into the woman I should be. Whatever that fulfilled in some way. Filled with wine or babies or biddies or winkles or cauliflower or triffids or aprons or cum. But for the imminent fulled of songs.

I sang biggest yellowist whispered sins low sweet lower. Lowdown deep of deep. Deep of the deeped that madness sadness tomorrow yellow sorrow.

"And a big yellow taxi drove Alison away. You don't know what you've got till it's gone. I am left with yellow. Every day yellow. A yellow cross the same height as Jason. I hate yellow. Yellow follows me. That doesn't mean, I mean. I blame my wedding dress. Yellow cheese cloth. Mrs. Quill shrieked when she saw it. *You are not a bride.* I don't care. I am infected with desolation. Yep. Fab whacking despair show. I believed the fairy stories."

Geraldine Burrow jotted nodded fiddled scribbled sitted unsmiling, but pretended pensive. Yacked her picky teeth. Yellowed fanger fangdango. Hid the fangs. At once. As third eye, middle blinked. She wrote on her notepad clipped to its clipboard. Third eye snapped its clip. Third eye burrowing me to a watery grave. Third eye owl-wising at me. Helped herself. Third eye helped. Third helping.

She closed her clipboard.

I wanted to press that mole through her skull and into her brain. Mushed. Smash the PVC and the yellow thing was yellow a thing you didn't think so you told me yellow not a thing, but, doubtful. Because. Right in front of me. The yellow thing on her desk. Monk said, yellow was not a thing. He sweetie-pied me. Master gobble egg yolking me all over me.

The Burrow reached over and fondled the blob. Her jewelry flashed. I shut my eyes. Unbearable swam in daffodil walls.

"Do you mind if I?"

Slid off the chair and climbed the walls. Smoothly. My cheek pressed to the daffodils. Too many to count, she loved the carroty colored centers. I crawling higher reached the ceiling. I looked at her over my shoulder. The Burrow golly shrinked. I did not lose my way.

She called,

"Enough of that nonsense."

I started sliding down daffodil cheeked. My slither breathtaking, no went to queen reality check, I admitted,

"Yellow scares me."

She said,

"Oh, I see. I see. Spooked by yellow. That's, well that is unbelievably interesting."

And I fell to the floor in the asking.

"You think so?"

Yellow Was A Thing

Yes, she thought so. I was Fucked. The room awed into a gaping silence. People died. I was not used to people dying. Should I tell her?

"I am not used to people dying."

"Who."

"Everyone."

Arggggg. The wave of daisy cushions, candle burned, wick in a pool of wax and caning prickle for seated.

My body stiffened. After I crept high and low in the airless. Spent my roar in that climbing creeping. Stiffer and tired and frittered at eighteen. Vison add sin sin sin to my sinned. A sinner braced random stuffed fuck everyone. Dead. Emotion said the wrong words. Passion expected too much banger sensation. Of nothing else to say. Except sing, dirge dared break the quiet of the daffydill wallpaper and cast a spell, dilly dang dong wonk round the wankers. I waited. Minutes zapped by. Time sped nearer to lunch. The sun brighting. I tempted to shout, to mimic that sungoddess and breakout with probable rasp wordy crystal balls in a beaky bird voice, in a fried on a wire voice of hesitant thunder wunder.

"What comes NEXT."

What resulted, after the after unspoken deep, after thought of pie, stodge steak, dumb plumsin formulating her thereafter.

Diagnosis? Actions spoke louder than. My body jumped the doom fisticuffs. My glassy shattered. Heart of gold and pathetic smile. Maybe the Burrow spent her childhood in a community of cabbage farmers. Or or or had a nauseating childhood as a ping pong champion. Ping! Idea. Where located the beginning in the gizzards, the mash brain grew a soul that mole told me she adopted rescue cats. And she envied a man's capability of peeing while standing. She definite sundried her own tomatoes. She informed me, she qualified as a Mensa candidate. Possibility she developed the three-step plan one two three a kick and a shuffle. She belonged to a Secret Society of Secrets. She slept with a knife under her pillow. Her the deadly fluke and me her lucky break.

I thought this. Because it helped. IT.

Diverted me. And the Burrow sat her goldy goldilocks flip in a snug chair. Her behemoth toothy tried to make sense of My Misery.

"You need to look *ecstatic*. It's the principal phase."

"In what?"

"Creating a cheerful life."

"How many phases are there?"

"Quite a few."

The Burrow trapeze cured the dumb decisioner, no. Got on with my lot. *Finish the song.* Let her honeyed a lecture. But. Nervous for she golded me, do you dream about her chipping her shoulder, turned blue and shattering her teeth. She convinced the girl to shine a normal flag and polish your wares anywhere and stockpile tins, ropes, vinegar, Scotch, snap at his heels, whatever you want, I can be the buzz. Then and then and then.

Half an hour left.

Blob on her desk. That precious treasure snored peaceful. Her trusty weapon of bony fingers primed to catch. Wordless her use of exaggerated tenderness. Geraldine Burrow reached for blobby. She lifted that yellow-watt object. My mesmerized it moved a wobble. Beated from within. A battery? Must be a wind-up squishy biff. The simple explanation Burrow soft, reverential. She putted her lofty nose into the aerosphere and whispered,

"What we have here…"

Both her palms turned up and aligned as a flatted pedestal. The Burrow balanced freaky bopper in the middle. She paused. Noticeable intake of gravity. Dialed a notch louder her talk imitating a majesty grand duchess.

"What we have here is The Only One In Existence. In the *entire* WORLD."

My mouthed a lower of disbelief. The Burrow shone like barley sugar. Paused for the buildup. I heard an orchestra playing a triumphal march. *Do you hear it? Yes*

The trained script singsong stuck in my craw. *What we have here.*

Ta dah.

The swollen lump, size of a deflated football, required did it, a puncture into the deeper cryptic yellowynatter. Of the Burrow announcing much gravy gravitus.

"What we have is a part, an extract of a Multi-Machine Synthemotion."

The what branded with a name. Marketed. Impressive. Tumbled of said gravitate Multi Multi Multi rolling boulders. These facets and machined morsels and floppy fragments. It certainly flopped sloppy bits. I summoned reaction interest.

"Uh. What's that then."

She held the multisynthing closer. The heart yellowy stalker lipped. I realized for certain. Porky blown me a kiss. My new best friended. Little clog fetus.

I tucked my hands under my thighs. No touching yet. Too slimy limey. My scrutiny distant bug eyes examined the proper peculiar of this oval ball. Muscular with soft edges. Single buttock and chunked. The thickness surface varied to depths of five to ten centimeters. A myriad of molecules cemented. Exterior fine of present queasy. Same as leather hide, vinyl upholstery, human skin. And covered with millions of tiny pores. Of honeycombed fleshy. Thought piece of tripe. This slash of triffid, same as a heart the human kind. Spherical with stalks and stems and rootlets and blunted projections, a possible planting. Into a temporary space of soiled.

And the front of the Multi-Machine Synthemotion, funneled tunnel of an anal whorl. Mouthy. Filled with sacs of liquid. Would it stamen sting with the stalkies? Could Multi-Machine Synthemotion sensed vibrations in a yellow. I wondered was it fertile. Carnivorous? A decomposer, a digester, a shitter, a stinger. Sensitive to stupidity. Could it spin, swallow, stumble.

Was I the prey.

Should I stock my shelves with anti-venom, tourniquets, vials of my blooded. Hell hell hell. Over-reacting with my common collective intelligence of an ant.

Geraldine Burrow letted loose five or six air kisses.

"Mwa mwa mwa. I love it to bits."

I mustered a smut of enthusiasm.

"Yup. It's amaaaazing."

Intelligent this pounding. This pummeled brain stretchy bread dough pound pound told. *It is a lump, just a lump, a smit interesting, but plopped LUMP.*

Or two she served tea and put lumpy on the glass topped coffee table. Reflected itself glass made doubled lump, tripled lump reflection in the mirror on the wall. And the yellow petals scatted on daffwallpaper multiplied lump of her hands togethered in a reverent impression of praying. To lumped. Of yellow was a thing. She began,

"Listen to me carefully."

I tipped my droplets of sweated drippings. All nerves.

"I'm all ears."

Ears covered me. Skin opening with ears in a flap. Eardrippings. Earguts of questioning cartilage question marks. Ears shouting.

What Next.

Agony it had to be agony you don't know fuck about agony I know yellow is a thing. It can't be. It can't be, it bloody is.

Her fingers trilled an arc movement. Around and around and around sphered. Both hands molded a sphere. From the air. She wholed the while her wily expanded.

"This device generates synthetic emotion."

I shaked a scrap of Incredulous. Collywobbles landed on the coir matting under my feet.

"It does?"

"Let me explain the basic brand name. This particular model is called the Core Luci-D."

Plenty of my collective more than blank.

"How do you spell that?"

"C...O...R...E"

"Core? You mean like apple core."

"Well yes if you want a literal meaning as in the central part of certain fruits containing seeds. I prefer the bigger picture. The center of the earth. The central element of humans. The spiritual seed essential to character and existence."

"Oh right *that* sort of core. I get it."

And she spelled.

"L...U...C...I...dash...D."

Next dashed emotions. Another gutting gut cored. The fatting peculiar smells a waft. It smelled fishy. Sea smells shell smells tooth smells shark smells.

I played serious along and asked careful,

"Where did The Core originate?"

She cleared her throat.

"My dear girl, this piece of genius is the latest development in psychoanalysis. Obviously, it's classified. Have you heard of Professor Nesbitt? You must have. No?"

Geraldine Burrow's tongue clicked disappointment. She winked. A wink and a wunk.

My picturebooked creation of Professor wanker Nesbitt. Such an elegant man in his cashmere jacket, the most superb silver buttons, kid leather loafers, the roundest glasses and thick lenses. But sistersky might comment *too congenial, make him eviler dirtier.* Dirty fingernails, hairy fingers, soggy bread for hair, pointed teeth could scratch glass, swam in a swamp, licked the envelopes, dragon breath so well-dressed in his nose ring, dragonboots straight from a fairy story. That inventor of the Core Luci-D.

The Burrow breathed insightful preparation. To divulge the facts. On this invention to fulfil my cure. Undevil me. Great. A butt that burped. Not gilded corngold, fields of heat, yields of wheat intervention as I imagined.

"Anyways," she swallowed Orange Pekoe. "The Multi-Machine Synthemotion technology emerged as a collaboration with several masterminds in a unique interdisciplinary research program developing the Core Luci-D. Yet the 'birth' if you can imagine, of the Core Luci-D, was accidental."

Her jewels noised crystals, chain-links clanked my blanked and her explaining,

"It happened through a series of ingenious experimental muddles, you know the type of mishaps mice, rats locked in cages, the vivisecting of bunnies and monkeys, keeping kittens in formaldehyde. The wonder of it when Professor Nesbitt discovered the organic value of concepts combined with magnetic energy creates artificial emotions. Can you believe it? Imagine the furor."

My stomach hurt.

"No."

I shivered social evil, such cruelty to pets. Where was that animal rights group. *When you need them.* But did not say. The sentiment. To the rabbidor garbling explanation keeper of the core.

"*And* Dr. Nesbitt made an interesting breakthrough."

Geraldine Burrow gulper rabbited spouting excitement.

"He managed to compound the spirit of emotion into a tangible form! So such feelings as glee envy mistrust optimism can be objectified."

I keeper of questions the confusion of thumb twiddled.

"Where is this tangible form. Do I have to fill it in? I am not expert at…"

"No no Shipley. Think of emotion as an object we hold in our hands."

My patience skipped.

"Where. Is. The. Emotion. Object."

She leapt to her feet. And imitating an Olympic torch bearer, the Burrow waved the Core Luci-D. That parked porker. She cried,

"Here! This spectacular apparatus."

What. What. What. Bollocks.

Jangle woman raving her rabbit sniffer. Bling too bright. Her strung of metal rattle made her somehow insincere. In sin. Her glisten fangness. Decided she the freaking. Scary biscuit. The windy moled eye of a dot. Labeled her a nutter. Conclusion most appropriate way to handle the situation what about.

Politeness.

"But it sounds ah intricate. I don't actually comprehend. Does the Core whatchamajig do magic tricks?"

"Professor Nesbitt created the concept lucid lucidity into Luci-D."

"Oh bully for him."

She shot me one of those looks. Of impatience and continued.

"Let me explain. Professor Nesbitt based the concept of the Core Luci-D on human elucidation. He combined this idea with valuable personal data collected to illuminate the nature of emotion."

My not too collective bright. Mutual dumb. Young budding knew. But could I believe this? Crocked hooey. And the lump chilled of. Vexed veins quite blue. String.

"Right. But..."

She interjected,

"And even more interesting, the word Core refers to the actual structure of a core. Meaning the configuration of a nucleus. Which in this case is the emotive spirit. In other words, an artificial emotional spirit. And the amazing discovery is the color of an artificial emotional spirit is gold. Exciting, isn't it?"

I trembled. My hands got sticky. Goldheat, fields of corn. Yields of wheaty wondered.

"Ummm but..."

"And scientists nicknamed the Core Luci-D the 'Lucy.' So clever don't you think?"

"Well yes..."

And such a distraction. I forgot to sing. I never wanted to sing my crazy ever never again. I forgot about yellow. No. Yellow was unforgettable. Eternal that cross to bear. Inside of intrigued and suspicious.

A gentle Burrow untied the ribbon and drew attention to various sectioned bits of the Lucy.

"Here and here and here. Please pay attention. It's compact, yet the complexity so so so unbelievably extraordinary. The exterior has grown a nest of overlapping loops. These loops unravel becoming roots and stems. Acting as conduits of spiritual emotion these attach themselves to the core of a person. They deflect electrical waves. Comparable to brain waves."

"But," I said. "I don't think brain waves are actually..."

"Yes they are," said Burrow firmly set. "Look closer."

"Is it alive?"

"No. Not really. Imagine the Lucy as an imitation organism."

Geraldine Burrow flipped the Lucy over.

What bizarre beneath. Expected underbelow. The underside. The underground. And so novel, biting the particular revealed every personal conglomeration. Ugh gunge worldy resembling earwax, dried flesh, beef jerky. And complication linked together with gristle threads. *Loops* she called them. Loopholed little lump. My worth my value my price My my my. Oh, she prettied thing up.

"The underside consists of a biotic engine. These threads penetrate human organs and the human spirit."

"Does it hurt?"

"It's not painful. Don't be concerned. Look here...the surface is a malleable substance. Touch it."

I inhaled a helpless urk loathed to feel the. Of an item, one feeling. Why the songs shrieked silence. She this yellow thing stopped me singing ridiculous so I. Reaching a tremble. Brave heart braver hand stroked outer. Surfaced. Textures abrasive to slipslither. Stickiness shifted against my fingertips. Gave a friendly squeezed diddle in the inners. Tickled the sog alien. I pulled my hand away. Moistness revolted me. My hangupper obstacle said,

"That surface gives me the creeps. Is it handmade?"

The Burrow yelper continuing her delighted.

"Yes! Absolutely. And so detailed. The process involves years of assemblage by apprentice technologists. They assemble raw emotions with a critical impact on spirit and also at the same time being a component of spirit. Many of the multiple functions reinforce consciousness, enhancing physical sensations and avoid errors when anticipating future emotional states. In other words, when you are on the verge of acting inappropriately, for example your chanting, causes the application of the Core Luci-D to adjust your emotions to the correct balance allowing you to stabilize."

"But why," I asked, "Is the Core Luci-D yellow?"

"That's not a genuine yellow."

"Yes. *It is.*"

"Right, but paler than a proper yellow. Such a striking primrose color. Professor Nesbitt's favorite hue. I picked the Primrose Chamber prototype because Monk informed me of your specific *aversion* to this hue. It's the old technique you know, reverse thinking. Achieves the opposite effect."

"Of what?"

"Okay that's a single example. Another is an activity to make stupid objects smart. Your problem is noisemaking singing etc. The reverse action is silence. Make silence your problem. Done. And your hatred of yellow combines a new emotional spirit. Anyway, in due course, you'll realize how your feelings can be altered by the Lucy."

The Burrow opened a cupboard full crammed of her rummage papers, overflowing containers and postage boxes.

"Ah here it is. An added component."

She handed me a golden pair of sewing scissors. Flash a twinkle polish of flawlessness. And I hung-held the scissors with the tippy tips of my fingers, as if holding a dead rodent.

I am screwed. I pondered if my scissor load valuable.

"Are they genuine gold?"

Geraldine Burrow laughed maniac he he har har. She found me diverting, ho ho rollicking vaudeville. Ha ha final funned the finish.

"No. No of course not. It's fool's gold. All that is gold does not glitter. Because. What is really fake. This is particular to the learning process. Imagine yourself as a rainbow with fool's gold at both ends."

"I can try, but it's going to be difficult." I replied.

With a pair of sewing scissors.

And funniest dubious itself to outer infinity I supposed. In the outhouse of defeat. The succumb needed to obey and progress to an improved woman. Fit and prospered. Wholly husky stoop by stooped and stepping by step. At least be thankful the Burrow a female person. But toughed reveler took no prisoners.

Her talked on, the instructions, read the leaflet. Bah humbuggery. I did not listen.

Women of the world tell me what to do. Ahem just a matter of twitching my witchetty grubbed.

Then the Burrow told me do here this. What the.

"Tonight, search your house and collect memorabilia that has profound significance to you."

"Ok I can do that."

Easy. Myself drummed doom always anticipating. The Worst.

She ignored my frozen Expression.

"You'll notice a piece of sheer material inserted at the front of the Luci-D."

"I thought it was pantyhose."

"No no this is synthetic skin. A shield protecting the vulnerable core of Lucy, which we called the false spirit."

She opened a desk drawer.

"When you are ready to begin, choose a quiet time. Draw the curtains. Turn off the lights. Gently lift the synthetic skin flap with a pair of tweezers. Put your objects and papers inside the Primrose Chamber. Please demonstrate this for me immediately."

"Where are the tweezers?"

"Here."

"Thanks."

Nibble went the tweezers. Ordinary ten cent tweezers. Bet she bought them at Teks. I peeped inside.

"I can see a buttery pulpy mass filling the interior."

"Yes. So interesting isn't it? Once the 'skin' is re-secured as firmly as possible, the Primrose Chamber processes your documents by transforming the genetic constructs of temperament into the form of an emotional control pellet. Can you visualize this?"

"No," I said.

Her weevil face fell. Down her, oh well. I visualized droll in my mind. Her orange tanned falling into a deep. The disappointment. For a short time. But she propped her encourage surfacing.

"Not to worry. We will get there."

Wild goose ideas smelled of freedom. So, who killed the honeychicken as she laid the golden popsical. Those that wandered lost.

I scratched at an old scar on my leg. The round mark, childhood gash from falling off a slippery slide. I wanted to sing. The desire returned, this raptor gripped me Sharp. Inside of adorable illusioning. Songfizz bubbled fast up throat.

Oh where oh where did my little dog go. This just a fantasy. Caught in a mudslide. No escape from reality. Nothing really mattered. Once I had a love and it was a gas.

Press pinched lips. Retained the bottled songs inside my gutsy.

As she repeated.

"The positive spirit generates agents to suppress negativity and negative emotion produces an overall adrenaline effect. This plastic adrenaline guides an overly emotional person towards a stable state owning completely falsified feelings."

"Won't people notice if I fake it?"

The world.

"Of course not," said this airily. "Your friends and family expect this. Let's conduct a detailed examination. Inside the chamber is a basin filled er, something similar in appearance to garden mulch. It is living fibers of feelings."

Aw thought bitty did they wriggled worms of grief, smiley, gloomhurt sanguine skeppy skep skepticality.

The Burrow stared at my disbelief. She continuing of determined.

"The Primrose Chamber examines your notes in the 'soil' and transforms them into what *I* have named The Core Pellet."

She put the ghastly thing in my hands. I held the Core Luci-D with shudder trembledness and almost dropped it.

Geraldine Burrow jumped to her feet. Paperwhite her whited out features. She gesticulated a shriek, as if she someone about to be pushed from a plane.

"Shipley! Please *please* be careful. Treat it like your firstborn child. The Core Luci-D is extremely fragile. It will disintegrate into liquid if dropped. And keep it away from extreme temperatures. If destroyed, a reconstruction of the Lucy encompasses a decade."

She calmed herself. Grabbed a gold pen. And formulated a list of simplified instructions. As she jotted them on a prescription pad. She recited aloud.

"Fill the Primrose Chamber of the Core Luci-D to capacity with your precious recollections and keepsakes."

"I don't have many."

"That's okay. Position the Luci-D under your right breast and undo the loops. They will automatically open to the correct length. And use these miniature clips to fasten it around your chest."

The Burrow handed me a small zip locked plastic bag filled with clips. Oooh skinclipped with buckteeth.

"Won't they pinch?"

"No no. Don't worry. Lie naked under a sheet of disposable paper. It doesn't matter where. The floor the sofa the bed."

I gloomed thoughts hospital operating table gurney. Pictured the snip.

"Please Shipley try to pay attention. Focus. Very important. For the most intense effect, keep the Lucy near your heart while you are sleeping."

Lie I had to lie. That possible an effortless action. Chewing off snippets that I knew. She pointed my ask at those stalks. And stems. And rootlets. And blunted projections. They fell, defeated. They interlocked into heaps of pendulum globules. She said,

"You don't need to touch the stalks and stems and rootlets and blunted projections."

"I don't want too anyway."

Memory of Bladderwort stuck.

"They have a mind of their own, those stalks and stems and rootlets and blunted projections. They sometimes grab."

What did blunter coiler grabbed? Would it tweeze the single strand of hair sprouting below my navel.

"Shipley you've gone so pale. You must not be afraid."

I was terrified.

"And listen. It's uncomplicated. Believe me. Such a unassuming formula and the results are so beneficial."

What were. The resulted exalted. And the process. Invasion infiltration of a blob spy sent to twist me. Mild disquiet happened. But for now, Ms. Burrow wrapped the Core Luci-D in bubble-wrap and laid it inside an insulated Woolworth's shopping bag.

"You can also wear the Lucy under your clothes. Anywhere. And swear on your grave you won't mention it to anyone. It's our little secret. The Lucy can't be ignored or hidden. So, pretend you are pregnant."

The Burrow presumed feelings I hated. Pretense. Pretender babe. The speculated guessing gamed her guess at me the gamer.

I might blow a gasket.

Instead. I recited The Confession of The Yellowing.

"One-eyed yellow idol broken-hearted woman.

Yellow God low hell.

Color-blind canaries.

Yellow beetle bug broach.

Mooned gaze at centuries.

Yellow straw.

Yellow silken scarf unaffordable.

Yellows leaves sticks."

My smarts preached.

"Nature-mother rarer applied gobs of yellow. And a million variations of sunsets and yellowed meadows. Yellow she skimped. Fuss scantly and selected. Like a lover's words yelling, brightly lit bathrooms attracted low flying flies."

She listened in a daze. I blithered on SO FAR.

"The conniption wife thinks. From out of the...off her head. I can't think of the word of yell reason hell yes ow."

The remoteness of my haywire stack.

"I mean. Rocket launches his missile. Whoosh such a never the same again follows wrenching tragic. And that death devastation. Blued. But yellow bit me. Fanger fanging. Of a. Voice to be flatted flat slaps into wildest blue yonderthere. Bride creeps her lurk tulle. Sin synthetic. Goes apeshit. Flip my Farrah Fawcett. Clouding. Bride of none. Hangs over my. Hang hanged me out to dry. God sees. On all fours diggle. Then. Flatted on my lay me down. Butterfly pinned to a specimen board. Legs apart, star-shaped girl bends knees up chested. Moves star arms alternate legs angel wings. Honeymoon of this honey not over the moon. Tries and tries. Faulty piece of the puzzle."

Obsession told the Burrow.

"That hellish God watched them butcher my lump."

In the telling, panicked.

"Alison says. *Wait Wait for me.* And I wait. She is late. No I am late. Or will she come am I the type. Who went. The disappear but. Why she calls, *follow me.* Alison says *move on.* She says *this is the extreme. Leave the ghosts forever.* Only cowards make plans. But my ghosts clamber and choke. *Come back.* I have these. Farewell obsessions."

Hello? Rules. I must ignore passions. Tweak. And erased infatuations. Safety faded to a safe space. I hung like a lone pear on the pear tree. I pierced my feet with rusty nails. I unhinged the gate. I crushed mince fed to the neighbor's cat. I cut Monk's bathrobe into shreds. I ordered a chastity belting from the forbidden forest. I got the belt stuck halfway up my thighs. I sobbed uncontrollably on his shoulder. Monk that time implored, for fuck sake pull yourself together!

Hostage shouted.

"And I have no plan. And that heaven so livid. Floods the ocean the sea the rivers the channels the tunnels the beds the boats. The tormented of foaming biblical it is. Ow. Water-lilies shriek in their beds. Those times. I make my bed, cry my river. And god strikes me are you done."

I began to sob. Geraldine Burrow jaded nonchalant. Her seen many mush sobbers in this consulting room. In my mind, a baseball bat clobbered. The Burrow heavy murderous. In her mangle of bracelets. A sympathetic paw on my arm, tucking the Woolworths bag under.

"You'll be fine."

"Do I need to leave a deposit?"

Hour consultation lasted an uneasy culmination of disbelief. She opened the door. I entered the waiting room and lowered my head avoiding the sight of that P. portrait and Mrs. Hodge shouting into the phone, "I said. Turn off the TV right this minute and finish your homework."

I walked on leg stumps pins and needled, weeping swelled my nose. Intensified my swollen in the mirror. Feral the bloodshot virus. Could. Not. Be. Me.

The Burrow called,

"Take the lift down..."

In the elevator, two embarrassed people moved to opposite corners, as I wept helplessly. Sobs trailed waydown river, leaving ghosted me to endure. Myself. And that stunned silence broken by the elevator's recorded message, *have a nice day.*

Christ.

The Pure Containment of Pathos

Okay. A pleasanter afternoon. Got myself a happied gallop. Smile. I Smiled. Slight wicked grin. Should avoided bottled sadness shit, the neediness self-obsession. SMILE. God dammit. I strode like an army general baring those gums. On the road to cheery. Cheered me yup. Skipped my chickadee. Not a soul invented the smile, ha ha ludicrous. A smile happened automatically. *Someone explain how cavemen invented the Smile.*

Of all the days, to be carrying lump Lucy inside a shopping bag, me in my Punjab, a checkered frump skirt and raw thwack of rubber thongs. A chanced meeting with Tiffany from school was it that long ago. Tiffany. I hated that name. We were not best friends. I looked up she looked past me. This streak of unspeakable cool. Height the issue. I wished Shipley born to be tall, born to be bad, not blue. I grinned false jollies delirious toothsome panting with desire for a shedding of popularity of sparkles disappearing before they hit. I stopped petrified, was I wearing my slippers, my nipples exposed, my pubic hair falling at my feet.

"Hi Tiffany. Wow this is a coincidence. It's me Shipley. Remember? From Year 5."

Tiffany of nodding hardly recognized. She helloooed a horror, not *her.* Her smile promised salvation, her expression did not. Glossy doll lips shone from strawberry lippy. I could smell a whiff as I inched closer kiss kissed the air. We were not even friends in high school.

"It's been years."

"No, it hasn't."

She acted friendly. Acting slowed for the red light. Do Not Cross.

"How have you been Tiffany?"

"Fine Shipley just fine."

Fine fine fine. Brief wave. I mustered some weak readies for a catch her chat.

"What have you been up to Tiffany?"

Been been been.

Sunglasses masked the impatience of her silver eyes, the eyes all the girls imagined were theirs. She eyed top to toe dowdy me. Her pierced scan girl. Me the skinner.

Tiffany's navy trim crisp blouse the impression of an executive banker special and anal. The stop light greened walking. Tiffany's high heels broke into a canter.

"Talk soon."

Faster and faster.

"I'm sooooo busy can't stop gotta run."

Rapid as a live bullet.

"I am sooo late. Appointment at three!"

Her words grew fainter and fainter.

"Lovely to see you. Bye bye Shipley."

The sheep of me baaaed,

"Goodbye Tiffany."

I knew then. The stealth of that façade. Tiffany shunning raggedyanne. I remembered her. Healthy Tiffany the cheer leader of hip her panties showing. Homeopathic girl, the earthy crunchy vegan ignored me the lackluster withered fruit. She the preacher of 'show me your palm and I'll trace your lifeline and tell you how ordinary you are and you will die in your sleep not scaling

Mt Everest. Her type cooked revolting mung beans smelling of the sewer. Her sort ate wheat grass custard. Absolute slop. Her typical cubed vegetables into pieces and pushed them around the plate. At fourteen, she changed into wild punk fishnets spiked green hair, and photocopied a fake ID. I tried to copy her, the dope I was, never invited to her parties. Underage weed druggy drank happy hour vodka two drinks for the price of one. She stole blocks of nut chocolate and baby oil and packets of razor blades from the supermarket. Toasted her skin. Sinister serenity sister. Then surprise surprise. She opened her heart to Jesus. A destitute carpenter. His miracle religion cured her acne. For a short time. I heard this from the local gossip. And in the end, Tiffany rejected the Lord Jesus Christ and ran off with a rich man.

A tear fell. Fool watching Tiffany of designer dress swirl from the waist, and leather shod almost running. Desperate to get away from shitty me.

Tiffany bitch moneyed up refused to acknowledge her absolute slutty drugged drunk hallelujah Jesus past.

Yes, I remembered Tiffany. I wiped my eyes.

Further along. Billboards advertising larger happiness.

Things go better with coke.

Tip topped bread kids love best.

Esso standard oil.

The boobs are real the smile is fake.

WOW true. On the boards depicting. To be ecstatic on fruited land, by speedboat sea, in a racing car, chiffon scarfed designer spectacles under the stars. The age of almost perfect contentment. A brave new world of persistent good fortune. Joyed without trouble. Happiness at the expense of grief. Pleasured without penalty. But where?

The mountain clung to that death of me.

Got myself home dried teary. I left the Core Luci-D in the bathtub to keep floppy moist cooler covered with ice cubes.

Delayed melting destruction. Later later later yes trialed the Lucy. Tied myself in knots.

Monk never home. Dishes stacked in the sink, newspapers fallen, washing powder Tide Attack Surf FAB ten kilos for his mother and cold stuffy. I stripped the bed, made the bed, had my cookie and ate leftovers and lay. Drowsy read Gulliver's Travels ooh classic enormous horn yawn halfway through fell asleep. Dreamt shit.

Gull, gigantic man. Unfitted inside the pickle house. He hounded the lilliput bookshelves. His huge thumb squeezed through the open door. Skimmed those books arranged according to color. Bright orange Penguin spines shone in a row. Here found that fat volume of Gulliver's Travels. Gulliver home from a long journey? No Monk and his wife, Et Cetera me surprised he is here, after so long.

"Hello Monk. Call me Et Cetera. You are Gull."

Monk lacked the imagination to be Gull.

He said, "I am not Gull."

But he truly true was. Samed ourselves sometimes as Gull and Et Cetera. My future. This couple the myth of us. Et Cetera warped me with the circumvented dreams. Of wife, Et Cetera. Cute name Et Cetera. Hinted of toughness, of endurance, a person disappearing into the distanced. But extras and sundries an endless list of a made-up woman remained etc etc etc. Unsuspicious interested casual. I asked him.

"Where have you been Gull?"

For months, the years crossed off the calendar.

"Aw, you know."

"No I don't."

He sounded tired.

"Settling arguments on the right way to whisk eggs. Peeing on fires. Selling my organs for a kilo of gold coins. I met sorcerers, flappers and a number of senile immortals."

I laughed etc etc. Et Cetera firmed criticalings.

"Friggin nonsense. You seem so different. Not yourself in that scarlet jacket and baggy pants. Your hair seems wrong. Those curls bleached corny. As if wood shavings are glued to your scalp. You are a lost spirit. And so much bigger. Too hulked for this shed."

I stopped the dream. Failed to remember why I did the same as her. Remembered none of the memories. This much I blur-remembered. I shranking shrunk skinny. Small. Halted the diminishment. The air con sucked the moisturizing from my body and the finicky flesh that once made me edible.

The size of a cat, upright I stood on two haunches. Catyface lay in the moth-to-the-flame bedroom. Gull grew his body tri-enormous. Why was I in this room? Shaking the linen. Discovered a fucked life. And holes. Or shake the fucking of life. And wack that moth with a fly swatter.

Et Cetera brewed a cup of coffee. In the lilliput putput kitchen. Difficult. As in. Perturbed. Et Cetera mislaid the coffee tin. The coffee pot? That stainless-steel coconut shape a kettle? The warm water? What *was* water? Where did it come from. Damn it. What caused water to be so heated, etc etc in the kitchen. Did we own a coffee bean. Played music of horns and flute solos. The Lucy sleeping in the bath. Horn tooted. Shhh. Storm on the way. Brain clouded every memory of crowded dreamtsleep. Those hordes of women existing without purpose. The presence of a woman had zero nada nooo effect etc. Unmentionable squandered disregarded etc etc etc. And my Et Cetera gene of that species. Bugger I forgot.

I growed mymanyselves even smaller. This reduction to size of a mouse. Shrinked some. As small as a fig. And that giant fig tree visibled from nowhere. Muchness collecting from under the tree. Memories? Figgy pud. Nuts? Rape victims? Unspent sperm? Tombs revisited? Etc etc etc Noises like the swish of a velvet curtain before a performance. This played on.

Et Cetera me etc, wanted to gather all the whooshing that ever existed. Fast trains, hurricanes, snakes, hairdryers, rockets, wizards, paperplanes, inhaling curses, fleeing, death etc etc etc. But what if Et Cetera me etc forgot her actions? Her lines. She would not remember that she could not recall contraptions, ideas, occurrences etc she forgot. This thought gave me a headache. I lay on the bed. How did I get to here? Didn't matter. The pieced of enduring human matter. I extinguished the candle. In the middle of the road a tip truck hurtling towards me. Et Cetera me etc etc etc nightmare ogre lorry in the bed running me over splat. With such criticism. And I refused to tell the bastards The Facts. The truth I imagined made her flattened dream-crap. For those myths belonged clang Et Cetera me etc. Once the wily crocodile, barefoot bohemian la la, sharp shooter, protective of the tin plate in between the brains.

The process of forgetting trapped, tied me to him. *Yes Master*. The eventual traptrick tighted. The exact way Gulliver. But different. Those slender ligatures of amnesia snaking around my thighs to armpits, my nodes, to her shuttered eyes, to my ambushed greying brains etc etc etc. And an absent mind waited for a sign of recognition.

"Gull? Gull? Gull?"

A gurgling sound. Nothing out of the ordinary. A cloud burst with the evidence that Et Cetera me etc wrought the ordinary exploded. Aye Aye Et Cetera me etc called his name.

"Gull Gull Gull Ggrrrrr."

This giant eye looked through my window. Excited Et Cetera me etc waved him away.

"You don't fit in here. You need to go on a diet."

His finger poked at my books again the Penguins. And Et Cetera me etc so small the size of a word on the page of a paperback. Gull boomed full of advice. His voice too loud.

"Find a beginning. Get to the middle. Stir the harking surroundings. Keep a tight hold on doorknobs etc etc. Go on."

I covered my little little ears. I couldn't go on. I kept forgetting. I got smaller. The size of a flea.

The list of me continued. On and on and on. The dream omen for a daytime napper.

I heard a squeak from the bathtub.

Monk came home. Dirty fingernails, muddy knees. Monk always went bit soppy gazed at me slept angelic.

"Wake up sleepyhead."

He gave me a present. This previous loved secondhand Jack-In-The-Box. Jack in a yellow clown suit, red pompoms running down his chest. Jack in its original paper carton. This boxed circus. It flotation on a cardboard wave. Of flawless preservation *Just you try me.*

I pulled the little lever. The winding crank that brought popping of Pop-Goes-The-Weasel. Almost snapped. This handle hung pathetic, this handle a broken wing.

"I broke it. Sorry."

"I'll fix it."

Monk looked for industrial tape handy. Fixed it. I wound and wound. And hoped. Against the wind. For a melody gone how long. The box stayed pangs of silent. And no bursting little bloke. *Come on Jack jump to it.* Jack struggled and struggled to surprise. To became a becoming of fully extended. But the bum. Jack's butt stuck. I cranked harder. Jack jumped up with arms spread. His Jester hat peaked of three corners had this hat.

Peeked-a-boo.

Jack booing. His toothy ever happiness. A terribled. That clowning smiled jester floppy hat. Donkey ears a tiny bell often tinkled *hee haw.* Jester the fool, bright starred incarnation of inspiration. Of wisdom, idiocy, skillfulness, stupidity, cleverness and whimsical. Jesters juggled distractedly dropped his balls one by one thudded.

Rice. Thrown that day.

The perfected fool. My hearted and minded faced the excruciating, the obscure, the intangible, the impractical. The perfect fool ignoring the obvious, the prudent, the premeditated. The perfection fool lacking respect for rationality.

Logic killed the jack-in-the-box. That discarded toys. The pure containment of pathos. I waited for Jack-In-The-Box to explode again but he never.

Until Monk asked questions how was it. At the therapy.

"What did Ms. Burrow tell you? Was the session worth the money?"

"I went over the time."

"Oh God we can't afford…"

"I'll hock the silver tea set."

"No need. I'll work extra hours."

"The consultation was Therapeutic."

"That sounds promising."

"You can't go in the bathroom."

"Why not?"

"She gave me a helpful machine. I can't describe it. I put it in the bathtub. You can't see it."

"How much did it cost?"

"Nothing. I have to return it when I'm finished."

"Finished what."

"I don't know."

Monk cleaned his fingernails and washed his knees in the kitchen. I did nothing for him. He hid razors and sharp objects. I consumed vitamins and protein powders. I said,

"I am bonkers."

He sighed,

"I know."

8

His Agony

Monk's agony blazed like a coal furnace from a ship's belly and the first mate doused the flames with a bucket of water and a shock rustled from his within. I thought, what a pleasure, a life lived with a catty wife. I obeyed he wanted. Antics rolling his eyes. I rolled over. The crackler mood alive. Heart of a heart, caught mangled in my femaleness, translated the agonized man. His Agony. But stalled his curious for a week. Curiosity tortured him. The wait rubbed my eyes. Each day loaded with whiskerbristled impatience. His unbearable hand hovering over the telephone desperate to dial. He honed a query phoning Geraldine Burrow. (Pearlmother drank of girls.) I overheard the call. Lead balloon. Landed. In my stomach pit. This muffled comfort. Monk strained and quavering.

"Geraldine Burrow? It's Monk Quill. Shipley's husband. Can I please schedule ten minutes with you? For an update on Shipley's progress."

And we went. Together.

Darling Street darling, flustering, three minutes late. His shirt stained hatred lateness perspired. Flayed his mucus. A swabbing and shot into the consulting room left me sat in the waiting room of shriek portrait.

When the receptionist nipped into the Ladies. I raced over to the consulting room door. Put my ear to the keyhole and listened and slid under the. *You never.* Unnoticed by Monk and the Burrow. Ha triumphant. I disguised myself as a standing lamp. Lamp with the curse. Burned impish pisher eyes in the corner. Lit like a neon daffbulb. A fancy one. My essential wobble disguised my head as a lampshade and my body hidden behind the wooden base. Monk moaned,

"I have a severe headache."

Geraldine Burrow offered Monk a glass of water, a Panadol, a seat, a *let's calm down.* The lamp included. The lamp worrying Monk might faint. He swallowed the painkiller. The Burrow asked,

"Who is Alison?"

Questlamp trembled. Gusts broke Alison. Waves carried her. I hung on. To my. Lighted bulb. Of eaves-dripper a drop, heard Monk. Gulped his words, throating attempted composure.

"Alison was Shipley's sister they were extremely close. She disappeared. She could be anywhere. Fergal, her husband, he says not to worry she'll be back."

Lamp outraged at such blatant.

Geraldine Burrow's safe chair swiveled ancient history behind the desk. Vinyl squeaked under her bony bottom. Liminal twat.

"Yes."

Was all. She said on the subject of failure. And Monk shifted in the wicker seat. Daisy pillows banished to a laundromat. Both chairs scraped the floor. Furniture creaked symphony of joints. Screech reverberating cruelty. His agony. Her indifference.

"Mr. Quill, please be aware, I've given Shipley a sixty-minute session. It's too early for me to comment and unsurprisingly, I can't tell you any of the information she confides in me. Whatever she says, pretend to believe her. At this stage, a better idea and a great deal of assistance for me, would be to hear *your* thoughts."

He unrealized me of furtive lamp giddy in the cornered. Monk's eyes. Lower slowed. Full somber, almost rolling from sockets. His hands pressed together in a praying bug mantis gesture. His nose wrinkled in anticipation of a toxic odor. Yes, his thoughts. I knew them. He thought nothing. He couldn't think of any. Bugger it.

Began the ploy for sympathy, this admitted my overheard.

"I am upset. I am distraught. I am scared for her."

Twit. Busted.

"I am troubled by recent events. Her agitation. My mother says…schizophrenia. I trust my mother's insight. This is unbelievably disturbing. I am in agony. But I keep my agony contained."

I pictured his agony transformed into a rabid reptile sunk in a vat of boiling venom. He went on.

"The marriage began with an act of violence."

My whooped knockout. The Burrow alarmed her mouth and suppressed a small cough ahem.

"Shipley hasn't mentioned…"

Monk dug out his shame. Almost a regurgitation. Worded careful throw up. Oooh vomit shim shaming it's way past lamp-me.

"Oh no, not that kind of violence. I'm ashamed to confess the situation is my fault. Blame me. My impatience. She's too small. Down there."

Private parts wink winked nudge nudged him on.

"We couldn't do *it*. Intercourse. I demanded Shipley go ahead with the surgical procedure. That is what I mean by an act of violence."

He clenched his knees together. At the agony of.

"They cut her."

Geraldine Burrow's eyes sparked. Freud applied here had to be. That sparking for the love of sweet Freud.

"Are you referring to a sexual problem? It's common in the early phases of marriage to experience certain difficulties. Freud had theories of women shrouded in obscure darkness. Woman unable to grow a penis or smoke a cigar."

Monk unsure and the lamp without a penile not surprised. A nasty and painful Bombshell. Demigod Monk whining,

"I'm not sure what that has to do…"

Fully equipped, the Burrow put her high horse on.

"Psychoanalysis removes the symptoms of hysteria. I developed a theory concerning Shipley's mania as stunted emotion accentuating repressed desires usually due to hysteria. Their discharge ended by depression. Her restrained thought formations strive for expression, for release and suppression converts into hysterical symptoms."

This complex diagnosis confused my Monk. Head in hands concealed his fancy in oily agony. As lampshade shady watching the contemptible Burrow doodle on her notepad. The Burrow under no circumstances burrowed for added information. Said her superficial advised him.

"Don't stress Mr. Quill. Why don't you have a baby?"

"I want too. But Shipley feels indifferent to babies."

"You must convince her. You and Shipley are investing in a lifetime together. I have no doubt you both will make the marriage work."

Lamp woman switched Alison's condition as the mad girl from atticus. Mental hissy fit germed me woeful. The lamp of me shocked myself and oh my godded. This vague prognosis. The menace of duration. Monk remaining unconvinced.

"Shipley frightened me after her visit with you. Apparently, she arrived home, in such a state. Sobbing. She told me about a peculiar object. Called a core something. She refused to show it to me. She raved on about apples and clandestine chambers. That the core would be beneficial. It sounded Completely crazy."

The Burrow sat on the rocker. She leaned on her confident expertise.

"Don't be too concerned Mr. Quill, fantasizing is part of the process. Imaginary objects are designed to diffuse Shipley's anguish."

"I don't understand what this means. Are you saying it's pure fantasy? But I smelt it. She keeps the damn thing in the bathroom. It smells horrible. And she babbled about a device named Princess I don't know, err, no, the Primrose Chamber. Whatever the hell that is."

Geraldine Burrow feigned astonishment.

"This process builds the fortitude to becoming a false individual. Yes. Fakery is the treatment."

My bulb a trembled, preventing a maddened flood of her poisoned artillery, watching Monk turn purple and. She. Went. On.

"Shipley told me that you investigate corresponding emotional colors. She said you isolated a particular emotion and it's yellow."

Geraldine Burrow sighed and avoided the subject of the Primrose Chamber.

"Yes yes Mr. Quill, we talked colors...blue means joy, red stands for stupidity and yellow represents despair."

Monk lost patience and started shouting,

"In the name of Jesus. None of it makes sense. I can't stand much more of this. She blames me for her madness and misery. I am the one in AGONY."

He clutched his head. His face got darker and darker. There was nothing else. But for him to hold his agony in. The Burrow tried to comfort him.

"Now. Now. In life, nothing makes sense. The other preposterous ideas come from Shipley's imagination. Many women hold their husbands responsible for a hopeless marriage. I can write a prescription for your agony."

My power cord wrenched from the wall. The Burrow screamed. We all screamed. I screamed.

"I heard Everything. Let me tell you Efficient energy output smokes a. Cigarette the beginning of half the way through butthead. I hear. Fling. I know unbelievable. She floats facedown. Life is a preposterous race. I think of her. All the time. Missing the grey matter. I the absurd. *Wait.*"

Quest enemy smelly hellhounds unknown strengths haggard badass. Geraldine Burrow proved an outrageous. Liar. I armed with huff bizarre. Sucked it up. Plagued itself selfish of pitiful. Love superstar celestial spacemagic wormhole. Put on that rubber bodysuit. Be the black dragon of the apocalypse. *Tell me about it.* And that shiny gold ring lingered. Unfaded, untarnished. It glowed brighter and brighter. As bright as hatred. Hate red.

You are such a child.

I wondered that day Monk almost began hated yellow. Made him nauseous. That beginning yellow supposed to do. But yellow wasn't Etc. This I showed him. The bomb I bought for a dollar. Yeh, at any Hell. Ow.

His turn asked the ah ha moment. Monk woe ridiculous loud whispered,

"What the fuck have we done?"

The Burrow ignored. And what remained was. Monk's appalled expression.

Hokey Pokey

Time of workedsleepworksleepworkedsleepworksleepworked-
sleep caverns below my eyes. Cleaner wore a plain blue uniform
zipper at the front two pockets. More scrubber Sadie jobs of.
Bathrooms, kitchens scrubbed. A rush, dashing, raced, hand to
mouth. Early morning to midnight. Shortcut cleaning. I wiped
sinks bathtubs with their clean dry bath towels. Left such a shine.
Sometimes I finished three-hour cleaning jobs in just over an
hour, charged for three. Quick and deadly and obliterated. Another day dusted porcelain puppies, paper flowers, elephant paw
ashtrays and wielded nasty hoovers up the stairs of a three story
six-bedroom house after eight hours forty dollars closed the front
door. Just stood on the landing blinded forgot. This exhaustion
obliterating memory. What town this house now sparkle cleaned.
Forgot location I lived? Put the keys into the ignition hopper car
jammed. A million shifts. Six nights seven nights nurseaided rose
at five. Sixteen hours nursing the goldies, the oldies bibbed like
babies. *Where are your falsies.* Bottled teeth. *Here dear open up*,
click bare gummed. Her toothy. And scalp balding *let me comb.*
Shudder showered *here you go dearie a flannel to wash your bristle
nethers.* Tough nursey. *Woman wipe yer arse.*

Old men and women undressed, bathed, showered,
dressed papery wrinkled skin. I dabbed antiseptic on bed sores.

Lifted heavy patients in and out of bed. From wheel chair to bed. On and off commodes. Strained my back. And I wiped and wiped. Shit from bottoms. Vomit from carpet. Slobber from chins. Tears from weepy eyes. Spilt cups of tea. I ran frantically down a busy road searching for a lost patient. Sometimes Sunday roast beef and rice pudding, TV in the sitting room, always a Shirley Temple movie showing. I made-up the old ladies. The ones that sat could not move. Just some powder. A bit of lippy. Thanks dear. Rouging powdering soft wrinkled faces. Bright red lipstick on thin lined lips. Feathery grey hair teasing up. Eyes brightened. Milky tea. Monte Carlo biscuits. One by one. Walking sticks frames simmered bent at the neck the knees. I put frail and chipped on the toilet. They clutched the metal railings. Blue knuckled. Stained white cottontails around their ankles. Me perched on the edge of the bath. Ran the cold-water tap. That sound of running water could trigger a pee. Many the wanderers wandering patients.

"They must be restrained," said The Sister In Charge.

I wrapped them trussed them wobble old dears mostly women in heavy canvas and tied them to the chair. This room of lost minds. Rocked stared meaningless days. Porridge custard slopped. Mrs Ross on a cruise ship bound for the Caribbean. All in her mind. Bony claw gripped my hand. Her sagging eyes. When does the ship dock. Scrawny lifeless batties. Ancient skeletal women. Curled in the fetal position. White sheets. How did they get here. One woman had had her vagina sewn shut. Another over-medicated woman masturbating furiously her nighty pulled up lying on her bed. Everywhere drooling. Gibberish. The man with testicles the size of basket balls. I made his bed. Neat triangular hospital corners. He unzipped aimed urine arc at me peed on me. I shaved bristling whiskers from the chin of a prehistoric nun. There was.

Somewhere. A glass eye on the bedside table. A pink rubber breast in the bedside drawer. Everywhere. Bluish feet. Thick curled yellow toenails. Split toenails. Dead white hair. Horrors lay ahead. Lay in wait.

And Monk at his gutters. Hours hours suckceeded Monk climbed a ladder. He scooped leaves, mudscum, bird droppings into a bucket for a living. He dirty fingernails grubbed knees a constant uncomplaining earned bigger wages than me.

I doom of feminist.

Feminism not a dirty word. Those ideals of self-actualization. Seeds of embryonic. Femaled mind of voiding me. Feet hit the floor fright the archangel heard her roar. Gone to the househumper hogs. Hard-won struggles a bunch of words floating around in my bloodwaters dumber of.

I had no concept of having it all. I had nothing to begin with. Oh, we ate enough. Spuds, fried mashed steamed, a treat lambchop or a takeaway. *Carry me away.*

Workingsleptworksleepworkingsleptworks and danced the drained dancer.

Monk said.

"Why don't you learn some country songs? Why don't you ever dance? Like that woman with the hunchback."

"Shar."

"She lets her hair down."

"No she doesn't."

"Why do you have to be so literal."

Christ why indeed.

I remembered her. Lovely Sharon Bee. Shar for short. Shar the Astonishing. She singsonged a left turn, a right turn, one foot in, kick yee-hah, let it beeee. Rollick woman radiant as can, a cancan. Her ancient sheets of reddened skin. Thick eyebrows and crooked teeth. Gummy haired. Each eye a pool of mud. That slight hump centered between her shoulders. Hunched. And her bulbous nose slapped on a face peppered with growths. Pus boil. The shamed of her. Ugliness meant a solitary existence. No chanced husband or lover. Ever. Just repulsion. Expulsion.

The day I met her. The 'No Trespassing' sign on her paling fence. An eye stared through a slat. Hello I waved. Said to her,

"You got a ton of leaves in your garden."

Shar Bee and me acquainted over a cuppa. She told me hunger overcame her. Five meals a daze day, handfuls of nuts, tubs of yoghurt, slabs of cheddar, cinnamon donuts. She ate large bites of bread and meat and turned pink from satisfaction. She told me her story. The nun of her.

"I invented my vocation, supplemented as a Bride of Christ."

Poor Christ. And her new nun name, a charming name, Sister Mercy Bee.

"Blah," she said. "I prayed to God. Hardly ever. Dear God let me be. Set me free. Make me whole and wholesome. Get rid of this damn hump. Chop off my goblin nose. Give me attractive bones and sinewy muscles and perfect skin and eyes the color of Windex."

God too lazy to improve her.

"Quite often. I shouted at God. Shouting nunned me. You fuckwit God. It's your fault I'm ugly. You do nothing else but blink and wink. You you you…"

At the memory, her fists clenched with exasperation. For God woulda coulda shoulda.

"He has so much time on his hands."

And Sister Mercy Bee formed a certain idea of the attributes of God.

"He didn't recognize me. I spotted him at the supermarket. Pushing a trolley. Sort of an old hippy with bright blushed skin and long white stringy hair. Rose colored horn-rimmed spectacles glinted on the middle of his nose. He wore Scholls with arch support and the predictable sackcloth robe tied with a length of rope at the waist. I mean you'd think he'd dress decent to go to the shops."

That untouchable God. Her mortifying flesh, kissed the crucifix, but not praying much. And God knew joys of heaven were an acquired taste. He never divulged to Sister Sharon this hogwash of *keep on dancing, live for today.* God ordered her to stay on her knees or go to hell.

"I spent ten years cloistered in that gun nunnery."

Nundom of postulancy. Noviceshipped the annual re-newal of vows. The final vowed. The pressure. The long days. The time God stole from her.

"I was forced to dress and undress covered by a bedsheet so that no other nun could see nakedness."

Four o'clock every morning, Sister Mercy Bee lay on the bare floor. The rattle rats of rosary. A chastising metal whip nipped her flesh. Her shorn head bloodied from razor cuts.

"We bathed in cold water and didn't use deodorant. We used pages torn from the telephone directory for toilet paper."

She grew old and bent, bowing before a plaster Virgin. And the fasting fainting mornings. Her empty tummy dreading broken bread and yellowing milk. Dismal food the nuns ate at dawn after chants and chimes. Unexplained bruises. Sister sister calling *help me help me* to that oblivious. GOD.

Until totally exasperated she made a final vow.

She vowed with a sniff,

"I have had quite enough of patience, virtue and soul searching. Phooey to crappy penance, to miserable mortifica-tion, to senseless self-examination. Good riddance to religion, to the dreadful purgatory shebang, to God, the Grand Silence,

Satan and the saints, sadly including my favorite, Saint Vitus patron saint of dancers. Hoo roo. Told the sisters I was off, oh boy, that didn't go down well."

The well again, down the well.

"Mistress Mother Superior tut tutted, such inappropriate language for a nun. Mistress Mother Superior said, How could you tell them about leaving? Are you impaired? You have no concern for your Sisters. You are selfish! Endangering their vocations. Never trust your own judgment! You are a poison spreading through the convent. If you hadn't told them you were leaving, we could have saved your glory."

We sipped our tea. Glory be. Shar opened a packet of Shortbread Creams.

Mistress Mother Superior frowned on Sister Sharon's dark night of the soul. The day of dispensation. Mother Superior inferior wept and wept copious crocodile tears. And the monstrous of this bloody divine comedy. Stupid God. A klutz. Sister Sharon Mercy Bee gave God a box of matches. Spiteful God, setting fire to Sharon. At the least.

"Or I snatched the matches and set God on fire."

Who to blame. Inferno Hellfire.

"Golly that mothership convent burned in the oak wood of unending lamentation."

Poverty chastity obedience turned to ash. Left behind forty singed nuns, blackened stone steeples, soot covered stained glass windows Holy Jesus Mary and Joseph a distant memory. So indistinct.

Sister Mercy Bee said,

"Freedom at last."

Glorious Sanctus Ave Maria. Final the earthly paradiso. For Sharon ex-communicated ex-nun. Sharon dropped the 'on' and the Mercy and retained the Bee.

Shar Bee began a new life and moved to Eden. She rented a clapboard cottage on Honeysuckle Drive. A mile from Monk and me. Her neighbors, a Seventh Day Adventist family with three daughters, Miranda, Millie and Mo. And behind her house, the Protestants with a pimply teenage son named Teddy. Across the road a married couple, Christian Scientists, the wife pregnant, having a homebirth, cheaper, didn't believe in the medical profession.

None of them ever said a word to Shar. A friendly nod occasionally. At this ugly woman. The upside-down crucifix nailed to her front door might be the reason.

Shar's occupation of leaf sweeper, alone. Dressed in baggy nylon pants, a loose shirt and flipflops. Shar in her yard. Swept in the misty season. Whoosh whoosh of autumn, an old wives summer, Halloween scary scary, enormous carved pumpkins and harvested fruitfulness. And fallen leaves. Everything falling, everything rusty, everything golden everything on fire. Shar kept sweeping. Sweep sweep. Often weep weeping. Saints preserved. To her it made no sense to wait until the last leaf fell. She watched the neighbors. When would they sweep? The neighbors waited for the last leaf to fall before raking their gardens.

"The last leaf fell," she said.

At last. The fall completed over. And dressed in red tartan kilts, the three little girls, Miranda, Millie and Mo, played in leafy mounds the color of peanut butter piled waist high. The children joyously flung armfuls of burnt gold in the air. They buried each other. They rolled around. They kicked light leaves. And disarray made a mellowmuddle I loved.

We. Shar and me watched Miranda, Millie and Mo. Memories of hokey pokey captured Shar. Not there, not here, not anywhere. But close to some beatific vision. Always a sham nunner. Mystical divined revelation. The idea of polka caught then and there.

"Do it," I said.

She twirled in a clumsy pirouette beside the mound of dead maple leaves. Followed by a small preliminary hop hopped. The heady slow turn of her head the hump following held the innocence of *look at me go*. Heel and toe, heel and toed staccato defiant pokey-mazurka. Elbows chicken-danced in the wind. Shar Bee probed the fiery deeps. Freedom confident on the outside. The number of reasons to frolic.

No more those stiff collars and moist randy priests *how deep are your bosoms.*

She told me.

"Father O'Brian pushed me into the confessional booth. Drooling. I kneed him in the groin."

Brought him to his knees. Proper genuflection! Ha God bossy said stay on yer knees. What if God's turn occurred.

A left turn.

Right turn.

One foot in. Kick.

One foot out. Kicky kick.

Shar whisked the hokey-cokey around. Like whipped cream. Like churned butter. Like scrambled eggs. But unbeaten. *That's what it's all about.* She bounced. Boiing boiing boiing, a light leap. Whoa. She tried going backwards and forwards. Yikes. Easy peasy. Hokey pokey. Knees bent, arms stretched. Made her nose smaller. Poof! The hump disappeared. Rah rah rah. Such magic. Worked better. Rollicking. Whoopee. Cheeks blushed. Rosy Shar blossomed and bloomed and put the whole self in. Slung the entire body out. Whoops. Shar skidded on. This habit that stuck. Shar fell on her knees. A pile of leaves cushioned her landing. Inelegant sight, Shar yelling,

"Bloody hell."

And who cared? Not a single person. Except the all-seeing idiot spying God. A blistering mutter, *get thee to the nunnery.*

Shar crouching fell of her polka dot underpants, she brushed off the leaves.

I noticed a shadow in the window of the house opposite. Shar's eyelids downward curled. Nosy neighbors. Deaf to the mingled melody of a sacred hokey pokey. Shar's pinions soared on high. She exclaimed,

"I don't give a toss."

Shefired the hot devil propane torch. Dry leaves went up in smoke. Another bonfire of her vanity. And hope adorned her mind. And her joyful spirit sped blazed uncontrollably. And glorious bliss sustained her. And she continued sweeping. Vigilant. Sweep swept away the weeper.

"Smile girl," she said. "I sweeps and sweeps and I don't care what these geezers thinks. Who has time for popularity? A strong woman stands alone. Next time around this ole ex-nun leaf sweeper gonna dance a country and western jig in me cowboy boots. Rootin tootin. Yee-haw."

Untangled My Chain

Constanted on the distant mountain sight clear from the bedroom window. Fergal tore love mistletoe kiss-any-where draped on The Yellow Crucifix. His erection. Fergal the cross to ward off fiends. Dove represented a soul, fish symbol of savior, snakes for evil who cared it didn't bring her Home

Alison, natural as lilies why that particular coffin flower. Okay red poppies grieved the lost. Girl trodden her stones. Night nobbled pelts raining. Again. Dripdropdripdrop rain seized asleeper. God cursed me dizzy dreamer. What night-dreamed sleeping drips. Weeping pings. *I dreamed life away.* Corned golding dream of honey meadow, ow. Hurt this dream of sexy Saint Sebastian winsome tied to a tree muscled shot with arrows. Saints dressed gergreat grrr in loincloths and. Lovely rope bound his hands. But the man would not be tied down.

Beauty and pain detached from each other. Glorious eagerness for the death I dreamed martyrs from martyrdom. The embodiment of female passivity blemished. The Virgin pierced, but pure. Erotic eros pleasure, la la la of pain. Super saddo-masochist sexy and spiritual ecstasy. All things to all men. That. I wore. A shirt of hair. Amulets of shark's tooth, bunnies foot, pearl earring. And yellow patched. Yellow Star of David on the lapel, on the knee, yellow banded right arm, inches below the armpit, on the left side of the chest. Humiliated the stigma on shame and in pain. Eyes burning raggy rage fixed to the ground. These badge beatings. Before leaving the building, put on the badge. Targeted. Punishment if the star creased of folded. Punished if a centimeter out of place. Penalized if attached with a safety pin. Haphazarded persecution changed to organized destruction.

I dreamt a wooden club beaten me. The beater smashed my skull. And sparkles, jelly babies, deadbolts, chux, five cent pieces fell from emptiness. Cha ching. The horror of empty jolted me and I woke screaming punching kicking. Him. Monk grabbed my wrists yelling,

"Shipley for god's sake."

The midnightmare of the tiniest bleatings.

"Sorry," I said. "Bad dream. Sharks. Beatings. Jews. Yellow stars. Money. Meadows. Headache."

I got out of bed and crashed into the wall. The way of the room. One two steps to the toilet. One two steps to bed. Monk had slight bruising. He groaned.

"Where is the Core thing?"

"The *Lucy* is in the bathroom. It seems to prefer the bath. I have to put my dreams and other tidbits…*precious objects* inside the Primrose Chamber before I see Geraldine Burrow next week."

"Right," sighed Monk playing along.

He put out his long wedge. Fullybig priggy prig. And I hugged the sheets. Heated the sheets musical. Sheets the symbol. Lit a match. Fired up the sheets. Dickie diddler dicked a dot to ditch his doppledanger. Add droned groaning. Me flat as a stingray on the dormant shore. My heaving ha ha body of ripples. The man made of sand. A million grains bristled my cells. And I had a poisonous spine. He nosed in bosom dumplings. My beautiful breasts. Palest rouge nipples shy and luscious pinked at the rims. Deadly as the seafloor. I laughed and laughed. Honked like a goose. Sting-goosed. Guffed guffle his wobbly eruptions. Tinny Minnie the moocher. Tinwoman tinkled the sandman. I asked, show the icon blued heaven for. How in hell would he know. I teased his shlong. At least madonna no longer bled. But. Gigglelady tempter tricked. Then. His head reversed the other way. My ears pinned back in a certain. My ears kinky. Liked nothing else in creation. Saint of the speared alive, fed my crazed eroticism neurosis. And the shriek of my songs yellowed my mind, minding yellow. Snaky hair. Two shades of yellow wallpaper. Yellow inked. Yellow funk.

I came with a towel in my hand. Sometimes, I came in my sleep. Bewilderblissed. So, Bleeding, What.

Him snored the night.

Sunrise. Morning uppity early dawned my whirligig. Yellower today, chink of light under the bathroom door. Chinked wisdom fields and mustard flowers unspeakable its name. The lucid Lucy jaundiced budding of sallow. To save me yellowed. Gone on goon gonner worshiped her. Sun of her disappearing but clang me from going. Kept me alive. Loosed me a little whittle.

I let the Lucy loose for a while. Gave it permission to explore miniscule shed. Not much room for it. Such a puzzle gooper.

And I reveled conceit. He didn't notice me watching, pretending to read his paper, his news and me expert at pretense. He misunderstood. My nothing to be said. To anyone but me. The silent watcher undetected. I caught the sight of Monk touching the Lucy! I watched his strangled strain. Peeking prodding inspecting at the want of me. This man picture of hesitation disbelief. I observed his thumbing. His thumb pressed it and quite revolted he pulled his hand away. Must be the wetty stickiness the dead skin of it. I waited before yelled sprung at him.

"Monk! What are you doing?"

Caught him wider open ha. He turned bacon gone green.

"Nothing sweetikins, just curious."

Huh I thought curiosity sinistered afraid of Monk husboat hubber hoonsbootie.

My persistent spied and a thought got at me. Well clobbered me. That the Lucy reeled him in. I caught him a couple of times, leaning in and *leering at it*. Plaster leer. His hand on it pressing. Again. Palm flat stroking. Sometimes I burst into the bathroom. I concocted an innocent excuse.

"I have to pee."

And then shouted,

"Monk what's the matter with you. Leave the Lucy alone for god's sake you are annoying it."

He jumped and bashed his forehead on the ceiling. *Serves you right.*

The time he didn't realize, I hid in the bed. A pillow bulge under the bed covers. Mellow my hard-hearted. Of restraint swelled. My left eye opened. Monk snuck into the bathroom. I murmured,

"I see you."

His body spun around. The fright of him guilty as a thief. His expression of haggard pickpocket. Bug-eyes and grubbed fingers reprimanding. His angered,

"I didn't do anything."

Blurt, I knew he was examining the Core. The man with his feedle wheedle. The grumble of blameless. I raised my,

"The Lucy is in the bathroom. Where else would it be?"
Crabby whined.

"Be careful where you leave the Lucy. It makes a mess. It leaves yellow *stains* everywhere."

He pointed at the bath with its peels almost gone. Scarce smears of paint mixed with splodges of yellow left on the sides and the rim.

"I can't get them off."

I thought of a brilliant. Idea.

"Why don't you ask your mother for some gumption?"

This marvelous. *Gumption*. Magnificent life somehow got me gumpery. The beginning of fortitude. *Gumption*. My excitement at the concept of pluck. This notion boning the path of resilience. Inevitable and I sang less. Fakery. My voice improved. Really! Really! I launched into operatic Boheme la la. This transformation into poet painter philosopher musician. Everyday life a bonnet old jacket chanced met him destitute flirted. Bought a passion fed the starving cunt with opera. And the lilacs died. We were young, we were crazy, at the low least, I established the bohemian look. I was. I was! *Dreaming*.

He asked me,

"Feeling better now?"

This frightened me. He posed as the sugar inquisitor. His plan to ruin the girl, puncture her tiredness, whack her with a fry pan. A fried mind. To get me ended. The soul-bowl Monk gripped. If I swallowed some soulfood. He grabbed the lot. Souped goo. But no no no no no me the piddle pooh. I drew myself up aligned my scrawny.

"I am improving didn't you notice?"

Habit hours, I rested for the entire afternoon. His recommendation. Monk said relaxation extremely helpful for the cultivation and revitalizing of emotions. For turning falsified of emotions, I must remain horizontal and sleep for as long as I could. Coma myself. After oaty lumped breakfast. After sogged a tomato sandwich lunch. After plump chicky roasted dinner. As much as possible, houred a billion days.

Mud on my a hem. Shuntled into jazz jazzy. Satin doll wigged me digged me as I skipped and flipping. Nobody's fool fooled everyone. Playing it cool. The unspayed cat on the rampage catting. My commando crawls. I wailed a plaintive restless rubbing my tail around his ankles. Stuck my bottom in the air. Wiggled my switcher-roonie rhumbas. I asked my sweetheart what lay ahead. The Cisco Kid told the silver banshee the future of a paper moon sailing on a cardboard sea of saw the yak, the yee-haw, in the vicinity of the Core. And the calmed tiddly do do done possible hummed wink wink.

Another day

Another day

Another day

Of daze hours. I lay on wax-proof sheetles. The Lucy beside me. Not quite ready to attach it. Onto my bod. Allowed lie its lay. The Lucy let it liar liar panted on fire. Those tentacles layer a small twiddle. A tickle. A wickle. Ooooh good vibrations vibrated its mwa mwa mehe desperate to grab at my hallucination began said,

"Let's go for a slither together."

But the Lucy scuttled without me. The luck of Monk at work or he probably accident tread and squish it.

Uninterrupted. The Lucy wormed along the short perimeters of the bedroom bump, the sitting room, the fried oniony kitchen, the peeling bathroom. It slinked along. Around and around. Many laps of the shedding. Surprised the brute. Discovered bloomed fungus. Different mushroom shades of yellowy. Uncountable these multitudes. The most peculiar yellows tracked me. And smelly minus daffy beaut, but sprouted foulness. I grew to love them, this proved a laborious process. Dissecting the scent. My sniffs told me yellow odors remained unprobed. For an odor never solidified. But I continued my investigation it rancid meat. Slime dirt. Turpentine soaked rags. Lemony piss. Cadaver fume yet sweet uprising. This clouded questioned. Identify disgusting through the asbestos walls. A water glass against the surface, I listened to the stink. The stench of it crawled into my hair.

What hair! That birdsnest. Uncombed sloven girl. Cavewoman. Neanderthal. Hairy untweezed brows. Armpit hair grew four meters, sweated screaming for razors and roll on pump spray lavender aluminum free. Oh crap too tired could not be bothered, no energy to looky nice. Browbeaten cheesed thighs to sugary of moist crevices, those rabbit ear folds. Where Monk loved to lick until I trilled trumpet sounds.

Incredulous, the Core Luci-D's stealthed her sought of. *What what what.* That fucked. The Lucy sidled marking my territory. Fucking with me. Laughed at me behind my vertebrae. Hooted till choking on saliva soup. A setup, set to snaked my soul, mebbe.

And the Lucy airborne stunned me. At night, the Lucy hung in the spell of the ceiling. In bed snuggle winter, I worried that Monk would wake and startle it and strangle me thinking I was the Lucy. Should I push the balloon away. I thought without eyes it insulated so bubble saw nothing. Sometime misery needed to know girl of me nearby.

In the shower, sang You're scared but you won't run, I raised my face at the hover above. The small circles of wafting as the Core Luci-D claimed the very atmosphere inside the pickle shed. It sneaked into the dead oven. It swarmed over cupboard doors, squeezed into drawers. That bandit ate my knickers. And I had no money to buy new ones. Sometimes the Lucy clambered onto the climb-over bed. Left a snailtrail of silver streaks. And Monk, too polite to ask about *those marks*. Christ, I thought, I would have to visit the Laundromat. Dollars it costed me. Shrapnel I failed to earn. Most possessions I stolen. The thieving of me keened. Yes, weekly shopping trips a wicked exercise stealing groceries decent in a long coat with holes in the pockets. Those selected items dropped to the hem. And my vinyl satchel with torn lining. In Target, I stole makeup, hid it inside the lining of my bag then paid for a packet of Tic Tacs, then exit as a surreptitious and slow figure into the Mall. A store detective woman followed me. This plump person wearing flesh colored stockings and a stern gabardine coat. She demanded to look inside my bag. I held the lining tight revealed an empty illusion. Her astounded. I fraidwobbled home knew my shoplifting days finished. For good.

3am I heard a muted gurgle. A burble of sappy. It spoken unbearable if the Core nagged me. But subtle the Lucy sounded a talk voice of prod. Unintelligible stuff throated of storm belches, lolly laughs, faint warbles of. It's intended. Rut me, shake my shoots, check the boolies, sponge those licks, soaked my bunch. Bozo revealed as wetted missiles aimed at bleeding me. Bled my brained. Pus pussy sizzled a heart. By which fate it primed me accept the rutted, the shot, the sponged of myself. To allow the disguised yellow blobber transform me into a behemoth sham forgery. I just might find luck happiness peaced. In the ending.

Or would this blob kill me yikes shit what.

For.

A huge wet tongue emerged. The canned kind, that Mr. Winkler sliced for his sandwiches. The suppled sop drippy. The Lucy slurped. The Lucy smacked its choppers. So hungered hungry. What god in heaven were its intensions. Should I phone Mr. Winkler let him know a tongue escaped from his pantry. Top shelf he stored tins of tongue. I hunted for a can opener.

Elastic tongue inched towards me. My girlscout fingers crossed. Be prepared. For the insert. The essential to find junk gather lucky talisman charm fetish idol totem today. And put it in. Into the inside horrid Primrose Chamber yellow mush. Synthetic emotioned to fake me. Imperative the I must I must claimed me. This fixation. The compulsion of unlucky. Unprotected from evil. No longer magical.

Find them, yes I ransacked the cupboards. Autumn for keepsakes. My yellow stuffy somethings. To feed treasured at the Lucy. Hokey Pokey? Poked around. Stuff I discovered. My keeper's old sheet music. Musical sheets the paper. My keeper played an accordion. He sang hymns of things. He made their tiny wings. Hold Thou Thy cross before my closing eyes. All creatures great and small. Shined through gloom and pointed me to the skies. Each little flower that opened. Needed Thy presence every passing hour. He gave us eyes to see them. The purple headed mountains. This was my story. This was my song. All that I dreamed. All that I prayed. All that I ever made. I gave to You today. All things bright and beautiful. Be stilled and know that I was. All things wised and wonderful. Praising my Savior, all the day longed. The Lord God made them all. Each little bird that sang. How great is God Almighty. He made their glowing colored. Great. Just extra great.

But this my keeper loved. To sing the song Daniel Boone was a man. Yes, a big man. Music of his that remnant from my childhood. Such a treasure. Shabby pages frayed the edges. The sepia picture cover of course. Daniel Boone. Of rugged and unfamiliar man. This man leaning on his shotgun. Kitted in a coon-cap lopsided, almost falling, its striped tail bushy resembling a dismembered rat. Daniel Boone was a man, a leathery man, leather skin fringed buckskins da dah. I conjured a chewed tobacco beef jerky kinda life. I pasted as a child believed. True life grinned cheek and grit. But the alternate I had. The choice minced meat man without. Beef honeycomb livery triped me. But hear the music. The few pages. A righted choice for murked Primrose Chamber. They of important matters. And that that that mattered. The deep meanings of lurk.

I opened my wardrobe. There. A shoebox. Sailed on a cardboard sea. Shoved darked in the depths. I rescued the box. Unfolded the torn. That box filled with old tax returns, photos, an iron key the lock lost a century ago, Alison's sapphire cross linked to a fine silver chain. Alison had said,

"Here. I don't need it. You can wear it when you get married. You know. Something blue, something of me."

And so, I adorned the borrowed blue, this her.

In the refrigerator. Ah ha a small container of chilled soup, noodle broth. Hint of ginger carrotted blend. Soupy got rid of the flu last month. Old grew a lid of mold. Soup told the story it slid down to the gullet this soup brimmed of nourishment. But I regurgitated the cloudy bleh. Gabble me, Monk's mother droned needed soup. Dispensable soup.

When then oh this the memory. I founded hidden under socks and sweaters. This drawing I did aged eight or nine years yes, in primary school. The drawing of a stick figure playing the piano. In tuxedo pants. White socks. Dots for buttons. This detail got carried away. Stickman lithe and limber did not resemble a person locked in a dress-suit. Hardly more than a caricature. Bow-tied colored it yellow with black spots. Vanity dashed in vain. A bumblebee cravat. Suited his florid face. Suit a serious ritual. My non-conformist pianist performed. I struggled as a bold innovator. I clung my endeavored. My decorous nonconformity. My unnatural exhibition. And I remembered to add cufflinks of pearl. Wow the grand piano the grandest with pert feet. Little circles wooden careful. Kept inside the lines had too. I drew a savage sun thick with yellow crayon. A scribbled sky. Of airy. And the piano player levitated on an empty space. I guessed distraction. Or bored. And forgot to draw the piano stool. This miscalculated the composition the balance of. I had drawn the pianist man a long long *long* way from that piano. Those ivories unreachable. I added extra-long arms. Three times the length of a normal limb. Arms straight as a chopstick. And even further this extension of long fingers, slender airborne sausages poised above the ivories. That tension of fingertips precarious touching the keys triggered music. Nimble musical notes flew. Neat notes danced around the sun. The child remembered. How thrilled my teacher was with this drawing. She pinned it on the class noticeboard. My pride of awkward lines. Faceless man. Long longer arms. The sun shone, a moment before the sound of music.

Hold on, I told the child of me. *Hold onto treasures tucked inside.* These fragile papers. Soup gone off. Silver links. Crowned of thorns. Vital impressioned. Loss. Absent necessities. Child's drawing. Furry hat sewn from the pelt of a dead raccoon. Childhood the songs, melodies, piano keys. Notes that danced like ants. Rusty key locking huge regretted. The value of a useless fragment.

I thought. Yellow wasn't a thing. But Daniel Boone was a big man. The hills were alive with guilt free sex. The first cut was the deepest. Then cried the songs of ummamumama suss-spish-oss minds. And I may asked herself, my god my god…what have I done? You Wonderful. You Marvelous. Liiiiiiggghhht burning in the fiiyaaplaahaace. Songs dying in my ransacked ready or not.

When you feel inclined, she had said.

The objects sapphire pepper tears silver soup key music drawing gathered together.

Choose a quiet time at home. I switched off the light. Waited for night. That waiting gamed again. Why. The Burrow told me. To wait until. Blimp noir here. The Lucy positioned on my bedroom dresser level with my face. Incidental it got there. Of all places.

"Hello Yellow,'" I said. "Are you hungry? If I feed you, what do I get in return?"

I always wanted something.

And the core Lucy-D began to swell, same as a pigpuffer fish of a sizeable belch, mushrooming a fairytale. The stalks, stems, rootlets extended to the length of a washing line. The Lucy reached for me, its larger and larger jello biddy advancing. Should I push it into the freezer. How dare it explode, how insidious the prodding sickies spirit. And it kept rising and undulated and oozed and dabbed and the roots grabbed at me. Was it appalled by this unmanageable body of mine. Should I sprinkle salt make it shrivel. The remedy worked for slugs and leeches.

Quick the loo, pain in my bowels began to break, wrenched lost this jelly bundle from my exit hole. A blip with imploring threads love me. A part of me. The Lucy expert at sliding under doors it filled the bathroom and I punched it, misguided for punching dough made it expand. The Lucy filler every available airspace, wrapped its stems around my body as if children playing Red Indians and I was the pioneer about to be scalped. *I can't breath,* I muffled and pushed and battered, *get off me Thug you have no right to cause me sorrow.* And the Lucy squeezed my fat.

Bloodseep and the mess of the Lucy and the emotion to suppress, to manage, to hide, to scrub, dobber cleaned grief and fear and resentment. Gumption ha. And I left spots of blood to remind me what was lost. And the Lucy shrank leaving oval marks on the walls, the impression of pressed by dyed scarlet cheeks or kissed by chubby lips. Of course, later when it was over, Monk was horrified by the madness, the vexing knowledge, I regretted being born female.

What me else remembered her rules. The Burrow's plain instructions. She said *put your objects and papers inside the Primrose Chamber of the Luci-D.* It shrunken into the size of a newborn football.

I prepared my mementos by folding the drawing once, twice, three times. The same with the sheet music. Careful not to tear paper already torn. Would they fit. Why nothing fit my fitted had a fit. Had to scrunch the lot. Untorn. The crucifix ow, my tears, the silver chain, the rotten soup, the key, the child's drawing, music papers Those tears.

The instructed what's. Wattage kept it low leveled. Mind a wonder pressed my nose against the Primrose Chamber of the Core Luci-D. That smell of atrocious grew sweeter. Old breath misted the skin-shield. Missed. Her relentless. The Burrow told me *gently lift the synthetic skin flap.* Ugh could untouchable. That moisted urk. Thank God for tweeze teasers. I touched soft avoided rip of skin-shield with the special tweezers. Wow the curtain opened.

I placed every precious inside The Primrose Chamber. Nose pressed to its stinky.

"Hello baby. Please dry my tears. Heat my soup. Untangle my chain. Carry my crucifix. Tell me how to reach the piano."

9

Pinched Me

I assumed,

You can never have too much lace. Lace threads. Flapper chic collected elegant woven and tatted crochets. Old-fashioned caps, shawls, collars, chairbacks, door knob, sugar bowl covers and modern boob tube, brazen crotchless knickers, stretchy tights and black mantilla. This needled and bobbined hung veil frills and reams of silkenstiff lowcut on my bosom enhanced the cleavage. The hollow indefinable division. A disagreement. The narrow deep riverspace, Monk preferred to nuzzle. Coincidence that his mother turned a little lacy and the flat dry creek. *Hey pinch me.*

I left the Lucy to her munch and crunch. Trusted without wonder or question.

Inevitable, the wait in shadows of hurrah. Six o'clock dinnertime raw chicken brining in a pot. I tucked slabs of brie in the chicken crevices, a sprinkle of allspice and cinnamon, brown sugar, a tin of apricots, a cup of wine, a cube of Maggi chicken stock, black olives, butter under the skin greasy as possible. My apricot brie chicken casserole with Rice-A-Riso.

Everyone's Rice-A-Riso was different. *Surprise yourself!* Monk loved his chicken din din. *Have yer chicken, chicken darl.* Every night, an experiment.

I tied my shoe in the loo.

Monk appeared covered in leaves. And bucked and fucked my fraudulent falsehooders slavered, *I love you.* Lied that my easy bitty smarted lies. Chewed lie into pulp problematic what I knew. Oooh rabid pleased with himself. Psst Monk.

"You look tired."

He shrugged *here.* Leaf droppings. The maze of me announced.

"We're having my Apricot Brie Chicken for dinner. Surprise surprise, I am the breast."

He spatted impatient, "Beast?"

"No breast B-R-E-A-S-T."

He wiped his hook nooky nose and for the thousandth time said,

"I don't understand. Do you mean abreast? And if so. With what?"

Caught his ho hum scorn *what in hell is she on about now.* I sat where I sat sometimes breathed and let the chicken boil over. The meat grew tender inside the cauldron burble bubble no angry way to say I sat where I sat. I refused to explain and dusted the furniture how it got unbelievable this worn and threadbare and holy and uglied. Ugly the lucid. Where could my. The camest. Lucidity. Days hussy sang,

"Come all without, come all within. Did not see nothing like the mighty sin."

He knew I glorified songs. The essential to want to sing. I accompanied the singing. He knew I liked my bitter sweet. Him the cup of meat. I came without. I came within nothing liked the mighty sin. Of a dog's meow. A horse's moo. Hurt the yellowing. Of gull Monk ogled my chew-chin-grin. I the dirty minx with his treeblock stuck up my path. My hide of a lovely rhino. She quite bananas. Spine bent peeled off a skin layer. Smartest banana in the world.

I presented my silver-tongue.

"It's part of the treatment."

Logical piggy pig pig requirement be. Destroyed. I climbed into my luminous, explanations were tiresome and my luminous was magnificent whatever it was, it was. Monk shaded his *here we go* eyes.

"I'm going out."

"Excellent. I need time alone."

As God my witty witless, Monk gone to visit a Fergal.

I could not think about him without thinking of her. She failed to cope. With pig pig. Left blood lippy written on the white wall. Alison slathered the words. In italics. In script. In lower case, in case, *pig pig*. Of All Days to disappear. My wedded hour. And this did not upset me. She hated weddings. I hated weddings now. Was I wrong for not probing more, with greater persistence. I thought she would come home someday, find me wearing our keeper's black twin set. The cashmere cardigan little golden sequins sewn circles, petals round the neckline, this memory of the keeper after her arteries hardened. Whipper keeper thought me the Jezebel. Her in sensible shoes, stocking straight seams, Saturday shortbread impending. Just around the corner after fifty years. Her deathly fell into a three-month coma. Bag for shit plugged in. A fluid drip, fed her soul which the witch prompt departed. This earth. Nothing to be said why mentioned the woman hung around even when they were dead, was I too harsh yesss I thought you unforgiving shithead, she squirted you out of her, splits the pain and that pushkin, but she never acknowledged your existence again. Yup. Unforgivable.

The blooded. Sat in a puddle of bloodmuddle. Of my confounded. Lost my everything. People said I terribly changed. Dearie. My damn paint pissed up against a wall. Dear. Complainer.

Bugger the warped waiting in the. Danger wizard lurked. Betrayal unsuspected speed and proud as a vampiress plunged into darkness. Smug phantom pounded glass, slammed its face, outsider trapped in ever funnish smoke. At least fantasy forgot the yellow. No, she said.

"I am the blighter yell yellow."

I yelled,

"I am lost."

Here built troll notes of girl in despair. And for no reason, for no reason was what this was all about. Everybody every jumped for joy. I thought.

Sun Day correct time for, the wearing of, could not put it off any longer. Timed set the buzzer for. The put on. The Core Luci-D. The Lucy dee dee. The attachment of the Lucy. Loops, gristle, wiggles eager reaching for me. Desire hungered cling myself. What was the process. I remembered the Burrow instructions. *For the most profound effect.* For the deepest. For the darkest yes. The Burrow instructed be a hairless bean. Her fucking directions as useful as vomit barf.

Started the shorn of me. But girl of girly whirly careful razored every single damn frump hair. Shaved my legs, pubes, underarms. Sheared of fluff. Razoring left armpit stubble. I hacked off my hair scissored hands pixie cut. I filled the bath, with hot water and bubbles. Rut shot buckshot sponged the soaking nuddy. And toweling dry, smelling of lavender and screams. I bullet ready. In my body disguise. Of I cream readied. For the Core. Would it really.

Her eyes lit like demented lightbulbs, if those existed no, Geraldine Burrow told me In Our Session,

"Position the Lucy under your right breast."

I was a breast. Just the one. But her Burrow lightning ordered me.

"Keep the Lucy near your heart while you sleep."

"I can't."

Horrors, could not sleep beside a gropeblob flogged of its inner Primrose Chamber thingy.

"Try."

Yellow was here. I named it Yell Hell Ow. You yell, its hell and cry ow it hurts.

I took off my T-Shirt, the unraveled cotton, raggedy skirt, torn lace brasicle, underpants. *Lace.* Thin waist. Bared without a fidget stitch buck me naked. My protruding rib caged lungs inflatable the foreboding breathed.

Her Burrow assured me,

"It's not painful. Choose a dark corner at home and undo the loops."

I drew the sarong curtains. Light chinked, invading the. Where the fuck were the loops refused to unlock those interlocked heaps. And the sheets the sheets, the peeps the peeps. I thought of pendulums swung inside Grandfather clocks you didn't find them these days. A post-it note what identified of globules here we are. My fingers digging into rubbery honeycomb its surface and cells softly parted ugh ugh gross the little buggers hiding. I rooted them out to the sound of quiet groans. The Lucy had grown a voicebox and senses. It felt my retching at the sight of the stalks and stems and toot rootlets and blunting projectiles. Fiddled and my faddled. Ouch. As loopy loo little unfurled intestines, they put up a fight what for, what was anything for. Yuk I almost yocked again.

"They will automatically open to the correct length. There is no pain associated with this action."

Yes, they opened. Praise Jesus. Loops uncurled the furl. Rhymester here of repeat hurling for the third time. Alien, I thought, staring at the Luci-D it's stalks and stems and rootlets and blunting projectiles spread waiting did it want a nest. Urk bile rose burning my throat. I could not bear to touch it.

Her Burrow boss.

"Lie naked under a sheet of disposable paper."

"Umm. Where?"

She replied, "Anywhere. It doesn't matter. Somewhere comfortable and quiet."

Not much to choose from. The baby mattress sofa or ruptured bed springs. Morning had. Broken. The sofa, the bed, echo. I unrolled a length of baking paper across the bed. What else.

"Use these miniature clips to fasten the Lucy around your chest."

The clips! The clips! Somewhere under the. Where could that fricking Woolworths bag. Be. My bumble in the darked. Unseen obviously. On my knees. Under the bed but recalled. The clips in my knicker drawer hidden indeed.

I held my breath and grabbed the Luci-D wriggley squirm and pushed it under my breast nifty clipped the tentacles to my flesh pinched. Wax-paper crackled my laying lay. As chickenshit fright regurgitated a puke it attached to my body gripped me grinner fear. I chewed the concept veg. I yawned a gobbed. I freaked a small. But lay with it, pouched on me. Revving the biological engine. Of the Lucy. The shaver bits of me lied on the wax-museum bed. The Lucy leech nuzzled under my. It prickled itched my skin. Its smell assaulted my hairless sweat fears fraidy cat. *Left Lucy on for hours worn the whatsit emotional rats nest. The Core Luci-D scratchy unexpected beast. Left welts on my skin clung to its clingwrap bubble.* Nest loopers my unravelling. Might sorted me. With its rooted stemmed conduits of apparent. Spiritual and Emotion hatelovehatelove-hateloveshit. Attached to my absolute core. The Lucy climbed out from in. The Core Luci-D for once on the outside. Blimey the hokey cokey. Heel hate and toe love heel hate and toe loved. A left turn. Cored. A right turn. Cored. One core in. Kick. One core. Kicky kicked deflect. And this yellow Core gnawing my strange itch sectioned. I became what-ho translucent ha ha harpy. *Yellow got even. Revenge an animal of untold uglier-horriblehideous.* A battery operated sea rushed over my brain, electrified curious, unable to wave. At me and my alien. What she said her Burrow pope statement.

"These threads, penetrate human organs and the human spirit."

The Burrow had showed me the underside of it. The underground. The Luci-D exposed conglomeration ugh mastication. Gunged crackle shifted my flesh box jerked. Hey Jack-In-The beef jerky. The complicated Core. Links of beefy threads. And she had called them lumps. No loops. Loop holed little.

Actions toasted.

Multiple parts of lucid. Tentacles reaching my countless holes. Bit at my nipples. Crawled its thriller worm into my rude, my navels. What lay beneath.

Bested way lost the plot. I tore off paper nuding myself. At the same time. Yellow forged me into a forgery. Of a dreaming of course I discovered happiness ha ha with no clothes on and there was. The sudden click of the FRONT DOOR OPENING.

I almost died of fright as Monk and Fergal walked through the door. The Lucy little octopus million gurgle, wrenched from me, OW, shrieked my skin the sieve, pain covered in red pustule holes, help. The Lucy left a trail of mucous and bolted in the direction of the bathtub. It moved nimble when cornered.

Had they seen? I grabbed a towel to hide my shame, to escape two sets of gapers. Monk his immediate covered Fergal's kiss-the-cook eyes. Monk of much glaring. He shouted too much.

"Shipley! What have you done to your hair? Why are you not wearing any clothes?"

"It's hot."

"No, it isn't"

"To *me* it is. I think the temperature is high. I need to cool off. I have heat rash."

I pulled on a skirt fast a crumpled shirt from overflowed washing basket. Blouse to cover my flaming gecko neck. Hoity toity haughtied. Noticed the biggest sausage sizzle inside Fergal's jeans. I ignored. The bloom behind his zipfly. This embarrassment Fergal raucous at me. Plonker splayed fingers over repulsive. His whisper urk.

"Aren't you pleased to see me?"

Hands in front of dobber, hid the wet patch. His wood wanked trapped in denim. I remembered That Day he wiggled it out so small and waved worm at me. *it it it*. Guzzle got me flapped. Should smack purple. Pulverize the porky. Pig pig. *Pervert* I had blazed. *Put it back.* Rat-tiddler inside it's caged. Weeny locked in metal teeth.

From that memory, I threw up projectile pastry meat pie for lunch warmed on his bare feet. Fergal's jaw grinned and bore it for the sake of another go at some point In Time. Monk mustering his agaped.

"Shipley! What's the matter with you. Here, Fergal go hose it off outside."

Monk busy boiling his boiler.

"Anyone for coffee."

What would Monk say if he discovered.

"Yeah, great," called smirk man, hosing his bare foot.

I pouted redder,

"I have to go out."

Chose a Maybelline shimmer lipstick Barely There. I was. Garbage held doubtful pills inside a plastic bag careful these precious pellet poo, *what should I do with you?* I booked another appointment with the Burrow. My head ponce higher proud refused to admit. Before I left the house, I touched doors and windows ten times. Fat happened wrong. With leaving and disheveled wondering if everyone discussed my bulge. That day lolled me. The pinched me pinny the pincher. Future fibbing plan. I had put on weight. On the body front. My blubber pouched on the outside. Rubber cushion rubbery. And heavy the sins. Of synthetic. I washed my hands. In the closed of the killing. Existed. Gave birth to. Pill of me. And worth nothing. And I the nothing, really the pill. Left the car, the bike, the fatted Lucy under a rag in the shed. I ran and ran embarrassment behind me. My Baby, I told them busybodies astonished at the ball of me. And greeted the neighbors.

"Hello Mr. Winkler."

Do you miss us Mr. Winkler. Sunlight poured through Mr. Winkler's sticky-out ears the cartilage as if on fire. Hosing and hosing in checked shorts and cable knit socks to his knees, game for the blaze, blushing at the sight of my see-through blouse stained from lemon juice.

Shar waited for dusk rake tomato sandwiches Coca Cola handy.

"Hi Shar Bee. In a hurry. Talk soon." *Come out come out wherever you are.*

Me and the pills rushed along twisted way Honeysuckle and running the bendy Eden streets. Daisy Drive, Pansy Turnpike, Gardenia Grove, Iris Road, Rose Red Dead End. Under the mountainous looming of Fergal's house. The times I imagined of bulldozers demolishing that atrocity.

I wept here camest the waterworks and hailed a, *you know* and everyone moved to the back of the bus.

Thought Happy Thoughts

This next consultation to discover what that Geraldine Burrow had to say about the test resulted. Consulting rooms on the fourth floor. Door marked Suite Number 5. I entered the waiting room. Waited. Familiar fronds fern brassy pot trickled length reached low table piled of magazines god help me smudges laced baby held princess. But I went on ignored loaded lace eyelashes *Don't stare at maniac me.* Smashed my terror of ready and waiting and sweating hands and the dead pills were they in the plastic bag I didn't know *do you have it yes I do da do da.* She shrieked center stage.

"NEXT."

Geraldine Burrow whipped her stuffy notes out, silent to her a while to recall. The truth significantly truer. I sat and doubted her legitimacy. Was this woman the Burrow for real therapist, a fraudster, gangster, minster, a mobster. Grew me double doubtings of her authenticity as in why I accepted Geraldine Burrow's authority.

Qualifications there, framed square three certificates above her desk and rigid hung exacting apart side by side. The middle certificate slipped a bit into its cardboard mount. The cardboard sea slipping by. Me staring a scrutiny eyeballs frog bulged. I could see a dab of failed glue the color of dirty mustard. Through a magnifying closer look. Yes these certificates flourished with script old style and stamped and embossed and deckle edged. But what if she photocopied certificates. That once belonged to dead therapists.

The Burrow noted my intense, my questioned. Her sight dulled by seen humanity. She patted her topknot. Her artificial fibrous clothed of nylon, rayon, polyester. The fake tan developed yellower. Ha. I snooty. She always overdid the jewelry queen bee jangled bangles, chains, leather tassels, diamantes. Ho ho ho gemstones manufactured to imitate the physicality, chemical, optical identity with natural minerals as found in nature in the natural world where. Yellow gems whoopee enabled smooth clarity for decision-making. Jewels boosted concentration. Shine increased energy. It offered relief from burnout, nervousness, exhaustion. This spectacle extracted me a jolted when the Burrow did a little clap. Fingertips this flutter.

"Shipley," she said. "How's the weather? Is it still raining?"

"You mean outside?"

I looked at my wet socks, sogged shoes, damp jeans. Holes ragged soaked from puddles and frays of no hope. Forgot the pellet for the while. Inside the room.

And remembered. Council workers blazed in yellow macs. The orange street light flickering stay or go. The road shiny from the puddles and signs yellow diamonds said SLOW and arrows squiggly two divided, a bent one pointed the other direction. Crossroad. Which route to choose, to merge, to bend. And yellow diamond of petrol pump, sexless figure walking, car skidding on curvy lines, warning. Not a through street. Exclamation mark! Everywhere signed a sign. Symbol of squirrel camel tractor kangaroo bump dip rough.

I guessed rain meant raindrops. Who cared if drops of cool gave me a rush. Wisdom the sword impaled the girl it ever, it soured, it singled me to. Like a yellow raincoat be glow seen. In the something anything fog. The godless grey. The stormy lash. The scurried yellow. Yippee brilliant bop such beauty deep. The gold goodygumdrops goldy-locked bully. From the black lagoon. Fin. Web. Gill. Sea Gull. Thought this etc etc. Ahhh stormed Anguish thinner weary. I kind of worn out now.

I spoke the way a thunderclap fell in pieces.

"I don't know. I never notice. Rain."

"Okay that's ok."

The Burrow I dim realizing might be shuffling the time-stream dragging her heels. She began a sort of speech. Her particular advice.

"Shipley. I think you should know. Joy cannot be shared."

And my speechless started.

"Really?"

"Yes. Do not waver from the source of joy itself."

"Okay. But."

She had more to say.

"Try to be aware of the flaws."

"In what."

"Your experiences! Seek the ruined flowers."

"Where."

"Find them for yourself. Concentrate on their significance. Process harmonious moods. Try to think sad thoughts, when you are sad."

"I am always sad."

"And think happy thoughts, when you are happy."

"I am never happy."

Definite her obvious roots showing depths of bleached curlies dry as hay. Hey. I didn't care in my desperate dying to show Geraldine Burrow the results from the Primrose Chamber. The Core Pills sized of a cockroach wrapped in a plastic bag used for Tip Top white sliced. Plus the remaining clips. Three clips left. Lost some.

Safe the pills, such pills played it as it lay. Plain and ever grey. Pilled way too ordinary. Surely it a great deal *interesting* to acquire excitement purple spots scary protrusions, a tuft similar to those old-fashioned kewpie dolls, transported me to a sixth dimension, an abandoned castle. To battle evil, unicorny fulfilled dreams desires, communicate awesome urgh. And top notch dueled monsterfish, realm thug, princess snowcone, sonicdash. What The Heck. Where the redbetter douchebag mortal enemy in dancer hoofs nestled in a spellbook. But no. Core Pills immobile in drab. Lifeless. Blame my faulted. Leaden, but it weighed nothing, their grim foretold me ashen. Of impatient.

"Ms. Burrow! Don't you want to know?"

"What about?"

"The Lucy!"

"Yes. *Yes.* Definitely."

The Burrow crossed her feet. Arms across her chest.

"Now. Let's remain calm."

I retrieved the pills from the sandwich bag.

"These appeared."

I dropped the oval greyish dum de dums onto her desk.

"I followed your instructions. I tweezed the shield-skin open. I put in my love. A sapphire cross on a silver chain, tears, the leftover soup, a key, my drawing and sheets of music."

The objects spoken showed the signs of hugest ordinary broken insignificant.

"The Primrose Chamber processed my objects and produced these sort of pills. I thought it a puzzling outcome. I expected a spectacular result. Are they really pills?"

Geraldine Burrow whopper pleased rubbing her hands together.

"Brilliant. Satisfactory. At least it's. Unexpected. You should be proud."

"But they are meaningless plastic beads. I'm disappointed. I expected a miracle from the mush inside the Primrose Chamber. Why didn't it rescue me? What am I supposed to do with these these these? Should I swallow them?"

Or throw crummy through the windowpane, leave them dissolving in the rain, shove into the drain, wash down ma throat swimming with whiskey, rummy, plummy knocked me knees.

"Listen Shipley."

I loathed to listen. Did anyone. Ever. The Burrow continued,

"The Core Luci-D fabricates compressed versions of your spirit and emotions. The pills are you. Yes you! The completed you. Emerges. Don't look so surprised. The pills transform into an imitation of yourself. Of course, you must ingest them. Get yourself returned to yourself. These pills are the bitter pill."

I baulked.

"What will happen to me? Are there side effects? I don't usually take pills. I might be susceptible to inner damage."

Liver kidney offal shrivel killer cave phobia of. My body inert on a cold slab. Bishops gawking at my pubes. Gutspill entrails destructed. Shagless girl marriage in blunder ruin.

"They are not a drug. The pills of you will interchange with the Core and grow roots that spread across your heart and your invisible soul. You will become an imitation of who you are purported to be. You will. You will. Exciting isn't it. You own a miracle. And a replica of you will be more believable than the real you."

"But what if I turn into a zombie?" I asked almost keen.

Fragile zombie partied with the bonies rinsed the bones, beyond the pale, for a zombie to die, flitted in my head, zombie scarred of love.

"And is it okay if I crush the pills and mix it with something sweet?"

Just a spoonful of. Teaspoon or cupful, undecided, honey or sugar or golden syrup to deconstruct the bitter. Helpful at a standstill.

Geraldine Burrow lost interest. She yanked the venetian blind a crooked screech. I noticed purple needled bruises above her elbow. Her medication chipped into her a flow into vague.

Elbows off the dinner table, Fergal often Roared. At Alison. Smashed her, bashed her. He believed. Alison belonged to him. That fog and steel the somber tombed her. Erected his gold horrible-ugly-hideous huh loss cross. In Full View.

The Burrow shuffled her notes. My eyes flicked sideways ah ha. Just blank fucking pages the real fake.

"Yes yes go ahead. It makes no difference. Do whatever you want."

She tidied her desk. She inclined into a little squeaky. I heard. A burp and windywoman said,

"We will discuss the outcome of the pill at our next meeting. You also need to return The Core Luci-D."

"Okay."

Straightaway, I planned revenge. Her biro clicked.

"Tell me about your week."

I thought again a predictable request and carried obedience, pretense of an expert, my story spilling for this occurrence tripped over my heart.

"I have lots of neighbors. Some of them are real. Mr. Winkler don't see much of him. Shar Bee leaves the house in autumn. Fergal troll owns Mad Mountain, I have to avoid. Yesterday, from the window, I watched two particular neighbors strolling through their garden. Both dressed in their Sunday clothes. They don't go anywhere except church. And picturesque, both of them, frail and elderly, him in a rumpled three-piece suit and her with white hair in soft waves, her complexion lightly powdered, resting her head on his shoulder, her face powder smudging his jacket. A magical couple. Her veined hand curling around his gnarled fingers pointing with his cane at the roses. I envy their tenderness."

My voice silvering across. Silver-tongue left a mark. The mirage of a better life as though I needed a nuclear bomb. Ruin plea of a girl letting her mind escaped. Somewhere.

"I thought of Alison. I miss her. Stick with it everyone told me, and I got destroyed."

The Burrow's eyes closed. I wondered if she had fallen asleep or trance self-induced yuck. But she yawned cracked her knuckles still with us.

"You know. William Blake enjoyed sitting with his wife in their summer-house. Both reciting passages from *Paradise Lost*. Blake said both of us free of troublesome disguises, as in the nude. He said we are Adam and Eve. He imagined they sat in the Garden of Eden. It scandalized his neighbors."

"But," I interrupted, "My neighbors weren't naked. God forbid."

"Your neighbors are a metaphor for nakedness. Examine the bare truth. The naked truth. Nothing to hide. What are you hiding? Expose yourself."

"I don't want to…I'm too self-conscious…"

Began uppity high hipper timed for the preach the lecture. Somehow, I inspired her monologue in full.

"We come into the world. Naked! Pure, our innocence sincere spontaneous defenseless. We have nothing to hide. We are on that trusting journey full of exhilaration wonder delight through the peace and calm of the Garden of Eden."

"Right," I said. "But…I live in Eden."

"We must rid ourselves of truth. Truth is a trap. It binds us gives us false expectations and obligations yes it does. We become draped in the woe of reality. This deliberate and methodical eradication of emotion."

Mistrusted could not rid itself listening to the Burrow of spit rant buster. And I wondered again again and again if she a fraudulent. Lollilike lady stored homophobic wolves in her cellar. Wallet stuffed with dupe dollars. Snubnose laden with loot. Nah. Bungdung burper she. Went. On.

"Mythology is a the symbol for nudity. The pure Core Luci-D grows synthetic wisdom and harmony as one and the same virtue. Nudity reflects the lies the revealed the feminine facet of the opposite of truth. Nudeness brings paradise of a golden age and deletes the burden of truth in a wolf's clothing. Nudity frees us from restrictiveness, it refines a higher consciousness the wistful ascent to fantasy naivety. The naked metaphor transcends the mundane. It inspires an uncluttered mind, enlightened thoughts. It gives us illusions, the ability to see what is not there, a realm, a sublime utopia. Naked means free from. Sin. Uncontaminated. To bask in magic. To ignore the fickle. To absorb falseness and become real. Our innermost beauty is naked without ribbons or bows. A fantastic lie walks naked in the light, shows untruth to the human race."

"Yes," I said. "It certainly does."

"So," said the Burrow descending from her lofty lies. "Be inspired by this image, bake, paint a picture, complete a jigsaw puzzle or write a poem. That might help."

Eek.

"Okay," I said.

Poetry.

I would rather die.

I Was A Pill

Home alone for hours, prepared myself to ingest The Core Pill.

Geraldine Burrow told me demolish ha ha. One pellet imploded in front of her very eyes. Not putting that bunger into my mouth. Others. Swill pills safe inside Woolies bag with these Burrow stuffies, *joy cannot be shared. Think happy thoughts. Think sad thoughts when you are sad.*

Righteous righty-oh. Even though braceleted arms yellowing a jingle enraged me.

Little little self-loather feebled a totter surveyed stall kitchen. Ummm destructive idea. The weapon wedding gift. I reached for the marble pestle and mortar. Heavy as my heart and knees bent. Heavyweight. This vestal bench buckler weighed the ton of bar bells and matched the grey granite of them. Greatest pleasure discovered a use for the pestle crusher.

I wished it held Fergal's balls. Giggley vengeance lurked forever.

My gripping pestle and me sweated brow and gritted teeth. Wowed as the girl I grown hefty muscle. Equipped for my smashed at the gobbet. I pulverized the pills in the mortar. Blitzed. Mortified. Exhilarated the pounded grinding it. Ground and grounded. The fine grainy finer. Ugh. The Core Pill transformed into powder like sheddings from a moth's wings. Grey powdery waterfall snow trickled through my fingers. Texture sight grains reminding me of old movies. The silent ones of graininess. B&W on flicker box TV with dials found it on the street. Television reeled the reel flickers such as Pandora's Box. The doomed anti-heroine Lu Lu a lustful imp. Twenties roared gangster epics. Chilled the blood. The idea if a bridge or skyscraper could not be bought, then steal it. And toughed guy/lady grainy flickering ground it downer.

Until.

The question for reasoning why existed these pills. Christ. What would smuggers do to me. I needed copious amounts of syrup to make powdery delectable but how to dissolve. And destroy the negative in my nothingness. Nothing ever turned out. Right.

Swallowing the powder, it winged down my throat. Million grains hard for a flapper's lollypop system of bitter to absorb. Pellet crushings hectic grew threads and suckers spreading inside the ocean of me. Spread fast exceptional at permeation. Lumpy distorted they eager infiltrated. Scientific allowable could do no harm I thought. Remember a scientist shaved me whittled me wider than a droughted prairie swept with tumbleweeds. Where a fire possibly started by a bolt of lightning. So, I receptacle for the dillpills powdery stuck swam my coffers. Beast pillpowders latched onto final heart. That shunned of happiness heartbreak harassment high-heeled heartache and happyless.

And what the what ha ha ha had to chuck the ridiculous ha.

Consequence of inadequate and overwhelmed evaporated. Poof smoked the magic gasp disintegrated to shitnothing. Done with soul weary. Let me live. Before I stopped. Breathing.

I imagined an alien crawled from my navel. This ticklish I laughed and laughed at the hole it left. I loved it to bits. A mosquito bit my ankle, of course I scratched the bite till it bled.

I ate packets of Smith's potato chips. Gleefulsalt swilling in my gut. Alone I dived into the ocean. I thought, lucky I combed my hair that morning and came up for air.

Nearby tenants pitched their possessions, furniture, mess on the pavement. I guessed unpaid rent. Accommodation difficult to find. Nests available high in trees. Those dole bludgers snuff and inhaled somehow. I pictured the final struggle. I sensed a greater need for security. I fancied lighting a cigarette. I coughed and stopped. This failure to cultivate smoking.

I foundling a falcon claw tangled in bird netting. The tug at freedom flight, its beak turning from side to side. Every good turn. I formed a conviction. Everyone looked after themselves and expected no assistance. I untangled the falcon, but possibly a baby raven and someone had too. Feel. This feeling of common tragedy. The bird bit me on the thumb drops of blood through this. *Let me go.* Trimmed my feathers. *Bring me my wits.* I believed understanding arrived when I got. Somewhere. Older. Died.

In the future. Pills soon deaded me crawling uphill his crooked mountainous later better late.

I embraced the imposter idea. The vanishing of every real. Re-realed unreal True. Converted to finicky faker girl. Under no circumstances got wacky or distraught or upset the appleycarted. Fake pleased everyone, the world, the universe. Simulated my rapturous rap rap ripper after power full faucet. Gossipy. Girl growled a sham so greater so womanly here. I sex-faked love *yes honey I came.* My uppance. I lusted ahhh beaten argh passion kiss kiss pride upped nose. This contrary canariness roused phony repentance. And he forgave me for burning down the marriage. And I concealed my bogus resentment said we were fine fine fine. I told bugsy Monk, no problem none. Practical him ever acceptance my sicker suck. *There is really nothing the matter.* With me.

Mock loathing mocked relief. Mild nervous depression dented the girl. And the shock tenderness of his lips brushing my cheek a la romance soap uptight. There there. Slight hysterical tendencies. What was a girl to do? Dabbled in grape tonics and country trips and exercised body and exorcised heart. I counterfeited a scared little inner.

"I am NOT afraid of ghosts."

"Fantastic," said Monk.

I created a deceptive self. A smoke screen. Of strongish declarations.

"I am strong. I am whole. I am not nuts anymore."

"Great," said Monk.

He checked the oven timer and arrange his pencils and notepapers. He flapped.

"Let us try to record our needs."

"Um. What."

"Important notes, grocery lists, dates, birthdays."

Monk made schedules, appointments, deadlines. Attempted productivity. In our lives. Him sorting color coding folders tax expenses birth marriage death certificates two lives filed in a two-drawer metal filing cabinet. He found the remaining pellet in the dresser drawer. Pellet lonely in the ziplock.

"What's this?"

"It's a present from the Lucy."

He avoided procrastination. As in delay tactics. And he switched to binding chopsticks, bunches of flowers and extension leads with elastic bands.

"We must give our belongings a home."

He filled plastic containers with sugar, spices, coffee, tea and stuck handwritten labels on each one.

"Look," I said. "You spelled cocoa wrong."

I pointed my helpful at 'COCO' at the sink full of dishes, towels dumped on the floor, a wind-up duck balanced on the edge of the bath and teddy kicked under the bed. Timed for.

Bed. Plumped the pillows and buttoned my nighty. Splitted second gap between wake and sleep this spaced of empty or timetravel to vacant space of zilch existing life without substance the body as a feather bone flesh absent in those seconds.

A roped light unwound from his eyes. Shouldn't he be squeezing my. We spooned. No I faced him and whoa his eyes gone. The sockets skin closed over. His eyes sneaked further and further over his cheeks, his neck, his nipples around me. Fizzled. Zero passion pissed off. A constant unavailability. I truly madly available just unavailable. To him anyone.

The fake of me still missed my sister. I unable to feign missing. Monk said what I felt was a draft from the gap between the door and the floor. Mine hiding tears acted blimey know-all scorn.

"I knew that."

What I sensed. The rug pulled from under. The antacid bubbling in my stomach. Christ the steam breath from a wild animal's nostrils. What animal. Let it be a pygmy hippopotamus, reason of impenetrable leather hide, herbivorous masticating spinach, lard muzzle, beady eyes and a body heavy enough to stamp out fires.

How to explain. Loss. The getting pissed push happened to the placid her. Did my sister detect the. Molestationer man. Faker fakery sugar-coated shaker faking resignation I pretended the loaded revulsion. For his damned actions. Inner voice said I hate him. But the grovel outer lied,

"I can deal with this. I really can."

Said it fast. I really can I really can I really can I really can can can can can. I really can. Twenty times and it sounded perhaps it sounded. Dishonest.

Dealt greater actions to control this quake of merry misery. Faked my vexed at the thought of a person's destruction. Instead substitute contrived rapture disguising silk flowers as holy spirit shamming artificial sweeteners, imitation of death. I shammed wretched tears flowed. Whoo golly. She yes in a better. I knew she would return and drag me to the other. But.

False yellow stuff tormented yeh hell ow yeah, I sing-songed Yeah Yeah Yeah sang The Beatles.

"Monk. Don't you realize how that lurid color tortures me?" Monk at the end of his. Me got worse. Hung onto. My sarcasm. No reason to suffer, I reasoned. In my subdued state. Steeped in serenity, brief jolly jolly submission the lot. Oh and laziness.

I never uttered a word of truth or performed truthful stuff ever again and that itself a whopping lie. Jigger girl helped myself to fat fibs. I faker so abled to sin, lie and cursed freely and delirious it of untrue.

The new optimism lead me to bake sorts of fancies. Fruitcake cookies topped with sugared dates and shredded parsley, *have you ever seen dyed porn pubes?* Cake dough the consistency of a turd salted instead of sugar. That old excuse. Beefed patties flavored with chopped tomatoes, peanut butter, lemon juice and cream curdled like baby vomit.

Dolly fisticuffs punched at emotion in our house. Retaliated when he yelled,

"You can't cook."

That tinny bite of spite. Existed. Tarnished us. The Relationship soiled with a stain impossible to remove red stains of beetroot rooted red wine. I scrubbed and bleached. I chipped at solid candle wax, tried brown paper and the iron. Monk plugged in the iron and switched it on.

"It's supposed to be fucking hot to melt the wax."

"I thought it turned itself on."

I wanted to iron his face into the carpet.

And my shocked,

"Monk! That's very unlike you. To Swear."

He replied,

"You drove me to it."

I was a terrifying driver. Crunched the gears and stalled. Tailgated, blocked gaps, hogged lanes and sped. Sometimes many many thrills *don't stop* me, accelerated, opened the window, hair in my face, stung eyes and the rush of danger. *Gonna go go go.* The corners, the race streets, caught a footpath, broke a side-view mirror.

Two o'clock in the afternoon of before and after. Small child stepped onto the road. Those enormous blue eyes. In front of my Mini. Wheels rather vacillated missed the clutch car skewed across the road spewing dust and litter. Spun the car 360 slammed the brakes and stalled facing the opposite direction. Rear bumper inches from a telegraph pole. I jerked the gears to neutral position. Such outrage almost killed a child safe untroubled wandering home. Incompetent to admit the fear but after the before I stopped driving. For a long time.

Shar Bee brought me a bottle of tequila and a bag of knitting. This a magnificent adventure. What a surprise, her bravery. Tearing from her house, a scarf obscured her face, she hailed a taxi, drove fifty meters along the road, hey presto a fiver.

"Whatcha bin upto."

I owned two shot glasses of print little skulled and crossboned on each glass. We clinked.

"Let us drink to."

Leaves, rosaries broken, string, false teeth, the last coherent thought, lovesongs attacked.

"Shar we gotta fake this drink to the obscure."

"Cheers."

Salutations to synthetic emotions.

"Talk to me."

"What about."

"Anything."

"Okay what kind of anything."

"The news."

Shar Bee read magazines and the newspaper. She said,

"Get this. Lost Spanish spaceship found eight years later."

"Where?"

"In a field of corn."

She flipped a page.

"Magician's stunt failed rushed to hospital."

"I hope," I said. "It wasn't the cut-a-person-in-half trick."

She laughed and raised her eyes to the heavens.

"Unusual fast bursts of sound on the radio cause extra-terrestrial speculation."

"Describe the sounds."

"Electronic moans."

"I haven't heard those in a while."

Shar Bee tore that article free.

"I'll keep this for later."

And.

"Apparently. Lavender water started leaking from Portuguese taps."

"Wow. I better buy more magazines."

"You'll get hooked," cried Shar Bee with glee clacking her needles.

"What are you knitting?"

"A pair of bed socks for Joe, the fireman."

Rainbow colors. A short silence. This ending of subjects to talk about.

After she left, I closed the sarong window and listened to the jackhammer in my head and another digging concrete across the road. I removed the Lucy from the bathtub. She fitted perfectly in that bottom dresser drawer. And a hot bath, simulated my tranquil with jasmine oils, steam, lit candles, the paint peels a short supply. Uncomfortable when Monk entered without knocking made me vengeful.

"You look beautiful darling," he said.

I sank. Phony vained easy mirror me. My vigilant was wary and watchful. Got me weary woeful worried, difficult to imitate that. I wondered where to get a tube of wrath. Smeared my skin with provoke vivacious cream to turn me opposite from surly to zesty girl. Kept tense timidity smothered. The pretense of an outgoing person. Regurgitated happier songs *happy days don't worry be happy so happy together you made me so happy love can make you happy oh happy day the happiest girl in the whole.* Yet. Tinged with remorse.

Every day me trundling the shame lie. Of self-assured self-congratulated propaganda. And Monk loved the idealized version of me. Gave me kisses left a hint of mint mouthwash. Impotent kisses of nips and pecks his birdy and I questioned the beakiness how would I find my meaning meaning meaning. *Kiss me. Again.*

Monk dribble grateful and on our wedding anniversary he said,

"I appreciate this."

And he thought he understood me when I said,

"Don't mention it."

Let me go cried as twilight spread me level. A dizzy un-conscious heap on a bye-bye bed. Let me disturb the many uni-verses. Run emptied street to one night stands in cheap motels. Knock back shots in a seedy bar. The old-fashioned cash register gobbled my thin dollars cha-ching. I planning my daredevil wear a leathery jacket starred and striped ballistic nylon deflected bullets and knives ride shotgun on a motorcycle chrome fenders black helmet flag flying. Engine throbbing between my thighs sped eight times faster than a girl should go. Go Go. Go. Pitch a tent in the sand swim naked in the salt surf laid in the sun. Allowed me some fun by opening the oyster self. But.

We agued tedious insidious.

The time of a nurses' aid working in sanatoriums where women were locked, a few died, went the crossover. I slippery and each day hopped to it. Bed sores, lippy and pudding. Rippled feet saw me sat on the edge of the bath winding my yellow ducky.

Dreaded old age.

Remembered.

Historical hysterical avenge paid Fergal. Fuming that an uninvited tongue licked itself into pale pubes. How he pinched me. Pinny the pincher. Bruised me. Pinned me to the floor of. I waited the chance. Showed appalling barbaric. I peed on his rug. Repugnant woman crouched and pissed and left my mark. A hot yellow puddle. Smelly signature soaked into immaculate white woolen. *Remember?*

Yellow fog rubbed against window. Yellow smoke supposed wisps but instead gobs muzzled my precise pain. As yellow slid along the mind streets. Yellow lamplighted yellow locks yellow hair yellow dress. Yellow sand sifted in the egg timer thought plenty of time. Only young once. Sometimes rubbish thrown in a heap.

Met my own killer face to cunt to create endless days that dropped a question on my pout. Visions. Opposite of hothead. I dared dither. Faced million indecisions. Should I. Knit a replica of Medieval armor. A bite-proof metallic suit. Dread of me undecided in the practice naivety, femininity, virtue. These substitutes for innocence. Cook fairy cupcakes self-raising understanding, of finally this knowledge risen. Gruesome. Sex tied to horror. Scary skeptical. Indecisive suspicious. Of unclothed vulnerable of undecided. Powerless of fight the stumbling blocks.

Monk said,

"You are way too thin."

My khaki shorts low on hips and T-shirt sized for a boy hand-me-down from Jason. (Fast forward the time of threat coming, vital to save my nephew.)

I ate a block of chocolate. Fruit and nut.

His butterfly squirming on a page in his scrapbook. A wasted life measuring with my wooden ruler. And last that dying fell.

Monk cried,

"Stop torturing me."

But I cheered the torturer. Cracking a whip. The circus trainer, the lion tamer. The fucking cake-walk.

He digressed.

"How should we begin?"

"But," I wrapped my shoulders in a golden shawl and replied, "We have *already* begun."

I asked him.

"How should we be."

My dusk lonely leant out windows. Ragged claws careful touching the ledges fifteen times. Scuttling across floors. Of wept and fasted as Monk calling,

"Do you want tea and cake?"

I complaining,

"Fuck. This cannot be. All. There is."

There must be.

There Had To Be More.

Than tea and cake and Lazarus back from the dead and a pillow pressed to my tears. I should have gone then. But I was short and afraid and humble. Would maybe running worth it. Bitten off his head with a grin. And him pleading,

"It wasn't intentional."

"I'm hungry," he said.

So, I lighted his way to bread.

"Need a loaf licker," he said. "To fill my hunger shed."

Spoke to me gently meant me no harm.

"Let me eat you," he said from under the bread.

I lifted the bread and he leaped on me in a flash. Entered me again, exiting me again, again, again and I said,

"Trust you is well-fed."

But he squeezed fate into a ball. Or he frittered time, this sting, life be worth a meaning equivalent to a magic lantern reflecting the Lucy and me, almost ridiculous, mostly the hoodwink of Reality, that loathsome alien.

Ah. Blew the Lucy a kiss. Headless nesting in the bathtub kept company with assortment of whiskers, pubic hair, a ring of faint scum. The Lucy began rumbled a snory grrr. The Lucy plump as a preggers, its worm surface crawled with grubs, the kind that wriggle from cocoons. The last time I held the Lucy, it leaked golden fluid into the palms of my. Made my hands crawled at skin shudder. But I extracted what I wanted, employed the skills to produce the pills and sang the squalid,

It ain't got long song.

I truly ruly loved it. The gun went off by accident. Sure.

Why did a person kill. Indecisive paused as a human brain's neuron tiddlies coded compassion, guilt, empathic pain yes. Why did destruction snarled into a thought of rip beat melted that toastie snubble. The problem of the Core Luci-D. Rid baggage blubber the Lucy but how.

Trigger. I lost a loved one unexpectedly. Trigger. Personal peeved and despair and inadequacy *you can't cook.*

Thought grew, hurt it, it hurt you, act now, make it happen, be the lone-wolf, be sympathetic towards that hobbly gobbly, outweighed the moral neurons.

What if I biffed the Lucy into a better shape. Sliced it and diced it. Transforming it into an acceptable ah, you know, they were doing that to me me me.

Hunted for a sharp object. Too light weaker the egg beater, the masher, the whip it stick, the peeler, the wooden spoon. When did we last. Spooned.

I extricated my treasures from the Primrose Chamber. The broth botch clefs links in the chain tick a ticka boon boon. Boon a big man. Thanked the Lucy for pellets of ingestion rioting in my innards.

Developed a contingency plan.

Raid a gun shop. Knee-jerk flee civilization. Fortify sandbag a cave to hole-up in. Aim carefully make every shot a headshot.

But the Lucy headless. Pointed my weapon at its Primrose Chamber. Would. It. Bleed. An infectious crimson shower. I heard a low hideous noise. The Core Luci-D shocked undead experiment. Fear deadened me examining the Lucy. Inert. Logical deduction overcame fears.

For. The. First. Time.

Choose the past. Question dilemma it created from human organs or evolved from a subterranean lava pond littered with skeleton friends surrounded by disembodied brains pickled in large bottles.

I pitied it. The choice throttling strangling stabbing by the executioner equipped with cords, a coffin and a brass bell. But the Lucy without a neck.

I cracked the Lucy with a harpoonspike. Fixed and punctured rubbery and throatgripped by my fingered ten. Kneeded the dough lump. Yawed a hole in its battered apple. Rule of thumbed. Struck dumb its flimsy shit meatiness. I the wench, wielded the blade. Sliced its tongue, its yellow maw, the Core. Cutlass killer lied lied lied. Mistaked funner fact and the Lucy left outside in the sun of foul. The brigs on fire liar liar antsy on fire. Burnished in my magic. Raked the firecracker. And ha ha ha ha the Core Luci-D frickin' disintegrated what lay beneath earwax, candle wax, dried flesh, beef jerky, gristle beefy threads. The Burrow called them. *Loops.* Loopholed little bumper. And it lay up-staring at the hard and bright and yellow. Huh hi heavens to betsy, whoops. The devil doer and done his best. Yo ho ho and a bottle of scum. Yo heaved ho fare it well. With it went objectified glee envy mistrust optimism. Bleh. Plunged me swift into the sullen smell. Here I slid on the road to hell. Held my nose. Retribution the sweety. Daisywhelpwhoopsa I howled my stuff pluck.

"That catastrophe is not my fault."

Apologies to Dr. Nesbitt, did he find it in a trinket shop, for the Lucy not coming home. And old Captain Nesbitt forced to brave the loss of dangerkid dynamic duo. What if. The man dangled from a helicopter in a rescue attempt. Pictured his bladder out of control. As he hung loosed.

I strained and poured the remains of the Luci-D into a large jar and put it on the windowsill. Prettier extra lucid and manageable. In the form of a fluid. Was it chemical commercial substance this as. Sunlight reflected. The liquid Core Luci-D Primrose Chamber. This a somewhat blinding.

Of Monk angried. Always hungry. Hungeranger. Monk nobbed in the gore. Manka Monkdiddy disbelieved my story. Kept squawking sat on his snout. Big nob said,

"You filled that bottle with olive oil, didn't you?"

He demanded confession. He spat it a spitter. And I howled. What the question of. Tell me why I howled for so long.

So long, baby.

10

Hello Baby Howled

My innards grew a multiple stock of ripe eggs. Did you ever as a small child call an egg, a googy egg?

Yes baby talk mine, Shipley's organ womb. Googies filled the ovarian reserve, reservoir a large body of water stored to prevent flooding, remembered sex education a bust.

Kinder surprised. Females of many different species laid eggs duh. The eggshell, the edible yolk, white, membranes, nucleus. And mine, the ova, a dozen eggs waited to be released, *pick me, pick me*. My eggs with a mind of their own, I tweezed the curtains open, rock and roll bubbies and shouted, GO. They rolled, they bounced off walls, they somersaulted and gyrated and them tinny sperms hovered. But eggs were choosy.

"Is yer DNA intact?"

Right ho billyoh boy oh boy. Eggs bound and trapped spermie spookers gotcha.

I thought of flowers in a glass vase, named her Crystal.

Bully for me, the hen trapping grit semen sundowners.

Eggy voices shouted,

"Get us new tadpoles to twizzle our rims."

The eggbomb timer ticked louder. Be aware of Insufficient years, for those leisurely googs shriveled with each passing.

And this withering gathered speed after the age of thirty.

Fertility raised a blooded red flag flip flagged at every lamble as she evolved into the mutton-girl.

And doomsayers bombarded women. Be wary.

What? Aging became this roll of a dice. But me not in any hurry for that bun in the oven. No ham unhurried. The spiced sweetened yum jazzed. But I married the harried. Hitched to a hungry man. The sweaty yeti pushed his yam in. Ha. Mammalian girl waltzed on her rainbow. Tucked into his pick. And as they say, it went ok. Who them said that? The doomed unknown, but I surprised myself for nohoped escaping that bullet. Eventual sorried an accident due. The lot of. What it took. He fired one shot.

I fell. A baby, the kite and a mother the broken string.

Of grounded opened. Quicker-sand under me. I sank of menstrual blood failed to appear. The late late late. By weeks. Must be the ham of his chaste pecks. But easy to wear white linen culottes without fear of stains. Bloodwhere. Today chuckled, always too late, last in line, angel crossed me off and ordered, take the test. Five bucks it cost. The high price of tomorrow. The test revealed a blip and the present drifting. Lucked positive.

But to be sure urgent stole another pregnancy test, slipped into my pocket and paid for cheaper cottonwool, jellybabies and quicktips. Tested again. Pee for Positive. Congratulations won the prize. Celebrated ate forty five jellybabies. Bellyache *just you wait*.

Future reality pregnant unimaginable womb gross flutter a moth trapped in there, that kicked vibrated stamping its feet, jerking its curls and flinging the placenta against my walls. I revisited the Family Planning Clinic. What should I say? *There is a grub growing inside me I can feel its living how can it breath?* Faced with the woman picture on the wall. Yes, I remembered the picture, soft drapery, a puppy somewhere frolic. Coo coo her peace veined eyes lowered coy. Hands cupped the watermelon stomach. Pumped to perfection. Kicked from within. Navel protruded, this a doorbell longing to ring. And my feet in the stirrups, her fingers tweaking the cervix yes yes its cherry ripe. Blood tested, positive.

Yoo hoo begotten an accidental baby. Why I asked. Did this happened. Ho hummed the ignorance. No surprise, my error of ruined the success of contraceptives. Hey I loved babies. The sudden ones. My baby would birth laughing a beautiful reckless, which way to summer, I planned to. Call her Awesome Polly, feed her apple pies and play her the ukulele. I told him.

"Gosh golly an accident."

That baby circumstance of dirty nappies, snot, curdled milk, projectile vomit. The present of awkward unpremeditated.

Thing.

Monk rang his mother without delay. Mrs. Quill in her dimity glow might not be pleased, but Granny pretending snuffle delight. Ahhh. Slight jumped for joy.

Motherhood crucial lifeblood hood wink, Monk fed me guff.

"Shipley."

"Yes."

"Mothering is the cornerstone of female identity."

His hand on my belly.

"Love begins and ends here."

He quacked his quack.

"You will not know yourself. Motherhood is a privilege and an honor for women. How do you feel?"

"Sick."

I combed my hair. He cracked his knuckles. I lit incense sticks. He jingled coins in his pocket. Hawk-faced ecstatic with the idea of Fatherhood. His own fleshed future of wail of shat and wee and softer talcum powdered a swaddle.

I dreamed.

Often quite nightmare baby bottles in the shape of hourglasses dripping breast milk. Dreamt ugh George Jetson pushing out a fetus as big as a whale. And on a stormy, I gave birth to twin chipmunks in a freight train.

"Kerouac is the father Monk. Not you."

Left the engine running. What if a wisteria hysteria birthed wistful buds. Or a sticky mess dropped from my privates. A blimp minus a nose this torso with a PVC brain.

I got thinner instead of fatter. For a short time weighed as much as a cupcake. Then reversed grown fatter and that rayon little ray of sunshine sundress didn't fit no more. Sometimes the buttons undone of shoulder blades jutting like defeathered turkey wings. And the bump unnoticeable even at seven months. The bump, an ant mound, round speed bump.

The shed for sale and a real estate agent arrived to price the joint his beadle eyes and smoothed shaven and patent shoes shone same as black glass. He glanced at the crib in the corner of the bedroom. The agent tried to please.

"Is baby asleep?"

"Not really."

Ain't born yet bozo.

Ollie and Molly sold the pickle shed. I found a rundown two bedder apartment on the ground floor suitable for a pram and bags of groceries, gas fire, thanked God in heaven for this proper house of linoleum floors, a real cooker and double the rent. Doubled over, thought labor pains, but Braxton hicks. Whatever hic. The new home on Honeysuckle, nearer the beach. And closer to Mad Mountain remained unmovable. We piled our boxes in a shopping cart, several trips, door to door and borrowed money from Mrs. Quill to paint walls a light yellow, the color of maggots and the woodwork, ultramarine created a fresh cheery interior.

"Its French style," I said. And set baits and mousetraps for the next life here as the biological fact, bile always surged upwards. Chin on my chest, I charged around the yard. I mixed eye of newt and radish liver salts. These dangerous spells for sickness mornings. *Apply pressure to the wrists. Eat ginger.* I ate knobs of ginger and bacon and brie with my fingers. I watched Three Men And A Baby ten times. Put bunned in the oven, cackling at least we owned a proper stove finally, an ancient gas Kooka four-legged machine. Made in 1920. A kookaburra picture on the oven door. Enameled and gas jets. I baked tasteless shortbread stuck fast to the tin tray. I slid a spatula under each and the biscuits crumbled to pieces. Monk's head on my belly.

"Are you crying?"

Sour petals withered bunch. Hey babe. Worn out further. By the lumped a lump and uninteresting useless soundless crumbs.

Remembered those aqua canvas patio chairs. I nicked them from Fergal's deck, in the dead of night, moss underfoot, a slight breeze, after we moved. I folded them and carried them home to roost. I put the empty chairs in our little garden, the size of a napkin and Monk said,

"Those are nice."

The beach walked along me, ate a peach, fancied myself as a mermaid siren. *Here I am, here I am.* Seaward. Sea-girls singing rollicking boat songs about. A mermaiden rose covered in mud. He married a murmurmaid at the bottom of the deep blue sea. Waves rode my landlubber sinking me. But gallant mated himself to redhot cookiemaid, my oh my. And I sank the bird on the wing. Go on getunderway. Heaved my anchor rocked rolling he. La la braved his beef. Show me the way to go homed. Storm weather skippered. Caught my panties in the stockblock. Ahh! He had a good time with. And I thought I glimpsed her. Teeth white and pearly. Her grey eyes. Her hair gone curly. In the garden shelling her peas. Sang birds high in the trees. Sang another. Sirensong *could I stay with you a while*. This place. Perked beyond space and time and time and space. Such a place. That sang every confusion. Magnificent times chat and wined and the sea. Alison's favorite color blue. Blueyellowblueyellowblueyellow. That mellow. She woke me. The week before my wedding day. She said *wait for me*. At her house, waiting wedding wheelie wine. I waited. For her. Late she was. Absent right when I needed her. Her fault. In some way, er why. I blamed on her. Did I? Did I? What if she. Discovered his rummage fiddledee. Caught me alone. Sinned and tarred that time. Took me to the mountaintop where he. Watched me, catched me, jumped my ju-ju. This shamed secret. I let myself go. Monk asked,

"What's wrong?"

"Nothing," I replied because the shame of a body secret. Teaser and caked. Nuclear bombed by a bullybiologist. Biologists asked strange. Questions. Like how long the hours of physical punishment torture degradation. How long measured the pranger. The pill, the bug, the bastinado. How long was the clitoris. This length of cockroach clit cunt considered representative of the yes no yes no picky sticky penis. Destroyed the want the lusting, throwing raw meat into a shark tank. Begone the sexed. And means, I begat. Cried shark shark sex snarky. Yo ho ho thirty men on a dead woman's breast. Gone the fairy pleasure of past experienced. The depletion of men stiffed and starked and sniffing wow. Godawful. I was stuck reading fantasy romance, erotic paperbacks. His castle. Gypsy witch appeased the celluloid beasties crazed from tenfold thirst and hunger raged into a local delicatessen. Monk the fiery kisser, squeezed my breast. A torrid short moan. The lively hand on his stiff member and blowjob lippers. Soft the enjoyment. Then rocket sperm downed a throat before. Rigor mortis concreted that foul organism. And the heroine fell off his cock.

Old soul daze, preggers girl sat and stared for a week at the bandaged Wedding Feast, stuck fast to the wall, nailed even to prevent a fall. Ahhh penniless. I had found that picture in a dumpster. Sometimes, I traced the torn and taped figures with my forefinger. Peasant wedding. Life not what I thought. Grandest passion banquet. Record time disappointment in a barn during springtime. YEH. Jolly the martyred groom and punching bag girlpope. This way of famine living. Moldy bread. Souped the picture. Two corn ears on mundane of self-indulgence HELL gluttony pissed. OW. Old blanket draped on the wall behind the peasantbride. Parody of fine fine fine woven tapestry. Door off its hinges as this serving tray offered. Off its head, the raking of hard grind and weary lives.

Child bumpkin sucked his thumb asked where did babies come from. Should I named. *Spit it out.* This having a baby. The Lucy. Insulted canary found the birdseed but lost the bowl. Braincells extinguished. I myself herself leery puppet. I hungered for soup and love and sucks and a landowner and a monk and a groom whoever.

Barefoot and pregnant clothed in a tropical cotton mu mu dress. The cottoned of swirl. Aloha palm trees swayed flora flowing six inches below my knees. Bluesky higher. How. Now. Whatever cow. Ha joked moo moo on me. That proved. Doodle-daisy hoolydooly faker married too young. It was that or burn. Losted me poor little everything. Bummer. Terribly terribly changed darling. Bloody washed away. Fuckit. *I told you so.*

The silence of a new freaking dumbfuck speechless. *Stop.*

The Remains Of The D

Hey silence sometimes happened to explain the immediate dishevelment of the inexplicable. So there. Silence was tricky to achieve. And you could not tug at silence. The idea of silence that would be powerlessness would it not yep. Silence stung and broke the. And silence developed into a superfluous stain on nothingness. You opened your mouth and nothing, ah, but drivel. But that was All.

A piece of blackboard chalk, a soul, a cake, a destruction equaled silence. Where you were, I knew, but I didn't know, in stifled and you went on, I could not go on, I went to a louder silence freak. You witnessed the gag, the smother, *shut up*.

Spawned regrettable the freaking accidental destruction of the Lucy. I didn't mean to be cruel. Yes you did. Would the murdered Core Luci-D reek revenge, but I was the sweet, yet non-fattening variety of vengeful, wicked, spontaneous. Dug two graves, my vengeance, a messed-up malice, sorry passive aggressive, apologized band-aiding the wounded. And I had to return the Lucy to the Burrow. With an explanation. Why what remained. The liquidity. Better this way of living the inferior.

Brought me to Darling Street, level four, Suite Number Five same same, knock knocked who there. Mr. Peebles of flaked beige, tapped at his watch and alarmed a fright at sight of me in the doorway. His shocked of Oh Jesus, not her. I aimed both eyes right at him War, I thought, Useless, I thought, did you have a friend in Jesus. No? Was it possible he might bolt. Again. Should I perform my zany air guitar? Of splashed it about and menaced anyway lowered my,

"Hello hallow Mr. Peebles."

I saw the gap in his trousers revealed a flash of cartoonish boxers. And I said blister beware words everyman everywhere wanted to hear.

"Your fly is undone."

He grabbed his zipper. Caught his death of, you'll be the death of.

"Gracious me."

And extra nervous, Podge behind the desk, fuzz of a buzz generalization. *Anytime now.* Geraldine Burrow called,

"NEXT."

Why didn't she shove that inside her shimmered. I blurted not that but. Louder.

"A tortoise passed me on a busy road. An angel shoved me through a shimmer. Silence is a new silence. Tucked between woks junked in sing sing. Smacked his delicate buds into the damned Well bloodmuddle heck of it. People said I was terribly changed. Bluer babe blinded. Middle in the stuck truck. That he would marry her. Ahhh, much sadness. The pee-niss frightness. It's gone the wrong way up. Heaving stuffed with lace. Hey Monk! I hated the groom on the floor raising a tankard. What if the knife slipped. Both of us side by side sitting on the aqua canvas patio chairs. Momentous times. Sapphire disappeared. Dearie. Lost me poor little everything. Dearie. *Dear me.*"

I was born missing. The garble garble misshapen life blurted,

"Say this forty times. Here come the angsty ants with acne. Hup hup."

Unstoppable blather.

"I performed unsafe obsessions. I discovered blood in my urine. Shoot me with a Snickers Bar. My eyes are still blood-shot. Still life. Heady. Bravo. Heart-pounding. Would this happen. Ask yourself. Could it? Be real. Hand me that knife. And relax."

Would she ask me to give her my unborn child? What did I want to be when I grew up. A girl in a sparkly leotard twirling a baton. A sixth-grade dropout. A clever clogs aren't you just. A killer. This was murder. I imagined a flamboyant inappropriate marriage to a mime artist or a rubbish collector or the owner of a baggage shop. *Stop it* he said to me.

"Stop it," said the Burrow.

I grinned corny, vengeance 'is mine sayeth the Lord' and presented the Lucy, remains of it, to Geraldine Burrow. Icky this Jar slow simmering sauce, liquid, gravy and crunchies, rice bubble shapes, threads of overcooked floating in the substance.

"Here. I'm sorry."

It looked like contaminated pee.

"Shipley!" she cried. "What have you done?"

Revenged, I done undoable revenge. The Burrow made an effort. Contained her incensed. Powerless poppy after fucking fabulous revealed. Her white knuckled fury Burrow wanted to, kick and beat and bruise foolish girl. I repeated the apologizing sorry sorry sorry. To the world. Morning had broken. Fucked faster went without food, water, semen, tinker tailors. Off again regrets. I had a few. Repentant gladwrap girl. But NOT. *Sorry.* No. How should I be? After repentance.

Her cheery determination disappeared. A livid Burrow ordered another Core Luci-D from The Institute of Face

Manifestation. And her balled of sunshine. Her dazzle. Her shakeahandy. Her goldy blindness. Her sungoddess gobs and gobs. Her gold turvey topsy enormous yellowing teeth threatened,

"I need to invoice you for the replacement."

Every threat gift wrapped revenge. Everyone paid for mistakes. Was it possible to suffer and not force a person to pay for it. And the unanswerable question. Landed a punch. The gouge price, *how much,* but the bankrupted girl tried graciousness.

"What will it cost me?"

Distance Never Changed The Love
I Had For You

Why. Hello. Dear. The meanie pointed at his toenail infection. Nicknamed him fungus Onk. Monk monotonous still hid behind an out-of-date newspaper every morning. Glowing in his rock cavity. The life of a glow worm equaled twenty minutes. Monk glad about the baby. Did I mention? His own flesh and blood and cells and fruit of the loins and breath and please let it be healthy and pure, this consequence fetus, nine months along. Dar dar de dar.

So far, Bub bump my bovine body. So far, left me stranded with. Translucent skin anticipated stretch marks. Quelled the war of me lying to Alison, to everybody, beat myself up. Leather whip of self-abasement. Today. I mean really? What was the point of Valentine's Day. Yuk clanger day of mawkish. Love. *Please don't make me say it.*

Monk, what a card, in the middle of the table. This card glittered desperate to impress. In the center, a red glitter heart shrieked Be My Valentine.

He wrote in red biro on the inside. *I wish you looked at me the way you look at Saturday, love Monday.*

But I worked every Saturday seven to four.

He wrote, *distance can never change the love I have for you.* But he was here.

And, *in my heart thinking of you.* XXXX.

I scraped the red glitter. Made a hole in the heart. Same as mine. Blue baby *breathe breathe breath.* Red sparkles dropped into my lap. I stood up, shook the glitter off my mu mu. Sparkle drifted didn't seem to land anywhere.

"Say it out loud."

"But it's on the card. Here, I got you a gift. It's an expression of my love for you."

I gave him a box of Cadbury Roses Chocolates. What you meant to me. Country Fudge, Caramel Crunch, Hazel Whirl, Golden Barrel, Strawberry Dream, Tangy Orange Crème, I didn't love you. The tang whirled the bitten, the dreaming a fudged life inside a barrel.

And his present, wrapped in tissue paper covered with a million hearts of dizzy. I tore at it, the soft tissue, oodles of hearts and unwrapped a tin of Quality Street Chocolate assortments. This purple riot. Treat.

"Thank you."

The toffee gropers encased in colorful crackly wrappers. Peanut Cracknell, Almond Octagon, Gooseberry Cream, Fig Fancy, Fruits of the Forest Crème sweets for breakfast. I removed a toffee. Long and thin like a little finger coated in a layer of milk chocolate.

"Thank you, Monk. They are lovely. Want one?"

I held the chocolate finger upright for the whole world to see.

I lay beside Monk. Immoveable bloat of me, almost upright on six pillows, princess felt the pea. And a churning potbelly. I felt the shape of a tiny hand embossed behind my skin. *Let me out* remembered. Memories made the mind ache.

A memory flamed and glared and blistered. The staring and glaring as hushed as the abominable mountain. Atmospheres and growing became oppressed by the glare. I blocked chinks, keyholes, shadows, gaps in the ceiling protected me from. Memory of girl flailing smacking at his mouth up her. His python tongue curled around my twatbody squeezing chicken neck vagina ugh.

I remembered tinned tongue stacked in Mr. Winklers pantry and a thousand tins tumbled down, swamping the day. High as the roof.

And Monk force-feeding a phony, no dead, no stuffed canary, no a hundred canaries, green canaries, blind canaries.

Darling. Oh me darlin...my sweet.

He tried and tried and tried the poke. Brickshit brutal. Unclenched my slam with a small incision and made a hole the exact size. For hubba bubba. Fucking fab infection, dabbed the wound with tea tree oil. Boredom dreamed husband deathly, what if he had left me in that damnation pickleshed. Samed as it always was. Tripe.

Let me hold you.

Booboo. Boohoo. Unconscious tampon, pull the string, pulled the other one. Breaked my spinal final. Evil spirits, keep them harmonied, offering suppertime night shifted. And miniature quill disturbed space and time. Bited rage against the machine. Wet filthed. Dreamrattle of a skeletoned party, second helpings, greek gargoyles, fierce god for a. There's a light burning in the. There's a light in the darkness of everybody's. Toy soldiers marched in jelloyellow. Shut the fucked upper. Girls played with matches. Touched herself touchy touchy touchy. Lay in the. X-Rayed scrag-end intense. Batgirl met the Burrow. The Core. The Lucy Luci-D goosey. In her head. Where. Was. She.

I do I do I do. Yes, to real stacked bitter masking. Of yellow jelly-woman climbing a cliff of no footing. The rocks broke under me and I fell into.

A broken morning.

Chipper dippy, the chipped Shipley waved him. Tainted. Off to clean them his gutters.

"Bye bye lambikins Got yer ladder and bucket and scooper?"

"Kiss me."

Smooched. His beautiful. His soft tiddle tongue. I licked mine his. He drew back and wiped his lips clean. His masked flabbergast.

"Bye bye boop-a-doop."

I learned to be wary of nicknames. The blondie fluff words. Descripted a girl. Was I wasting my time, uppity yup. I went to the bed I got out of. Hard to reach past my bellyache, my did the fondle my cherry pit. The way she demonstrated. But difficult to pip the buzz button into deep. *Why don't you just give up. Give it give it. Tick tock.*

Spoiler. I fell apart. Body of desiccation collapsed, as if a fragile porcelain cup hit a solid surface, smacked the dependable, cracked the unforgettable. Breakable crashed on unbreakable. A trail of lace, pebbles, heartworm intestine, ribbon veins, peanut pancreas, bean bladder laid in bits everywhere, nowhere.

And the sinking woke pieces of me at midday. Sewed myself together with stem stitches. I made the bed. I cleaned the house. *What else could I do?* A lump of grey mold floated on top of old tea. The routine cockroach ran around in circles. *Can't do that unproductive.* I whacked it with a dustpan. Ruminated up his. Packet of flour riddled with moths, turned into maggots, not sure of the actual entomology, but writhing muck. I threw the lot in the trash. This kitchen a better size, picture rails, room for The Wedding Feast, did I mention it? I trod on a strawberry. Strawberries fell sometimes. As a newborn, I had a strawberry birthmark on my womanly bit. That unthinkable. But the reasoning of marked. Would this little squirming inside my wombikins be stained? Like The Me.

Walked and walked. Bright and hard sky and sun, struck like an axe. Hours, breathless, feet dragger. At the very end of my witless. Adrift. Should I visit Shar Bee? Maybe this preference for bobs of weirdness. Shar didn't give a toss, had no toss to give, forgot about the toss. Once she said to me,

"I don't give a rats arse."

"Does a rat even have an arse?"

"A small one," she replied. "Like the postman's."

I pictured her. Every week, Shar danced around her backyard, the pile of dead leaves and she lit a bonfire, inspired the fire brigade to show up, hoses at the ready. Shar loved firemen. She fed them shortbread creams and mind boggling pork ribs smoked in hickory chips. They wiped their mouths, shook her hand, shook greasy fingers said,

"Fire restrictions in place. Fines apply. What if a flame escapes and you burn down the entire neighborhood? Don't light anymore fires this year. Wait for winter."

Wait. Was about the raking and the last leaf and fall and she lit another bonfire.

What else could she do.

I greeted the hello sightseer of traveling Gull and forever woman Et Cetera. And the rest. And so on. And so forth. A madcap invention of paranoia, person vanished to a stipple on the horizon, but endless sometime. She multiplied her crowded infinitesimal. Left me a list of instructions. Left her teeth marks on lead pencils, chewed everything, the unspecified items, odds and ends etc etc etc. I often searched for her etc etc etc. In vain.

Go on chat to Mr. Winkler, bent snap, picking his beans. Basketfull filled to brim a squillion and me wishing for beans. He straightened, dropped his shovel, a glancing at bulb girl on her wander. I smiled. Splendid man, his chins like tree rings, his neck the color of multiple coats of varnish. Mr. Winkler made a claw hand scratching at the emptiness, the air, this half grimace wave, *hello young lady.* He shuffled, embarrassed at the sight of my preggers.

Body weighted this life inside slowing me. *What else could I do?*

I turned toward a worse idea. The Mountain. Interminable scowled and evil. Found myself fretting somehow. At the foot of that escarpment. The grueling path leading to once her house. And Fergal still lived there even after. I wondered why. He chose to stay in the cold sprawl angled. An immense. Its ostentatious shot from cliff and the edge. And my outrage at what he he he did, constructed a human sized cross, right where. He painted the cross yellow in memory. What memory! Not Alison's beloved color. Sicked the shriller yellow. That yella cross lied. My older sister was not. That gone.

She must maybe returning to. Soon I hoped. Lost items got. Somewhere. Alison told me that she locked herself in. He the murmurer,

"Open the door my love."

"I can't," she said.

"Can't means won't."

Was what you meant.

The oblivious and remorseless firmament. Imagined she slipped, her plummeted, skidding vertical rock-face. Hinged her fallingstar, so fast it sparked. But no body. Did the sea bind her with seaweedy arms, held Alison under. Her long brown hair rose in horror. While. Sea of incessant. The headland, the murderous mountain.

You heard it first HERE. Over a million years, the killer mountain turned to iron, the highly magnetic type and it sucked the metal deposits from the inside of the human brain and turned everyone in the vicinity nuts. That explained everything.

Yet Mount Mad peeked the beach of stretch sandy grains told every story of the earth. Did Alison ever think of us, side by side, sitting on those aqua canvas patio chairs? Crow circled, murder of crows blurred against. Precipice of the cliff, reflecting a metallic sheen. Clearness of two sides for now facing my future face down in dirt.

That memory and. She said, this to me. Not questions just thoughts.

"The edge is a bizarre and beautiful situation."

"What if I had never got to see the sea."

"I should not be weary of life."

"Because,"

"I need peace."

"Because of the healing in the repetitive chorus of the sea. It is calling to me."

"No, it is not." I said. "Why are you talking such nonsense?"

And bumping to cold yellow cross. Yellow crossed and crass. So ever since I hated. Yellow. My horrified and railing at Monk,

"How dare that bastard erect such a morbid hideous reminder."

Of her missing. Of my missed. Monk held me.

"Don't go getting overexcited. You always do."

"I bloody do not."

My agitated always did. She needed peace.

"The world does too."

She had that from out of the blue. Went into her blue. I should hate blue. That would be logical. Blue etc etc disappeared.

Gave in. Not today. *Go no further.* I started for home, support me to the exhausting around.

In the future, a confrontation. I planned to grill Fergal, along with his fucking sausages. But the comfort of a satisfying memory of the day he. That hour he stormed me. Unrelenting theme song Jaws, the grip great white shark sang to the soundtrack of a dishwasher, waterfalls, spin dryer. And after the storming lick, with both hands, he adjusted his ponytail and went to the downstairs powder room. To wipe his dick. Under no circumstances confessed. Nobody knew. That I peed on his precious rug. Left a nasty yellow mark. And that yellow so full of nastiness snigger.

How Alison walked through the door and said,

"What's this stain on the carpet?"

Fergal lied,

"I spilled a glass of wine."

He sweated revulsion, his brain screaming filth. His face flipping to wishy-washy, *there is nothing going on here,* why he changed the subject. That week. And the Wedding after. He didn't have a clue how the mark got on the rug. Spiffy banned from the house.

"Some other animal," I said. "Must have wandered inside."

Someone's pet cat or dog unable to control itself. An incontinent being, of course, four legged, squatted, yes that plausible the explanation. Had to be. A pathetic creature. *Don't tell.* Monk. And while Alison peeled apples in the kitchen, I punched Fergal where it hurt the most.

went under

Further the struggle seemed to be led somehow. But not as far as I wanted to go. You were not listening. Why I sang, what I screamed, the songed in no brainer.

I did what I was told. I got hysterical. I said, *I do.* I lost my sister. I got sliced. I dried myself thoroughly. I sang and sang. *When it comes to being loved...* I got told to shut the fuck up. I retaliated. I talked to a doctor. I swallowed the bitter pill. I malformed. I forged myself. Engorged myself. I lived a lie. I sacrificed a lamb. I murdered the Lucy. I filled my womb. I developed expectations. I hated yellow. I worshiped yellow. I became said hello yellow. And yellow lied. My life of a liar. Because none of it made. Sense. Except help.

No sounds today, not even birds chirped and mediocrity. This silent spring. About nothing, except blue sky and white monstrosity perched on the cliff. Monk told me, I was not welcome at Fergal's house. Not after that bother with Jason and the absinthe. Poor kid, the isolation. Alison always read 'Jason and the Argonauts' aloud to Jason. The man's quest for a miraculous ram with a golden fleece. *Gold.* He ploughed a field with dragon's teeth. *There had to be an easier way.* Jason loved that bloodthirsty myth. Jason said,

"Super-cool check it out knock it off scaredy cat."

The guilt of him vomiting. Everyone got silly under the influence of alcohol.

This memory changed my direction, *turn around, switch the dial back*. Reversed my mind. And I turned to face the highup house, the cliff. I would venture closer. She might be home, she used to be. *Then go to her,* the notion. Climb the steeped hill towards that forbidden. Even from here, I noticed the empty driveway. Under, went my breath.

"He must have gone to the shops. Thank God."

Visions of undertakers, hands carefully folded behind and measured steps under grey top hats gliding. One foot in front of the other, concentrated heel-and-toe, this process of walking towards a severe death. The power of. Gone.

I kept going. Weaker struggled along almost vertical ground. Steeper the way of gravel and dirt and sludge must have rained, rocks and ants moving in a single file. Pack animal insects. Sped a swift lizard, distant cicadas and so many flies *nosing in*. My shoulder collided with boulders. Dirt clung to my nails, clawed my zig zagged way. Up way ahead only the yellow cross, its arms outstretched, appeared pleased with itself. Yellow welcomed. Daisies sunshine shone straight into my eyes. I squinted. That afternoon of blonde brick church. I blinded the wretched shaded my eyes. The screen door opened. Jason in a white T-shirt and a baseball cap. He stood on the deck. What could he. I waved. He saluted like a tiny admiral.

Goodbye.

Waves bore her. Jason hopped off the veranda. Little lighted feather. He strode over to the precipice and stood motionless. In front of the yellow cross. At the utmost edge. Of what the fuck was he doing?

I walked faster. Tried to run. My head throbbing, thoughts racing, nobody home. Jason alone, too young to be left on his own.

The house a great distance and that small figure. I stumbled, grazing my knees. I began crawling. A bit further up the Mount Mad. That tortoise ran faster than me. Sun dress loosed ballooning. Wished for a rope tied to my hands and a muscleman to drag my bulk through the dirt, past the gnarled trees bent low to the ground, well-trodden, someone warning who what the watchful creeping from trunk to trunk. Faster than me. A shadowed paranormal. EEK *Lucy.* But I killed it!

Slow too slowed, body, legs crumpling must. Quicker to reach him. The cruel sun-sea beamed from behind a darkcloud. Brainer hammered through childhood. *Jesus wants me for a sunbeam.*

Monk preached inside my head. *Have you thought it through Shipley. Never undertake a thing until you've.* Thought it through. Or you would go under. But a tired pregnant woman must focus on the wonders of the universe. At the edge of a quizzical and wondrous. What if I never swam in the sea. What if I never saw the sea again.

The wondered of sudden pain, how brown cow OWWW caterwaul of. The stomach hardened and my groaned depth yell of me. Hello doubled over. Agony dazed the contraction. Truth for once ripping through. Disturbance. The stream cream. Screamed. Five minutes. Ten fingers ten toes. Every minute a scream. Monk said I was a scream. A drag, a hoot, a drama queen. Was I in.

The contraction ended. An inner bossed, *this isn't happening. Don't you believe it.*

Still.

I keeping hurt, my creeping forward. Through bee stings, skittering dead leaves, twigs brushed sharper and sharper. Armslegsface. The fallen crackling dirted beetles scuttled under rocks. Undergrowth of moist dead plants decomposing tried. Humus layer fed the soil. But glued me. Throb brutal stopped and I lay for tender cheek on damp matted. Earth. *Speak to me*. The beautiful stench of rot and droppings and decomposing. Then propped on my elbows, strained shadows, where was Jason. *But I thought I was close.* So near, so far, so near, so far. Twisted path. I inched on, pushed my hands knees forward, like a shuffling furry animal on its last legs.

Seconds.

Another pain contraction ripping gained. Fell felled onto my side. Would there be side effects. Yes. Breath ratcheting an electrocuted sound. Beast guttural. Rose from my. Squat. Suffering removed a canker, at last, kept going HELL got over. *Or go under.* This wail-grief beached whale. Head lowered imagined struck by. Hammer or hatchet or bludgeon *there's a hole in the bucket!*

I reached out and pressed both hands to a tree trunk, left me with bark indentations on my palms. Shaped of a heart and flecks of tenacity, Be My Valentine. Tree-sap urgency sapped, grunting growled me to move forward. This forest risked of helpless. In the power of fate, unable to see the forest for the trees. Flux of time faced death. A complication, what was I thinking climb that. Climb every mountain, she'll be coming round the.

The rounded ball. At nine months. Mount Mad pushed me to its miserable center. Core of girl such a different structure of lucid. Disturber of lucidity. The simpled applecore. And the precise solution of none. Her the appropriate ideal to the enigma of female identity. Passivity perceived as a chosen state. Female response to entrapment. Veiled yes. This masked. Caught between angelic submission and monstrous assertion and.

There's a hole in the blinkin' bucket

Itchy trickled. Ruptured the membrane. Wet myself. Fluid streamed YUCK screamqueen down my legs. A kind of leaking gush of pale yellow. My waters had broken. Morning had broken. *No.* Could be wee. They said it difficult to tell the difference between amniotic fluid and urine. My punishment for every destroying of the Core Luci-D.

You always cried for weapons. I cried for a dagger, release me from my misery quest to rescue the boy. Owned flesh and blood.

Baby wanted to push. *Not now.* Me longing. The longed for an eagle to whisk me, detach me from cling side of Mount Mad. The lower half of my body strained, bore down, was I about to. Shit. Reason announced pushing stage this. (Like in a maternity hospital those panting women flat on their and purple faced. Stirrups always handy trussed spread em lady, cunt blowing in the air conditioned as. Fetus head crowned royal. And groups of medical students rushed in rubbing hands with glee and sanitizer.)

Lost my voiced. Teeth gritted ground spare grit my heard a, "Don't push."

God said, *don't push when you feel the urge. Don't hold your breath. Don't lay on your back. Don't let someone hold your legs back. Don't count the minutes of a push.* God had a lot to say.

Half-way safest for slow controlled birth. Sacrificial lambikins. Burnt offering top of the Mount Mad told Alison,

"Bring me your son, your only son and sacrifice him."

"To what?"

"How would I know?"

Chopped enough wood, loaded the donkey, worshipped the expanse. The boy asked,

"Where is the lamb."

"God will provide," she said.

God interfered as usual. Alison told me later

"It was a close one."

As I. Fought for breath, fight for old life, new life, child life. Mustered a yell, but feeble,

"Jason Jason. Wait. *Wait for me.* Don't go near the."

I hated waiting. I couldn't see him. Would he find me? Maybe hear my brittle voice. *Distance Can Never Change The Love I Have For You.* On the cliff, the ugly house. Both lucid, pompous. How much time did I have? How far apart would we become? *Distance can never change the love I have for her.* How dilated was that hole? *There's a hole in the.* Ten minutes, three minutes and another doubling over. A stream of blood ran down my leg. I wiped the blood with leaves and grass. My imagination went crazy. Alison's inflamed love for Jason, the wanting him to be with her. This her opportunity. Alison, the mother cyclone of wanting. The wanting willy willy whirling at me. I shielded my eyes, felt the grabbing squall, my arms not long enough to reach the cliff edge, to STOP HER, to catch Jason. Alison seizing him. The strong of stronger wanting strength, than hey what Hercules. Tall grass frothed around me. Wind chill legs bared. Teeth chattered ground to dust. I did not mean for it. To Happen Like This.

Would I be alright. I agreed yes alright when he asked me. I smelled fire brimstone hellish. I wanted to cry, where was the boy. Anybody. A voice of her lied,

"He is at school."

But he was there. On the threshold. About to.

I vomited strands of wool a beastly yellow ball. A cat full of fur balls. Lay in the tufted, must have swallowed some wooly, that many longest years ago. But it woolen remained in my gut festered jest.

I ascended Mount Mad, kamikaze, crawled for a while, for a long longer time on my grazed knees such agony. Monk that time of my slicing, claiming his private agony. But nothing compared. To bleeding, collapsing, melting. I cracked of desperate, crying,

"Wait."

But he disappeared.

Eyes dimmed and there. Her skipping leaping seaweed hair. Eyes bloomed blue cornflowers came towards me, from the steep. Hippydress wings flower flew at me. Reached for me from the sea. On an island of water its inevitable circle. Waves raced you know and her swift reached my side, my combustible help me help me. Why are you watery. And me bled bloodmuddle.

No discontent, no disenchantment, not for this. We stayed where I lay. On the grass under the sky slither of placenta oozing out. So much blood lost. Too much for a body fading. No possibility of joining the dots. And what dots. Just reddish trembled tiny fists wailing. At me. Wailed *don't leave me don't go.* Specific creatures incapable of birth. I thought I lost. You.

Alison whispered in my, she held hands, slipped away. *Look at us.* Magic girls, witch bitches, hearts' desired. My wrote the entire whatever off as experience. The hellish fun of it. Cruelty and charming and suffering hee-hee hilarious. At The Same Time.

I called, "Life then. What is it."

Everyone said goodbye. Who might that be, Monk chortled, Au revoir chickaboo.

Why. Good riddance. Dear.

And Mr. Winkler,

Bye bye neighbor.

Shar Bee hooting,

Listen kiddo, you is what you is. Ta-ta.

Strong women stood alone.

The skeleton friends said,

One last farewell drink.

Gull and Etcetera said

So long little girl.

Mrs. Quill shuddered *urk* at the wet of me breaking.

Geraldine Burrow asked yet another unanswerable question,

Shipley what have you done?

And Thank God. Simple Fergal said, *Let me taste your ware.* Fergal said, *Ciao.* Fool Fergal, *Let me see your penny.* Finger pressed to his lips,

Shhh don't tell.

Happy Valentines. Why I heard Monk calling,
"What's the matter?"

Monk was here watching us creeping together, we must
over the earth, we were the earth. We kept on creeping burrowing like rabbits. I glanced at him and he moved closer crikey.
"For God's sake what are you doing?"

And he fainted. My sainted aunt. Could die dying. It
couldn't be helped. I crept over him laid my trail of blood
across his starched. Later. *Catch you. Snot you it's me,* what
a person said breaking up with. Or deathbed. Sad about it.
Never see her again. Or indignant hang up the phone, slam a
door. Fare thee well. Type of expression two lovers in a movie
said. Term unsuitable for use in daily life. Bye bye baby flir-
tatious. Bon voyage. Ship sailed long journey. So long. Dear.
Get-up-and-go. Gumption! Keep it real. And dried me off.
Alright of. Casual relaxed.

But I did not go under. Towels under me. Hands tugging.
Blood jammy sticky, a voice saying,
"Push slow. Not long now."

Pushed my grubby knees wide. Split me. Wider open to
the world. Supposed to suck on a breath mint why. Increase
breathing or was that poise and posture. But I curled, a sharp
stone against my spine. Didn't think I did think about. I went
for a walk and now this. The pain it searing hot blood cold.
And the boulder baby moved through that hole, zoomed down
my tunnel, light at the end of. Its tinge hazelnut head. Emerged
alone. What did I expect. Did it blink. In the natural daylight.
And she here. Caught the baby. Wrapped him in a bright green
jacket. The breeze gentle. The woman wore runners and a leotard. Khaki cladded shirt tied in a jaunty knot at her waist. A
sweatband held her feathered hair. A jogger saved us.

"She's a healthy girl."

Babythesea the slippery seal. Parcel of emptiness, no! Full of sounds, cried that usual wha wha wha.

I held her in my arms. This fragile theory of soft skin and strength loved, I held her in my.

An ambulance siren, unbearable yell, it loud fire police murder shocking. Caught a brilliant reflection. Got to us saved us in time. It took to snuff out a candle.

"I thought you were a ghost. I mistook you for my sister."

"I was going for a walk when I found you."

In labor, in a state.

"Did I make a mess?"

Monk in the mud, went under.

"Is this your husband?"

"Yep. He's asleep, just leave him."

Really.

The intention, I meant to scrap it without satisfaction, an unreal halting, not respectable, you crying with happiness, but a disappointing hoot with everyone feeling like they'd been stabbed.

But I changed, because a woman changes her mind and I minded and cast in myself, we peaced a shush under those bleached skies, the uproar burst from a mound of soil *imagine baby*, rollicking boulders and little pebbles under trees gone silvery white, even pure clouds at the edge of the babble babble babble *ceasefire*.

I wasn't in the desert or on a busy road or on land sea or solid. I wasn't anywhere. But the sense of my risen from struggle and blood and trite me said,

"Life can only get better!"

Wind in my face, high on a perch and you calling.

Bested way. Best of luck.

Acknowledgements

This book owes its existence to the exceptional Stevan V. Nikolic, Editor, Adelaide Books. My incalculable thanks for his encouragement and for publishing YEH HELL OW.

For their support, I am eternally grateful to Desmond W. Ferguson, Karyn Maslyn and Chris and Helga Holland.

To these hardworking champions of short stories who published my fiction and gave me the confidence to write a novel, thank you and deepest appreciation Halimah Marcus Electric Literature, Christopher James Jellyfish Review, Jonathan Cardew Connotations Press, Blake Butler The Fanzine, Scott Waldyn Literary Orphans, RW Spryszak Thrice Fiction, Michele Seminara Verity Lane, Tomek Dzido Founder STORGY, Felix Garner Davis Malevolent Soap, The Quail Bell Crew, Margaret River Press and Overland, guest editors Craig Bolland and Mandy Beaumont.

And to Ben, Sasha, Hannah and Katherine Rose love you to the moon, sun, all the stars, spirits, extra-terrestrials whatever else is up there and back. It's been fun!

About the Author

Judyth Emanuel was one of three winners in 2017 Victoria University Short Story Prize for New and Emerging Writers. Her fiction has appeared in Joiner Bay, The Margaret River 2017 Anthology and literary journals online Electric Literature Recommended Reading, Literary Orphans, Verity Lane, Intrinsick, The Fanzine, Quail Bell, STORGY, Jellyfish Review, Connotation Press and in print Overland, Thrice, Malevolent Soap and Adelaide Literary Press. She was short listed for the 2017 Neilma Sidney Short Story Prize, selected as a finalist in the Pulp Fiction Raven Short Story Contest, semi-finalist for the Conium Review Flash Fiction Contest and shortlisted for the Margaret River Short Story Prize. In 2016, she was awarded a Residential Fellowship at Varuna Writers House NSW. Her collection was suggested for the Writer's Victoria Personal Patron's Scheme. In 2013, she was accepted into the One Story Writers Workshop at the Centre For Fiction in New York.

For a number of years, Judyth worked as a cleaner, nurse's aide, housewife, graphic designer, art director and managed an artist-run gallery. In her thirties, she painted outsider watercolors. Her paintings were exhibited in London, Los Angeles, Barcelona, Boston Sydney and many other places. In the past, she lived in Kuwait, Saudi Arabia, London, Cyprus and

Boston and now resides in Sydney, Australia and New York City. She married three times and has three children.

Judyth graduated BA Visual Communications at Sydney College of The Arts, BA Fine Arts at National Art School and MFA in Creative Writing at The University of Technology Sydney.

She is currently completing a collection of short stories and working on a fictional travel memoir.

www.judythemanuel.com

https://www.facebook.com/judyth.emanuel

@judythewrite